Outcast

Outcast

Louise Carey

First published in Great Britain in 2022 by Gollancz
an imprint of The Orion Publishing Group Ltd
Carmelite House, 50 Victoria Embankment
London EC4Y 0DZ

An Hachette UK Company

1 3 5 7 9 10 8 6 4 2

A CIP catalogue record for this book is
available from the British Library.

ISBN (Trade Paperback) 978 1 473 23275 4
ISBN (eBook) 978 1 473 23002 6
ISBN (Audio Download) 978 1 473 23006 4

Typeset at The Spartan Press Ltd,
Lymington, Hants

Printed and bound in Great Britain by Clays Ltd,
Elcograf S.p.A.

www.orionbooks.co.uk
www.gollancz.co.uk

For my father, Mike Carey

Part 1

Part 1

Prologue

'Jeanie sent me,' Yasmin Das says.

Cole frowns. 'I don't know a Jeanie.'

'She said you might say that. But you did, once, and it's about time you were reintroduced.'

Cole doesn't know whether to be excited or alarmed by this information. He was only just thinking that he needed to learn more about his forgotten past, and who better to fill him in than someone who knew him personally? But Cole's day job, before he lost all memory of it in the MindWipe, involved subjecting children to a programme of corporate mind control – and during his time off, he masterminded a false flag attack that left dozens of people dead. He can't help feeling that anyone who knew that past version of him very well is not someone he'd like to meet.

'What does she want from me?' he asks Yas. 'And why is she contacting me now?'

Yas gives Cole a look that he finds hard to read. 'She wants your help. When you were working on the Harlow Programme, you used to feed her intel from inside the Black Box. She'd like you to do it again.'

The words hit Cole like a blow. It's not just that this is one of the first pieces of concrete information he's had about his missing years; it's also the fact that Yas knows about his role in InTech's covert programme of mental manipulation. It's bad enough thinking about the Harlow Programme in the privacy of his own head; hearing Yas, someone he likes and respects, talking about it out loud is almost unbearable. He hates that she knows about his time in InTech's most highly classified research and development lab – learning about his past almost isn't worth the shame of having to talk about it with other people. He has so many questions that, for a moment, he can't respond.

'What? How...?'

'Jeanie filled me in on the details,' Yas answers, noticing Cole's confusion but oblivious to his discomfort. 'You and she were trying to halt the programme's progression, but then she lost touch with you. Now there's—'

A knock on the door cuts Yas off mid-sentence. Cole is turning to see who could be calling this late at night when she grabs his arm.

'Don't answer that!' she hisses. 'Listen, we don't have a lot of time. There's something brewing in the Black Box. Something big. Jeanie wants to stop it, and she could really use your help.'

She digs in her pocket and hands him something: it's an oval of white plastic with a silver button in the centre, hanging on a length of cord.

'Take this and hide it,' she says. 'You can use it to get in touch with us if you need to, but it's for emergencies only.'

Cole has seen things like this device in retro technology exhibits – it's a patient tracker, used in the days before MbOS technology to help dementia sufferers who strayed from their homes. He's impressed. The tech is so archaic that it won't be blocked by any of InTech's firewalls or detected by their scanners. He takes it – then, at a loss for what to do with it, puts it in the fruit bowl on his kitchen table. There's another knock on the door, louder this time. It snaps Cole back to attention; his professional interest has distracted him from the most obvious problem with Yas's plan.

'Yas, even if I wanted to help you, I don't work at the Black Box anymore,' he points out. 'There's nothing I can do.'

The furtive expression crosses Yas's face again. Cole finally identifies it as chagrin. 'Yes. About that,' she says. 'You asked why Jeanie was getting in touch now. It's because it might be her last chance for a while. We've been monitoring the chatter at the ICRD and Kenway has decided to – well – he's putting you under house arrest.'

Panic spikes through Cole. 'What?'

'I'm sorry,' Yas whispers. 'Really, I am. This shouldn't be happening to you. But there's a way you can use it to do some good. Or get revenge, if that's your thing.'

Shouting from outside, now: 'Neuroengineer Cole! Open the door!'

'Yas,' Cole hisses through gritted teeth, 'what is going on?'

'I have to go!' Yas replies. 'We know Dr Friend is going to request you be reassigned to the Black Box. If you're in, then once you get there, look out for our man on the inside. From what I've heard, he needs all the help he can get.'

The door bursts open, flying from its hinges. Cole whirls around: four armed guardians enter the flat at a run, their weapons trained on him.

As the guardians cuff him, they turn him back towards the open window. Yas is gone.

Chapter 1

Everyone has always called her Fliss, except her mother.

One of Fliss's earliest memories is of her mum correcting her when she tried to shorten it, the lines on her worn face deepening into a disapproving frown. 'You're *Felicity*,' she said. 'Felicity Loh. It's a good name. A proper name.'

By which she meant an old name, one from before the Meltdown. But they're not living before the Meltdown, are they? And besides, her mum told her that *felicity* meant happiness, and Fliss found herself resenting that, as though the name were a standard she had to live up to. She's not happy, not most of the time. Who is? And so, she started calling herself Fliss, and after she left the settlement at Gatwick and joined the crew, everyone else did the same.

Fliss has been thinking about her mother a lot today. It's probably because she's out teaching Josh how to hunt drones, and teaching is something Mum has always been good at. They're perched on the roof of an abandoned house, one of a row of identical houses – she, Josh, and the rest of the crew. Josh had wanted to wait inside one of them, in the shade; the heat is already becoming oppressive, and he's a redhead who burns at the mention of sunlight. But Fliss had insisted on this position and, since she's the leader, Josh had to agree.

'You need to brace yourself against something or the recoil will knock you over,' she tells Josh patiently. 'It's not like in the movies.'

The crew don't have a television of their own, but many of the settlements they stop at do and occasionally, when times are good, they've traded some of their food or meds for the chance to watch a film. Fliss likes the westerns best. They're all from long before the Meltdown, but the stories of bandits and frontier towns remind her of life in the wasteland. The gangs of outlaws are even a little like her own crew, though they have it easier than she does. Cattle rustlers only have cowboys and sheriffs to contend with. Fliss and her crew have the corps.

'I know it's not like in the movies,' Josh snaps back. 'I've seen you do it, haven't I?'

Fliss feels an answering stirring of annoyance, which she tries to suppress. Her mother is endlessly patient, and taught Fliss how to dress wounds, snare rabbits and scale trees with a supply of gentleness that never ran dry – even when Fliss was cross or slow. Of course, this particular lesson would horrify her. They never attacked drones at Gatwick; their philosophy was to avoid the corporations' notice as far as possible.

'I know you have, Josh,' she replies, calm as she can manage. 'But you won't know what I mean until you've tried it yourself. Here—' She takes the gun from its holster on her belt and shows Josh the stance again: legs slightly apart, back braced against the chimney stack, left arm supporting and steadying her right. 'Like this.'

Josh copies her, making a gun out of his thumb and index finger and squinting along it into the sky. He fires off a volley of imaginary shots, then mimes a drone going down in flames.

'I get it,' he says. 'Now give. I want to try.'

'If you're going to fuck about, I'll take you back to camp,'

Fliss retorts. 'Maybe I should have let Gabriel or Sonia handle this one after all.'

She glances at them as she speaks. They're sitting with Ben on the flat roof, sharing a canteen of water. Sonia only rolls her brown eyes – she doesn't have any more patience for Josh's idiocy than Fliss does – but Gabriel shoots her a look of mute appeal. He has a soft spot for Josh, who is the youngest and newest of the crew. Fliss doesn't relent; Josh may be a kid, but he needs to know this isn't a game.

He sobers immediately. 'I'll be serious! I promise.'

She hands him the gun with a show of reluctance, and he takes it reverently, making a big deal out of it. It lies in his palm, compact and dense, its once-shiny surface flecked with rust. Fliss oils it regularly, but it was old and beaten up when she got it.

Josh curls his fingers around the handle and takes up the stance she showed him, pointing the gun at the sky to the east. Then he sights along the barrel, squinting into the flat stare of the sun.

Fliss watches all this approvingly. She had her doubts about letting Josh get his hands on the gun. It's the only working one the crew has, and he has a tendency towards recklessness. But he's been begging to learn how to use it since he joined them, and Ben did barter for a shotgun from some traders in Crawley the last time they passed that way. It doesn't work yet, but with a bit more tinkering it might, and the crew could use another shooter.

A dark speck comes into view, silhouetted against the light. At the same moment, Fliss hears a high and steady humming, still distant, but coming their way. The delivery drone is heading straight for them.

'It's here,' she says, with satisfaction. 'Right on time.'

All at once, Josh's arms start to tremble. The gun is probably heavier than he was expecting it to be, but Fliss knows that's not the only reason.

'What if it's armed?' he asks. His voice is a high whine that matches the sound of the drone's motors. He coughs, embarrassed.

'They're never armed on this route,' Gabriel tells him, affecting not to notice Josh's discomfort.

'But what if it is? What if they've noticed what we've been doing?'

'They haven't,' Fliss chimes in. 'We've been careful.'

This is true. The crew have a rotation of drone routes that they change up regularly. They never strike the same flight path twice in a row, or twice at the same point. They leave as long between hunts as they possibly can. And this route is one they know well. One of the big corporations uses it to ferry staple foods from the agricultural zones in the south over to London: the delivery drones carry grains, pulses, occasionally root vegetables – nothing valuable. There's no reason to think the drone would be armed. But still...

You can't always tell the armed drones apart from the normal ones, not by sight. You know when you've hit one though, because it's the last thing you'll ever do. Usually. Some of the corps just put regular guns on theirs, and in that case, you might get away with a chestful of scars or a chunk out of your ear, like Ben has. But Thoughtfront put heat-guided missiles on their really important shipments, and some of the pharmaceutical corporations use even nastier things. Things that can melt your skin off and leave you choking on your own lungs.

It's how Fliss's predecessor died. Fliss was little more than a kid herself when it happened, and she tries not to dwell on the memory, but occasionally an image from that day will resurface. It was only her, Harry and Sonia in the crew then, and they were trying to snag a shipment from AviLife – painkillers and birth control, but they were hoping for antibiotics, too, which are rare as hens' teeth and far more valuable. Harry had been closest when they brought the drone down, so he'd got the brunt of the gas when the little cannister exploded. Fliss, to her shame, had run. Sonia, too. They'd returned several hours later to find the shipment melted and Harry... In the end, she and Sonia had been too afraid even to bury him. The crew wear gas masks when they go to collect a drone now – Fliss traded for them herself – but she hasn't hit an AviLife shipment since.

Overhead, the sound of the drone is getting louder, and Josh's shaking has intensified. The kid is all swagger and no substance; he's been boasting about his imagined prowess with a gun for weeks, and now that it comes to it, he's running scared. Fliss could remind him that she did *tell* him this was a serious business. Instead, she squeezes his shoulder.

'You'll be OK,' she says.

He takes a deep, shuddering breath, and thumbs the safety off. The gun wavers a little, but he steadies his right hand with his left, like Fliss taught him, and finds his target. The drone is closer, larger. But it's not time yet. Timing is everything. Fliss has drilled into him, again and again, that he has to wait until it's almost directly overhead. He pauses, gauging the distance. Beside him, Fliss counts down slowly from five in her head. When she reaches zero, she feels Josh tense up, and he fires.

The recoil takes him by surprise, as Fliss warned him it would. He does not stagger, but his right arm flies backwards, and the shot goes wide. He fires again, and a third time, chasing the drone across the sky. But he has no better luck. It's above them, and then it's gone. The sound of its motors recedes in the still air until all is silence again.

'Fuck,' Josh says. Fliss knows he's aiming for angry, but he just sounds shaken.

'Don't worry about it.' She takes the gun from his hand and holsters it again. 'We'll try again tomorrow.'

Fliss steps away from him, gazing into the sky to the west. She can still just about make out the drone, a dark spot on the horizon. In the crate it carries, there is flour or potatoes or lentils, maybe even some spices or sugar. Enough to feed the crew for a month, with plenty left over for trade. It's out of the gun's range now, but she can still see it, drifting lazily along in the pitiless blue of the sky. Fliss almost wishes that it had shot back, and that she and the crew had been forced to flee in a hail of bullets. In fact, it's very rare that they lose someone to attacks from the delivery drones. Most of them just fly right by – too high to reach, or gone too fast to catch. Mostly, the corps ignore them. Somehow, this makes it worse.

She's about to turn away, to go and retrieve her rucksack for the trek back to camp, when several things happen at once. There's a muted pop behind her, and something flies past in her peripheral vision, almost too quick to see. An instant later, the distant drone drops from the sky like a stone.

'Uh, Fliss?' There's a note of fear in Sonia's tone.

Fliss freezes in place rather than spinning around to see what the matter is. The pop was quiet – if she'd been talking, she might have missed it – but it has set her heart hammering. She knows what a gun sounds like.

'Good shot,' a man says. His voice is a hard drawl.

The hairs on the back of Fliss's neck rise. There aren't any settlements in this part of the wasteland; the only other people likely to be out here are rival crews. Crews don't tangle with one another often – the wasteland is large, and there are enough things trying to kill its inhabitants without them turning on each other – but hostile takeovers are not unheard of. If that's what's happening here, if another crew like the Grins or the

Red Flags has come to swallow them up, then the others might yet survive, but there's no hope for her at all.

'You can come down,' the voice adds. 'We're not going to shoot.'

Well. That's unexpected. Fliss turns slowly to see who has got the drop on her. Two figures, a man and a woman, are standing in the middle of the potholed street. They're wearing sleek, black body armour and close-fitting helmets that obscure their faces. They're both armed – the man with a pistol, and the woman with an enormous thing that looks a bit like a grenade launcher, which she carries mounted on her shoulder. The man has his gun trained on Gabriel, Sonia and Ben, who are still sitting where Fliss left them, exposed on the flat roof. Fliss shoots Sonia a warning look. *Stay still.* The strangers have the upper hand, here. Run, and they're likely dead.

Josh has darted behind the chimney stack. 'We're armed,' he calls, acting the tough guy. 'So, you'd better back off, or—'

'Shut up, Josh,' Fliss says. Her voice is calm, almost inflection-less.

These two aren't from a rival crew; she can see that at a glance. They're corporate: her scavenged handgun won't even begin to cut it. With a jerk of her head, she orders everyone down to the ground. The others slip off the flat roof, while Fliss scales the wall beside the chimney breast. She has to put her back to the strangers while she climbs down, which makes the space between her shoulder blades feel tight and itchy. If they wanted to shoot her, though, they could do it just as easily to her face. As soon as she reaches the ground, she turns back to them, showing her hands.

'We'll leave,' she calls. 'We want no quarrel with you.'

'Smart girl.' The woman is speaking now. There's some kind of distorter in her helmet that makes her voice sound thick and robotic. 'But you've got nothing to fear from us. We just want to talk.'

Which is an odd opening gambit from someone so heavily armed. Fliss's eyes must betray something of her thoughts because the woman laughs, the sound a low gargle, and unships the grenade launcher from her shoulder. 'This? I didn't bring it to threaten you. I thought I made that clear when I shot down your drone.'

Fliss boggles. She'd assumed when she saw the two that the shot must have come from the pistol. The grenade launcher is massive, and it just downed a drone that was over a mile away. To hit something from that distance, with that force, and to make as little noise as a snap of the fingers? It's impossible.

'What do you want to talk about?' Fliss asks.

'We've been following your crew's activity for some time, and we want to go into business,' the man replies. 'We have weapons and resources, and you have a talent for shooting down drones. We'd like to make use of it.'

'Here,' the woman says. 'A gesture of good faith.' And without further preamble, she offers the launcher to Fliss, holding it out to her with both arms, like it's a child.

Fliss's mind whirls. This feels like a trap. No one has ever given the crew something for free, least of all a corp. In the wasteland, you scavenge what you can get and steal what you can't. She thinks, again, of her mother, of what she would say if she could see Fliss with these two corporate goons.

You can't win against the corps, Felicity, and you can't bargain with them. They aren't human. All you can do is run, as far and as fast as you can.

It's advice that Fliss has disregarded, time and again. She has stolen from the corporations to feather her nest and fill her belly, and she's always managed to come out all right. Working with them, though ... That's new. It feels risky. She looks to the rest of the crew. Sonia, Ben and Gabriel look back, waiting on her decision. Josh only has eyes for the grenade launcher; Fliss isn't sure whether he's staring at it with fear or lust.

She thinks about it for a long, slow minute. You can't trust a corp. But it's not like the crew are in a position to be turning down offers of help, whatever their source. She steps forward and takes the launcher from the woman's arms. The woman's hand brushes against Fliss's own as she does so. It feels human enough.

'I'm listening,' Fliss says.

Chapter 2

'I want everyone to bring their A game tonight,' Tanta's team leader says. 'This is an important assignment, so keep your minds on the job.'

He's looking at Tanta when he says it. Reflexively, she adjusts her uniform, straightening her lapels and tugging the hem of her shirt down to cover the body armour beneath it. She's not used to dressing in formal wear; the collar of her white shirt feels like it's cutting off her air supply, and the tailored black trousers impede her freedom of movement. But it's important she look the part.

There's a soft chime in her mind as a notification comes through, and she touches a finger to her temple, summoning her Array. The AR display glimmers before her eyes, bright in the dim interior of the van. T minus two minutes. On the seats beside her, her colleagues shift uncomfortably in their ties and waistcoats. Their team leader, Senior Guardian Porter, is sitting facing Tanta. His waistcoat is too tight for him, and his red face gleams with sweat. Evidently the formal wear doesn't agree with him, either.

'Now, I know some of you are a little new to this,' he continues. There's a collective creaking as the rest of the guardians turn in their seats to look at Tanta. Porter is being his idea of subtle, but she is the only new person to have joined this team for years.

'I want to reassure those people that it's normal to be nervous,' Porter says. 'This may all seem daunting at first, but if you keep your head down and follow my lead, you'll be fine. Got it?'

There's no one else he could be addressing, so Tanta forces a nod, eyes on the floor. Her cheeks are burning. She's been working in Porter's unit for two months – ever since Douglas Kenway demoted her from the InterCorporate Relations Division to the community guardians – but she still gets a pep talk every time she goes out on any assignment more challenging than gate duty. She's sure Porter means well; he probably has no idea how to speak to a teenager and has assumed that because Tanta is young, she must need babying. Most of her colleagues in the unit are in their fifties.

'Good,' Porter says. He looks like he's going to continue with his lecture, but the vehicle slows to a stop. They've arrived. The van's double doors swing open and the team climb out into the cold night air. They emerge outside the southern face of the Needle and file in through its staff entrance. The slender pyramid with its jagged spire is InTech's corporate headquarters, and during the day it plays host to thousands of office workers who are occupied with everything from high-level trade meetings to maintaining the corporation's main server room. Tonight, however, it is playing host to activities of a different kind.

It's Foundation Day, the anniversary of InTech's incorporation, and this evening the Needle has been transformed into the venue for the biggest party south of the riverbed. The skyscraper glows like a beacon, warm and inviting. In the restaurant and event hall near its apex, servers are busy pouring champagne into crystal flutes and arranging platters of canapés.

At the other extreme of the building, in a dingy security

room on basement level one, Tanta and her colleagues cluster around Senior Guardian Porter and await their orders.

'I want you all to set your 'scape security apps to record,' Porter begins. 'I'll be down here in the command centre, monitoring the footage as it comes in. I'm sending you your individual assignments via MindChat now. Most of you will be on the external doors, checking 'scape idents and conducting bag searches.'

There's a collective groan as everyone receives their instructions. No one likes being on door duty, especially in this weather.

'Can't we check IDs from inside?' asks Wright, one of Tanta's colleagues. 'It's not like a few gate-crashers will be the end of the world.'

Porter fixes him with a glare. 'Director Kenway himself will be at this event, and these security arrangements have his seal of approval. If any of you have a problem with them, you can take it up with him personally, got it?'

The protests subside into half-hearted muttering. One thing Tanta has learnt since joining the guardians is that she isn't the only one who dislikes Douglas Kenway. He still runs Residents' Affairs, the division responsible for the community guardians, alongside his new role as Interim Director of the ICRD, and he has a reputation among the rank and file for being both quick to form grudges and slow to give them up.

Porter looks them all over, nodding to himself. 'Didn't think so,' he says. 'Now, does anyone have any questions?'

Tanta coughs. 'I haven't received my assignment yet, Senior Guardian.'

The Senior Guardian's glare melts into a patronising smile. 'Ah, yes, Tanta,' he says. 'I've got a special job for you.'

Tanta hefts a platter of canapés in one hand, a tray of drinks in the other, and suppresses a sigh. Foundation Day is usually a celebration that she enjoys. The lights and fireworks are comforting at the dark tail-end of the year, and most CorpWards and wagers get a day off in honour of the festivities. Even during the times when she was too busy to take a full day away from her training, the general air of revelry and cheerfulness was always enough to lift Tanta's spirits in the past.

Not this year. This year, her bad mood could sour milk. When Senior Guardian Porter had kept her behind in the command centre, she had hoped – for one brief, shining moment – that he was going to give her something interesting to do. A guest to tail, some intelligence to gather, an important message to deliver. Instead, he had told her he wanted her to be a waiter.

'Given you're still recovering from your injury, I think the stress of working security at such a high-profile event might be a bit much for you at the moment,' he had said. 'I'd like you inside the venue instead, helping the servers. Make sure none of the guests get too rowdy.' He'd winked at her. *Winked*. 'I'm sure they won't give you any trouble.'

Tanta had only nodded in reply, not trusting herself to speak. *A bit much?!* Her injured hand has been out of its cast for weeks, and as for stress, she has held positions of greater responsibility than Senior Guardian Porter ever will in his life. She could tell him things about corporate duty and sacrifice that would shock him to his core, for all that she's less than half his age. Though of course she can't, really. Her service record is classified: more senior employees than Porter might try and fail to access it. So, he had sent her off to hand out drinks and direct drunken guests to the toilets, and Tanta had bitten her tongue and let him do it.

She's in the event hall now, a vast, open-plan room on the penultimate floor of the Needle. Smart dinner jackets and flowing evening gowns fill the space with elegance and colour. Servers, Tanta among them, flit between the parrot dresses and penguin suits, topping up glasses and offering around food. The venue is almost the highest point in the city, topped only by the penthouse apartments of InTech's board members, one storey above. Floor-to-ceiling windows line the entire room, offering a sweeping panoramic view. There's a large group of guests clustered around the ones to the south, admiring the twinkling lights of InTech's flats and skyscrapers.

No one is looking through the windows on the opposite side of the room – in fact, people are going out of their way to avoid them, giving the crowded hall a lopsided appearance. Tanta doesn't need to be an ICRD agent to know why. The windows to the north look out over the riverbed, filled with barbed wire and gun turrets, to the city beyond – Thoughtfront's side of the city, where no InTech employee has been welcome since the Bridge Gate closed and relations between the two corporations took a turn for the worse.

Even the guests unlucky enough to be positioned closer to the northern windows avert their eyes from the offending view, without ever speaking a word on the subject. This isn't the time to be dwelling on the cold war between InTech and Thoughtfront; it's a party. Tanta is the only one to find her eyes drifting towards the riverbed and its impassable bridges again and again. It's hard to believe that less than a year ago she was on the other side of that no man's land, infiltrating Thoughtfront's side of the city for the sake of her corp. That was a harrowing time, but she can't help looking back on it now with a pang of yearning. She'd rather be back behind enemy lines, with all the danger that entails, than stuck in InTech as a glorified security guard.

The indignity of her new role would be easier for Tanta to bear if InTech's threat level were low; then, she could at least take comfort from knowing that the ICRD didn't really need her. Unfortunately, the opposite is the case. Tanta knows more about the dangers facing her corporation than most. It was her investigation two months ago that uncovered the reason InTech and Thoughtfront are at each other's throats in the first place: a false flag attack, carried out by Cole but orchestrated by parties unknown, designed to trick each corporation into thinking the other was moving against it. But even if she'd had nothing to do with those events, she'd still be able to read the signs that something is amiss.

Ever since the summer, the mood on the south side of the city has been tense and anxious. InTech's Communications Division is ruthlessly efficient at coordinating media blackouts, and even the most public catastrophes of the summer – the Ward House fire and the viral attack on the sleeper factory – have been successfully passed off as tragic accidents. But not even InTech can explain away the closure of the Bridge Gate.

Tanta is too young to remember much about the original split between InTech and Thoughtfront, but she knows it was bad. Thoughtfront was once InTech's military research subsidiary, and it took with it much of its parent corp's expertise in weapons and defence systems. InTech remained a powerhouse, retaining an edge over Thoughtfront in the quality of its mind-based operating systems and its intelligence networks, but the parting of ways still left it more vulnerable than it had ever been. For years, residents on both sides of the bridge had worried that the split was the prelude to all-out war – that InTech would try to take its wayward subsidiary back, or Thoughtfront would seek to secure its independence by striking against its former parent. That fear receded over time, but it's back with a vengeance now. And for all InTech's spin, everyone can feel it.

The threat of war would be enough on its own to explain the unease gripping InTech's side of the riverbed, but for the last two months, it has been exacerbated by more tangible hardships. Two weeks after the Bridge Gate closed, the rationing began. Tanta – like all InTech residents – awoke one morning to find a quota card on her Array, limiting her weekly purchases of food and other essentials to a pre-determined set of items. Since then, the restless atmosphere in the city has curdled into something more volatile. The restrictions have been billed as a temporary measure to help InTech build up emergency reserves in case of crop failures – a precaution, nothing more – but even the most unthinkingly obedient CorpWard can see the cracks in that cover story.

When Tanta is on guard duty at the Outer Gate, or out on patrol, the tension in the air is palpable; here, in the halls of power, everyone is doing their best to pretend it doesn't exist. It isn't working. This party is ostensibly a chance for InTech's elite to relax and celebrate another successful year of business, but the laughter in the room is a hair too loud, the lulls in conversation strained and awkward. Unspoken fears linger in the pauses, giving the atmosphere of festivity a feverish edge.

On the streets, the anxiety Tanta senses is formless, compounded by uncertainty, but the mood of the party is different. The people in this room know things about the causes and nature of this crisis that the ordinary residents of the city don't – Tanta is sure of it. The sense of this knowledge, pervading everything and yet still out of reach, makes her skin itch. InTech is facing a new threat, something bad, and Kenway is too spiteful, or too afraid, to let Tanta come back to the ICRD and find out what it is.

Tanta is about to make another circuit of the room when a woman in stiletto heels bumps into her, interrupting her thoughts and almost knocking her over. She steps lightly aside, reflecting that her balance and reflexes are wasted in saving platters of appetisers from going flying.

'Excuse me,' the woman murmurs, then stops to help herself to what's on Tanta's tray. Tanta has never met the woman before, but she had enough lessons on InTech's power structures during her ICRD training that she recognises her: she's Harpreet Toor, Director of the Trade Division.

'It's no trouble,' Tanta replies. She's about to add 'Director', an instinctual gesture of respect, but stops herself. Director Toor has no idea who Tanta is – there's no point in letting her know that isn't mutual. Director Toor selects a small bowl of caviar, her hand wavering as she reaches across the platter. She looks dour, her lips set in a thin line, but her brown eyes are unfocused. She's very drunk. And not happy drunk, either.

Tanta watches the Director as she walks away, thinking fast. The upper echelons of InTech's management are in this room, drowning their sorrows and letting their guard down. If she wants to find out what insider secrets she's missed since her demotion, she's unlikely to get a better opportunity.

She waits a moment, then follows Director Toor into the crowd. There was a time when what she is doing now – abandoning the job she has been assigned to eavesdrop on InTech's top brass – would have seemed an unimaginable breach of protocol. Unimaginable in a literal sense: Tanta's Harlow Programming, the programming Cole took out of her head, once made such uncorporate instincts anathema. But her Harlow Programming is in ruins, and since she lost it, she's found herself doing unimaginable things on a regular basis.

Harpreet Toor is making her way over to a little knot of fellow Directors. Tanta spots Douglas Kenway in the group, and hastily drops her gaze. He doesn't strike her as the kind of man to pay much attention to serving staff, but she still has to be cautious. He and the Directors around him are talking intensely, but without animation, and accepting top-ups of champagne whenever they are offered.

They're standing near a table filled with discarded snacks and empty glasses, so Tanta busies herself with clearing it. It gives her an excuse to keep her head down, and to listen in to their conversation. She blinks a few mental commands, enhancing the audio on her 'scape. Keen as he was to oust Tanta, Kenway hasn't dared risk the awkward questions that would arise from demoting one of the ICRD's most promising young agents permanently. Technically, her role with the CommGuard is part of a temporary work shadowing scheme, which means she still has all her ICRD intelligence-gathering software.

'... extent of the problem,' Toor is saying. 'I warned catering about the shortages, and they still decided to go ahead with the original menu.' Her tone is pointed. Out of the corner of her eye, Tanta sees Kenway bristle. He's still Director of Residents' Affairs, so an event like this technically falls within his remit, though she doubts he had much to do with organising it.

'It's a party, Harpreet. Enjoy yourself,' he says, in the tone of a man who isn't taking his own advice. 'Leave catering to manage their own business.'

'It seems they are unable to do so,' Director Toor replies acerbically. 'I mean caviar, Douglas. Caviar? You must see how this looks.' She drops her voice to an angry whisper and her words are lost in a crash to Tanta's left as another guest drops his glass. She edges closer, moving around the table.

'... attacks haven't let up in almost two months,' Toor continues, 'and our warehouses are starting to run low on essentials. The residents are a hair's breadth from rioting as it is, and if word gets out that you've been serving champagne and foie gras at executive functions—'

'We're not discussing this here,' Kenway snaps, and Toor subsides, glaring at her champagne flute as though she would like to fling it into Kenway's face.

<<Tanta. How's it going?>> It's Porter.

<<Nothing to report, Senior Guardian,>> Tanta returns, wishing him away with all her might.

<<There's a UAV delivery coming into the kitchen – more

wine for the revellers, I think. Mind giving it the once-over for me?>> Tanta grits her teeth. Trust Porter to send her running off after a delivery drone – and just when she was starting to learn something!

<<Of course,>> she replies.

She edges her way through the crowded room, heading for the service door to the kitchens. The brief snatch of conversation she managed to overhear before her manager's intrusion was frustratingly light on details. It has told her little she didn't suspect already, though from what Director Toor was saying, InTech's food shortages are worse even than Tanta had guessed. And what are these attacks she mentioned? As the Director of Trade, Toor oversees the corporation's export and import networks, and the agreements it has with agri-pharma conglomerates like Bayanto and food production corporations like PGU. Could Thoughtfront be targeting InTech's supply lines, or its trade partners? And if it is, then how on earth has InTech allowed such a state of affairs to continue for this long?

Tanta sets her tray down outside the entrance to the kitchens and hurries through into a close, airless space full of people, smells and steam. InTech's automated defence turrets are programmed to shoot down any unauthorised UAVs in the corporation's airspace, so checking the delivery drone is just a formality. If she's quick, she might be able to get back out to the party in time to catch some more of the Directors' conversation.

She threads her way between the stainless-steel worktables and rows of ovens, dodging line cooks. There's a drone loading bay at the back of the room – a hatch in the exterior wall through which UAVs can shuttle in and out, ensuring the kitchen is constantly supplied with everything it needs to keep the biggest event venue in InTech's part of the city running. The drone is already waiting on the platform when Tanta reaches it, a huge delivery crate clutched in its mechanical talons. She slides the crate free.

The first clue Tanta gets that something is wrong is that the crate is far too light. She puts it on the workbench next to her and pops the lid; it's empty. She's about to ping Porter a query when she realises that the lid she's just removed is, by contrast, heavier than it should be. She turns it over. Six thick, black cylinders have been taped to its inside, red wires snaking between them.

Tanta goes still, motionless as a mouse crouching in the shadow of an owl. Then, swiftly and carefully, she raises her index finger to her forehead and summons her Array.

<<Senior Guardian, there's a bomb in the delivery crate,>> she sends. <<We need to evacuate the——>>

A *whump* rips upwards through the building, cutting Tanta off mid-message. It's more a sensation than a sound, a rumble of thunder that shakes the space behind her eyes and inside her chest. The building shakes, too, swaying as though it's been hit by an earthquake. The blast rings Tanta like a bell, leaving her jangled and confused. For an instant, she thinks the improvised explosive she's holding has gone off, but that's impossible – she's still alive. She braces herself against the workbench, focusing on one thought and one thought only: she must not drop the bomb. If it detonates, then she and everyone on this floor are dead. Her jaw locks as the shockwaves from the explosion hit, and she tastes blood.

Then the motion subsides, leaving behind a ringing in her ears and a distant sound of shouting. Tanta stays where she is, her thoughts racing on ahead of her. Judging by the direction and intensity of the shockwaves, the blast came from several floors below. No doubt about its source: a bomb has hit the Needle, and a second – the one Tanta is still gripping in one hand – could explode at any moment.

She pings Porter again. For a second, her Array flickers and vanishes, replaced by a flashing error message, but her 'scape reconnects in a heartbeat.

<<We need to evacuate the Needle,>> she repeats. <<There's a second device up here.>>

There's no response to her hail. Tanta risks a glance behind her: the kitchen is still full of servers and chefs, milling about in confusion and dawning fear. No one has noticed her standing in the corner with the unexploded bomb. Through the kitchen's porthole window, she can see guests wandering around in the hall beyond, looking dazed. The majority of InTech's upper management are at this party, and just one storey up are the residences of the board themselves. An explosion on this floor would be beyond disastrous; the shockwaves could knock the entire corporation to its knees – not that she would be around to see it happen.

For an instant, Tanta is paralysed by indecision. She knows what she needs to do here – clear the building, disarm the bomb, inform the ICRD – but protocol dictates that the Senior Guardian on duty should initiate those steps, not her. She needs Porter's permission to proceed. Without him...

Tanta shakes her head violently, physically dislodging the thought. Porter isn't answering her calls, and she can't risk lives waiting for him. The Needle has a building-wide emergency MindChat channel. She signs in, using her agent privileges to push her message out to everyone in the skyscraper.

<<Evacuate the building,>> she orders. <<This is not a drill. The emergency lifts are in the southeast concourse. Take them down to ground level, then get to a safe distance.>>

She sets the message to repeat. Then, she turns her attention back to the bomb, blinking an image capture of the device. Everyone in this part of the building needs to get as far away from here as possible, and assuming the two bombs were supposed to detonate together, they don't have long to get clear. She might be able to buy them more time, but she can't do it alone, and there's only one person she can think of who might be able to help.

<<Cole? Are you there?>> She's half-expecting silence in return. Cole isn't allowed to respond to personal messages while he's at work, and since his arrest, he's at work all the time now. To her relief, she gets a notification from him moments later.

<<I'm here. What's—>>

Tanta sends him the image capture immediately.

<<What is that?>> he asks, tone wary.

<<It's a bomb. Do you know how I can disarm it?>>

<<Shit! Tanta, what's going on?>>

<<Can you help me deactivate it or not?>> Tanta can well understand Cole's alarm, but there's no time to explain things to him.

<<Um. Right. OK. Maybe. Let me access your 'scape.>>

She grants him the permission he needs, her free hand flying across the air as she inputs the haptic commands. She feels a prickle at the base of her skull as Cole starts viewing her feed. There's a tense pause once he's in. Then he sends:

<<Zoom in on the device and give me a second. I need to think about this.>>

Tanta does as he asks. <<I can't give you much longer than that.>>

While Cole inspects the bomb, Tanta sends out another call to Porter. Like the first two, it goes unanswered. That, and the error message on her 'scape, suggests that the first bomb must have been on basement level one. That floor of the Needle houses not only the security command centre but also InTech's main server room – the interruption to Tanta's 'scape connection was probably caused by the explosion ripping through the machines that host the Inscape system.

Tanta feels a pang of almost-grief for the Senior Guardian. He wasn't a good team leader, but he meant well. She can spare him no more thought than that – there isn't time. The server outage will be a problem for the corporation, but not an insurmountable one. Tanta's 'scape is already back online, transferred to one of InTech's many backup servers. Far more concerning is the fact that the command centre is where the generators that power the emergency lifts are stored. If they're too badly damaged, she'll need to find another way to evacuate the building. Tanta racks her brains. Wright was on door duty on the staff entrance. He'll be the closest – if he's still breathing. She pings him.

<<Guardian?>>

<<Tanta?>>

Tanta lets out a relieved breath. <<I need you to go to the command centre and check the power to the emergency lifts,>> she sends.

<<What's going on?>> Wright sounds confused – and scep-tical. Tanta is the most junior member of the unit, and he's not used to her issuing commands. <<I heard an explosion and—>>

<<Mobilise the others. We're evacuating the Needle.>>

<<But shouldn't Porter be the one to—>>

<<Porter is dead. GO. NOW!>> Tanta sends, putting as much authority as she can into the order. If everyone waits around for Porter's go-ahead, the building will blow up with all of them in it. She turns her attention back to the bomb.

<<Cole?>>

<<OK, I think I can help,>> Cole replies. <<Do you see that disc in the middle of the explosives?>>

Tanta does. It's a pale, grey dome, small and compact.

<<The bomb itself looks homemade, but that thing is an InTech anti-theft device,>> Cole continues. <<The corp puts them on some of its UAVs – they're set to explode if the drone

28

is tampered with. Someone must've repurposed this one to act as a detonator for the other explosives. It'll be set to a timer, but you should be able to deactivate it.>>

<<How long till it goes off?>>

<<I don't know.>>

Tanta imagines grains of blasting powder falling through an hourglass. She hopes they're moving at a trickle, not a rush. <<I'm ready. Tell me what to do.>>

<<The first step is to detach it from the lid – gently – and turn it over.>>

Tanta does as Cole orders, though touching the device feels a lot like forcing herself to stick her hand into a bear trap. The disc is stuck to the lid of the crate with some kind of glue, and for a terrible second Tanta thinks that freeing it will set it off, but it comes loose with a soft snap. She turns it over; there's an AR control panel on its underside. Someone has clearly tried to destroy the panel, scratching at the marker code beneath it in an attempt to render it unreadable to the Inscape system. But the code has been etched onto the plastic casing of the device itself; the readout is glitchy, but legible.

<<What now?>> Tanta sends.

<<OK. OK.>> Cole sounds like he's barely restraining himself from panic. <<The AR menu should be simple enough. You're looking for the override system. Find that, then input your 'scape ident. You still have agent privileges, right?>>

<<Yes.>>

<<Then your ident should work to override the detonator. In theory.>>

Tanta doesn't like the sound of that. <<In theory? What if it doesn't?>>

<<I'm sorry, Tanta – that's the best I've got.>>

Tanta hesitates. If her ident doesn't disarm the bomb, could it detonate it instead? She's weighing up the risk when the device in her hand starts to beep.

<<Oh, fuck. Tanta, do you hear that? That isn't good.>>

Tanta hardly needs Cole to tell her that. It seems the decision has been taken out of her hands. She finds the override system and taps in her ID. Her finger hovers for an instant over the *submit* button.

<<Here goes nothing,>> she sends. She smashes the button, her finger jabbing through it and onto the casing beneath.

After she's done it, she realises her eyes are screwed shut. She opens them again. She's still here, and so is the Needle. For the first time since she contacted Cole, she tears her eyes from the bomb, looking behind her. The kitchen is empty; the hall beyond it, too.

<<Tanta?>> It's Cole.

Tanta sends him a mental nod – enough to let him know that it worked, she's alive – then switches to another channel. <<Wright,>> she sends. <<How are those lifts?>>

<<All fully operational,>> he replies a moment later. <<Evacuation is halfway complete.>> Tanta's outburst must have done its job; he sounds afraid, but he's no longer questioning her hastily assumed authority.

<<Excellent work,>> Tanta sends, then shivers. It's a Harlow Programme command phrase, and it slipped out before she could catch it. Her old mentor used to use phrases like this on her frequently – *excellent work; you've exceeded everyone's hopes; I'm very disappointed in you* – and there was a time when just hearing one was enough to flood Tanta with euphoria or dismay. It's one of the ways InTech keeps the CorpWards in line – one of the ways it kept Tanta in line, back when her own programming was operational.

She's angry at herself – not for the slip of the tongue, but for her indecision of a few minutes before, when she was faced with the unexploded bomb. In situations like that, every second counts, and Tanta wasted precious moments worrying about protocol when she should have been taking action. Greater even than her frustration is her unease. She knows why she hesitated. It's been months since the Harlow Programme was removed from her head, but its echoes remain, and they're still trying to tell her what to do, insisting that the chain of command is more important than her colleagues' lives – and her own.

Another message from Wright cuts across her thoughts. <<Tanta... how the hell did this happen?>>

Tanta doesn't answer. She's wondering the same thing.

Chapter 3

Tanta is the last one out of the Needle, forty-five minutes after the evacuation began. She has barely moved a step in all that time, apart from the brief walk from the kitchens to the emergency lifts, but she's mentally drained, strung out by tension and the after-effects of adrenaline. Her feet crunch on glass as she walks through one of the fire exits. The Needle is still standing, in spite of the explosion that rocked its foundations, but it looks a lot like she feels. There's an ominous cloud of smoke billowing from its open doors, and the shockwave has shattered windows throughout its ninety-five floors, spraying the surrounding streets with shards of broken glass in a radius around the epicentre of the blast that's probably half a mile wide.

The first thing Tanta does when she gets outside is check on the rest of her unit. They're still shaken by Porter's death, but they've recovered well from their initial panic. Wright has assumed command of the team and is doing a decent job of keeping up morale; he has established a security perimeter around the building and has the rest of the guardians super-vising the cleaning crews who have arrived to sweep up the debris. The guardians are also holding back an increasingly vocal throng of onlookers. The crowd is fractious, shouting questions at Wright and the team and trying to push past the perimeter they've created. Not an ideal situation, but at least it gives her harried colleagues something to focus on besides the explosion. Once she's sure that Wright has everything under control, Tanta takes herself across the road from the Needle and waits.

She has already notified Kenway of what has happened; she's expecting a summons to the ICRD for a debrief, so she's surprised when she sees him shoving his way through the crowd towards her, Harpreet Toor by his side. Toor's gait is steadier than it was when Tanta saw her last; evidently the shock has sobered her up. She greets Tanta with a curt nod; Kenway only glares at her.

'Are you Tanta? The Acting Senior Guardian?' Toor asks.

'Yes, I'm Tanta. I coordinated the evacuation,' she replies. She was never supposed to be in charge, and claiming a title that isn't hers will only give Kenway another excuse to be angry with her.

'Let's talk over here,' Toor says, drawing Tanta and Kenway aside from the crowd. When they're out of earshot of the onlookers, she addresses Tanta again. 'You were the one who found the second device, yes? Have you told anyone else about it?'

'No one in the building,' Tanta replies. 'While I was disarming it, I asked for a technical consult from a colleague in the Black Box – Neuroengineer Cole.' Kenway's jaw clenches. Toor, who must know nothing about Cole or Tanta's history with him, nods, satisfied that anyone working in InTech's most classified R&D lab must have a high enough security clearance to be trustworthy.

'That's good,' Toor says. 'You shouldn't mention it to anyone else. The official account is that there was an electrical fire in the server room.'

'Understood,' Tanta says.

'Good job in there,' Toor adds. 'I'll leave your Director to debrief you.'

She walks away, leaving Tanta alone with Kenway and his look of intense dislike.

'I placed Cole under house arrest for a reason,' he says. 'He's a security risk. Involving him in something like this was a breach of protocol. I'm disappointed in you.'

Tanta flinches, hardly needing to play up the extent to which she feels the sting of the command phrase. She restrains herself from pointing out that her breach of protocol likely saved Kenway's life. It's important that she continues to act the part of the obedient CorpWard, meek and submissive. If Kenway – or anyone else in InTech – ever finds out that her Harlow Programming has been removed, she can kiss her newfound mental freedom goodbye. She murmurs an apology, her eyes on the ground.

'See that it doesn't happen again,' he says. 'Dismissed.'

Is that it? Tanta thinks. She was expecting Kenway to have hundreds of questions for her about the sequence of events. In fact, and despite her dislike of the man, she was looking forward to them. She hasn't had an ICRD briefing in months, and she misses the intensity, the forensic focus on details, the speculation on players, motives and means. She had already started examining the circumstances of this attack in preparation, arranging them in different configurations in her head to see if one could shed some light on what has happened here. But Kenway is turning away from her.

'Director?' she says.

'What?' he snaps.

Tanta knows she should leave this alone. It's not her job to investigate this case, and it won't help anyone if she tries – least of all her. But although Kenway has kicked her out of the ICRD, he can't suppress her instincts. An empty delivery crate, rigged with explosives, that somehow made it through all of InTech's UAV countermeasures: Tanta is drawn in by the mystery of it – it makes her pulse race and her mind whir with possibilities. She can't help it.

'Would you like me to examine the drones?' she asks. 'Perhaps I could—'

Kenway starts walking before she has even finished her sentence. 'Go home, Junior Guardian,' he calls over his shoulder. 'You're not needed here.'

Tanta watches him leave, struggling to swallow her anger and dismay. She just disarmed a bomb that was about to blow out the top of the Needle, for god's sake! Many of InTech's Directors – perhaps even the board themselves – are only alive because of her intervention. She wasn't expecting a pat on the back, but a thorough debrief would have been nice. She masters her feelings at last, with difficulty. Exhaustion flows in in their wake. Suddenly, the raw night air is too cold, the shouting of the crowd too loud.

Tanta is turning in the direction of her flat, about to take Kenway's advice, when a familiar face appears in the crowd. Reet sprints towards her, wrapping her in warm, strong arms that smell of rosewater and cinnamon.

'Tee!' she gasps. 'I'm so glad you're OK!'

Tanta leans into her lover's embrace and just for a moment, all the tension and disappointment of the evening drain away. She's back in the Ward House, Reet holding her close in their shared bunk, sheltered by a blanket fortress that protects them from harm.

The effect lasts as long as Reet's arms are around her. It is only when her lover releases her that Tanta realises how strange her presence here is. She knows Reet's schedule like the back of her hand: she should be on shift at The Rotunda, InTech's premier enhanced hospitality venue, right now, not outside the Needle comforting her.

'What are you doing here?' Tanta asks.

Reet colours. 'I – I heard the explosion,' she says. 'I wanted to make sure you were all right.'

Reet has always struggled to keep her feelings hidden, especially from Tanta, and Tanta can tell that the question has embarrassed her. The sight of her lover's all-too-legible face, an open window onto her thoughts, fills her with a rush of affection. Perhaps Reet is ashamed of having left work early, but Tanta is touched by the gesture. She kisses Reet gently on the lips.

'Sorry, I'm still in guardian mode. I didn't mean to interrogate you. It's really good to see you, Reet.'

Reet's hazel eyes brighten. 'You too.' She takes Tanta's hand, drawing her away from the shattered building. 'Shall we get out of here?'

In former days, she and Reet would have gone up to the roof of the Ward House and sat there talking, probably until the sun came up. It's been two months since the Ward House burnt to the ground, but they've yet to find a similar spot. They decide to head to a bar, a luxury that Tanta is still getting used to. Reet is The Rotunda's Senior Manager now, and her allowance has increased as a result. Suddenly, they can afford to go out for drinks or meals on a regular basis. Tanta knows she should be grateful for these new freedoms and comforts, but she often finds herself thinking wistfully of the Ward House, with its narrow bunks and hard mattresses.

Tanta presses close to Reet as they walk, relishing her warmth. The night is cold but clear; even here, in the centre of the city, they can see the stars. She feels a quiet sense of companionship settle over her, like a dusting of snow – beautiful, but fragile.

As they draw closer to the bar, she realises she's reluctant for the walk to end, for anything to interrupt the sweet silence, the soft weight of Reet's arm around her shoulders.

'Do you want to talk about what happened?' Reet asks her, giving her a squeeze.

Tanta's heart sinks. She knew that the spun-glass bubble of contentment couldn't last. The last thing she wants to do is talk to Reet about the frustrations of her evening – it's a conversation that can only end badly. In the past, when she was feeling low, it was always Reet she would turn to, but that is changing. There are times, like this night walk, or when they're making love, that Tanta can pretend she and Reet are as in-sync as they always were. She's ignoring the obvious, though: more and more, sex and silences have become easier than actually speaking to one another. Tanta hesitates before she replies, but she is still so used to their old, easy confidence that keeping her own counsel feels like treachery. After a silent struggle, she blurts out:

'I was hoping Kenway would debrief me, but he didn't. He just sent me home.'

'Because you need to rest,' Reet replies.

'No, because he didn't want my help. He said so himself.'

'It's for the best, Tee,' Reet says instantly. Her tone is gentle, but decisive. 'If Douglas wants you resting up right now, then you're exactly where you need to be.'

Tanta experiences a savage stab of self-pity at Reet's words. She knew she shouldn't have said anything, and here is her punishment. A familiar tangle of emotions constricts her chest. Her lover used to know exactly what to say to make her feel better, but that hasn't been true for a while now, and she should stop torturing herself by looking for comfort that Reet can't give her anymore. Of course Reet would defend Kenway; as far as she's concerned, he's family. Tanta remembers how she used to feel about InTech and its Directors, the love and loyalty that were the strongest forces in her nature – or in what she had thought was her nature. Reet has the same Harlow Programming in her head as Tanta once did, only hers is still fully operational – and still manipulating her judgement.

Reet kisses her cheek. 'It won't be forever,' she says, anxious to reassure. 'Next time the ICRD gets busy, I'm sure Director Kenway will want you back on the front lines.'

Tanta nods, the knot in her chest tightening. It would be pointless – even dangerous – to say more. If word gets out that she's anything less than a model employee, happy to serve her corporation in any form it deems fit, then the brass might start asking questions about Tanta's own Harlow Programming – questions that wouldn't lead anywhere good for her. She can't risk saying anything that would give the game away, even to Reet. She turns the conversation, keen to get off the subject.

'How did you get to me so fast, anyway?' she asks. 'I thought your shift didn't finish for another hour.' She's still curious on this point; it's not like Reet to leave a shift early, for any reason.

Reet looks away. 'When I saw what happened on the news, I left Shirin in charge.'

Tanta wasn't trying to catch Reet in a lie, but she realises with an uneasy start that she has. She slows, looking at her lover's face. There's another blush spreading over Reet's cheeks, and an awkward, furtive expression in her eyes.

'I thought you said you came because you heard the blast,' Tanta says.

Reet reddens further, looking wretched. 'It was both.'

'Reet? What's going on?'

'What do you mean?'

'Come on. What is it?' Tanta tilts her lover's head down so that their eyes meet. 'You can tell me.'

'I made it, Tee,' Reet says, the words tumbling out in a rush. 'I applied to the ICRD's agent training programme last month, and I didn't say anything to you because I didn't want to jinx it, but I just found out last week and ... I got in. I'm going to be an agent!' A smile breaks across her face, lighting her up like a bulb. It's gone in an instant, replaced with worry. 'I was waiting for the right time to tell you. I know you've been having a hard time at work and I was hoping I could wait till things got better. I didn't want you to find out like this,' she finishes miserably.

Tanta is stunned. She knows that she and Reet are not as close as they were, but she never imagined she'd miss something like this. It does make sense of a few things, at least: Reet's swift arrival at the scene, and her lack of curiosity about what happened – she probably heard all about it from another agent. And she called Kenway *Douglas* – they're already on first-name terms.

'I know the timing is awful, Tee, and the last thing I wanted to do was make you sad,' Reet continues. 'But now that I'm a Probationary Agent, I can finally help you like you helped me! I'll let you know whenever there's a good job opening. I've already told Douglas about how you helped me with my training, and ...'

Tanta reaches for a suitable response to all of this and finds ... nothing suitable at all. She stares at Reet, searching for pride and excitement that just aren't there. She's jealous, of course, as Reet worried she would be, but she loves Reet too much to begrudge her this success, which she has dreamt of for so long. Reet has worked hard to become an agent, training every morning before work and often staying up late into the night reading the ICRD's procedural regulations. She has wanted to serve her corp in a higher way than as the manager of The Rotunda for a long time.

But is it really Reet who wants that? Is it Reet who voluntarily sacrificed sleep and leisure to mould herself into a more perfect tool to serve InTech's needs? Tanta isn't sure, and it is that uncertainty, rather than envy, that holds her back from happiness. *Reet's not really Reet*, she thinks, not for the first time. The joy that lights up her lover's eyes and animates her smile is not hers, but a cuckoo feeling decoyed into her brain by the Harlow Programme.

But she's letting her own emotions ruin what ought to be a celebration. Rousing herself, Tanta forces a reply. 'Reet. It's OK. I'm happy for you.' It's a bridge too far – she realises it as soon as the words are out of her mouth. Reet is the one person who always knows how Tanta is feeling, and she can tell that Tanta is insincere.

Her face crumples like a stepped-on paper cup. 'I shouldn't have said anything,' she says. 'I knew it wasn't a good time.'

'No. I'm the one who should apologise. This is great news. Really. I didn't mean to spoil it.'

But Tanta can see she's only making it worse. 'I – I'm just tired, Reet,' she says. 'Really, really tired. I should do like Kenway said and get some sleep. Can we take a rain-check on that drink?'

'Sure, Tee. Of course. Whatever you need.'

'Thanks. I'll talk to you tomorrow.'

Tanta leaves – flees – before her lover can say another word.

She does not go to her flat, despite what she said to Reet. She wanders back to the Needle instead, where the crowds and the cleaning crews have finally dispersed, replaying their conversation in her head as she walks.

It would be easier if she could blame Reet for their growing distance – then she'd at least have somewhere to direct her anger – but she can't. It's not Reet's fault that Tanta has lost her Harlow Programming, or that Reet has kept hers – it's just a quirk of fate, something over which neither of them had any control. Tanta knows all this, but it doesn't make it any easier to bear.

The worst part of it is that she understands Reet as well as she ever did – better, even. Tanta's mind flicks back to her moment of indecision in the Needle, the insidious pull of corporate duty and protocol that haunts her still. She remembers what it was like to have the Harlow Programme in her head, and so she knows exactly how wide the gulf between her and Reet is, and how impossible it is to bridge. She longs to be honest with Reet, to re-establish the closeness and the mutual support that have sustained them both for so long, and at the same time she understands why she can never be open with her again.

Reet's promotion is an added cruelty because it has come too late. If she had been accepted into the ICRD in the summer, she and Tanta would have been colleagues. They could have shared theories together, even partnered up. Maybe then things would have worked out differently, and Tanta would be tucked away with her lover in a conference room right now, discussing the strange UAVs and their explosive payloads, rather than wandering the streets and pondering her unanswered questions alone.

The thought stings. Tanta had to keep Reet in the dark about her first case because Reet wasn't an agent and now, just as she has encountered another mystery she'd love to solve, their positions have been reversed. Reet likely knows a thing or two about the attack on the Needle. She probably knows the truth about InTech's food shortages, too. But she won't breathe a word about these things to Tanta, and Tanta won't ask her. Reet is loyal, loving, fiercely protective – of InTech and of Tanta both – but the joint objects of her affection have never been in conflict before, and Tanta can't ever put her divided loyalties to the test. It would be cruel, but more than that, she doesn't dare. Because she knows, deep down, which of them Reet would choose.

Chapter 4

Douglas Kenway is as unhappy as a man who has achieved his dearest personal and professional ambition can be. When the board offered him Jen's old post as Director of the ICRD two months ago, he'd had difficulty restraining his jubilation. He'd coveted it since the start of his career, and he had wanted to see Jennifer Ash destroyed for almost as long. To have realised both dreams at a stroke seemed too perfect.

As it turned out, it was. Kenway leans forward in Jen's old chair, rests his elbows on her old desk, and tries to calm his nerves. His introduction to the ICRD has not been easy. He arrived in the midst of several crises at once. The Bridge Gate had been closed, bringing all communication between InTech and Thoughtfront to a halt. The Ward House had burnt to the ground, taking with it a sizeable proportion of the corporation's Harlow Programmed Corporate Wards. And Jen had just been exposed as a Thoughtfront mole, calling into doubt every project she had ever signed off on.

Kenway has spent his first months on the job fighting these fires, with little time for anything else. He has had to recall every agent on field duty to check that they haven't been compromised, acquire more CorpWards for Arthur and his experiments, and repulse Thoughtfront's increasingly brazen assaults — or try to.

The corporation on the other side of the riverbed has been taking full advantage of InTech's confusion. Not long after the Bridge Gate closed, gangs of unaffiliated bandits began harrying InTech's UAV supply chains, and there's little doubt in Kenway's mind as to who is funding them. The food shortages that Harpreet talked of at the party are worsening by the day, and the rationing he has instituted in response is only a sticking plaster. The Communications Division is putting the best spin on things that it can, but InTech's side of the city is a step away from starvation. And Harpreet was right on another count, too: the corporation relies on a diet of bread and circuses to keep its residents in line — now that the bread is running out, civic unrest is sure to follow.

Thinking of Harpreet brings a wave of anger. She accused Kenway of ignoring the extent of the problem, but that's not the issue. He recognises it all too well — it's just that his hands are tied. When Jen was running the ICRD, Kenway used to take a deep satisfaction in her ever-dwindling resources. More than a decade of relative peace had made the board complacent: they slashed the ICRD's budget every quarter, despite Jen's cautions, and Kenway never cared to back his colleague up — in fact, he'd relished her discomfort.

Now, that same lack of funding has become his problem. He's in no mood to appreciate the irony. The board have realised their error, at least, increasing the ICRD's budget tenfold, but it has come too late to reverse the worst of the decline, and much too late to prevent this latest disaster. Tonight's explosion had a lower casualty rate than the attacks the corporation experienced over the summer, but the threat to InTech itself was the greatest yet.

The Needle is not only an icon — the emblem of InTech's

corporate authority – but also its headquarters in a more practical sense. Most of InTech's Directors were at the Foundation Day party, and the entirety of the board were on the floor above. If the second bomb had gone off, it could have taken out all the corporation's leaders in a single stroke. The board have been taken to new accommodation now, of course – evacuated by a team of guardians who answer only to the conduit. Kenway has not been briefed on their location, which he takes as a very bad sign. They are losing trust in him and, honestly, he can see why. Thoughtfront (and it must have been Thoughtfront) has struck at the seat of InTech's power with impunity – a strike that the ICRD could neither anticipate nor counter – and it happened on Kenway's watch.

He has been summoned to an emergency meeting with the board's conduit to discuss this escalation in Thoughtfront's hostilities, which is the only reason he's still hanging around in the office at this hour. At the appointed time, he takes a lift down to the ICRD's basement. Ordinarily, meetings with the conduit would be held in the Needle, but it's closed, for obvious reasons, and the basement of the ICRD is as blast-resistant as a nuclear bunker. It may be right next door to the bombsite, but there's no safer place for the corporation's top Directors to gather.

Kenway strides into the room with a confidence he doesn't really feel. You need to project the things you want to be true about you, he has learnt; act as though you know everything, and other people will believe it. Or that's the idea, anyway. The board never seem quite as convinced by his certainty as he'd like.

This floor of the basement is usually used as a gym but has been hastily repurposed into a conference suite with the help of a folding table and chairs, giving it the appearance of a war room in a disaster zone. The conduit – a drab, grey man in middle age – is waiting for him, along with Arthur Friend and Harpreet Toor.

Kenway doesn't bother to return his colleagues' greetings. He has no time to waste on feigned cordiality – not towards them, at least. He wishes the board's Representative his gravest 'good evening', however. The conduit, as usual, acknowledges Kenway's entrance with nothing more than a blank-eyed stare.

'Report, Director Kenway,' he says, before Kenway has even sat down.

Kenway delivers his report as smoothly as he can, making sure to dwell on the positives: the fact that the second bomb was defused before it could do any harm, the low casualty rate. He praises the swift action of the community guardians – their quick-thinking and professionalism reflect well on his own good sense as their Director – but keeps Tanta's name out of his account. The board have not forgotten the way the young Corporate Ward saved the Harlow Programme and exposed his predecessor, and Kenway hasn't, either. Pleased as he was with Jen's downfall, he is never going to trust the agent who brought it about. Tanta betrayed one manager – who's to say she wouldn't do it again?

'The first device detonated on basement level one,' he concludes, 'resulting in the only fatalities of the night – four Server Engineers, and a Senior Guardian working in the command centre. There was also some minor damage to the main server room.'

The conduit sits up straighter at this, turning towards Arthur. 'Will the damage to the servers have any impact on the security update, Director?' he asks.

'Not at all, Representative,' Arthur replies. 'The damage was extensive' – he shoots a cool glance in Kenway's direction as he gives the lie to his understatement – 'but our backup servers in the data zeppelin are still fully operational. It has been moored just outside the city walls as a security precaution. The update will have to be rolled out from there, but it is still on schedule. The final human trials will take place the day after tomorrow, with the update itself going live in one week's time.'

The conduit nods. 'The update must take priority over all other concerns,' he says. 'It is vital to InTech's continued viability.'

Kenway returns Arthur's glare with interest, but in truth, he's relieved. The security update makes him uneasy, but he knows its importance to the board, especially given the state of affairs in the city, and the fact that it can still go ahead is good news. He is just starting to hope that he'll be able to escape from this meeting with his dignity intact when the conduit turns his watery eyes back in his direction.

'Director Kenway. Tonight's attack represents a lapse in internal security that cannot be tolerated. The UAVs evaded the city's automated defence turrets and reached the Needle without being intercepted. How do you account for these failings?'

Kenway blinks. The speed with which the board have gone back on the offensive has caught him off guard. 'My engineers are still combing the scene,' he replies, trying to gather his thoughts, 'but based on the available evidence, it would appear that—'

'*My* technicians have also visited the scene, Representative,' Harpreet cuts in. 'And they have discovered something of interest.'

Kenway turns his glare from Arthur to her. Harpreet is trying to undermine him – probably gunning for his position in Residents' Affairs. As the Director of Trade, her role is prestigious, but her security clearance is still lower than Kenway's – the only reason she's been attending these emergency briefings at all is because of the recent attacks on InTech's supply lines.

'It would assist in the coordination of a more *effective* response if Director Toor cleared future site evaluations with me directly,' Kenway returns icily.

But the board are not to be put off by this attempt to put Harpreet in her place. 'Proceed, Director Toor,' the conduit says.

'According to my officers' analysis, the UAVs were able to circumvent InTech's security measures because they carried valid InTech idents,' Harpreet says. 'By checking the serial numbers lasered into the drone casings, my team determined that both vehicles were stolen from us within the last two months.'

Kenway's heart sinks. 'Then it would appear that the incident at the Needle is linked to our recent spate of thefts,' he says, keen to regain control of the conversation.

'Two hundred missing shipments in sixty days,' Harpreet fires back, 'is hardly a mere "spate of thefts". And now it seems Thoughtfront is using the UAVs it has stolen to launch direct attacks against the highest tiers of our leadership! This is unacceptable: what is your plan of action, Director Kenway?'

Kenway is certain that Harpreet has overstepped here – presuming to ask questions and deliver admonishments on the board's behalf is not something they usually tolerate – but the conduit doesn't so much as murmur. He stares at Kenway fixedly, waiting for his reply.

Kenway feels a stirring of panic. 'Director Friend's UAV anti-theft measures have so far proven ineffective,' he says. 'Perhaps a further round of modifications will—'

'Director Friend's anti-theft measures are not the root of the problem,' the conduit interrupts. 'Thoughtfront is blockading our supply lines, and now it has assaulted our headquarters. You are responsible for InTech's intercorporate relations, Director Kenway, and it falls to you to coordinate a response to these outrages.'

The conduit's tone is as expressionless as always, but Kenway can sense the board's anger behind his words. He tries to think logically about how best to placate them, but his indignation threatens to drown his other thoughts. It isn't *fair*. He has done everything he ought to do to counter the drone thefts – vetting the employees with access to InTech's trade schedules, changing all of the corporation's delivery routes and timetables. They simply should not be possible – and yet the board still blame him for their continuation.

'All of our intelligence networks indicate that the thefts are the opportunistic work of unaffiliated bandits, Representative,' Kenway says at length, trying to sound reassuring. 'It's likely this cowardly attack came from the same source. While it's almost certain the agitators are being armed and encouraged by Thoughtfront, there's no evidence that it was directly involved in the blast. It can only be a matter of time before—'

'We do not have time, Director.'

Kenway subsides into humiliated silence. The conduit's eyes flicker to and fro as instructions from the board pour through his router.

'Director Toor tells us that the Corporate Ward Tanta played a significant role in evacuating the building after tonight's attack,' the conduit says at length. 'Has she been briefed on the broader situation?'

Kenway's heartbeat pounds in his ears, making the conduit's voice sound tinny and far away. It isn't the first time the board have asked about Tanta. In the aftermath of the Ward House fire, Kenway had simply told them she was exhausted after her ordeal and that he'd moved her to the community guardians to give her a chance to recover. But that was two months ago; he can't keep claiming she's indisposed forever.

'Tanta is still participating in the CommGuard shadowing programme,' he says. 'A period of lighter duties may be advisable, in light of all she's been through.'

'Surely not still, after all this time,' Arthur exclaims. 'Improved emotional resilience is one of the main advantages of the Harlow

48

Programme, and Tanta is among the most promising of her cohort.'

Silently, Kenway wishes a number of unspeakable fates on the doddering old fool. Aloud, he says: 'Even so, an assignment of such an important and sensitive nature, so soon after her valiant work in exposing Jennifer Ash, might prove too much for her.'

The conduit pauses to process this for no more than an instant. Then: 'We think not. Director Kenway, you will reassign Tanta to the ICRD and make use of her talents to investigate this matter. Perhaps she will succeed where others have failed.'

Where I have failed, you mean, Kenway thinks savagely. This galls him more than anything else. The board would never have told Jen what to do like this. They gave her complete autonomy in the running of the ICRD, when they've been breathing down his neck ever since he stepped into the role. But then, look what that licence cost them. He supposes, bitterly, that they are determined not to make the same mistake again. Jen is gone – Kenway gave the termination order himself, and was very particular about ensuring it was carried out – but even in death, his predecessor continues to thwart him.

He nods. 'Of course, Representative.'

There's nothing else he can say. The board were always going to insist that Tanta be brought back into the fold in the end. He can take comfort, at least, in the knowledge that he has laid the best groundwork he can for her to fail. Months spent telling the board that she's not ready, that he fears she won't be able to cope with an assignment of this magnitude – it will come as no surprise to them when he is obliged to report that, regrettably, she wasn't up to the challenge.

And Kenway is absolutely determined that she won't be. If he was keen to keep Tanta beneath the board's notice before, he's desperate now. It's clear from the way the conduit talks about her that the board see her as future management material – and that future may not be so distant. Despite the difficulty of the role, Kenway likes his new directorship, and he intends to keep it.

It won't be hard: he'll send the girl down some blind alleys, ask her to follow up on leads that other, better agents have already investigated and found useless. If she does, by some fluke, find out something of value, then it shouldn't be difficult to pass the credit on to someone else, or take it himself. And after a few days of frustration and failure, he'll tell the board that Tanta has not managed to justify their hopes. Of course, by then he's sure he will have found a solution of his own to the attack on the Needle and the drone thefts both. Then he'll have the double satisfaction of proving himself to the board, and seeing Tanta bumped back down to the bottom of the ladder, where she belongs.

Chapter 5

While Kenway is suffering through his meeting, Cole is waiting for one of his own. Tanta asked for his help in disarming the bomb at the Needle over an hour ago, and he's been watching out for her from his living room window ever since, tense and anxious.

While he waits, and to distract himself from his worry, he plans how to break out of his flat. This has been a regular evening activity for him since he was placed under house arrest two months ago. He'll get home, eat dinner, and then turn his mind to thoughts of escape. As a challenge, it has offered plenty to occupy his attention. Douglas Kenway and his community guardians have taken extensive precautions to keep Cole secure – there are sensors on his windows, a lock on the outside of his door, and covert bugs hidden throughout his living space.

Cole thinks he knows where most of the cameras and listening devices are now, and he has a good idea of their ranges and lines of sight. He's probed for weaknesses in their code as well, moving carefully and cloaking his Inscape ident to avoid detection. After many weeks of thought and planning, he has worked out a way to shut them down for at least a couple of hours – plenty of time to break through the bars on his window, smash the glass, and jump out. Unfortunately, Cole lives on the fifth floor and, unlike Yas or Tanta, he couldn't scale a building if his life depended on it.

He's not seriously intending to put his plan into action – he doesn't have the guts – but it helps to while away the long hours when he's not at work. Just as Yas predicted, Cole has been reassigned from the ICRD to the Black Box, and he's not happy about it. He misses Tanta, and being back at the scene of his old crime is no picnic, either. Though he lost most of his time in the Black Box in the MindWipe, the memories Cole does have of the place are not pleasant ones. The way Tanta looked at him when she discovered that he was the architect of the Harlow Programme... He doesn't want to think of that every time he arrives for work in the morning.

And, of course, his job also makes the possibility of escaping even more remote than it otherwise would be. Cole is not only InTech's prisoner, but one of its most valuable assets. Planning his breakout is like plotting a burglary in reverse: a heist where he is both thief and plunder.

No, all things considered, he's not going anywhere any time soon. Still, house arrest isn't so bad in the grand scheme of things. Cole reminds himself, frequently, that plenty of people have it worse. He tries to count his blessings. Some days that's easier than others.

A knock on the door rouses Cole from his thoughts. Relief floods through him. He knows it's Tanta immediately: she's the only person he knows who keeps such insane hours, and the only one who would bother to knock.

'Come in,' he calls. He's grateful to Tanta for acting as though his home is still his own, a space where he has control over who enters and when. One of the blessings that Cole always counts twice, when he's in a mood to count, is the fact that Tanta is still able to visit him. She has to disguise the social calls as security checks, of course, but being a guardian means that she has the clearance level to come in without triggering an alarm. There's a soft beep as the digital lock on the door recognises Tanta's 'scape ident, then a *shunk* as she draws back the lock – an actual deadbolt, annoyingly, and not some digital lock that Cole could bypass in a heartbeat.

'This is a random security check, Resident,' she says as she walks in. 'Are you storing any restricted items in this domicile?'

'No, Guardian,' Cole says. He's powerfully glad to see Tanta safe and well; he's missed her more than he'd like to admit. Cole's world has become very small since his arrest, its boundaries narrowing to the walls of his flat, his office, and the car that shuttles him between the two. Tanta breaks up that monotony; she's his only visitor, and a welcome source of news about the world outside the Black Box. Their meetings are also the only chance Cole gets to make adjustments to the dummy system he built within Tanta's 'scape that mimics her lost Harlow Programme. He's been maintaining it ever since her original programming was destroyed last summer, deleting itself from her MbOS for some reason that Cole still doesn't understand.

'Are any of your activities in this domicile in contravention of InTech's end-user licence agreement or community guidelines?' Tanta demands, her tone stern.

'No, Guardian.'

'I'm going to search your residence now,' Tanta informs him. She makes a circuit of the flat's small living space, checking each room in turn.

'OK,' Cole replies.

As he's done many times before, he walks into the bathroom and turns on the shower as high and hot as it will go, letting the steam fog the mirror. Then he sits on the floor, leaving the door open. Tanta joins him a few minutes later. There's a narrow alcove just outside the bathroom, a place where one can sit out of sight of the camera at the far end of the hallway, and she positions herself within it, crouching with her back against the wall. For the first time since she entered the flat, she smiles at him.

'It's good to see you,' she says.

'Likewise,' Cole replies fervently. 'So, what happened? Is everything OK?'

'I'll tell you all about it,' Tanta replies, 'but let's check in first. Are you safe?'

This is a routine Tanta insists on whenever she visits. She never knows when she'll be forced to make a hasty exit, so they need to get the most important questions out of the way first. Cole's position in InTech is perilous; they both know it. It wouldn't take too much to tip him from being an asset to a liability.

He nods. 'For now. How's your dummy system holding up? Has anyone questioned your programming?'

Tanta shakes her head. 'No problems so far. Any word from Yas?'

'Zilch.' This question is more a matter of habit than anything else. Cole has told Tanta about Yas's visit two months ago and shown her the communicator she gave him (which he has wedged down the side of his mattress) but so much time has passed without him hearing from her, the mysterious Jeanie, or their 'man on the inside' that he's beginning to wonder if he ever will.

'I'm still looking into what she told me, though,' he adds. 'As much as I can, anyway.'

Yas's radio silence hasn't stopped Cole from trying to find out what she was talking about – if anything, it's piqued his interest further – but his progress has been slow. Arthur Friend doesn't trust him, and he's been attempting, as far as possible, to make use of Cole's genius without telling him anything about the projects he has him working on.

Cole's job now mostly consists of debugging code and fixing software for the other neurotechs, work which, although difficult, can be accomplished without the need for much context or understanding. It makes learning anything useful about the goings-on at the Black Box a challenge. It's also mind-numbingly boring, involving all of the most tedious parts of a neuroengineer's job, while leaving no room for the creativity that used to make that job enjoyable for Cole.

'I hope you're being careful,' Tanta warns him.

'Always.'

The check-in over, Tanta frowns at Cole, scrutinising his face. 'You need to get more rest,' she says. 'Dr Friend is working you too hard. You look exhausted.'

Cole scoffs. 'Pot, kettle.' It's useless for them to give each other advice on self-care. Cole is a prisoner and Tanta is lying to everyone she knows; more sleep isn't going to help either of them. 'Now fill me in,' he says. 'Do we still have a corporate headquarters?'

'Just barely,' Tanta replies, with a faint smile. As she recounts the night's events to Cole, he finds himself thinking with nostalgia of their old partnership. Helping Tanta disarm the bomb earlier this evening was terrifying, but exciting, too, reminding him of their exploits when they were undercover together in Thoughtfront territory. He misses working in the ICRD with her. Looking at the animation on her face as she tells him about the things she overheard at the party, he knows Tanta feels the same.

'Kenway wouldn't even let me stay to inspect the intact drone,' she finishes, with uncharacteristic gloom. 'Even though I disarmed it.'

'*We* disarmed it,' Cole replies, pulling a face. 'And you probably aren't missing much. They'll just take out the flight recorder, check its path, and trace it back to whoever sent it: child's play. Not worth your time, if you ask me.'

That earns him a chuckle. Then Tanta pauses, her index finger flying to her temple to summon her Array. 'There's another patrol in the area,' she says. 'I should go – I'll try and check back soon.'

'OK.' Cole rises as Tanta does. 'Hey,' he adds, as she turns. 'Thanks for visiting.'

He tries not to show how reluctant he is to see her leave. These brief meetings with Tanta are often the only real human contact he has all week, and he's depressed by how much he has come to rely on something so fleeting. It says a lot about the quality of his days now that these late-night tête-à-têtes are the only highlights in them.

After Tanta has left, Cole tries to do as she suggested and rest, but it's a vain effort. Arthur delights in summoning him for work at inconsistent times, and knowing that he will likely be jerked awake by an armed guardian some time between the hours of five and eight in the morning does little to help him drift off. In the event, he's lucky. The guardians come for him at eight thirty, allowing him a halfway-reasonable amount of sleep.

His good fortune lasts until he reaches his shared office at the Black Box to find Arthur waiting by his desk. Cole is working under his direct supervision, and it's one of the things he hates most about his job. Arthur has been poisonously jealous of Cole ever since Cole created the Harlow Programme. Now that Cole is his prisoner, he takes a petty satisfaction in making his life miserable. He forces him to stay late and arrive early, to curtail lunch breaks and forgo vacation days, reminding him of his place with a litany of little tyrannies.

'Ah, Cole,' Arthur says, flashing him a smile that would look benevolent if there weren't so many teeth in it. 'I'll need you to stay late today. Sarah is off sick, so I've assigned her tickets to you.'

One of Arthur's favourite power plays is a nasty rule he has dreamt up whereby Cole isn't allowed to go home until he completes every task on his docket. Usually, this isn't a problem – most of the work Cole is given is simple enough that he can race through it – but occasionally, the good doctor likes to surprise him with a deluge of extra tickets, forcing him to stay into the night.

The worst part of this for Cole, as Arthur no doubt knows, is that someone else always has to stay with him. When this happens, his colleagues resent him for it, and he has the discomfort of having to endure their cold stares and angry mutters on top of their usual wariness. Cole's role in designing – and attempting to sabotage – the Harlow Programme is classified, but he's sure that Arthur has told his co-workers enough about his chequered past that no one will dare risk becoming friendly with him.

Cole nods an acknowledgement of Arthur's order; he's not about to give him the satisfaction of any other kind of response. He sits down at his desk and puts on the MbOS port that allows him access to the Black Box's systems, turning his back on the conversation. Arthur sticks around for a few minutes, but when he sees that he's not going to get a rise out of Cole, he leaves him be, stalking off with the rest of the department to their morning meeting.

The instant he finds himself alone, Cole glances sidelong at the doorway. The corridor outside is empty, as is the rest of the office. This is a rare opportunity: it's not often that he's left unsupervised, even for a moment. When it does happen, he has learnt to make the most of it. He shucks his MbOS port again and moves over to the door, as though he's going to the bathroom. Once he's out of sight of the security camera trained on his work area, he makes a beeline for the absent Sarah's desk.

Then, with a familiar thrill of daring, he slips her MbOS port over his eyes.

As he told Tanta last night, Cole has been looking into the Black Box's research projects. Despite what he told her, he's not being as careful as all that. The risks he has been taking are serious ones. If Arthur ever caught him snooping through classified files like this, he'd be lucky to escape with his life. Cole may be useful, but in the corporation's eyes he's also dangerous; the instant he gives the powers that be grounds to suspect him of further treachery, he's sure they won't hesitate to act.

For the first month of his house arrest, Cole limited his detective work to his own tickets. He reads code like other people read fiction: fluently and without hesitation, so even when glitching programme fragments were sent to him carefully shorn of their illuminating context, he could usually still work out where they were from and what they were intended for. And sometimes, for all their care, one of the other neurotechs would forget to redact the departmental identifier from an error report. Cole knows how to read those, too.

The approach taught him more about the comings and goings at the Black Box than he was expecting – certainly more than Arthur ever wanted him to know, but Cole realised a few weeks ago that he had learnt all he could from it. His own workstation is walled off from most of the Black Box's systems, and the most sensitive of the lab's research and development projects never come anywhere near him. He could have abandoned his own amateur sleuthing at this point and waited for Jeanie to make contact. He could have given up on the whole thing. But some of Tanta's investigative instincts must have rubbed off on him, because instead, Cole decided to start doing this.

He scrolls through Sarah's files, cloaking his Inscape ident as he goes, just as he does when he's probing the cameras in his flat. There was a time when the recklessness of his behaviour would have made Cole dizzy with fear; he's faintly alarmed by how little it bothers him now. He understands the danger he is in on an intellectual level, but that knowledge feels remote from him. Perhaps he's depressed and looking for a thrill – a man holding his hand over an open flame to remind himself of what it's like to burn. Or perhaps he's trying to recreate the exhilaration and danger of his brief stint in the ICRD.

Both these motivations likely have some part to play in Cole's furtive investigation, but he knows they're not the real reason he's pursuing it. He's driven by more than ennui or self-destructiveness: he wants to make amends. The last time he worked in the Black Box, he created terrible things. If, or when, Jeanie does call on him to help her sabotage whatever atrocities are being dreamt up here now, he wants to be ready.

Cole is looking for two things: firstly, clues as to the nature of the big project Yas told him about, and secondly, some hint of who Jeanie's 'man on the inside' could be. He's yet to find an answer to the second question, but on the first, he's made some headway. From the scraps of information he has gleaned from his own work tickets and stolen from his colleagues, Cole has managed to compile a list of almost every project in the Black Box. He daren't risk writing this list down anywhere, but his memory is good enough that he can keep it in his head. He updates it now with the project notes he finds on Sarah's workstation, though she's involved in nothing more remarkable than developing a new suite of pseudotransmitters for the MoodZoop app. Cole's hopes weren't high, but he's still disappointed: Sarah's was the last workstation in his own office he hadn't checked, and investigating the other teams in the building is going to be much harder.

It's all the more frustrating because Cole is certain that Yas is right. There *is* something brewing in the Black Box, but so far, he's only been able to intuit it from its absence. Cole has matched each project on his list to a floor, an office and, in most cases, a set of named staff members, and there's someone missing. In all his digging, he has never yet come across any work from Arthur Friend himself. He must be working on something: Cole has heard him talking about how busy he is, and once or twice he has even cancelled meetings to 'focus on his research'. But whatever it is, it's so sensitive that he won't let Cole – or anyone else, for that matter – catch so much as a glimpse of it.

Cole is about to open Sarah's system messages when the sound of footsteps in the corridor outside sends him scrambling for his desk, his pulse thumping in his ears. He regains his chair just as a figure appears in the doorway. It's Neal Ortega, looking awkward. He's tall, with brown skin a few shades lighter than Cole's own, and a mop of black hair. Cole has seen him around, but never spoken to him before. He's a Neuroengineering Assistant, which is a glorified term for an intern. He's completing a work placement in the Black Box as part of one of InTech's neurotech training programmes, but he's not experienced enough to do any project work himself; he spends most of his time acting as a guinea pig for 'scape updates or going on coffee runs for the other neuroengineers.

'Um,' says Neal. 'Sorry to bother you. Dr Friend sent me down here to supervise you.'

Cole shrugs, affecting indifference. He slips his MbOS port back over his eyes, hoping Neal won't notice the way his hands are shaking.

There's a creak as Neal steps further into the room, then the sound of him sitting down. For a few minutes, they sit together in silence, Cole pretending to work while he gets his breathing back under control.

'You're – you're *him*, aren't you?' Neal asks. 'Neuroengineer Cole?'

The intern speaks so quietly that at first, Cole doesn't realise he's talking to him. He nods once, without turning around.

'I read about you,' Neal says. 'I mean, I read something *by* you,' he continues, when Cole doesn't reply. 'On my neuro-engineering course. It was a paper you wrote about extending MbOS pseudotransmitter pathways into the limbic system. An analogue study using rhesus monkeys.'

Cole remembers the paper: a juvenile effort that he penned before he was out of basic training. It was probably the beginning of his research into what would become the Harlow Programme – though, of course, the papers on *that* are classified.

'I just wanted to tell you that it changed the way I thought about the Inscape system,' Neal mumbles. 'It was ground-breaking.'

Cole is embarrassed – both by Neal's praise and his own coldness. He takes his MbOS port back off again and looks at the intern. Neal is staring at his feet, his cheeks flaming.

'That's kind of you to say,' Cole replies. He wishes Neal would shut up. He seems like a nice young man, and being seen talking to Cole won't do any favours for his career. He's about to return to work when Neal glances over his shoulder, then rises from his chair and crosses to Cole's desk.

'I, uh …' Neal fidgets, chewing on a nail. 'I showed your paper to a friend on my course, and she liked it too.'

'That's good to hear,' Cole says, wondering where this is going.

'Yeah. She said that maybe I should talk to you about it.'

'Well, now you have. And I'm flattered, Neal – really. But I'm sure Director Friend told you the same thing about me as he told everyone else. You shouldn't be talking to me, because I'm—'

'A security risk. I know,' Neal says, dropping his voice to a hoarse whisper. 'But my friend's a bit of a rebel.'

A feeling like an electric current thrills through Cole. He had given up hope of ever hearing from Jeanie's 'man on the inside', but unless he's badly misread this situation, he's standing right in front of him. Only he's more like a teenager, and he clearly doesn't have the sense he was born with. Internal security has been tightened since Cole returned to work at the Black Box: this office is bugged with almost as many listening devices as Cole's flat. Neal may already have said too much. Cole shifts in his chair, putting his back to the camera above his desk.

'Your friend isn't called Jeanie, is she?' he whispers.

Neal lets out a whoosh of pent-up breath. 'Yes!' he says, much too loud. 'I've been trying to find a time to talk to you for days, and—'

Cole stands up, scraping his chair back noisily across the floor. 'Not here!' he hisses. He can see now why Yas told him that Neal would need all the help he could get.

Lunch time, he mouths. *Talk then.*

Aloud, he says: 'I can't help you, Neal. If you have questions about my research, ask Dr Friend.'

Neal gives him a single, nervous nod and flees back to his seat.

Cole spends the rest of the morning in a state of feverish anticipation. Neal stays with him for another hour, until Arthur's meeting concludes and the rest of the team return, but to his credit, the intern doesn't so much as look Cole in the eye again, let alone speak to him. Cole can't even be sure that Neal understood his message until lunchtime rolls around. He arrives early and takes his normal seat in the canteen – at the far end of the table furthest from the door. As usual, the rest of the table is empty – If Neal does turn up, there'll be no one to overhear their conversation. It's not an ideal place to talk, even so, but

62

they'll be safer in the noisy canteen, where there are cameras but no listening devices, than they could ever be in the office.

Neal walks in fifteen minutes later, when the lunch rush is at its peak. Cole watches him out of the corner of his eye, his heartbeat uncomfortably loud. Neal skips the queue for the vending machines – he's brought his food in a paper bag. Most of the tables are busy. He scans the room for a moment, apparently searching for a free seat and then, with a convincing air of resignation, crosses to Cole's table.

Cole feels another jolt of excitement as Neal approaches. This is really happening. The intern is about to sit down next to him, but Cole waves him off with a subtle motion of his hand.

'Opposite,' he murmurs. 'And keep your head down. You don't want anyone to figure out that we're talking.'

He follows his own advice, darting only the quickest of glances at Neal before returning to his sandwich. The boy looks stressed, biting his lip and fidgeting. Cole fights down a wave of highly inappropriate amusement. Neal reminds him of himself when he and Tanta first started going on covert assignments together. He would never have considered himself cool under pressure, but seeing how anxious Neal is makes him realise just how much he learnt and improved in the brief time he and Tanta were partnered.

'Relax,' he says softly. 'No one's looking at us. Just eat your lunch.'

Neal forces his shoulders down and complies. Cole has more questions than he can safely ask, but he makes himself wait until the young man looks a little calmer before he speaks.

'So. Jeanie asked you to contact me,' he says, after they've sat eating for a while in silence.

Neal dips his head in a slight nod.

'What can you tell me about her?'

The intern looks up again, confused. 'Is this a test? She said you'd help me.'

That was presumptuous of her, Cole thinks. *As far as I can remember, we've never even met.* 'It's complicated,' he replies. He pauses, trying to think of how to explain the situation without getting into decades of old history. 'Jeanie and I have mutual friends, but I don't know her personally. I'll help you if I can, but I'd like to know more about what I'm getting into first.'

Neal looks uncertain at this, but he does his best to answer. 'Well, I found her in a forum on the old web,' he begins.

Cole's interest is caught at once. If Jeanie knows her way around the old web, she could be a neurotech herself, or something similar. Most of the servers and cables that used to host the pre-Meltdown internet have long since fallen into disuse, but parts of the old web are still there, if you know where to look and have the skillset to access them. Cole has done it himself: when he was in basic training, he and some of the other neurotechs used to dig around in the ruins of the net in their spare time.

'Is that where she recruited you?' he asks.

Neal nods again. 'I read an essay she wrote about corporate power structures and how they rob us of agency in our own lives, and it made me re-evaluate a lot of what I thought I knew about society. The corps act like they're our friends, but they're not accountable to us at all, you know? We didn't choose them to run the world, like people used to before the Meltdown. They've replaced freedom with consumer choice, and it's been so long that we've all forgotten the difference.'

Neal's eyes are shining as he speaks. It's been a long time since Cole has heard this kind of revolutionary talk. When he lived in the Ward House, some of the other CorpWards would talk like this sometimes. They'd hold late-night political discussions, railing against the injustices of a system they were just beginning to understand. Cole would always listen with interest; he never had any friends among his fellow wards, but on this topic, and this one only, he shared their sentiments. The corporate system is rigged; you can't grow up in a place like the Ward House without knowing that instinctively.

Their InTech minders didn't encourage such talk, but they didn't actively repress it, either. In Cole's experience, life tended to do that for them. The radical young wards grew up and got jobs, and that put paid to most of it. When the collapse of corporate society means the loss of your salary and health insurance, it stops being something to daydream about. Neal's young enough that he has less of a stake in that rat race, so his idealism makes sense. Still, Cole is surprised. Neal is the first person he's met who has ever gone so far as to act on it.

'I was just talking to her and thinking about it all at first,' Neal continues. 'Jeanie had some questions for me about the work I was doing here, but I'm too junior to be involved in anything interesting. Or, at least, I was.'

'What changed?' Cole asks.

'Dr Friend made me his personal assistant,' Neal replies. 'It's not as exciting as it sounds. I mostly just get him coffee, but recently, he's started asking me to bug-check some of his code. He told me it's for a security update to the Inscape system, to make it more resilient to viruses.'

Cole draws a breath; Neal has just told him more about Arthur's work in a minute than he's been able to learn in two months. 'That sounds like a big job for just two people,' he says.

'It is,' Neal agrees. 'I've been working fourteen-hour days, and he only brought me on board with the project a week ago. Before that, I think he was trying to design the whole update by himself. It's highly classified, and I' – the trainee pauses, glancing around the canteen – 'I think he's lying about what it's for. It was actually your paper that made me suspicious.'

Cole looks up at that. 'What do you mean?'

'I've never seen the update in its entirety, so I can't be certain, but I think the changes it will implement are too broad to only be aimed at addressing security flaws. I've read the code again and again. I don't know for sure, but some of it looks as though it's designed to stimulate the incursion of pseudotransmitter pathways into the limbic system. I checked it against some of the sample code in your paper and – I'm pretty sure.'

There's a hint of pride in Neal's tone that reminds Cole of himself again. He's felt that thrill of scientific discovery before. 'That's concerning,' he says. More than concerning. MbOS architecture is designed to interface with the brain's visual and auditory processing centres; it has no business in the limbic system, the seat of emotion and memory. No ordinary security update should be so invasive; the only programme Cole has seen that extended so far was Tanta's Harlow Programming. He thinks he has an idea, now, why Jeanie came to him about this. Yas told him that he'd fed her intel about the Harlow Programme in the past. Could this 'security update' be some form of modification to his work?

Neal frowns. 'I just couldn't understand why Dr Friend would *lie* to me. So I talked to Jeanie about it, and she said that it could be something big – and that whatever it was, InTech's residents deserved to know about it. I told her I wanted to help her find out what was really going on. And she told me to talk to you.' Neal looks at Cole expectantly as he finishes speaking, as though Cole is about to propose a brilliant scheme to uncover whatever Arthur is up to. The trainee clearly believes he is some kind of rebel mastermind.

Would I be in this situation if I were? Cole thinks.

The rational part of his brain reminds him that he's well out of his depth here. A notional freedom fighter who lurks on the old web isn't much help to them in the here and now. Cole is a known traitor and Neal is just an intern. But Cole has been out of his depth since Yas's visit, and it hasn't stopped him yet.

'The next step,' he hears himself saying, 'is to gather more information.' He's surprised at himself: it sounds like something Tanta would say. 'We need to find out exactly how this update works, who it's for, and what it's designed to do.'

He's terrified that Neal is going to ask him what they're supposed to do *after* that, but to his relief, the trainee only nods.

'Arthur isn't storing the update on the Black Box's main systems, is he?' he continues. If he were, Cole is sure he would have found it by now.

Neal looks impressed. 'He sends me segments of code to check on data cards. He's never let me edit the update directly, but I've seen him working on it. He uses an MbOS port connected to a hard drive in his office. I don't think I can access it, though.'

'I can,' Cole says, a little in awe at his own daring. He's had enough practice recently, hacking into the workstations of his colleagues. 'Is there a time that Dr Friend's office would be empty – some time when we could examine the update undisturbed?'

'This evening,' Neal says immediately. 'He has a meeting with the board every week at eight.'

Cole starts. He wasn't expecting Neal to suggest they make their move so soon. 'Let's wait till next week, then,' he says. 'It'll give us more time to prepare.'

'We don't have that long,' Neal replies. 'Dr Friend only asked for my help in the first place because he had a tight deadline: the update's almost ready for launch.'

Unease twists in Cole's stomach. 'When is it going live?'

Neal casts another nervous glance around the canteen. His eyes come to rest, at last, on Cole's own. 'Four days.'

Chapter 6

Tanta sleeps late the following morning. She's exhausted – both from her exertions at the Needle and her not-quite-argument with Reet. When she wakes, bright autumnal sunlight is spilling through the blinds in her bedroom, and there's a message from Kenway sitting at the top of her Array.

Tanta's first response is weary annoyance. This must be a reprimand of some sort. Perhaps Kenway is still peeved that she asked for Cole's help with disarming the bomb, or perhaps – and this thought sends a spike of alarm through her – he has discovered that she is visiting her old partner on the sly.

She opens the message. <<Come to my office at the ICRD immediately,>> it says. <<I have an assignment for you.>>

The words trigger a surge of excitement, which she tamps down with difficulty. An 'assignment' could mean anything. Kenway may simply be changing her patrol route or, worse, getting her hopes up only to saddle her with to some even more menial task, like the 'special job' Porter gave her at the party.

But he wants to meet me in the ICRD, Tanta thinks. *That has to mean something!* She tries to suppress the thought. She shouldn't care about this as much as she does. Jen betrayed her, Kenway cast her aside, and the only reason she became an agent in the first place was because she was programmed to love serving her corp above everything else. She shouldn't want to return to the ICRD, and yet she does, with an intensity that rivals the way she used to feel about Jen and about InTech.

She doesn't know if she just misses the interest and excitement of her old life, or if this is yet another example of the remnants of her Harlow Programming still exercising their phantom control over her free will. Either way, she can't change how she feels; she's tried. She checks the timestamp on Kenway's message. He sent it more than half an hour ago; she had better not keep him waiting any longer.

<<I'm on my way now, Director,>> she sends back, rolling out of bed and hunting for some respectable clothes.

The walk doesn't take her long, which is just as well. It's raining despite the sun, a drizzle that steadily increases to a downpour as Tanta goes. She's on the road leading up to the ICRD when she notices a knot of people clustered at the base of the Needle. At first, Tanta takes them for more onlookers, come to gawk at the aftermath of last night's blast. It's only when she gets closer that she hears the chanting and sees the placards some of them are holding: crude, home-made things that are wilting in the rain. She narrows her eyes, zooming in on one. It says, simply: *We Want Answers!*

You and me both, Tanta thinks.

Tanta hasn't been back to the ICRD since Kenway demoted her to a glorified beat cop last summer, and a wave of nostalgia hits her as she walks through the open plan office to his room. She has been through so much in this office, experienced extremes of happiness and misery here. She knew that coming back would be painful, reminding her of all that she has lost since being exiled from the ICRD, but she wasn't expecting the excruciating sense of hope, a feeling so strong that it sends pins and needles through her fingers.

69

Thankfully, the office happens to be almost empty; none of Tanta's former colleagues are around to witness her return. In other respects, though, the similarities between this meeting and the last time she was in the ICRD are striking. Kenway is sitting in the same position behind Jen's old desk, leaning back in his chair with insolent ease. Tanta has had some opportunity to get a bead on him by now, though, and she can see the cracks in his façade. Kenway's thinning, tawny brown hair has a few more streaks of grey at the temples than when she saw him last, and there are purple pouches of skin under his eyes. He may look as self-satisfied as ever, but his new position is clearly taking a toll on him.

'Tanta, I've decided to reassign you to the ICRD,' he says, his voice as smooth as oil. 'You are reinstated as an agent with immediate effect.'

Joy rises through Tanta like bubbles in a glass of champagne. She's back! She's fizzing with happiness, but she refuses to allow it an outlet. It would be dangerous to give a man like Kenway any insight into her feelings. She gives him a formal nod. 'Thank you, Director. I'm ready to help the ICRD in any way I can. You said you had an assignment for me?'

'Yes.' Kenway leans forward, steepling his fingers on the desk. 'It relates to last night's incident. The UAVs that targeted the Needle were our own models, stolen from us a month ago. Bandits have been targeting the Trade Division's delivery drones for several weeks now. They're likely armed by Thoughtfront, and standard anti-theft measures have proven ineffective at deterring them. I'd like you to investigate this matter further.'

Tanta listens to this brief with outward impassivity, but her mind is racing. Suddenly the rationing, and the attacks Director Toor mentioned at the party last night, make sense. If Thoughtfront is targeting InTech's supply lines then it's no wonder it's been a struggle to get food into the city. From what

Kenway is saying, it sounds like these are the first drones stolen by the bandits that InTech has actually managed to recover; the assault on the Needle, bad as it was, could be a chance to unravel their entire operation. But if the thefts have been going on for weeks, then Tanta has been brought onto the assignment at a very late stage. She'll need a lot of information to get up to speed.

'What are your working theories on the thefts?' she asks. 'Do you believe the bandits are also responsible for the attack on the Needle, or do you think they sold the drones on to a third party?'

'I assigned you this case so you could find the answers to those questions,' Kenway sneers, 'not pester me about them.'

Tanta quails under this insult. She's only just arrived back in the ICRD, and already she's getting things wrong. She tries to rephrase. 'Apologies, Director. I only wanted to know what progress your team had made on investigating the thefts so that I can better direct my own efforts.'

'I'm very disappointed in you, Tanta. I wasn't expecting you to need so much guidance. I thought you could handle this, but if the task is proving too confusing for you, then I can certainly reassign you elsewhere.'

Tanta feels a sick pang of distress. Kenway is disappointed. She's messed up, somehow, though she doesn't know how, and now he's going to send her back to the community guardians. She opens her mouth, intending to stammer out an apology. She'll endeavour to do better; she'll give the assignment her all; she'll—

A puzzle piece slots into place in Tanta's mind. It is as if the room and its occupants come properly into focus for the first time. She closes her mouth again. She has figured out what's going on here and she's disturbed she didn't spot it before. She suspects that the ghost of the Harlow Programme got in the way, just like it did in the Needle, nudging her onto the old, familiar path of obedience before she even realised it was happening. This is what scares Tanta the most about the remnants of her programming. The thoughts that haunt her mind do not feel alien. The voice in her head urging respect and loyalty – the one telling her that if Kenway is angry, the fault *must* lie with her – is her own.

Kenway knows how eager to please the Harlow Programmed CorpWards are. He drove Tanta into a state of confused distress on purpose and then, when she was already reeling, he used a command phrase to try and seal the deal. *I'm very disappointed in you.* Tanta can still remember how she used to feel when Jen used those words. The pain and misery were almost more than she could bear. She would have done anything to avoid such censure: recusing herself from an assignment would have seemed a small price to pay for securing her manager's approval. And that, of course, is exactly what Kenway wants. The odious man is still waiting for her response. She raises her head and looks him straight in the eye.

'I misspoke. I understand the assignment perfectly, Director. I'm eager to get started.'

Kenway looks taken aback. He recovers quickly, however. 'You're sure, now?' he asks, voice dripping scorn. 'It seemed rather too much for you a moment ago.'

'Not at all,' Tanta replies demurely. 'I couldn't possibly turn down this assignment, Director. After all, the board asked for me personally, didn't they?'

She sees the moment her guess hits home. Kenway's eyes widen, the smug, oily look wiped from his face. It's back again a moment later, of course. Kenway is good at hiding his emotions, but Tanta is even better at ferreting them out.

'They have been in contact with you directly, then?' he asks, his tone clipped. Tanta says nothing; she only looks at him –

a cool, appraising look. Her silence is far more effective than either a confirmation or a denial. After attempting to stare her down for a couple of seconds, Kenway makes a sudden, violent sweeping motion with his hand, waving Tanta towards the door.

'Very well, then,' he snaps. 'You're dismissed.'

Tanta feels a rush of fierce pride – she's won! – but it passes quickly. She may have kept control of herself, and the case, but her position remains perilous. Kenway is setting her up to fail, and just because she's survived this first encounter doesn't mean he's going to stop. She needs to find out what's she's dealing with here. She'll get no help from him in that endeavour, but perhaps she can glean something from the ways in which he is unhelpful.

She stands her ground, ignoring Kenway's dismissal for the moment.

'Permission ask a question, Director?' she says. He makes an impatient gesture of assent.

'Do you have a list of the UAVs that were stolen? If I had their serial numbers, then I could—'

'That's classified,' Kenway shoots back. Tanta has the impression that he was almost hoping she would ask, just so he could refuse her.

'What about details of their flight paths?' she pursues.

'Tanta, this meeting is over.'

'One last question, Director,' Tanta says quickly. 'Is there footage of any of the attacks?'

A spasm of annoyance constricts Kenway's features. 'If there were any footage, don't you think I would have reviewed it already?' he snaps.

'That's all I needed to know,' Tanta says. 'Thank you for all of your help.'

She turns with military precision and marches from the room. Kenway hasn't given her much, but he has still ended up telling her more than he intended to. He was furious by the time she left, and not just at her incessant questions. These bandits are clearly making his life very difficult indeed, and if the board have started making suggestions about how he handles the investigation, then he must be struggling with it..

The question that finally made him lose his temper was about the footage, and he hadn't said that it was classified or irrelevant, but that it didn't exist. That's a sign that whoever the bandits are, they're running a tight operation. Most drones are fitted with wireless security cameras as standard; the fact that there's no footage of the attacks *at all* suggests that the bandits are aware of the cameras and targeting them deliberately. It also suggests that they're armed with weapons systems advanced enough to take them out.

It's not a lot to go on, but it's a start. She'll talk to Cole again, ask him what kind of tech you'd need to bring down a drone, and work the case from that angle. Then, if Kenway will authorise a reconnaissance trip into the Unaffiliated Zone, maybe she can investigate the sites of the attacks for herself. Tanta feels the beginnings of confidence as she plots out this course of action. It will be a struggle, she knows, but with perseverance and a little luck, she just might manage to succeed where Kenway is so clearly hoping she'll fail. Then, perhaps, she can use the fresh store of goodwill she'll accumulate with the board to make her position in the ICRD a more permanent one.

She's halfway across the office when the door opens and Reet walks in. The last thing Tanta needs is another almost-argument, but it's too late to duck into a conference room – Reet has already seen her. Tanta shoots a harried smile her way, trying to look too busy to talk. To her dismay, Reet heads straight towards her. And then she hears Kenway step out of his room.

'Ah, this is good timing,' he says. 'Hold on a moment, Tanta.'

She freezes in place. *What can he want now?* The greasy quality is back in Kenway's voice. He has some new twist of the knife in store for her, Tanta's sure of it. She stays still, waiting for the other shoe to drop.

'I forgot to tell you about your new team leader,' Kenway continues. 'You'll be reporting to her on this assignment.'

Tanta's stomach gives a sick lurch. She stares at Reet; as always, her lover's face gives the game away before she's said a word. Her cheeks are flaming scarlet, her eyes downcast in a look of acute embarrassment.

'I believe you two know each other already,' Kenway says.

Chapter 7

'I want you to know that I didn't ask for this assignment. Douglas gave it to me. I did tell him about our relationship outside of work, but he said it didn't matter.'

Reet has ushered Tanta into a briefing room and created a secure MindChat channel for them to use, but she still hasn't met Tanta's eyes. Tanta nods, but doesn't reply. She's too angry – not with Reet, but with Kenway. Of course he would say that their relationship didn't matter; he's probably ecstatic about it. Assigning a trainee to be Tanta's team leader is exactly the kind of stunt Kenway would pull to undermine and humiliate her. The fact that this particular trainee is someone who Tanta practically trained herself is a bonus.

'I think it'll be nice to work this case together, Tanta,' Reet continues seriously. 'I mean, even though I'm officially your team leader, you taught me so much. It'll be more like we're partners, really.'

Actually, Tanta realises, she *is* a little annoyed with Reet, who, despite her intelligence, doesn't seem to have figured out what is going on here. There's no way a junior agent like her should be managing someone like Tanta; if anything, it ought to be the other way round. But instead of questioning this reversal of the chain of command, Reet is playing along.

Like she's programmed to, Tanta thinks. Perhaps a year ago, if she had been in Reet's shoes, she would have done the same. Now, the power plays at work here seem so glaringly obvious that it's hard to restrain her impatience that Reet can't see them too. And Reet's management speak is starting to grate on her. She's insisting on calling Tanta by her full name – presumably in deference to ICRD protocol about the strict separation of the personal and the professional. She's also still referring to Kenway as *Douglas*. It sounds creepingly obsequious to Tanta's ears, but she makes herself remember how she used to gush about Jen and tells herself that Reet's behaviour is no different.

Tanta realises, with a rush of shame, that Reet has taken her silence for sulkiness. She is being unprofessional and hurting her lover's feelings into the bargain.

'You can still call me Tee when we're on duty, you know,' she says now, forcing herself to smile. 'Just don't kiss me or anything.'

Reet laughs, relief showing bright in her eyes.

'But we're not partners,' Tanta continues. Frustrating as this situation is for her, she knows how important working in the ICRD is to Reet. She doesn't want her lover's first experience of managing an assignment to be ruined because she's too chary of Tanta's feelings to do the job properly. 'I'm flattered, but you've got to remember you're my team leader, Reet. That's the role Ken – Director Kenway has given you. So, you can give me orders, even pull rank with me, and I won't be offended. Just tell me what you want me to do.'

'Thanks, Tee,' Reet replies. Her tone, warm but business-like, reassures Tanta; clearly, she knows what being a team leader entails, and is willing to do it. Tanta suspects she was only waiting for permission.

'So, where should we start?' Tanta asks. 'Do you have the serial numbers of the stolen drones?' She's hoping Reet might have some of the answers Kenway withheld from her before, but she's out of luck.

'Douglas hasn't briefed me on that yet,' Reet replies. 'He's asked us to liaise with the UAV engineers at the Needle, first. We can work the case from there.'

Despite their conversation in the briefing room, Reet spends the whole of the short walk to the Needle quizzing Tanta on MindChat, asking her if she has any theories about how the attack there could have happened, and what she thinks their next line of investigation should be. Tanta answers as best she can, amused in spite of herself at this pairing of the uninitiated with the ill-informed. Reet's a green recruit, and Tanta's own brief from Kenway was so confusing that she's still not sure exactly what they're trying to achieve here.

The protesters Tanta noticed earlier are still outside, and the knot of people has grown in size. The Needle is surrounded by AR security cordons, and there's a line of guardians standing between the demonstrators and the front entrance. Tanta and Reet hurry through the virtual tape, each signing the obligatory NDA that pops up on their 'scapes' readers as they enter the building. They ignore the crowd and its shouted questions, though Tanta can still feel its presence at her back even after the doors close behind them.

A white man comes to greet them as they cross the lobby, introducing himself as Senior Technician Phillips. From his profile, Tanta can see that he works for Residents' Affairs.

'My colleague and I have been assigned to this case,' Reet says, showing Phillips the Agent badge on her profile. 'What can you tell us?'

'Well, the UAV that hit the basement was destroyed in the explosion,' he explains, 'but we've been examining the intact one upstairs.'

He leads them to the lifts and up to the top of the building, where a temporary workspace has been erected in the middle of the event hall. A dozen UAV technicians, explosives experts and engineers mill around in the space, their hands darting in front of their faces as they input data on their 'scapes. In the centre of the room, a number of objects have been laid on a fold-out table, as if in state. There's the drone that Tanta intercepted and its explosive payload, alongside some blackened fragments of burnt plastic.

'What we know so far is that the drones were intercepted en route to the city from Sodis, and subjected to some kind of hack,' the Senior Technician says.

Reet is nodding, her expression intent, but Tanta catches herself thinking: *well, obviously.* Sodis is InTech's Southern Distribution Centre, a dead-and-alive company town on the south coast. It's filled with warehouses and staffed by sleepers, their conscious minds shut down while the routers connected to their 'scapes direct their bodies in the monotonous tasks of filling orders and stacking crates. Sodis is the source of some forty per cent of all the city's imports, so the fact that the UAVs came from there is hardly surprising. And 'some kind of hack' is vague in the extreme. Does this man know anything that basic deduction couldn't tell them already?

'Do you know where on their route the UAVs were intercepted?' Reet asks. The information would be valuable, if they could get it – it would give them a starting point for identifying the bandits' base of operations.

'It's impossible to tell, unfortunately,' the Senior Technician replies.

Tanta remembers something Cole said when she visited him last night. 'Wouldn't that information be stored in the drone's flight recorder?' she asks.

Phillips looks annoyed. 'That was the first thing we checked, but the logs have been scrambled. They're unreadable.'

'It seems odd that the thieves would scramble the flight logs,' Reet says. 'Why not just delete them entirely?'

'Because that's impossible,' Phillips replies. 'InTech flight recorders are tamper-proof. You can't damage the recorder or delete the data within it without frying the drone's engines.'

'So this was a workaround,' Tanta summarises. 'If the logs were just scrambled, can we unscramble them?'

Phillips rolls his eyes. 'You can try,' he says, 'but they're gibberish; none of my guys can make sense of them.'

Tanta thinks of Cole – she's sure that he would be able to wrest something of value from the bowels of this machine. Kenway has already told her to keep him away from the ICRD's work once, but it's clear that the technician from Residents' Affairs is not going to crack this on his own; he doesn't even seem inclined to try.

<<My last partner was a neurotech, and he was really good at this kind of thing,>> she sends to Reet. <<Maybe we could bring him in for a consultation?>>

Tanta sees Reet read the message; her shoulders tighten and her eyes flick Tanta's way, but she doesn't respond. 'Keep trying. Ping me if you make any progress,' she says to the Senior Technician. Then she turns and leaves. It is not until they're outside the building that she sends a reply.

<<Douglas already told me about your old partner, Tee, and he said we weren't allowed to consult with him on this. Sorry.>>

Tanta feels a familiar cocktail of emotions well up inside her: frustration, chagrin, rage. She forces them back down, reminding herself that Reet doesn't have any choice but to toe the line on this. It doesn't make the feelings any less intense, but it does help her to keep a lid on them. Personal considerations aside, she's surprised Reet isn't more concerned by the Senior Technician's lack of commitment. It's vital they solve this case: the stability of the entire corporation is at stake, not to mention the lives of its residents. Tanta was expecting Reet to veto Cole's involvement, but if they don't bring *someone* else on board, they'll get nowhere.

<<What's our next move, then?>> she asks, trying not to sound snippy.

<<It's eighty kilometres from here to Sodis,>> Reet sends back. <<That's a huge search area but it's a start. Maybe we could requisition some guardians to sweep the route?>>

<<Over that distance, we'd need hundreds. The people we're looking for would see us coming.>> Tanta doesn't want to undermine Reet, but her idea is untenable; a search like that would be needle in haystack territory. It also neglects the obvious: the intact drone is the best link they have, if not to the terrorists who attacked the Needle then at least to the bandits who supplied those terrorists. Why begin their investigation with a search when the evidence they need is already in their possession?

Reet chews her lower lip, her eyes darting from side to side. Then she catches herself doing it and forces her features smooth again. Even though she's still irritated, Tanta notes this transition from anxious to unreadable with approval. She's spent hours coaching Reet on keeping her emotions hidden, and it's good to see it paying off.

<<Let's make a circuit of the flea markets. If the bandits are selling the UAV shipments they've stolen, we might find some of the goods there,>> Reet sends.

Tanta hesitates. She's unwilling to shoot down a second idea so close on the heels of the first, but she can't let this plan pass without comment. <<Shouldn't we ask someone else to examine the drone's flight logs, too?>> she hazards. <<It's a strong lead, Reet. We can't afford to ignore it.>>

Reet frowns. <<I'm not ignoring it, but Douglas told me

we should leave the technical side of this investigation to his engineers. They know their stuff, and I trust their expertise.>>

The words are pointed, a rebuke. Tanta realises that her doubts are beginning to sound uncorporate and bites her tongue on further disagreement. <<OK. Shall we split up so we can cover more ground?>>

That suggestion Reet agrees to at once; Tanta suspects that she, too, would like nothing more than to escape this conversation as soon as she can.

The city's flea markets are ephemeral things, transient bursts of noise, colour and commerce where unaffiliated traders and InTech residents mingle, distinctions of class and corporate affiliation temporarily set aside. The largest of them are found on the outskirts of the city, in the courtyards of the huge tower blocks that house InTech's poorest residents. Such residents are keen to trade with the unaffiliated. Their wares – pre-Meltdown artefacts and curios, handmade jewellery, wild fruit scavenged from the Unaffiliated Zone – are both fascinating to browse and cheap to buy. Most unaffiliated accept chit as currency, but they'll take barter goods just as readily, and the things they want aren't hard to come by in the city: food, clean water, over-the-counter medicine.

Tanta has never seen an unaffiliated person selling supplies boosted from a corporate UAV. There's no market for such things, which InTech residents can order easily through their 'scapes or buy in the nearest supermarket. And it would take a pretty stupid bandit to risk selling stolen InTech supplies within InTech's own territory. Tanta doesn't mention any of these thoughts to Reet, who's probably well aware of what a long shot this is already. She's voiced her reservations about this plan once; repeating them would only sound churlish.

But after most of a day spent trawling through one dead-end

market after another, picking through boxes of woven scarves and scavenged coins and racks of antique mechanical devices and finding no red flags whatsoever, Tanta's reserves of patience are running dry. She's half an hour into her fourth market, this one a collection of stalls set up along the bank of the riverbed, close to The Rotunda, when Reet messages her.

<<How's it going?>>

Tanta threads her way through the crowds, glancing at the boxes and crates the unaffiliated traders are using to store their goods to see if she can spot any InTech watermarks.

<<Nothing yet,>> she replies. <<You?>>

<<Same here. Let's keep going.>>

Not for the first time, Tanta sends a mental nod rather than risking a reply. This search is almost pointless, and meanwhile, back in the Needle, the drone and its payload are just sitting there, being pored over by idiots. They have another lead – a far better one than this – and Reet is ignoring it because of office politics! *Not office politics,* Tanta corrects herself. *She has a direct order from her manager. She* can't *ignore it.* This thought is no less annoying for being true. Kenway's orders are disingenuous and unhelpful; he's not acting with the best interests of InTech or the success of the assignment in mind.

The last time Tanta was put in this position by a manager, of course, she and Cole had simply gone behind her back. The memory still carries traces of guilt, but nonetheless, Tanta is tempted to counsel the same course of action here. The only thing that restrains her is the knowledge that Reet would never agree to it.

She channels her feelings into her work, throwing herself into the fruitless search with renewed focus. There's nothing suspicious among this collection of stalls, but Tanta scans the faces of the stallholders, letting her gaze soften to catch the details. Most of the merchants are thin almost to the point of gauntness, their eyes alert and hungry. Tanta spots one or two with Inscape profiles of their own – former InTech residents, most likely, who have lost their jobs or businesses. They leap out at her from the crowd, their AR outlines making them more vivid than the 'scapeless people around them. Her stomach gives an unpleasant flip whenever she sees one of these residents-turned-unaffiliated, but she forces herself to keep looking regardless.

This is another thing that has changed for Tanta since she lost her Harlow Programming: she never used to notice all the people the corporation has rejected, those for whom it has no place anymore. She used to believe that InTech, in its benevolence, had a place for everyone. Now, she seems to see them everywhere. It shames Tanta to see how many of the unaffiliated merchants are visibly sick or malnourished, just as it shames her to think that she never noticed this before.

<<Tee,>> Reet sends, interrupting Tanta's thoughts. <<I think we should call it a day. I've checked and double checked every market I've come across, and I can't find anything.>>

She sounds defeated. Tanta feels a rush of pity; Reet may be the captain of this impossible boat, but they're stuck in it together.

<<That's OK,>> she replies, trying to sound reassuring. <<We'll try again tomorrow.>>

<<No, I don't think we should. We're getting nowhere with this.>>

Though Reet is downcast, her pronouncement makes Tanta hopeful. Perhaps now, she will be more open to considering other avenues of investigation.

<<If we haven't heard anything back from the Senior Technician by tomorrow morning,>> Reet continues, <<I'm going to go to Douglas and tell him we've hit a dead end.>>

Tanta's optimism evaporates. An admission of failure is exactly what Kenway wants; he will need no better excuse to kick Tanta off the case, and Reet with her.

<<Are you sure that's the best course of action?>> she sends. <<Maybe we could interview some staff over in Sodis first, see if they can shed some light on this?>>

<<No, Douglas already did that,>> Reet replies. <<They've all been ruled out as potential leaks; he sent me the notes this morning. Tee, I'm stuck. And ICRD protocol states that when an agent has exhausted all leads, they should refer to their line manager for appropriate guidance. So that's what we should do, right?>>

Tanta pushes aside her annoyance that she is only just hearing about these interviews *now*, and tries to marshal her thoughts. She recognises the singsong, recitative quality in Reet's voice. She is falling back on protocol to show her the path she ought to follow, just as Tanta would once have done. She thinks back to how the old Tanta would have felt and thought, were she in Reet's shoes. She won't be able to reason Reet out of her adherence to the rules, but perhaps she can convince her to rethink her interpretation of them.

<<We haven't exhausted *all* our leads,>> she returns, choosing her words with care. <<There's still the scrambled UAV flight logs to consider.>>

<<That's why I said I'd wait till tomorrow,>> Reet sends back. <<If the Senior Technician hasn't cracked them by then, Douglas will want to know.>>

<<What about bringing in another perspective? A new pair of eyes might spot clues the technicians have missed.>>

<<I already told you, Tee: we can't talk to your old partner about this.>>

The annoyance in Reet's message is clear. Tanta pushes on anyway. <<Not Cole, necessarily. We could ask Dr Friend for his assistance. Maybe he'd loan us one of his engineers?>>

<<I don't see why one of Dr Friend's colleagues would be able to find something Douglas's guys haven't. What is this *about*, Tanta?>>

Tanta considers. Reet isn't buying anything she has to say, but she can't just let the matter drop. Backed into a corner, she tries another tactic.

<<Don't you think that Director Kenway has been a little unclear about this assignment?>>

<<I don't know what you mean. Or what this has to do with what we're talking about.>>

Tanta almost groans aloud in despair. It's like talking to a brick wall! Did she really used to be like this?

<<I *mean* that I don't think he's given us the information we need to do a good job,>> she sends back. <<Do you remember when I asked you this morning about the thefts, and you said you hadn't been fully briefed on them yet? It's things like that. We don't have all the facts. Why do you think that is?>>

<<I don't know, but I'm sure Douglas has a good reason.>>

<<But what if that reason is>> – Tanta gropes for the right word – <<political, rather than strategic?>>

<<What are you talking about?>>

Tanta takes a deep breath, steeling herself. She has a heady, reckless feeling that what she says next isn't going to make things any better, but she's come too far not to take the plunge. <<I don't think Director Kenway *wants* us to succeed, Reet. I think he's making the assignment difficult for us on purpose.>>

There's a long pause before Reet replies. When she does, her tone is harder than Tanta has ever heard it before. <<You mean he's making it difficult for *you*. Be honest, Tee. You think this is all about you, don't you?>>

Tanta is floored. <<OK, yes,>> she admits, <<I think he's setting me up to fail. Not because it's all about me, but because Kenway and I have a history, that's all.>>

<<Call him *Director* Kenway,>> Reet snaps. Tanta is so taken aback that she doesn't respond.

<<Fuck, Tee,>> Reet continues. <<Douglas warned me about this. He *told* me you didn't like him. When he said you resented him for sending you to Residents' Affairs, I told him he'd misjudged you. I *defended* you! I guess I was wrong.>>

With a cold, distant feeling, Tanta thinks back to the day she was introduced to Cole – and her meeting with Director Ash immediately afterwards. *He is arrogant, incautious and untrustworthy,* Jen had told her. *So, I'd like you to keep an eye on him for me.* Cole was dangerous, so Jen had tried to sabotage Tanta's relationship with him from the start, to make sure that if it came to it, Tanta would know without question where her loyalties lay. It shouldn't surprise her that Kenway has done exactly the same thing; there may be a new Director in charge of the ICRD, but he's working from the same playbook.

Reet, that's ... That's not ... I didn't ... Tanta dismisses the rebuttals and explanations as they occur to her, knowing that she has already lost. There's no denial she can give that won't make her look even guiltier in Reet's eyes. She can no more convince Reet to doubt her manager's intentions than the old Tanta could have been brought to question why Jen would have wanted to undermine her relationship with her partner on her first day.

<<You need to get it together, Tanta,>> Reet sends. <<I know how much being an agent means to you, but you can't see Douglas as your enemy: he's your manager. You know that's insane, right? We're all on the same team.>>

Her reasoning is so exactly what Tanta's would have been, once, that hearing it feels like looking into a mirror at her past self. She grits her teeth. <<Yes,>> she sends. <<I know that. I'm sorry, Reet.>>

<<It's OK.>> Reet sounds gentler, now. <<Just ... just try to

87

like him, will you? I think if you got to know him, you'd realise that he's not like you think he is.>>

Tanta doesn't respond to that. She could spin Reet a tale about how the surprise of the transition from guardian to agent has put her on edge, making her start at shadows. She could beg for a second chance, promise to do better, to treat Kenway with the respect he deserves. She's pretty sure she could make Reet believe it, too. With anyone else, that's exactly the play Tanta would make here; after all, it's what she's good at. But she loves Reet too much to lie to her.

<<I appreciate the apology,>> Reet sends, some time later. <<And I'm sorry too, for snapping at you. I'm a little new to this. And I – well, I'm still really happy we're working together.>>

Tanta doesn't respond to that, either. It hurts her to stay silent, but it's that or correct Reet's misunderstanding. She wasn't apologising for the fight; she was apologising for what she's going to do next.

Chapter 8

Neal steers clear of Cole for the rest of the day. Cole knows it's safer that way, but he still finds the wait until the evening maddening. It's not good for him to be alone with his thoughts at a time like this – it will only sap his resolve – and yet thinking is all he can do.

Uppermost in his mind is Tanta. That the 'security update' Neal discovered is linked to the Harlow Programme in some way, Cole is all but certain, but the exact nature of the connection remains an open question. There's a chance that it's a new version of the programme, designed for future generations of Corporate Wards. That would be bad enough, but Cole is even more terrified by the alternative. If the update is designed for Tanta's cohort, then she could be in imminent danger of discovery and reprogramming, and Cole has no way to warn her about it. The dummy system he's rigged up in her 'scape won't stand up to scrutiny from a professional. If she's called into the Black Box for adjustments to her Harlow Programming, one of his colleagues will realise she doesn't have it anymore.

Anxiety on his own behalf comes a close second to his worries about his friend. There's a part of Cole that still can't believe he is really doing this – conspiring with an anti-corporate agitator and her recruit to steal information from the most secure

R&D lab in the city. It seems insane. It *is* insane. He doesn't have the skillset for this kind of thing; he's not working for the ICRD anymore and even when he was, he had Tanta to watch his back and make sure he didn't do anything stupid. He and Neal are engineers, not spies.

These thoughts chase each other round and round in Cole's head, worrying his mind like dogs with a bone. As is his habit, he takes refuge from them in his work. Usually, the chores that Arthur throws his way are too trite to offer Cole much of a distraction, but today he has the added challenge of leaving each task on his docket precisely 99% complete. Cole goes to work on his tickets like he's assembling a ship in a bottle, layering in fixes, edits and workarounds with painstaking care. From the outside, his work list looks infuriatingly incomplete, a jumbled mess of wood and wire. But one tug on the right string of code, and the masts will rise, the sails unfurl, and the whole thing will be finished.

Today, Arthur's rule that Cole can't leave until he's cleared his tickets is going to work in Cole's favour. He stays at his desk all afternoon and into the evening, apparently accomplishing nothing at all while the office empties out around him. His colleagues can all access his workstation remotely; as the clock on Cole's Array inches closer and closer to eight pm and his docket remains stubbornly full, he receives several expectant glances, which grow in pointedness and irritation as time ticks on. Despite Cole's nerves, when Neal appears in the doorway at last, it's almost a relief.

'Dr Friend just left,' he announces to the room in general, careful to avoid meeting Cole's eyes.

'Then I'm going home too,' a woman says. Several of her colleagues nod in agreement, getting to their feet.

'Wait,' says a man. 'What about him?' He jerks a dismissive thumb at Cole. 'Someone needs to wait with him.'

There's a collective groan.

'I'll stay,' Neal offers. 'I haven't finished my unit tests for today anyway.'

The others need no further convincing. There's a rapid exodus, everyone leaving in a scramble of grabbed coats and hasty goodbyes, as if they're worried that Neal will change his mind. Neal returns their farewells affably; Cole remains hunched over his desk, pretending to look at something on his 'scape. After a few minutes, silence falls over the office.

'Are you done yet?' Neal asks. It's his way of asking if Cole is ready to get started; the bugs are still on, so they have to be careful what they say. They're on the clock. Arthur works late – it's likely that he'll return to the Black Box after his meeting with the board, which means they have a couple of hours at most to find what they need.

Cole holds up a hand, fingers splayed: *give me five minutes.* Speed won't help them if everything they do is recorded. Now that he and Neal are alone, Cole finally has a chance to take care of the cameras and listening devices without the worry that anyone will realise what he's doing. He came up with the workaround he has in mind while planning his breakout from house arrest, but it will work equally well for the Black Box's bugs, which are the same make and model as the ones in his flat.

The footage the bugs record is divided into date and time stamped files and sent to a secure folder on the Black Box server. Cole can't edit or delete the files themselves – they're locked and protected to prevent such tampering – but the folder's data storage permissions are easier to hack. Once Cole has found his way in, he cuts the folder's data storage limit in half and disables its automatic overwrite function, so that new footage cannot replace the old. The cameras and listening devices are still recording, but once the folder fills up, in a few minutes' time, what they see and hear will no longer be saved anywhere. He'll reset the storage limit before he leaves tonight, and no one will be any the wiser; even if someone realises that some time stamps are missing, they're more likely to put it down to a server clock error, which happen from time to time, than deliberate sabotage.

Cole waits out the intervening minutes in tense silence, watching the folder's storage space vanish before his eyes. When it's full, he breathes a sigh of relief and leans back in his chair. The sense that InTech is no longer watching him is incredibly liberating.

'Cameras and bugs are dealt with,' he says to Neal. 'Let's go.' He flushes with embarrassed pride at Neal's admiring glance. He never used to be so good at circumventing security systems, but there's nothing like practice to hone your skills.

They meet their second obstacle when they reach the stair-well. The door to the stairs is locked; the scanner set into its lintel will recognise Neal's Inscape ident and admit him, but any attempt to walk through it on Cole's part will trigger an alarm. Luckily, he's had the entire day to think of a solution.

'You'll have to go through and disable the scanner from the other side of the door,' he tells Neal, with more confidence than he really feels. 'I can talk you through it.'

He explains to Neal where he will be able to find the manual override, and how to trigger it in a way that will make it look like a glitch. Once they've finished investigating, they can reset the scanners and delete the record of the shut-down so no one even knows it happened. Neal has displayed an impressive level of calm up to this point, and although he looks nervous as he listens to Cole's instructions, he shows no sign of wanting to back out.

He walks through the door and disappears up the stairs. There follows a tense wait. Cole can't risk sending Neal any further instructions via MindChat; he just has to hope the intern has understood him. Sure enough, after a little while the light on the door scanner winks out. Cole waits a minute before following. He tells himself that he's making certain the scanner is really off, but in truth, he's trying to calm his nerves. It hits him, suddenly and with great force, that once he crosses the threshold into the stairwell, he'll be out of bounds, trespassing in an area of the Black Box that he has been expressly forbidden from entering. If anyone sees him, he won't be arrested or even MindWiped. Arthur won't give him the chance to betray InTech a second time.

He climbs the stairs as quickly and quietly as possible, expecting at every turn to run into a colleague who happens to be working late, or even Arthur himself, returned from his meeting early and coming to check up on him. When he emerges on the second floor and sees only Neal, the sense of relief makes him a little unsteady on his feet.

Arthur Friend's office is actually two rooms off a private corridor at the back of the building. They try the one on the left first; with the scanners still shut down, the door swings open to admit them easily enough. For a few moments, the interior of the room is too dark for Cole to see anything: then, the automatic lights blink on. The room is just as Cole remembers it from the summer. It's one of the nicest offices in the Black Box, large and well appointed, with a carpeted floor and a narrow window that looks out on a sweeping view of the city skyline. It's spotlessly clean, and almost completely empty. There's only a hardwood desk, a plush chair, and a row of filing cabinets up against the back wall. The cabinets all have manual locks, and it looks like Arthur must have taken the key with him, because there's no sign of it in the office. Cole is scratching his head over this when Neal takes a pen from his pocket.

'Tip one of those filing cabinets upwards, would you?' he says.

Cole does so, manoeuvring himself awkwardly behind the

one on the far left so that he can tilt it up and back. Neal crouches at the base of the cabinet and starts fiddling around with the pen. Cole hears a series of scratches, followed by a satisfying *clunk*.

'All done,' Neal says.

Cole looks at him with new respect. 'Where did you learn to pick locks?'

'I didn't – I just shifted the rod that controls the cabinet's locking mechanism,' Neal explains. 'We've got the same kind of cabinets in our office, but we can never find the key. I've seen the neurotechs do this a bunch of times.'

Cole has known a lot of engineers in his time, so it comes as no surprise to him that Neal's colleagues would turn to lockpicking over simply cutting a new key. He puts the filing cabinet back down and slides open the bottom drawer. It's filled with a jumble of data cards, office stationary, and old equipment. If the hard drive Neal mentioned is in here, it could take them a while to find it.

He and Neal exchange a look. 'You search through these,' Cole murmurs. 'I'll check the other room.'

He glances at the clock on his Array. It's already been almost an hour since Arthur left; if they don't find something soon, he'll have to call off the search.

The other room turns out to be a surgical suite, with white walls, bright angled lights, and a counter full of racks of medical instruments. There's an operating table fixed to the floor in the centre, and a bulky thing that looks like a long, stainless-steel cabinet behind it. Cole stops in the doorway, struck immediately by the temperature change. The suite itself is unremarkable – a facility that researches mind-based operating systems needs places where such systems can be installed – but it's colder than the corridor outside by several degrees. That, and the cabinet, finally make Cole twig: the room isn't an operating theatre. It's a morgue.

The mortuary cabinet's freezer unit hums softly in the silence. Cole spends a moment psyching himself up before he opens it. Even so, as he swings open the door and pulls out the drawer inside, he can't help but clap a hand over his mouth, stifling a moan of horror. The body within is horribly burnt, and so small that it can't be fully grown. Its head has been smashed, the skull caved in on one side. The top of the head has been surgically removed, exposing the brain. Wires snake through the grey matter; Arthur must have been examining the corpse's 'scape.

…Only those wires aren't the right gauge or colour to belong to the Inscape system. His gorge is rising, his mind reeling, but Cole has worked on enough MbOSes that he can see that at a glance. The corpse doesn't have an Inscape, but a MindEye, the Thoughtfront equivalent. At the same instant, Cole realises that he knows the identity of the body before him. The burns – and the head wound – were his first clues, but the MindEye completes the picture. It's the agent Tanta fought last summer, the girl who was hardwired with a rival Harlow Programme of Thoughtfront's design. He never met her, but he remembers Tanta's descriptions of her well enough – and he remembers her death at Tanta's hands, in the fire that consumed the Ward House.

'Cole, I've found – oh my god.' Cole turns; Neal has come into the room and seen the body. He looks like he's trying not to vomit.

The trainee is holding a slim black rectangle with a fold-out MbOS port. Cole takes it from his hands, slipping the port over his eyes. He's expecting the contents of the hard drive to be as chaotic as the contents of the filing cabinet, but once he bypasses Arthur's security, he finds only one file inside. It's called *Harlow 2.0.* The words root Cole to the spot – they're more terrible, in their way, than the sight of the agent's corpse.

'This is it, Neal,' he murmurs. 'Good work. We just need to copy the update, and then we can get out of here.'

'Keep your voice down!' Neal hisses. Cole feels the intern grab his arm and pull him up against the wall, out of sight of the frosted glass window set into the door. Footsteps in the corridor tell Cole what is going on without Neal having to explain. Dr Friend has returned.

Chapter 9

Cole stands stock-still, trying to keep his mind in the present. Arthur is metres from where they're standing; if he comes into this room then Cole and Neal are both dead. But for a moment he is adrift, lost in the horror of what he's seen.

The footsteps grow louder. Cole takes off the MbOS port and glances at Neal; the trainee stares back, rigid with fright. Both of them are doing their best not to breathe. Just before they reach the lab, the footsteps halt. Cole listens, straining his senses. There's the creak of an opening door, then a *snick*. Arthur has gone into his office. Cole releases the breath he was holding, feeling as though he might collapse; his whole body is shaking. He tiptoes back over to the cabinet and slides the corpse back inside.

Beside him, Neal reaches for the handle of the door. Cole lays a hand on his arm. He's as keen as Neal to beat a hasty retreat, but there's something they have to do first. He waves the hard drive, shooting the trainee a significant look. This is what they came here for; they can't leave without it. Neal mimes slipping the drive into his pocket, but Cole shakes his head. They can't risk taking the drive with them, either: Arthur would notice it was gone. But Neal is close to panic, and this game of charades has gone on too long already.

Quickly, Cole puts on the port again and accesses the file

inside. He selects *download*. A message flashes up in front of his eyes: {*Access denied*}. The drive must be locked to prevent its contents from being shared outside of the Black Box's systems. It was the same with the data cards he and Tanta found when they were investigating the original Harlow Programme.

Neal pokes him: *are you done??*

Cole shakes his head again: *not yet*.

Then an idea strikes him. He might not be able to download the security update to his 'scape, but can he send it somewhere else? He opens it again, this time selecting *upload*. As he expected, the message he gets this time is different: {*This programme file is locked. Sharing beyond the local server is prohibited. Do you wish to continue?*} His hands trembling, Cole selects *yes*. He's stumped for a moment about where on the Black Box's server he can hide the update, but the answer is obvious, when he thinks about it. In other circumstances he might have paused for a moment to admire the elegance of his own solution, but right now he doesn't have the time.

He enacts his plan, gives Neal a thumbs-up, and together they slip out into the corridor. They're racing down the stairs to the ground floor when Cole remembers the security system.

'Neal!' he hisses. The trainee has drawn ahead of him. 'You need to reset the door scanners!'

Neal whirls around and dashes back up the stairs, while Cole throws himself the last few metres along the hallway and into his shared office. It's faster than he's moved in a long time. When he regains his desk, he's gasping, and his chest feels several sizes too small for his heart. He sinks into his chair, trying desperately to get his breathing under control. Once he's suitably calm, he puts the finishing touches on his work tickets, emptying his docket with a few flourishes of missing code. He has just finished when Neal comes back in, looking far less exhausted by his sprint through the Black Box than Cole feels.

'What did you do with the update?' the trainee asks.

'I sent it to the security footage folder,' Cole murmurs. 'I can't access it there, but you should be able to. Do you have a way of getting it to Jeanie?'

Neal nods. 'Leave it to me.' He swallows. 'Was that a *body* we found in that lab? What was—'

'I need to fix the cameras,' Cole jumps in. 'Let's talk tomorrow.'

He's left it longer than he should have already; he was only waiting for Neal to return. Working quickly, he goes back into the folder's data storage permissions and resets all parameters to normal. Before he leaves, he sneaks a look at the update; it's been uploaded correctly. He renamed it with nothing more than a date and a time stamp, so it will blend right into the surveillance footage until Neal has time to retrieve it. As Cole returns to his own workstation, Arthur walks into the room. Cole darts a glance at him out of the corner of his eye, trying to read the doctor's mind in his features.

'Still working on Sarah's tickets, Cole?' Arthur asks. 'It seems there was a small server outage earlier. I hope you didn't lose any work?' He sounds mildly hopeful at the prospect. Cole holds in a sigh of relief; Arthur noticed the disabled scanners, then, but he hasn't read anything into them.

'Some,' Cole replies. He's surprised he's calm enough to answer at all. 'But I'm finished now.'

'Finally,' Neal retorts. 'I'll let the guardians know.'

Five minutes later, Cole is on his way home with his armed escort, amazed that the break-in is over and that both he and Neal survived it. He doesn't know whether to feel elated or terrified. On the one hand, they succeeded. Cole is a prisoner in his own home, with cameras tracking his every move, yet tonight he managed not only to escape the corporation's gaze, but to pull off a feat of espionage which would have impressed

99

even Tanta. On the other hand, what he found during his brief, stolen freedom has confirmed some of his worst fears.

Arthur is working on a new version of the Harlow Programme, and for some reason, he's using Thoughtfront's rival mind-control technology as his guide. It's a baffling development – and a disturbing one. From what Cole and Tanta learnt over the summer, Thoughtfront's version of the Harlow Programme is far more primitive than the original. It's also more psychologically damaging. Cole remembers Tanta's accounts of her fights with the Thoughtfront agent – the girl was barely human.

Cole has no idea why Arthur is interested in this less advanced version of InTech's own programme, and that's what frightens him most of all. For all that he and Neal have discovered, they still don't know what this update is meant to achieve – or who it's intended for.

Chapter 10

The crowd of demonstrators has been dispersed by the time Tanta gets back to the Needle, so there's almost no one around to see her as she slips inside. She tries not to think too hard about what she's doing, letting the momentum of her decision carry her through the foyer and into the lift to the top of the building.

It's not just that she's disobeying orders from her direct superior. That's bad enough, waking echoes of shame and panic in her de-programmed brain that buffet her like strong winds. What makes it immeasurably worse is that the direct superior she's disobeying is Reet – her lover, her soulmate. The thought of Reet's look of hurt and betrayal when she finds out what Tanta has done is almost enough to stop her in her tracks.

She does stop when she reaches the double doors to the event hall, looking cautiously through the glass. Most of the engineers have given up and gone home, but Senior Technician Phillips is still here, prodding at the surviving drone with a listless air. *You could turn around*, a voice inside Tanta says. *Go back to Reet, apologise properly, and put this behind you.*

And what would happen then? Reet would go to Kenway in the morning, tell him they have no new leads, and Kenway would kick them both off the assignment. He'd send Tanta back to the CommGuard, if she was lucky. Maybe Reet, too, but Tanta isn't going to do her friend the disservice of pretending that she's motivated by concern for her.

The truth is, the idea of being exiled from the ICRD again fills Tanta with terror. There has been such a lack of certainty in her life recently; her own thoughts are strangers to her. Wanting to be an agent, to put her skills to use, is one of the only desires she has that the loss of her Harlow Programming hasn't altered beyond recognition.

She expected it to. In the months after she was busted down to the community guardians, she kept waiting for that drive to follow the twisting thread of a case to its end to shift beneath her feet, just as everything else had been doing recently. It hadn't; in fact, it had only grown stronger. Tanta missed the ICRD, and not just because she was bored as a guardian. She missed it because being an agent is part of her. The realisation had been bittersweet: bitter, since it had only come once that aspect of her identity had been stolen from her; sweet, because she knows so little about herself now that every revelation is precious.

As an ICRD agent, she can keep doing a job that fills her with a sense of purpose. More importantly, being an agent gives her power that she simply did not have as a guardian – including the power to help Cole. Over the past two months, Tanta has been growing increasingly concerned about him. His isolation and Dr Friend's mistreatment are taking a heavy toll – when she visited him last night, he looked close to despair. But the more she thinks about it, the more Tanta begins to see a way through these difficulties. It won't be easy or pleasant, but she can walk this tightrope of an assignment and come out unscathed on the other side – and if she's very careful, and very lucky, she can bring Cole with her.

She pushes the doors open and marches into the hall, holding her head high.

'Working late,' she raps out to the Senior Technician. 'That's commendable: this is a high priority case. I need to take one of these UAVs back to the ICRD for additional tests.'

She picks up the intact drone as she speaks, as though the idea that the technician would refuse has not even occurred to her. For her plan to work, she needs to look as though she was born in charge, to exude authority. Phillips looks irritated at the interruption, but not suspicious.

'All right,' he says. 'I just need to clear it with your manager.'

Damn. Tanta was hoping the fact that Phillips recognised her would be enough to convince him to hand the drone over.

'Sure,' she says, without missing a beat. 'I'll get you his contact details.'

'*She* sent them to me when we spoke earlier,' Phillips says.

'Oh.' Tanta feigns sudden realisation. 'The woman who was with me earlier isn't my manager. Douglas Kenway is.'

The Senior Technician blanches. 'I – I didn't know he was involved in the investigation directly.'

'Oh yes,' Tanta says. 'He's managing both of us. Like I said, this case is important: the brass are watching it closely.'

Kenway is not well-liked in the Residents' Affairs Division – Tanta learnt as much from her time as a community guardian. He has a reputation for ruthlessness even among those who don't know him personally. She's sure Phillips falls into that category; he's probably never even seen Kenway before, let alone spoken to him. Tanta is half hoping he'll let her take the drone on the strength of Kenway's name alone, but the Senior Technician recovers quickly.

'OK, then,' he says, shoulders tensing at the prospect of speaking to someone so high up the corporate ladder, 'what's his ID?'

Tanta makes a show of accessing her Array and opening

MindChat. 'One moment,' she replies, her eyes tracking back and forth as she looks up the details she needs. 'It's Douglas_ Kenway5431.'

Phillips summons his own Array; there's a long pause while he tries to decide what message to send. His lips move and stop, move and stop, as he drafts potential authorisation requests and then discards them as too long, too curt, or too familiar. Tanta reads his lips out of the corner of her eye.

Hi, Director –

Director Kenway, I have a request here from one of your agents –

Hello Director, you don't know me but I'm – No, that's stupid.

She waits, looking bored. She almost feels sorry for the Senior Technician, though his hesitance is a good sign. He's already rattled, which means he's unlikely to think too carefully about what happens next.

The MindChat ID Tanta gave him sounded as though it *could* belong to Douglas Kenway. In fact, it's out by a couple of numbers and an underscore, turning it from a valid username into a string of gibberish. While she was calling up her MindChat, ostensibly to find Kenway's details, Tanta was actually checking to make sure the ID string she had made up wasn't in active use by anyone else. The last thing she wants is for some other Douglas to get the Senior Technician's message and give the game away.

Phillips is still starting and discarding messages. Tanta lets the wait stretch out to thirty seconds before she says:

'These tests are actually quite time sensitive, so if you don't mind...'

The Senior Technician darts a glance at her. 'Sorry. Just finishing up.' He resumes mouthing words: *...if you could let me know whether that would be OK, I'd appreciate it. Sorry to bother you.*

Finally, and with a relieved air, he makes the haptic command for *send*. For a few moments, nothing happens. Tanta waits, watching for the infinitesimal changes in his posture and expression that will tell her that the error message has come in: *User not found*.

She starts to tap her foot, lightly, on the floor. The look Phillips shoots her way this time has a harassed quality.

'I think there's been an error. My MindChat says it can't find him on the system?'

Tanta gives an exaggerated sigh. 'Let me give it to you again.' She repeats the ID before Phillips can reply. It's better for her to do this out loud than through MindChat or a text-based service. More plausible deniability, and it makes it that much easier for the Senior Technician to believe he has simply misheard her.

After he has tried, and failed, to contact Kenway a second time, Tanta asks, 'Do you need me to spell it for you? D-O-U-G—'

'I know how to spell it!' Phillips snarls. 'I'm not sure *what's*—'

'We don't have time for this,' Tanta breaks in. 'The Director asked me to get this back to him by the end of the day. Do you really want me to have to explain to him why I couldn't do that?'

The Senior Technician has started to sweat. Tanta sounds completely calm, but inside, her senses are heightened and her pulse is elevated. The success or failure of her plan hinges on this moment. It's vital Phillips believes that what comes next is his idea.

'Look.' She softens her tone. 'Whatever this technical issue is, I'm sure it's resolvable. I have to get back to the ICRD *right now*, but if you can think of some other way to get the approval you need, I'm willing to hear it.'

'Um – uh—' Phillips's eyes flick from side to side as he thinks. 'In urgent cases, I think I can get approval retroactively. If you could—'

'That's great,' Tanta says warmly. 'I'll ask Director Kenway to ping it over to you as soon as I get back to the ICRD.' She pauses, letting a slight frown crease her forehead. 'With any luck, he'll be able to weigh in on whatever is causing this technical fault, too.'

The approval from Kenway is never going to arrive, of course, but by the time the Senior Technician realises that, she'll be long gone. She flashes him her most dazzling smile.

'I really appreciate your help on this,' she says. She turns away, the drone still tucked under her arm, and strides off.

As soon as she is out of sight of the hall, she breaks into a run.

Reet pings Tanta when she's halfway up the stairs to Cole's flat, but it's just to tell her that she can clock off whenever she's ready – it's late, and most of the traders in the markets will have packed up their stalls by now. It's the sort of message that requires no more complicated response than a mental nod, for which Tanta is grateful. She was afraid Reet was going to suggest they go for drinks after work, but evidently she'd like a little more time to cool off.

Tanta knocks on Cole's door, as she always does, even though he cannot open it from the inside.

'May I come in?' she calls. There's no point in maintaining the security sweep ruse any longer; she's an agent, now, and her clearance level would let her visit Cole whenever she liked, were it not for the fact that she's been explicitly ordered not to.

'Tanta?' Cole's voice sounds rusty from disuse. 'Of course.'

She draws back the bolt, waits for the 'scape scanner above the door to recognise her ident, and walks inside. Cole looks even worse than the last time she saw him. There are dark circles under his eyes and his expression is groggy, as though she has woken him.

'Are you OK?' she asks, forgetting, for a moment, the urgency of her purpose in coming here.

'I'm fine,' he answers, unconvincingly, 'and I'm really glad to see you, but what are you doing here?' He shoots a meaningful glance towards the camera above his door. In reply, Tanta unhides the Agent badge on her public profile.

'I need your help with an ongoing investigation,' she says, and in spite of the circumstances, she allows a smile to break across her face. 'I'm back in the ICRD, Cole!'

Cole returns her grin. 'Hey, congratulations! I knew Kenway would come to his senses!' Abruptly, he sobers again. 'But are you sure I'm the best person to ask? If you want to hang onto that fancy badge, I'm probably not someone you should be talking to.'

'Your concern for protocol does you credit, Neuroengineer, but you're the only person I *can* ask,' Tanta replies. She raises her voice as she says it, pitching her words to carry to the audio devices nestled around Cole's living space. Kenway is going to know she was here soon enough, because she's going to tell him. Rather than trying to hide the conversation that's about to take place, Tanta has decided that the best way forward is to use it to her and Cole's advantage.

Like it or not, their exchange will be recorded, and given what she's about to do, someone will be examining the footage sooner rather than later. But if Tanta treads carefully, and gets Cole to do the same, the encounter need not reflect badly on either of them. It will be a delicate task, though, a question of shining the right light and casting the right shadow over her words, so that anyone listening will hear only what she wants them to.

'Even though you're currently subject to heightened security arrangements, Director Kenway still recognises your value as an asset,' she says. 'Now, I can't tell you much about the case I've been assigned because it's classified, but I'm hoping you might be able to help me with it all the same. My team leader and

I have been trying to make headway on this all day; it's time sensitive, and we're getting desperate.'

'O … K,' Cole replies. He's clearly thrown by the change in her tone from friendly to formal, but he knows Tanta well enough to guess that she's doing this for a reason, and that she needs him to play along. 'I'll help any way I can.'

'I know you will,' Tanta says. 'And believe me, I wouldn't be asking if there was any other option. But InTech needs you.' She walks into the living room and puts the drone down in the middle of Cole's coffee table. He walks over to inspect it, frowning.

'This UAV's flight logs have been scrambled,' Tanta says simply. 'Do you think you can repair them?'

Cole raises an eyebrow at her. Tanta can read several different questions in that eyebrow – *what's really going on here? Why come to me about this? You know I'm a neurotech, not a drone engineer, right? When are you going to drop the act and start talking like a normal person again?* – but she can only answer one of them.

'None of the drone technicians who have examined the flight recorder so far have been able to make any sense of it. With your mind, and the way you've worked with me for InTech's good in the past, I thought you might be able – and willing – to take a look.'

The eyebrow comes down again. 'I'll give it a go,' Cole replies. 'It could take a while, though.'

Tanta seats herself on the other side of the coffee table. 'That's quite all right. I can wait.'

Cole's first thought when Tanta turned up at his flat, less than twenty-four hours after her last visit, was that his chance to warn her about Harlow 2.0 had come sooner than he was expecting. His encounter with Neal Ortega, their break-in at Arthur's office, and the things they found there, have been swirling around in his head all evening, leaving it clouded as muddy water. When he heard the knock at his door, he was eagerly anticipating the relief of being able to share these troubling thoughts with someone else.

Tanta's entrance had put paid to that idea. It's clear she's on a mission, and whatever that mission is, it involves her speaking *to* the cameras and listening devices in Cole's flat rather than working around them. Cole can't afford to talk about any of the things on his mind in InTech's hearing – it would put both of them at risk. It seems it would also disrupt whatever Tanta is planning, though just who she is trying to convince with her 'InTech Needs You' speech, he isn't sure. He plays up to it as best he can, though, feigning an enthusiastic readiness to serve his corporation and trusting Tanta to make all clear in time.

In fact, he really is intrigued when Tanta shows him the drone and tells him about its scrambled logs. It must be one of the UAVs that attacked the Needle; he's been wondering about what happened there ever since he helped Tanta disarm the bomb, and he knows she has too. This is his chance to help both of them find out. He gets to work straight away, shifting the body of the drone into his lap and giving it a once-over. It's battered, but intact. He's going to have to take it apart to get to its flight recorder, a satisfyingly physical task that will make a change from his usual work.

Of course, hot on the heels of this realisation comes another. Cole hasn't worked on a physical machine in years, and his flat proves it. He doesn't own so much as a spanner.

'Um, do you have a screwdriver?' he asks Tanta. She gives him a sceptical look.

'Of course, no reason why you would,' he mutters. He's going to have to improvise.

A few minutes of digging around in his kitchen produces a small, dull knife, which will have to do. Cole uses it to loosen the screws in the drone's base, then slides off the plastic panel and lifts out the black box from inside. It is neither black nor a box: it's an orange cylinder like a battery, designed to be easily visible in case the drone is ever destroyed and it needs to be recovered from the debris.

From this point on, Cole is on more familiar ground: the drone's flight recorder has a 'scape interface, a fold-out port that he slips on. The readout is no-frills, designed for engineers only. Cole scans the lines of text, narrowing his eyes. When Tanta told him the data inside had been scrambled, he hadn't been sure what to expect. In a worst-case scenario, the black box could have been damaged beyond repair, its contents destroyed or rendered unintelligible. That was unlikely – InTech's flight recorders are tamper-proof and virtually indestructible – but not impossible. What Cole encounters is far more interesting.

'The logs have been encrypted,' he tells Tanta. 'It's really quite clever. Whoever did this couldn't destroy the black box or erase the data it held without scuttling the drone, so they ran its contents through a cipher instead. Quite a tricky one, by the looks of it.'

'Do you think you can break it?' Tanta asks.

Cole doesn't reply straight away. The answer is almost certainly yes – any cipher can be unravelled with enough time and patience – but it's not the most relevant question right now.

'How long do I have?' he asks.

'Till morning.'

Cole pushes aside his weariness at the prospect of the long night of drudgery ahead of him, and checks the clock on his Array. It'll be dawn in eight hours; in codebreaking terms, that's no time at all. The hardest ciphers can take months to crack. Some have puzzled cryptanalysts for years. The analytical programmes on his 'scape will speed the process up, but he's not sure that will be enough. All in all ...

'It's not impossible,' he says.

Tanta nods, accepting his assessment without question or challenge. Cole is struck once again by her trust in him, which seems to have endured despite him having done very little to deserve it. Then he turns his mind back to the task before him, keenly aware that there's no time to think about anything else.

He starts by downloading the scrambled data from the flight recorder to his 'scape. The drone's logs look like a wall of text in an alien language, an impenetrable forest of nonsense words and symbols, but Cole has had some practice in parsing such things. Codebreaking is good mental exercise for a neuroengineer, and Cole cracked his share of encryption algorithms on the learning app back at the Ward House, both during his studies and for fun.

The most important factors in breaking a cipher are how much computing power you have to throw at it, and the nature of the key used to encrypt it in the first place. An encryption key functions much like a physical key – albeit one that's a mile long and has a hundred billion teeth. It fits into the lock of a ciphered text, and when it turns, the text turns with it, revealing its true form.

Encryption keys are too long and complex for their structures to be guessable by the human mind alone – and that's where computing power comes in. First, Cole must write the algorithm that will enable his MbOS to generate possible forms for the key, then set it to try each possibility in turn on the drone's logs until it finds one that fits. MbOSes are powerful machines, able to calculate millions of possibilities a second, but the process could still take hours or even days to run, even if he speeds it up by fine-tuning the code as he goes. A thought occurs to him, and he turns to Tanta.

'Do you have any copies of uncorrupted flight logs that I can see? Ones from drones that haven't been tampered with?'

Having a plain text log that he can feed to his algorithm will make it easier to reverse engineer the encryption.

'Hold on; I'll try to get hold of some,' Tanta replies. She puts her index finger to her temple to summon her Array. Cole returns immediately to his work; there's no time to waste on waiting. He'll have to push on, and add in the new data if and when Tanta comes through with it.

Cole likes a challenge but writing an algorithm like this is not a task in which he can take much pleasure. An encryption key is just a long string of numbers, really, and there's nothing elegant about crunching numbers endlessly until you find the right ones. The algorithm will be a huge, blunt instrument of a solution, if it works at all. Still, he tries to make the code as simple, and as graceful, as he can. Coding is Cole's craft, after all, and anything crafted must bear its maker's mark, in one way or another.

He spends four hours creating the algorithm. It will take far longer to run it and, glancing at the clock, Cole sees that he doesn't have much time left. He sets the thing going anyway. He'll let it work for as long as they have; if it hasn't found the encryption key by morning – and it's hard to believe that it will – then at least he'll know there's nothing more he could have done.

He dismisses his Array and stretches, becoming aware of his hunched posture and aching limbs. He has barely moved for most of the night, and his joints are stiff from disuse. He gets up and walks into his tiny kitchen, intending to make himself a coffee. There's still hours left till dawn, and it will be hard to stay awake now that it's just a matter of waiting.

'I've found some sample logs,' Tanta calls from the living room, her voice startling in the deep silence that has fallen over the flat. 'I'll send them to you now.'

There's a soft chime on Cole's Array as the logs come in. He opens them, flicking through each in turn as he waits for the kettle to boil. They're short, terse lists of longitudes and latitudes punctuated by times and prevailing weather conditions. And then he freezes, hit by an idea with the force of a ten-tonne truck.

He starts to pace up and down the kitchen, coffee forgotten. The logs are short – the cipher he's been trying to decode is hundreds of times their length. It's pretty standard for encrypted texts to vary in length from their plain text equivalents, but even so, the disparity here is startling. It's as though whoever intercepted the log didn't just scramble it, but also mixed it with the contents of an encyclopaedia.

Which raises a question in Cole's mind. Hands trembling a little with a combination of excitement and fatigue, he resummons his Array and opens a linguistic analysis programme. He runs one more check. What he finds makes him laugh aloud. The solution to the encryption is so simple, a hundred neurotechs could have spent a hundred lifetimes looking for it, and never found a thing.

'I've solved it!' he announces to Tanta, who has come over at the sound of his laughter. 'Well, not quite,' he amends. But he knows how to, and that's the hardest part.

'Well done, Neuroengineer Cole,' Tanta says, her tone still oddly stiff and formal. 'I knew I could count on you. Send the logs back to me, and I'll take them straight to Director Kenway.'

'Not yet; I said I'd almost got it,' Cole reminds her. 'I know how they were scrambled; I haven't unscrambled them yet.'

'How were they encrypted?' Tanta prompts him.

'They weren't.'

'But I thought you said—'

Cole is unable to contain himself. 'That's the beauty of it. They *look* like they've been encrypted. Any neurotech or mathematician worth their salt would *assume* they'd been encrypted – and

113

probably drive themselves up the wall trying to find the key to decrypt them. But it's a ruse. Have you ever heard of steganography?'

Tanta shakes her head.

'It's cryptography's poor relation,' Cole says. 'If encryption is the equivalent of locking a message in a box, steganography is more like throwing a rug over it and hoping no one will see it.'

'So, it's easier to solve.'

'Yes,' Cole says, 'but not using a decryption programme. Everything I've been doing for the last four hours has been a complete waste of time.' Far from resenting the loss of his evening, he feels the urge to laugh again. The sleep deprivation probably isn't helping his judgement, but he's delighted by this solution, which has hidden from him in plain sight all this while. It's the opposite of everything he found boring and blunt about the encryption key algorithm: simple, elegant, and witty. It's the kind of workaround he would dream up – which is probably how he figured it out.

'No one would ever look at a wall of text like this and assume it *wasn't* encrypted,' he continues. 'If they ran traditional analyses on it and found no solution, they'd likely just assume they didn't have enough processing power to find the key.'

'*You* didn't,' Tanta points out.

'Yes, but I—' Cole stops, checking himself before he slips into arrogance, but Tanta could already see where he was going.

'You're a genius,' she finishes dryly. 'So, if the logs aren't encoded, what *has* been done to them?'

'Essentially, they've been flooded with white noise,' Cole says. 'Whoever tampered with them filled them with random characters and numbers, disguising the original contents.'

'And that's a process you can reverse?'

'Yes. Probably within a few hours.' The logs are something like a giant wordsearch, or a jigsaw puzzle where most of the pieces are red herrings, never meant for use in the final picture. Designing an algorithm that can sort the relevant information from the junk around it will take Cole a while, but a good deal less time than breaking an encryption.

Tanta sags back into the couch. Her obvious relief makes Cole alarmed: it's rare to see any lapse at all in her perfect poker face. If even he can read her expression right now, the stakes on this must be incredibly high.

He gets to work right away, fingers dancing across the air in front of him as he types. With the scrambled logs cracked and the first flush of excited triumph abated, he finds himself thinking again of Neal Ortega and their harrowing discovery in the Black Box. It's impossible to say anything to Tanta now, but Cole needs to find a way of warning her about Harlow 2.0 soon.

'Tanta,' he says, as casually as possible, 'Do you think we might be able to talk again, sometime this week? I—' How to phrase this? *I think InTech is planning another Harlow Programme – or maybe something worse. And god help me, I think I'm going to try and stop them. You in?* '—I could do with seeing a friendly face.'

Tanta shoots him a look of real solicitude, but her tone is light when she replies. 'If Director Kenway says that's OK, then sure.' She's still performing for the bugs, playing the good, obedient CorpWard. Cole knows there's nothing else she can say with so many eyes on her – he's not even sure why he asked. For now, Tanta's equivocal reply will have to be enough.

Chapter 11

Sometime in the dark, mutable hours before dawn, Douglas Kenway is dragged unwillingly from a dreamless sleep. He opens his eyes, blinking in a darkness that has robbed the room around him of all definition. The clock on his Array informs him that it is four am. A notification is blinking insistently before his eyes. It's from Tanta.

Kenway props himself up on one arm, confused and irritated. Messages from subordinates shouldn't be coming through at this hour: he thought he'd set everything on his 'scape to mute before he went to bed. He brushes the notification away, too annoyed even to wonder why the girl is bothering him this late at night.

It refuses to budge. Assuming his MbOS is glitching, Kenway swipes at the notification again. And then he catches sight of what it says:

<<I'm sorry to bother you so late, Director Kenway, but I think we ought to meet urgently. Could you come to the ICRD as soon as you receive this?>>

That's infuriating enough; the presumption of the request makes Kenway's blood boil. But it's topped by the last line, which the CorpWard appears to have added almost as an afterthought: <<You'll be pleased to hear that I've found a break in the case.>>

Everything Kenway feared when the board instructed him to give Tanta the assignment is encapsulated in that line. He can almost feel his career prospects dimming at the sight of it. Tanta was not *supposed* to find a break in the case! Kenway took some pains to prevent her from doing so: he gave her only a partial brief, put her under the command of an inexperienced manager, and then sent them both haring off after dead ends. That Tanta has made progress despite these obstacles – and produced a lead from an avenue of investigation Kenway had thought fruitless – is bad news indeed.

Kenway was one of the select few who was briefed on the original Harlow Programme, and when he first heard about it, he had actually thought – the memory brings a bitter sneer to his lips now – that the programming would make his job safer. Surely, he had reasoned, a perfectly obedient, perfectly loyal worker would never seek to undermine their direct superior?

Obedience and loyalty are fine things, as is talent, but they'll only take you so far. Kenway became a Director the same way all his colleagues did – through sheer and unflinching ruthlessness. Wards programmed to serve the corporation out of a sense of love and duty, he had thought, would be incapable of exactly the kind of behaviour that helped him to rise through the ranks.

Well, he'd been wrong. He learnt that lesson after what happened to Jennifer Ash, but it seems he still hasn't learnt it thoroughly enough. The Harlow Programmed Corporate Wards may not be ruthless, but they are dangerous. He sees, now, why the board are so keen to expand the programme. Tanta and Reet and the other CorpWards are coming for Douglas Kenway, and for everyone like him. They're not conniving or cruel – just completely, maniacally devoted to their jobs. They'll make him redundant, and they'll do it courteously, kindly, and with cheerful smiles on their faces.

How many times has he heard the conduit say that the Harlow Programme is the future of the corporation? And how many times has he agreed, pleased to be able to butter up the board with this flattering estimation of their foresight? It's only lately that Kenway has come to realise that the future of the corporation looks a lot like the barrel of a gun, and it's pointing straight at him.

He gets dressed in a tearing hurry, then spends almost as long as it took him to get ready deliberating how he should play the meeting that's about to take place. He briefly considers instructing Tanta to come to him, to remind her of who is in charge. But he's already working to her timetable – specifying the location of their conversation would be an empty gesture. Ordering Tanta to resubmit her request for a meeting via her team leader would be another way of asserting his authority, but while confronting her with her breach of protocol would certainly be a relief to his embittered spirits, it would also mean that Reet would be present for their meeting. Kenway is not at all sure he wants a witness to whatever is about to come, especially not another CorpWard.

In the end, the only thing he can do is order an executive taxi – and curse Tanta out roundly while he waits for it. Kenway arrives at the ICRD half an hour after Tanta sent her message, a delay short enough to indicate to the board that he's taking this 'break in the case' seriously, but hopefully long enough to have made her impatient.

She doesn't look it. When he reaches the fourteenth floor, she is sitting outside his office, her hands folded demurely over a dark, dented thing with six broken spokes. She looks up as he approaches and smiles at him. Kenway stares at her, trying to interrogate that smile, but he can find no smugness or triumph in it. It's like a wall, and all the CorpWard's thoughts are on the other side of it. He smiles back, his own more like a snarl, a weapon: *back the fuck off.*

He knows he needs to find some way to assert his power over Tanta, to regain his slipping grip on authority, but he wasn't expecting this meeting, hasn't prepared for it. He is unbalanced; for the moment, his store of stratagems is empty. The fact that Tanta drops her eyes and waits, respectfully, for him to open the door to his office and usher her inside, somehow only makes this feeling worse.

At first, Kenway sits behind his desk while Tanta stands to attention before him. This gives him the absurd feeling that she is towering over him, however, so after a moment he gets back up again, clasping his hands behind his back in what he hopes is a commanding attitude.

'What have you found?' he raps out. He's trying for an imperious tone, but the words sound tired and sullen.

In reply, Tanta holds up the broken drone. 'This is one of the UAVs that attacked the Needle last night,' she says. 'When Reet and I visited the scene yesterday afternoon, the Senior Technician working there told us the vehicle's flight logs were unreadable.'

Kenway gestures for the girl to continue. He'd made quite sure that particular lead was a non-starter before he sent Tanta and Reet to follow up on it. He has already read a report on the drone from his Head of Engineering: the best minds in both his divisions have been working on its flight recorder nonstop for the last twenty-four hours and discovered nothing of value.

'Reet instructed us to search the city's flea markets to see if we could locate any of the goods that had been stolen from this or the other UAVs,' Tanta continues, 'but we were unable to find any.'

'Does this catalogue of dead ends have a point?'

'Yes,' she says, unperturbed. 'My team leader was of the opinion that we should return to you and seek further guidance, but I disagreed. So, I took custody of the drone from the Senior Technician on your authority and took it to my old partner to see if he could make any headway with it.'

Kenway feels a wave of incredulous relief. The situation is far better than he had hoped. Driven and dedicated she might be, but Tanta evidently lacks any sense of politics. In her over-zealousness, she has played right into his hands. 'That,' he says, 'was a flagrant violation of my direct order. You're off the case. Leave the drone and get out of my office. I'll send through details of your official reprimand later.'

Tanta does not so much as blink. In fact, she gives no sign of having heard Kenway at all. There's a pause; she stares at Kenway levelly. 'Don't you want to know what Cole found out?' she asks him.

'You can send me the details later,' Kenway snaps. 'Breakthrough or not, your conduct was unacceptable. I'm *very* disappointed in you. I will be taking over the case from here.'

The command phrase, at least, has its desired effect. But though Tanta flinches, she does not turn to leave, as he had hoped she would. She doesn't stop staring at him, either.

'No,' she says. 'You won't.'

Unease begins to reassert itself in Kenway's mind. 'What did you say?' he asks.

'You won't be taking over the case. That is to say, I don't think you want to, Director.'

Kenway is fast losing his grip on the reins of his temper. 'What are you talking about?'

'The board were pleased when I told them what I'd found

out. They want to meet with us both tomorrow evening for a full debrief.'

Kenway's whole body goes cold. 'You – you've spoken to the board?' he asks. He curses the words as soon as they're out of his mouth; they sounded weak and wavering. He should have seen this coming. He thinks back to the notification from Tanta, which woke him up despite him muting his 'scape before he fell asleep. At the time, he'd assumed his Array was glitching, but that wasn't the reason. There's one type of notification that's programmed to come through regardless of the settings on Kenway's 'scape, one summons that can never be ignored. He retrieves Tanta's message, noticing now what he was too sleep-addled to see before. It's tagged with a discreet footer in pale red: *push notifications enabled on the board's authority.*

Tanta still hasn't blinked, Kenway realises. Her cool green eyes, at once clear and impenetrable, bore into him, making him shift from foot to foot. 'Of course,' she continues, as though Kenway has not spoken, 'what happens in that meeting is up to you. Right now, the board are under the impression that I was following your orders when I asked Cole to assess the drone. They're impressed with your leadership and foresight; you authorised me to take a calculated risk, and it paid off. You'll see from the security tapes that my meeting with Cole was carefully managed. He never learnt anything that could have compromised the assignment, and I supervised him the entire time. The whole thing reflects very well on you.'

'But I *didn't* authorise you to meet with him!' Kenway explodes. He needs, desperately, to regain control of this conversation, but the stark contrast between his rage and Tanta's matter-of-factness only makes him sound more unhinged.

'I'm sorry you feel that way,' Tanta says, 'and if you'd like to tell the board that, I defer to your authority to do so. Personally, I believe that everything I did was well within the *spirit* of your instructions. You asked me for results, and I delivered them. I was intending to tell the board as much: I really couldn't have done it without your guidance. But if you'd like to give me sole credit for the breakthrough that just blew this assignment wide open, that's entirely your prerogative.'

There's a long silence then. Kenway lets it stretch. He tries to keep his expression thoughtful, as if he's mulling the issue over, but in reality, he feels like he's been winded. Tanta has won the match before he even realised what game they were playing.

By having the board's ear, she's ensured that Kenway can't throw her to the wolves without risking the same fate himself. She's even offered him a reward to counterbalance the threat: back her up, and he can share in the credit for her success. Which reminds him that he still doesn't know exactly how resounding that success is.

'You haven't told me what you found out yet,' he says.

'Of course!' Tanta's eyes widen a fraction, as though the discovery upon which the whole of this meeting hinges had simply slipped her mind. 'The logs Cole recovered from the drone tell us exactly where it was when it was brought down. We know where the bandits attacked it: seventy-five kilometres southeast of the city, just outside our Southern Distribution Centre.'

Kenway feels his shoulders tense. It's a good, solid lead – the best anyone on the case has been able to find so far. It's no wonder the board are pleased; this is exactly the kind of progress they demanded of him at their last meeting, the one where they insisted he give the assignment to Tanta.

Back then, the idea of the CorpWard succeeding where his other agents had failed was Kenway's nightmare scenario. He was willing to go to great lengths to prevent it – even at the risk of allowing the drone attacks to continue – but now that it has happened, he finds himself forced to change course. He can't afford *not* to let Tanta succeed, because she has manoeuvred him into a position where his triumph is contingent upon her own. He'd be impressed, if he wasn't so angry.

'What do you want?' He hisses the words through gritted teeth.

Tanta tilts her head to one side. 'I want to serve my corporation to the best of my ability, Director. Isn't that what all of us want?'

Kenway has never been in this position before – he's usually the one extorting someone else, not the other way around – but he's been on Tanta's side of the table enough times to know what's happening here. This dance, these sly references to doing what's best for the corp, are unnecessary; surely Tanta knows that she has already won? 'Fine,' he says. 'And how do you want to do that, *specifically*?'

He's expecting Tanta to ask for a raise, or a promotion. 'By continuing to work the case with Reet,' she says. 'Oh,' she adds, 'and I think it would be prudent to bring Cole back into the ICRD as a permanent technical consultant. With your permission, of course. His assistance with the drone proves he can be trusted. I think his house arrest has lasted long enough, don't you?'

The expression of innocent enquiry on her face looks so genuine that Kenway is only able to see past it by an effort of will. Freeing Cole is easily done. Kenway put the order in place, and he can lift it again. With the help Cole has just provided, it won't even be a hard sell to the board. Leaving Tanta on the case is likewise an easy choice. It would be foolish, really, to do anything else. He supposes he should be grateful she hasn't asked for something harder to deliver, but instead, it makes him uneasy.

The way this meeting has gone leaves Kenway in no doubt

that Tanta has manipulated this situation intentionally, playing him and the board with expert precision. And yet her demands make no sense. She has him by the balls, and she's asking for nothing she doesn't have already. If Tanta's designs were obvious, he could at least take comfort from the fact that he understood them. If she were trying to rise through the ranks, or feathering her own nest, or looking for favours she could call in down the line, Kenway would feel he had the measure of her again, and could disregard her plans, or thwart them, as the situation required. But the fact is, he has no idea what Tanta wants – she seems to want almost nothing – and that scares him. He opens his mouth to ask her what she's playing at, then thinks better of it.

'Done,' he says. 'Now get out of my office.'

To his intense relief, she does. As the door closes behind her, Kenway dials up the opacity on the smart glass windows to 100%. When he's sure that no one can see him, he picks up the drone from where Tanta has left it on his desk and begins ripping the blades of its propellers off one by one, like he's tearing the wings off a fly. The methodical violence of the action calms him, helping to clarify his thoughts.

While it's true that he doesn't understand Tanta, it's clear to Kenway that he has underestimated her. He assumed her Harlow Programming would make her easy to control, but there's something different about her, something that sets her apart from the other CorpWards he has encountered. She's more cunning than he ever would have given her credit for.

He demoted Tanta to the community guardians, and she somehow managed to impress the board enough that they restored her to the ICRD. He treated her as nothing more than a minor irritant, and she outmanoeuvred him effortlessly. He assumed she was like the other Harlow Programmed wards – driven, but without guile – and he couldn't have been more wrong. The clearest thought of all in Kenway's mind, as he lays the dismembered drone back on the desk, is that Tanta is none of the things he thought she was. The only thing he's sure of is that she is a threat to him. And this time, he must deal with her permanently.

Chapter 12

Cole doesn't see or hear from Neal at all the following morning. At first, he assumes they'll speak at lunch, but there's no sign of him in the canteen, either. Cole stays there the full hour, just in case, but he never shows. By the afternoon, he's stewing in fear and doubt, veering between the hopeful conviction that Neal is simply working somewhere offsite, and an equally certain foreboding that something terrible has happened to him.

Neal told Cole that he would get the update they found on Arthur's hard drive to Jeanie, but not how he was going to contact her – or what would happen next. What if something went wrong during that hand-off, or while Neal was preparing for it? Cole has no way of knowing, and even if he did, no way of sending help or raising the alarm. He's adrift, separated from his co-conspirator and ignorant as to his success or failure. The tenuousness of his connection to Neal, and through him to Jeanie and Yas, is terrifying.

A message from Tanta would at least take his mind off his gnawing worry, but she's gone silent, too: he hasn't heard from her since she left with the flight logs he helped her unscramble last night. The day dribbles away, light fading from the sky as afternoon slouches towards evening, and still Cole doesn't see anyone except the colleagues he shares his office with, and no one speaks to him except to give him more work to do.

The lonely monotony is a return to his normal routine, but after all the excitement and alarm of yesterday, it's jarring, making Cole feel almost as though the covert trip to Arthur's office with Neal, and his midnight visit from Tanta, were things he dreamt.

At four pm, he's trying to take his mind off his mounting anxiety by fixing some bugs with the ticketing system when a voice behind him nearly makes him jump out of his chair.

'You can all leave early today. Take the evening off.'

Cole spins around. Arthur is standing behind him. There's a mumbled chorus of 'thanks' and 'goodnights', followed by a collective rush for the door. Cole rises to his feet, intending to follow the grateful crowd of neuroengineers out of the office, but Arthur lays a hand on his shoulder.

'Not you, Cole.'

Cole stiffens, hands curling involuntarily into fists. Arthur probably just has some more work for him to do; there's no reason to believe he has any other motive for keeping him behind. Well, aside from the fact that Cole was engaged in anti-corporate espionage in his office less than a day ago.

'Dr Friend?' he manages to croak. His heart is hammering so loudly he's surprised Arthur can't see the veins in his neck and temples pulsing in time with it.

'I've just assigned you a dozen new tickets,' Arthur says. 'See that you have them completed by tomorrow morning.'

Cole takes a deep, steadying breath. He's so relieved that it's all he can do not to laugh aloud. He's not going to be arrested! Which still leaves the question of where Neal is, but his narrow escape has made Cole bold, and now that Arthur is in front of him, he thinks he can see a way to ask about his co-conspirator that won't look suspicious.

'Uh, I'm not allowed to be in the office unsupervised. A trainee stays with me, usually. I think last time it was Neuroengineering Assistant Ortega?' He looks at his feet as he says it. With any luck, Arthur will assume he's embarrassed.

'Yes, I'm well aware,' Arthur replies. 'Neal has been helping me test a software update. He'll be downstairs in a few minutes.'

Cole nods mechanically, his mind racing. Neal has been here, in the building, all this time? Cole didn't see him arrive, and he got here pretty early. Perhaps the intern has been staying out of his way on purpose, the better to avoid suspicion. But then, why offer to watch Cole now? He's sure there are other junior employees who could do the job.

Arthur is still standing behind Cole's chair, and Cole realises with a sinking feeling that he intends to wait there until Neal arrives. It's another insult; a reminder that Cole can't be trusted alone, but he's too preoccupied to be nettled by it. He turns back to his work, trying to mask his tension, but the tickets Arthur has assigned him, although time-consuming, are too easy to calm his thoughts. He's acutely aware of Arthur's presence at his back; the doctor is so close that Cole can hear him breathing.

'It's good of Neal to agree to supervise you, isn't it?' Arthur remarks. 'He really is a model employee.'

'Mm,' Cole replies. If Arthur is trying to twit him with his own lack of work ethic, he's barking up the wrong tree; Cole has never concerned himself with all that corporate bullshit.

A strained silence falls between them. After a few minutes, it occurs to Cole that this is the longest he has spent in Arthur's company since the night that he and Tanta broke into the Black Box last summer. Arthur speaks to him several times a day, to mock him or increase his workload as the mood takes him, but his visits are always short. He hates Cole; he's certainly never deigned to babysit him before.

'I'm very pleased with him,' Arthur says. The pause between

this and his last comment has been so long that it takes Cole a moment to realise he's still talking about Neal.

'I don't know him all that well,' Cole hazards.

'Well, no, you wouldn't. Neal is more my handiwork than yours. I consider him something of a protégé, in fact.'

Cole's pulse spikes again. That doesn't sound good. What if Neal has actually been spying for Arthur this whole time? Maybe the break-in was an elaborate sting, and Arthur is just waiting to get Cole and Neal together before he reveals the ruse and calls the guardians. That wouldn't be like him, though: Arthur may be a tyrant, but he's no fool. He wouldn't waste time engaging in amateur dramatics over something this important.

Cole shifts in his chair, pretending to call up something on his 'scape, and risks a glance behind him. Arthur is staring at him, and there's a faraway expression on his face that Cole hasn't seen before – not that he can remember, anyway. There's smugness in there – in Cole's opinion, Arthur always looks smug – but something else, as well. He almost looks...

But Cole doesn't have Tanta's knack for reading people, and he can't complete the thought. All he knows for sure is that Arthur has something on his mind, and since he won't shut up about Neal, the something must have to do with him. Then Cole hears a tread on the stairs.

'That will be him now,' Arthur says, as though he and Cole have been chatting all this while, rather than hanging around in awkward silence.

Adrenaline hums through Cole, making his palms sweat and his muscles tense. If he has been discovered, he will have to fight. He casts his eyes around the office, looking for something he could use as a weapon. Arthur carries a stun baton on his belt now, a 'security precaution' that he takes great pleasure in wearing in full view whenever he and Cole are in the same room. The doctor is an old man; Cole's no fighter, but he's reasonably sure he could overpower him if he had to. Of course, the success or failure of this desperate course of action depends on Neal. If he really is who he says he is, one of Jeanie's freedom fighters, then he'll help. If he's been playing Cole since the beginning, then Cole is already doomed.

For an instant, Cole contemplates striking Arthur now and making a run for it. His mind whirls; he feels sick and dizzy. And then his thoughts come screeching to a halt as Neal walks into the room. At first, Cole is relieved to see him. There's a spring in Neal's step; he doesn't look as if anything is wrong. But then he turns to face Cole, and Cole realises that he was mistaken. Something *is* wrong. There's something terribly wrong with Neal himself.

His eyes are fever-bright, and the smile stretching his lips is one that doesn't belong on a human face. It's the painted grin of a child's doll: it comes from the world of inanimate objects and on a living, breathing being, it's grotesque. Cole sees all this in an instant of queasy horror, before Neal turns from him and looks at Arthur. The trainee's back straightens as he stands to attention.

'Good evening, Director!' he says. The sound gives Cole another shock. It's Neal's voice, but it, too, is *wrong*. It's as if this man is not really Neal, but an actor playing him in a pantomime, instructed to over-inflect every word and enunciate every syllable.

'Ah, Neal,' Arthur replies. He sounds completely unaffected by Neal's wrongness. 'I'd like you to watch Cole for me until he's finished with his work.'

'It would be my pleasure, Director!'

'See that he doesn't slack, won't you?'

'Of course, Director!'

Arthur pulls the stun baton from his belt and hands it to Neal, who takes it with as much enthusiasm as if he has won the lottery, and the doctor is handing him his winnings. 'If he *does* slack, or if he tries anything, use this to keep him in line.'

'Will do, Director!'

Cole feels a sick jolt of fear. Arthur wears the stun baton to prove a point; it's a display of power – nothing more. He's never actually *used* it.

'Arthur,' he begins indignantly. He half rises from his chair.

Arthur nods, and the next thing Cole knows, he is on the floor, his body on fire. His limbs stiffen, spasm and jerk, no longer under his control.

'I was hoping you'd give me an excuse.' Arthur's voice sounds distant and satisfied. 'Well done, Neal. You did an excellent job.'

Cole looks up, through the waves of pain, to see that Arthur is beaming almost as widely as Neal. Suddenly, he recognises the expression on Arthur's face that eluded him before: it's pride. And not the kind that goes before a fall – fond pride, like a father has for a son. Or an inventor for the success of his latest experiment.

Understanding shoots through Cole, worse than the shock from the stun baton. He knows what's wrong with Neal, and the knowledge is so awful that it feels like he's losing his memory all over again. A trapdoor opens in his mind and he drops through it, into freefall.

Neal is more my handiwork than yours.

Cole doesn't remember much of his previous relationship with Arthur, but he knows how jealous the doctor is of him, has relearnt it the hard way, through weeks of insults and petty cruelties. Cole has never forgiven himself for creating the Harlow Programme; Arthur never forgave him either. It was a feat of neuroengineering that cast a long shadow – one they have both spent the rest of their careers trying to escape. But while Cole has been desperate, ever since he learnt the truth about his role in the programme's creation, to repent for it, all Arthur has ever wanted is to surpass his success.

Arthur hasn't come to arrest Cole for treason. No, he's here to gloat. He has finally perfected his answer to the Harlow Programme, his own magnum opus, and now he's here to show it off.

At last, Arthur's interest in the Thoughtfront agent's programming makes sense to Cole. He was so distracted by its obvious inferiority to the Harlow Programme that he never spotted its one advantage: it may be blunter and more primitive than InTech's version, but what it lacks in sophistication, it more than makes up for in speed. It took InTech more than a decade to see results from the Harlow Programme. Neal has been programmed within the space of a day.

All of these revelations clash and roar in Cole's head like waves. He remains utterly silent, drowning in horror and pity. He wants to seize Arthur by the throat and strangle him – but that wouldn't do Neal any good. In fact, Neal would rush to stop him, and against Neal and the stun baton, Cole doesn't stand a chance. As has already been amply demonstrated, he wouldn't make it out of his chair. Slowly, Cole climbs to his feet. He bit his tongue when Neal shocked him. His jaw aches and he can taste blood, making speaking an effort, but there's something he has to know.

'Who's the software update for?' he asks. His voice is barely louder than a whisper.

'What?' Arthur snaps.

'You said Neal was helping you test a software update. Who are the end-users?'

Arthur frowns. Cole can see him considering whether or not to answer, weighing up the security implications against his desire to rub Cole's nose in his achievement. But he's in a boasting humour, and the information Cole has asked for is hardly sensitive by itself.

'It's a city-wide prototype,' he answers. 'Everyone below the level of Director will be receiving it. Including you, Cole.'

Cole opens his mouth, then shuts it again. There's nothing he can say, no accusation he can hurl at Arthur that won't make clear to him that Cole knows about the Harlow Programme, and about their shared past. That would be suicidally stupid, so he says nothing.

'I want those work tickets finished by morning, remember,' Arthur repeats. 'Chop chop.'

He flashes Cole one last, terrible grin, and stalks out of the room.

Chapter 13

Fliss sits up in her sleeping bag, woken by a beeping from the touchscreen phone in her jeans pocket. The inside of her tent is dark, but it's time to get up: she and the crew have another drone to hunt. She checks the details she has been sent on the phone's cracked screen, calling up the little map as she has been taught to do. The crew are a blue marker to the south; they're camped out near Ditchling today, on what's left of the old downs. A timer at the top of the map tells Fliss that they have less than forty-five minutes to make it to their target, a red arrow hovering over Albourne. They'd better get a move on.

She puts on her body armour and pads outside. Ben and Sonia have already turned on the solar lanterns, and Gabriel is cooking breakfast on the portable stove by their pale light. The stove and lanterns are new additions to the camp, as are the sleeping bags and tents. Some of these things are loot from all the drones they've been taking, while others, like the phone, are equipment from their new benefactors.

Life has been good for the crew recently: Fliss's bargain with the two strangers has paid off in spectacular fashion. Fliss sometimes catches herself gazing around camp with a sense of unreality, unable to believe their good fortune. It was less than two months ago that the crew shared a couple of leaky tarps by way of shelter and an assortment of scavenged rags and blankets for bedding. Most nights, their old heater would die, and Fliss would be forced to go out foraging for wood so they could have a fire. And now look at them! Solar-powered lamps, a working stove ... Their camp has been transformed, and in so short a time that the change feels almost magical. In spite of these boons, however, Fliss still isn't living up to her name. She's not happy.

In some ways, she's more on edge than she was before.

She walks over to the rest of the crew, snagging a piece of bacon from the stove and dancing it back and forth between burnt fingers.

'Eat up quick,' she says. 'We're moving out in ten. Josh! Get your arse in gear!'

Josh appears, blinking muzzily, at the mouth of his tent. 'Fuck off, Fliss. I was already awake.'

While Josh gets ready and the others eat, Fliss goes back into her tent and drags out the heavy lockbox that houses the crew's new weapons. These are another gift from the strangers. They have given the crew a handgun each for emergencies, plus the huge, shoulder-mounted blaster the woman was carrying when Fliss first met them. Fliss had thought this was a grenade launcher when she first saw it, but it actually fires a high-speed net capsule. The net gun is much more effective at downing a drone than a bullet or even a grenade could be. The capsule is laser-guided, and when the net bursts out, it tangles itself in all of the drone's rotors at once, bringing it down without damaging it. Keeping the drones they hunted intact was never important to the crew before, but it matters to the strangers, so now they have to take it seriously.

It's not like the additional requirement has hurt their strike rate. Since they started going hunting with the net gun, the crew have barely missed a shot, and every hit has brought their quarry down at once, its cargo unharmed. The strangers have never told Fliss who they work for, but she can take a reasonable guess from the quality of their weapons alone. It's common knowledge even among the inhabitants of the wasteland that Thoughtfront's military hardware is scary stuff – cutting edge in the bloodiest and most literal sense of the term.

Her suspicions about her new partners are one of the reasons Fliss has been so tense lately. Another is that their fancy new weapons are now the only ones the crew have. Before he handed them over, the man insisted on taking Fliss's own salvaged pistol, and the rifle Ben had just picked up in Crawley. This had gone against the grain for Fliss – the rifle wasn't even functional, but the handgun had once belonged to Harry, and she'd had it almost since she joined the crew. She had complied, because she couldn't argue with the new guns' superiority, but it was only after she gave the old weapons up that she found out about the catch.

The strangers didn't tell them about it, but the crew figured out pretty early on that their new guns don't work all the time. When they're out on the strangers' business, visiting the coordinates they send Fliss on her new phone and shooting down the drones they find there, the weapons function flaw- lessly. But when Josh tried to shoot a crow a few weeks ago, his handgun wouldn't fire, and the bird had cackled at him and flown away. Fliss had laughed too, at the time – Josh is the kind of person who likes to shoot or throw stones at anything that moves, so she'd been rooting for the crow – but afterwards, in her tent, she had worried over it. She took the crew out hunting rabbits the next day, with the same results.

Fliss isn't sure how the guns *know* what they're being aimed at, but somehow, they do, and it seems they will only fire at things the strangers want them to hit. It's not a huge problem, though – the strangers send them after so many drones that Fliss and the crew don't need to catch rabbits anymore. They have so much food and medicine that it's been a challenge to offload the excess, and they've had to widen their range just to find enough settlements to sell it all to.

They have everything they need, and there's a kind of thrill, besides, in their new weapons' effectiveness that compensates for the crew's loss of choice in their targets. Drones no longer pass them by, or hurt them. They have tools for disabling anti-theft mines and armour to protect them from bullets. All in all, and in spite of the loss of the pistol, they're doing much better since the bargain than they were before. Still, Fliss can't help worrying about what might happen if they meet someone or something that needs shooting, and the new guns refuse to play ball.

She keys in the code on the lockbox and flips it open, then gathers the crew around to dole out the weapons. She gives everyone a handgun first. They're a little too shiny for Fliss's liking, but they're also sleek and light. Next, she takes out the net gun, which she hands to Sonia. Josh looks sour.

'That's bullshit,' he protests. 'I'm a way better shot with the nets than Sonia.'

'Fuck off, Josh,' Fliss retorts amicably. 'Sonia's shooting today, and that's the end of it.'

Josh does have a point. Since Fliss took him out to practice that first time, he has improved immensely. He turns out to have a good eye, now that he's over his nerves, and he has been the shooter on most of their recent hunting trips. He's not careful, though; he may make most of the shots he takes, but Fliss has seen him miss before because he was showing off, trying to down the drone without looking, or from further away than necessary. Other times he's been flat out distracted, sighting after grouse and foxes in the bushes when he should have been watching the sky.

'All right, everyone, listen up,' Fliss says. 'You've done this enough times now that you know the drill, and probably some of you are starting to feel like you can ignore it. So, we're going to go through it again.'

There's a collective groan, but there's no real heart to it. To an extent, Fliss knows the crew find this patter reassuring. They expect her to act the brusque drill sergeant, barking orders and doling out sarcasm with a liberal hand. It's a part Fliss plays well, and the others usually settle into their corresponding role of the long-suffering cadets with equal gusto.

'Tell me your roles,' Fliss orders, raising her voice above the grumbling. 'Ben?'

'Lookout,' Ben grunts. He's a scrawny guy of about eighteen, not much good in a fight, but with keen eyes and a surprisingly carrying voice. He'll be stationed at a little distance from the rest of the crew, to keep an eye out for trouble and shout his head off if he sees any.

'Got your binocs?' Fliss asks him. 'And your gas mask?' He nods. 'Good. Sonia?'

'Shooter,' says Sonia, hefting the blaster onto her shoulder as she speaks. 'Got the net gun, and I got a gas mask, too.'

'I'm running,' Gabriel says, as Fliss turns in his direction. 'For my sins. Got my gas mask, and got my, err, feet.' Fliss snorts. None of the crew like being the one who runs after the drone and brings it and its cargo back. It's the most tiring task, and the most dangerous, which is why they rotate it between them.

'And I'm here to make sure you idiots don't fuck anything up,' Fliss concludes.

'I still don't see why I can't be shooter,' Josh grumbles. There's a belligerence in his tone that Fliss doesn't like.

'I'll put you back on the net gun when you stop fucking about,' she says sharply. 'For now, watch Sonia. You might learn something. Have you got your mask?'

'I have a question,' Josh says.

Fliss raises her eyebrows at him: *well?*

'Why can't we use the new masks?' he asks. 'They're lighter, and they don't smell like dogshit.'

This raises a chuckle from Gabriel, though Sonia shoots Josh a withering glare. It's true, the old masks do stink. They're the one bit of kit the crew still use from before Fliss's bargain, and they've had them for years. Fliss traded for them herself, and has maintained them religiously ever since. She cleans their filters every week, but they're old, and wearing them makes every breath you take taste of mildew. It's true, too, that the strangers have given them new masks, with digital displays and automatic sensors. They're lying in the box they came in, untouched.

Fliss flashes Josh a smile, one that shows all her teeth. 'Joshua,' she says, 'Remind me: who gave us the new masks?'

Josh gives her a blank look. 'You said it was Thoughtfront.'

'Yes, I did. And why did they do it? What's in it for them?'

'I dunno.'

'Exactly. You don't have a fucking clue. Tell me something: if a Red Flag raider offered you his canteen, told you to take a good, long swig, would you do it?'

Josh wrinkles his forehead, his expression halfway between confusion and annoyance. Fliss wonders if she's made the hypothetical too difficult for him. 'Nah,' he says at last. 'He might've spat in it.'

'You're right, Josh. He might have. Or he might've done something worse, because the Red Flags aren't our friends, are they? You know who else isn't our friend? Thoughtfront – them and every other corp out there. They may be helping us right now, and right now, we could use the help. But that doesn't mean we can trust them.'

Josh smirks, trying to cover his embarrassment. 'Bit paranoid, aren't you? Everything else they gave us works fine.'

Fliss buries her head in her hands. 'But not all the time,

shit-for-brains!' It's bad enough when the guns conk out – Fliss isn't going to take that chance with the masks, which are far more important. 'You weren't here the last time a crewmate got gassed, Josh, but I was. Trust me, you don't want to see something like that happen to one of us, and you sure as shit don't want it happening to you. We're using *our* masks because this is life or death, and I don't want us putting all our faith in people who were trying to kill us less than two months ago. Got it?'

Josh nods, and Fliss decides to leave the subject there. His face has gone as red as his hair, and there's a fine line between giving him the kick up the arse he so desperately needs and inviting mutiny.

She's about to tell the crew to move out when a black car comes into view, its sleek, urban design out of place on the muddy downs. This is another thing that puts Fliss on edge: she hasn't seen the woman since the day she first met the strangers, but the man hangs around camp like a bad smell, turning up at the most inconvenient times to collect on his end of the bargain.

The crew are allowed to keep all the cargo they find, but their agreement with the strangers is that they hand over the drones. The man visits at least once a week to collect them, watching jealously while the crew load them into the boot of his corporate car. It doesn't help Fliss's sense of unease that the man always knows exactly where the crew are camped, without ever calling ahead. It stands to reason he's tracking them through the guns, or perhaps the phone, but that doesn't make his appearances any less unsettling.

'We're heading out to a target,' Fliss tells the man as he approaches. 'If you've come for the drones, you can get them yourself. They're in my tent.'

'Actually, I've come to observe your skills in action.'

That takes Fliss by surprise – the stranger has never come

with them on a hunt before. 'Why?' she asks, her tone polite but guarded.

'Your little team has an impressive strike rate,' the man replies. 'You've successfully captured more UAVs than any of our other subcontractors, so we're considering expanding your role.'

Josh grins at this indirect vindication of his talents, but Fliss makes no reply. Perhaps the man expects her to thank him, but she's not inclined to. Her first thought is that him coming to watch the hunt is a bad idea. Another vehicle in tow will only make them more noticeable, and drone hunting is a risky business – it's better to have people around you who you can trust. She briefly considers saying so, but quashes the impulse. She can't afford to piss the strangers off. And if expanding the crew's role means sending more drone coordinates their way, she's not going to complain about it.

She shrugs. 'Fine by me. Come on, then.'

The crew's own vehicle is a beaten-up old truck. It was another gift from the strangers and has been modded so the crew can drive it normally, without the need for the headware all the corporate types have. Usually, Fliss would drive, but this morning she lets Gabriel do it. She spends the trip watching the stranger's car as it whispers through the wasteland behind them, craning her neck to peer through the truck's grimy back window.

She tells herself she's just making sure the man doesn't lose them, but really, she wants to keep an eye on him. For her, the crews' newfound prosperity is alloyed with dark and formless suspicions. Why do the strangers want so many drones? And if they really do work for Thoughtfront, then why do they need the crew to hunt them? Fliss is in a constant state of anticipation, waiting for the answers to these questions to leap out and ambush her.

The rest of the crew, of course, are acting like all their

birthdays came at once, but they're suckers for free stuff. Gabriel loves the truck with a passion that borders on obsession, Ben and Josh can't get enough of their shiny new guns, and even Sonia has expressed a quiet approval for the portable stove – and the bacon it has made possible. They're too busy with these new toys to think about the strings attached to them; Fliss can't think about anything else. The guns are the best they've ever used – when they work. The crew can hunt just as they used to – when the stranger doesn't invite himself along for the ride. There's always a price. Right now, it's a small one, but prices have a tendency to rise. Fliss isn't sure what she'll do if the strangers ever ask her for something she can't afford to give them.

It doesn't take them long to arrive at their destination. The truck's electric engine is fast and silent; they hiss through the wasteland at incredible speed, a metal ghost. Fliss tells Gabriel to pull up a few hundred metres shy of the coordinates she received, concealing the car in a sprawling tangle of bushes that have spilled out from the hedgerow and spread across the remnants of the road. As they're all getting out and putting on their gas masks, the stranger slides to a halt behind them. Fliss is worried the man is going to ask a lot of questions, or otherwise get in her way, but he only lounges against the boot of his car and watches their preparations in silence.

She has the crew follow her at a distance while she scouts ahead, scoping out the area the drone will be passing through. Her heart sinks as it comes into view: the overgrown verges of the old path they're on drop away, revealing a bare stretch of bridge and, beneath it, a corporate-maintained trade road. Fliss curses under her breath. Many drone routes loosely follow the paths of the corporate roads, so it's not the first time the crew has hunted within sight of one, but they're a lot closer to it than she'd like. To make matters worse, she can see a metal box on the far side of the dual carriageway. Two guns protrude from it, and it's topped by a security camera. As Fliss watches, the camera's glass eye narrows and the guns twitch like the antennae of a hungry insect, following its gaze.

She turns to the crew; their nervous expressions tell her that their thoughts are running on the same lines as hers. The stranger has walked over to join them.

'We can't take the drone down here,' she tells him. 'We're too exposed.'

'If you're concerned about the defence turret, you needn't be,' he replies. 'It's one of ours. It won't shoot.'

Fliss nods, somewhat reassured, but Sonia pulls a face. 'Aw, Fliss,' she protests. 'The middle of a bridge still isn't a great mark, is it? What about traffic? Last thing we want is witnesses.'

'Then you'd better ensure you don't leave any,' the stranger says.

Fliss resists the urge to glare at him; it's not a helpful contribution. 'I didn't choose the mark, Sonia,' she says, with a pointed look at the stranger. 'But anyhow, there won't *be* any witnesses because we're going to be smart about this.'

The crew straighten up as she speaks, waiting for her to lay out the plan of attack. 'Ben: I want you up in one of those trees on the verge, keeping an eye on the trade route. If you see anything, and I mean *anything*, give a whistle and we'll fall back. Sonia: stay here by these bushes and line up a shot from cover. Gabriel: get ready to leg it. I want you to snatch that fucker out of mid-air – got it?'

The three of them nod and move out.

'What am I supposed to do?' Josh asks sullenly.

'I said you were here to watch, didn't I?' Fliss snaps. 'So, watch.'

She heads off to help the rest of the crew set up, leaving

Josh and his bruised ego behind with the stranger. First, she cross-checks Sonia's position with the coordinates on her phone, making sure she'll have a clear shot. Then she runs over to where Ben is perched on a branch at the top of the verge, his binoculars already glued to his face. It's still early morning, and the road is clear for now. Fliss shimmies up the tree to join him, then checks her phone again.

'We've got ten minutes,' she tells Ben. 'Keep an eye out to the south.' It's the direction most of the drones they've taken over the last two months have come from. There's a big corporate warehouse complex down that way, on the coast, not far from where the crew are camped.

She waits with Ben while the time drains away, scanning the sky at anxious intervals. The drone is two minutes out from their location by the clock on Fliss's phone when she feels him tense up beside her.

'Fliss,' he murmurs. 'We've got company.'

Fliss follows his gaze. There's a light utility vehicle coming down the road towards them. It's gunmetal green, and it looks official.

'Good looking out, Ben,' she murmurs.

She takes the binocs off him and squints through them, the world going large and blurry for a moment as she readjusts the sights. Then the car leaps into focus. There looks to be two men inside – both corporate types, with guns and helmets. Fliss twitches the binocs upward, searching for the drone. She finds it sooner than she was expecting – and it's in the worst place it could possibly be, flying directly above the car and matching its speed.

'Fuck,' Fliss hisses. The car must be a security escort: there's no way they can take the drone out safely now. 'Give the signal, Ben. We need to—'

The crack of a pistol drowns out the end of Fliss's sentence.

The car veers off the road, its left front tyre bursting in a cloud of dust. A second shot takes out its windscreen. Through the binoculars, Fliss sees a spray of red shoot from the chest of the man in the front seat. The lenses bring the violence shockingly close: she can see the man's face contort in pain, his lips moving as he screams something to his crewmate that Fliss is too far away to hear. Convulsively, she jerks the binocs away from the sight.

Something else red rushes by in her field of vision as she does so. She's about to grab Ben's arm and run – if someone is shooting at them, they need to get out of here – but she stills herself with an effort, seeking out the flash of colour. The twin circles of the binoculars swing left and right, finally settling at the bottom of the verge. Josh is crouching at the edge of the road, his handgun drawn. He's taking aim at the car again.

'WHAT ARE YOU DOING?' Fliss shouts.

She's too far away for Josh to hear – that, or he's decided to ignore her. She drops from the branch and swings herself forward like she's on a trapeze, breaking into a sprint as soon as she hits the ground. By the time she reaches him, though, it's all but over. The car is a crumpled mess of metal and glass, a bloody figure slumped in the front seat. Josh turns as she reaches his side, an expression of flushed excitement on his face – and that's when the back door of the car opens and the other guard leans out.

Fliss reacts instinctively. As the guard draws his sidearm, his eyes fixed on the beacon of Josh's flaming hair, she raises her own gun and fires. She may not be the best shooter on the crew, but she's no slouch. The bullet hits the man in the chest, making him sag back into the car. She fires again, and a third time, panic taking her outside of herself so it's like she is looking down on the scene from above. She can see herself shaking.

Fliss has been in hairy situations before – many times – but she's used to shooting at drones, not people. Lots of crews don't worry too much about the distinction, but up till now, it's one she has always managed to preserve. When her magazine is empty, she rushes back into her own body, the force of her return almost knocking her onto her knees. Beside her, Josh is whooping.

'That was insane! Did you see me take the one guy out, Fliss? Did you see what I did to the tyres?'

Without a word, Fliss takes Josh by the arm and drags him back up the embankment. He follows willingly enough, still enthusing about the red wreckage he has made of the car. When they are back on the road overhead, safely screened by the bushes, Fliss spins him around and takes hold of him by the shoulders. She wants to shake him until the gleeful expression drops off his face and some good sense falls into his head, but she settles for shouting instead.

'What were you thinking?! You could've got us all killed!'

'I thought you'd be happy,' Josh protests. 'You said we didn't want any witnesses. And it was—'

'I said you should *watch*, Josh! What part of that did you not understand?'

'But—'

'Calm yourself,' says a cold voice. 'The boy was acting on my orders.'

'That's what I was trying to tell you,' Josh finishes.

Fliss turns. The stranger is standing behind her, with Sonia and Gabriel in tow. They're crouched at his feet, and clearly Josh isn't the only one disobeying Fliss's instructions today, because they have the remains of the drone between them, tangled in a net like a fly caught in a web. They're poring over its open delivery crate, their eyes wide.

'Fliss, *look!*' Sonia says.

She picks up the crate, tilting it to show Fliss what's inside. It's filled with blister packs of pills. Fliss catches sight of a few names before Sonia puts the crate down again – Thanafen, Vitamorph, Penicillin. It's enough to tell her they've hit the mother lode. Antibiotics, painkillers, birth control – medicines like this will go for a small fortune in the settlements. Fliss and the crew could easily live off this one shipment for weeks.

It's an impressive haul, but it isn't enough to dull the edge of Fliss's rage. Sonia, Gabriel, Ben and Josh are *her* people. That the stranger had the gall to boss them around in the first place is bad enough – the fact they just did what he said, no questions asked, is worse. Fliss feels the dizzying vertigo of freefall. She is losing control of this partnership; she's losing control of her crew, and that *cannot happen*.

She opens her mouth, intending to tell the stranger where he can shove his orders – and maybe to follow the suggestion up with a physical demonstration. Then she shuts it again, to give her thoughts time to catch up with her tongue. As much as she wants to vent her anger, losing her temper will only erode her authority. She needs to keep the stranger on side, and though she's still furious at the stunt he and Josh have just pulled, she can't deny that it has worked out in the crew's favour. A line does need to be drawn, though – and in no uncertain terms. She looks the man in the eye.

'Next time, you clear shit like this with me in advance. Understood?'

He nods. 'Of course. On that subject, there's something I'd like to discuss with you. My colleague and I have been impressed with your work for us so far, and your performance today confirms our good opinion. We'd like to offer you and your team a more sensitive assignment.'

The knot of unease that has lain coiled in Fliss's stomach ever since she first made her bargain with the strangers tightens.

She suspects she knows what kind of work the man means, and she's certain it won't be to her taste. She hesitates, thinking of the mangled mess of the car and the two men inside it. Then her eyes slide back to the crate full of meds, and her thoughts turn to more pragmatic considerations.

Fliss is under no illusions that she can trust the stranger, but if the rewards of the work he has in mind are anything like their haul today, then perhaps she can live with getting her hands dirty on his behalf. Their partnership has only brought the crew good things so far; she's not ready to end it just yet. The decision is too important to be left to her alone, though. She turns to the others.

'The big isn't shuffling a scamp game here,' she warns them. 'We draw on this, we're like to get wet. I'm for counting straws.'

The crew don't often speak in cant, but with the stranger at her elbow, Fliss feels a sudden need for secrecy.

'Short,' Josh says immediately.

Sonia shrugs. 'Short. Long as the wire's live.'

Gabriel nods; he goes with the consensus on most things. That only leaves Ben.

'Bunk, if you want,' Fliss tells him. Ben isn't built for violent work; she wouldn't blame him for wanting to sit this one out.

Ben looks from Fliss to the rest of the crew, his expression conflicted. 'And bunk the wire, too? No chance. Short.'

'That's settled then.' Fliss forces her own doubts down to the bottom of her mind – and with them, the queasy memory of blood spattering against glass. 'What kind of "assignment" did you have in mind?' she asks the stranger.

In response, the man waves them all over to his car and opens the boot. Inside is a different kind of haul to the meds they've just recovered from the downed drone – armour, ammo, and a thick, grey tube on a tripod that looks like a rocket launcher. Fliss's smartphone beeps, and she pulls it from her pocket. There

148

are two messages on its cracked screen. The first contains the map and timer Fliss is used to; the second is a photograph of a girl about her age, with dark hair and green eyes.

'I think it's about time you hunted something more challenging than drones,' the stranger says.

Chapter 14

After her confrontation with Kenway, Tanta finds herself with time on her hands. She doesn't like it. She'd much rather throw herself back into the investigation – both for its own sake and because the last place she wants to be right now is alone with her thoughts – but until her meeting with the board in the evening, there is nothing for her to do.

She goes back to her flat and tries to sleep, but the early morning traffic is in full flow by the time her head hits the pillow, and after an hour she is forced to give the effort up as pointless. Her long night poring over the encrypted flight logs with Cole, and the showdown with Kenway that followed it, has thrown out her internal clock and left her full of nervous energy. She decides to use some of it up by wandering the city, wearing out the time before dawn in a restless, purposeless walk that leaves her no more inclined to sleep than she was before.

Not so long ago, Tanta would have looked forward to the day of freedom before her as a rare opportunity to spend time with Reet, but now the thought of seeing her lover is the main source of her disquiet. As the sky brightens and the city wakes up around her, Tanta tries calling Reet on MindChat a few times, but gets no answer. She's torn between worry and relief at this radio silence. She desperately needs to talk to Reet, but every time she thinks about trying, she can't even imagine where she'd start.

Reet's trust in Tanta has always been unquestioning; Tanta knows this, because she used to feel the same way about Reet. And now she has lied to Reet, gone behind her back, maybe even jeopardised her career. Every apology and explanation Tanta frames in her mind ends the same way, in faltering silence, as she is brought up short, time and again, by the inadequacy of words to excuse such a monumental betrayal.

I did it for InTech, she thinks. *For the case*. But she knows that's only half true. She did it for herself, too, because she hated being shut out of the ICRD and she wasn't about to let Kenway demote her again. The game Tanta has played to get to this point is not one she would have thought herself capable of two months ago. Kenway and Reet are her superiors in rank, and she has deceived them both – and for personal gain, no less. She doesn't regret her actions, but she can't help feeling queasy about them.

It is these thoughts that prevent Tanta from dropping into the ICRD to visit Reet in person, though it's an easy walk from her place. Instead, she finds herself falling into the familiar path of one of her old security patrols – a wide circuit that takes her up Commercial Street and over to the southwest of the city, towards Inspire Labs. She needs to head that way eventually anyway, to pick up Cole for their meeting, but she has hours to spare. She dawdles along the route, dropping into a café for lunch and visiting a supermarket to pick up groceries for her flat.

She's glad she decided to do this so early in the day. The shops have been packed ever since rationing was introduced, the sudden cap on supply producing a corresponding surge in demand as residents scramble to stock up on essentials. In the wake of the attack on the Needle the situation has only got worse: the queue outside the supermarket snakes all the way down the street.

The line is restless, sending up a murmuring like a hive of angry bees. The shop is operating a one in, one out policy, and there are two guardians in full body armour on the door, searching people as they leave, which makes things even slower. Sour looks thrown at these guardians become muttered imprecations as the wait drags on. Several people break out of the line to question them – 'How long are we going to have to wait?'; 'Is there even any food *left?*' – but they brush all enquiries off with the same response:

'Be patient, Resident. You'll get your allocation, just like everyone else.'

When Tanta is two people away from the front of the queue, one of the guardians has a whispered conversation with someone inside the store, and the shop's steel shutters roll halfway down.

'The fuck?!' the man in front of Tanta yells. 'It's not even four pm!'

'This shop is closed for today,' the guardian replies. 'You'll have to go somewhere else, Resident.'

'Where do you expect us to go? Is anywhere else any different?'

'Have they run out of food?' a woman asks. 'You said there'd be enough for everyone!'

The muttering of the queue grows louder. At some point during her wait, Tanta realises, it has dissolved from a line into a crowd. Despite the guardian's announcement, most of the shoppers show no signs of leaving. Some of them are eyeing up the windows of the store with a speculative air, as if they're measuring a jump.

The guardians tense, squaring their shoulders as they face off against the throng. The one who spoke grips the stun baton on her belt.

'Disperse, Residents,' she says. 'I won't ask again.'

Tanta backs away. She's never seen anything like this before. The community guardians are supposed to keep the city safe: seeing them threatening a crowd of InTech's own people feels wrong. It feels like chaos.

InTech is losing control of the situation. The harder the corporation tries to minimise and disguise the impact of the attacks, the more out of touch it seems. And things are only going to get worse. Tanta thinks of the protesters outside the Needle. If what she's seeing on the streets is any indication, Kenway's rationing isn't working, and neither is the Communications Division's spin campaign. People want food, and they want explanations. How long before they refuse to take a closed door and a guardian's 'no' for an answer?

To her chagrin, this sense of foreboding actually reassures Tanta. It encourages her that she's doing the right thing by challenging Kenway – and by going over Reet's head. Not that her lover is likely to see it that way.

When the shadows lengthen and the light turns golden, Tanta quickens her pace. Before long, the looming bulk of InTech's flagship R&D compound comes into view, dark against the setting sun. The sight of it makes her feel better than she has in hours. She hurries through the gate. It has been a day of doubt and disquiet – a lonely day – but there's a friend waiting for her inside. Cole, at least, will be pleased to see her.

The hour Cole spends with Neal is one of the longest of his life. He works in strained silence, his limbs still aching from the shock he got from the stun baton, not daring to even move from his chair. Neal watches him – actually stares at him – the entire time, a placid smile stapled to his face. He interrupts his vigil only to answer the door; when he returns with Tanta in tow, Cole *is* pleased to see her – not just because he's missed her, but also because being alone with Neal was terrifying.

She smiles at the sight of him – a reassuringly human smile. 'We've been summoned to a meeting with the board's conduit,' she says.

'A meeting? About what?' Cole's pretty sure he can guess the answer. This must have something to do with the attack on the Needle, and the encrypted flight log that Tanta visited him about last night – though just what the outcome of that visit is, he isn't sure.

Neal frowns. The frown is as disturbing as the smile. Again, it looks too static, almost inanimate, as if Neal's face is a mask and his real features are trapped beneath. 'Dr Friend instructed me to watch Cole until he is finished with his work,' he says. 'He told me to see that he doesn't slack.'

'That's OK; I'm acting on the board's authority,' Tanta replies, unruffled. She makes a gesture, presumably viewsharing the documentation with Neal. When his expression doesn't change, she adds, 'Dr Friend will be at the meeting too, so you can clear it with him personally, if you'd like?'

Neal relaxes at this. The frown vanishes and the smile slides back into place. 'Great!'

Cole casts a sidelong glance at Tanta, wondering if she's finding Neal's reactions as unsettling as he is. If she is, she gives no outward sign of it; Cole supposes that, never having met the intern before, she has no way of knowing how out of character he's acting.

'I'll order us a car,' she says.

They leave the Black Box together. It's an awkward trio. Neal clearly still considers Cole to be in his custody despite what Tanta has said. He and Tanta walk on either side of Cole, like a pair of guards, and Neal won't put the damned stun baton back in his belt. With Neal beside him, there's little Cole can say to

Tanta about what's really on his mind, but her presence does give him courage. Once they're all wedged uncomfortably into the cab, he decides to make the most of their short journey.

There's no way Arthur could have realised it – he has no idea that Cole even remembers the Harlow Programme's existence – but he has given Cole an opportunity. Cole still doesn't know whether Neal managed to pass the Harlow 2.0 file onto Jeanie before Arthur tested it out on him. If he didn't, then this time alone with the intern could be Cole's only chance to learn about how the software works, and what it does. The insights he'll be able to glean from simply talking to Neal won't be as useful as what he could accomplish by investigating the programme directly, but they'll be better than nothing.

The idea of using Neal like this, after the way Arthur has used him already, makes Cole sick, but the feeling is lessened by the conviction that it's what the old Neal would have wanted. He was committed to exposing the truth about Arthur's 'security update'; he risked his life to try. The least Cole can do for him is to honour and continue that commitment.

First, though, there's a more personal matter he must address: why on earth hasn't Neal reported him as a traitor? Harlow 2.0 seems to have given him a full-scale personality transplant, and yet he hasn't breathed a word about their conspiracy, their secret trip to Arthur's office, or what they stole from inside. Given what Arthur has done to him, it's unlikely Neal is concealing what happened out of self-preservation. What, then?

'Neal?' he says. The trainee turns his blank smile Cole's way. 'You know what we talked about yesterday?'

For the first time that evening, the shadow of a more complicated expression crosses Neal's face. 'Yesterday?'

'Yeah,' Cole prompts. 'We had lunch together.' A new thought occurs to him. 'You – you don't remember that?'

There's a flash of alarm in Neal's pale brown eyes. 'I... I

don't...' And then the smile comes back on like a light, burning the doubt away. 'Never mind! Was it important?'

'No,' Cole manages. 'Not important.'

He fights off a wave of rage and disgust. Memory loss? Hijacking Neal's brain was monstrous enough, but Arthur hasn't even made a clean job of it. Cole knows what it's like to reach for a memory and find nothing in its place – the sickening sense of freefall when the trapdoor of your own mind opens beneath you. Neal may be a shadow of his former self, but Cole recognised that same fear and confusion on his face. Neal was a good person. He had Cole's back, helping him at a time when Cole didn't have anyone else to turn to. And now his mind has been put through a shredder.

What angers Cole the most is that Arthur doesn't seem to have chosen Neal as his guinea pig because Neal rebelled against him. He used him without hesitation, almost without thought, simply because he needed a test subject, and the intern was both handy and expendable. The destruction of his entire personality was just a by-blow.

You don't know *his personality has been destroyed*, a voice in Cole's head suggests. *This could be temporary*. It isn't, though. Cole can tell just from talking to Neal that there's no easy route back from this. He might recover, but Cole doubts he'll be able to do so while the programming in his head is active.

Even through his fury, the neurotech in Cole still manages to be disappointed at Arthur's lack of scientific vision. Cole isn't proud of the Harlow Programme – it's one of his greatest shames – but he's too clearheaded to deny that it's a delicate and complex creation. An addition to the Inscape system that manipulates the feelings of its users while leaving their person-alities and skillsets largely intact is – and Cole uses the term advisedly, without arrogance – a work of genius. Arthur's attempt

156

is a grotesque pastiche by comparison, mental reprogramming by blunt force trauma.

Of course, Cole has only his own first impressions to rely on for this assessment. If he's to draw a conclusion with greater nuance, he'll need to take a more methodical approach. Clearly, Harlow 2.0 has impaired Neal's episodic memory and emotional responses, but how have his other abilities fared? He tries another conversational foray.

'We were only talking about a paper of mine,' he says, 'investigating pseudotransmitter pathways in the limbic system.'

'I've read that paper!' Neal replies. He looks into the middle distance and recites: 'Pseudotransmitter pathways in the limbic system: an analogue study with rhesus monkeys.'

'Yep. That's the one. What did you think of its conclusions?'

'The paper concluded that MbOS extension into the limbic system was theoretically possible under the following conditions. Firstly—'

'I know what the conclusions were,' Cole interjects. 'I wrote them, remember? But what did you think of them? Did you agree with the findings?'

'The paper was a useful contribution to InTech's ongoing neurotechnical research and development. Its findings were valid, and its methodology was sound. Future investigations of this type would better serve the corporation by the inclusion of a control group for greater rigour.'

All of which is technically correct, and suggests at least that Neal's intellect hasn't suffered, even if he sounds like he's swallowed a textbook. But the old Neal told Cole that the paper completely changed the way he thought about the Inscape system, responding to it with a scientist's curiosity and enthusiasm.

'What did *you* think about the paper, Neal?' Cole probes.

Neal's drawn-on smile falters, then reasserts itself. 'I just told you.'

A memory flashes into Cole's head of the recording he and Tanta watched the night they broke into the Black Box, the night they learnt that Cole created the Harlow Programme. *Can you elaborate on that for me, Tanta? Was Heinz right or wrong to break into the pharmacy?*

That depends. Was the pharmacy one of ours?

'Thanks, Neal,' he says heavily. 'Good talk.'

It *was* a good talk – or at least, an informative one. It's already given Cole a few theories about how Arthur's programme works, and what it does. The first, and the hardest for Cole to swallow, is that he's been kidding himself. Sure, Harlow 2.0 is less sophisticated than the original, but in the essentials, it's not so different from his own creation. It exists for the same purpose: to instil in its subjects an absolute and unquestioning obedience to corporate authority. The second – and this is even more disturbing – is that it seems to do so at the expense of almost everything else.

Tanta is glad when the taxi finally pulls up at the ICRD. There was heavy traffic on the way, so the ride took a while, and Cole spent the entire time engaged in a strange and desultory conversation about a scientific paper with his guard, a discussion that Tanta could neither participate in nor follow. It has done little to calm her nerves. She would have liked the chance to talk to Cole alone before their meeting, and the presence of Dr Friend's lackey has made that impossible. He insists on following them inside, too, accompanying them all the way down to the temporary conference room in the ICRD's basement.

They find Dr Friend waiting outside the room; it's the first time in quite a while that Tanta has been pleased to see him. He looks up when they come in, his benignant smile at Tanta souring into irritation when he spots Cole and his escort behind her.

'What are you doing here?' he snaps.

'The board have asked Cole to join our meeting,' Tanta explains. She glances behind her: the odd young man is still hovering next to Cole, looking expectantly at Dr Friend. 'Your colleague would like you to confirm that Cole is released from his work for the evening,' she adds.

Dr Friend waves a hand at the man in a shooing motion. 'Yes, confirmed,' he says. 'Good job, Neal.'

Tanta stiffens at the familiar command phrase. If she'd known this Neal was a CorpWard like her, she would have felt a little kindlier towards him. His concerns allayed, Neal leaves. It's too late now, though, for Tanta to take advantage of his absence to fill Cole in on what's going on. Dr Friend is here, and he has questions of his own.

'Tanta,' he says, his voice soft. 'Can you tell me why the board have asked Cole to this meeting?'

Tanta suppresses a shiver – whether of nervousness or disgust, she can't tell. Now that she recognises it for what it is, Dr Friend's manipulation seems transparent, and transparently self-serving. Knowing that doesn't stop the echoes of her programming waking up at the sound of his voice, though, needling her to answer him truthfully. It's what she's planning to do anyway – there's nothing to be gained by lying – but she resents the impulse, all the same. It didn't originate with her, and a part of her wants to disobey it on principle.

'I believe Director Kenway requested him, Doctor,' she says, looking him in the eye. 'His input could be useful to a case we're working on.'

Dr Friend doesn't like that at all; his face flushes with anger. But then Kenway himself arrives with the board's conduit, and the respectful murmurs of 'Representative', and the general bustle of entering the conference room, forestall any reply he might have made.

The board's conduit is as Tanta remembers him: pale and paunchy, with watery blue eyes and mechanical movements.

'Director Kenway,' he says, his voice a dead monotone. 'Tanta informs us that you have a development to report.'

Kenway, sitting stiff and erect in his chair, clears his throat. His usual oily expression is gone; his face is wooden, and he doesn't so much as glance at Tanta as he replies. 'Yes, Representative. The investigation has made progress.'

Tanta listens closely while Kenway speaks, alert for any sign that he might be reneging on their bargain, but he simply outlines Tanta's work so far, and artfully insinuates that most of it was his doing. The only fireworks come when he mentions her trip to discuss the flight logs with Cole, which he presents as a stroke of genius on his own part.

'You ought to have cleared that with me in advance!' Dr Friend interrupts.

'Time was short,' Kenway shoots back, his voice tight, 'and Neuroengineer Cole's input was needed. Your agreement was hardly in question, but if I presumed too far on your sense of corporate duty, then I apologise.'

With her Harlow Programming operational, Tanta was never in a position to understand most of the political manoeuvring that went on in these board meetings before. Now that she does, she is both shocked and impressed by Kenway's brazenness. There's nothing Dr Friend can say in response, and he knows it. His face grows thunderous, but he only nods.

'Given Cole's material assistance with the case,' Kenway continues, pressing his advantage, 'it is the judgement of the Community Guardianship Office that his heightened security arrangements may safely be brought to an end. He would also be of considerable use as a technical consultant to the investigation going forward. *If,* that is' – he inclines his head in Dr Friend's direction – 'Director Friend will approve his transfer to the ICRD.'

This proves too much for Dr Friend. 'I will not,' he says. 'Cole is dangerous, and—'

'Overruled,' the conduit interjects. 'We are satisfied that the Corporate Ward will be able to contain any risk posed by the Neuroengineer. She has done so before.'

Tanta glances at Cole to see how he is taking this news. A part of her is worried; she has interfered with his life and his work, and she never checked with him how he felt about it. As soon as he meets her gaze, though, she knows she needn't have been concerned. The look of incredulous relief on his face is unmistakable.

'Continue, Director Kenway,' the conduit says in his dull, flat voice.

'Considering their performance on the case so far, Tanta and Reet would be excellent choices to head up the investigation.'

The conduit gives a single nod. 'Acknowledged. Is there anything else?'

Tanta is expecting a prompt 'no'. Kenway has already said everything they agreed to, and taken far more credit than he deserves.

'Just one more thing,' Kenway replies. He looks at Tanta as he says it, flashing her a broad grin.

Tanta's stomach clenches; Douglas Kenway being in a good mood is never a good sign.

'As mentioned, our work thus far has identified a possible location for the bandits' base of operations,' he says. 'They appear to be located closer to our Southern Distribution Centre than to the city. Given the centre's strategic importance – it houses our regional archive, and there has been unrest in the area before – historically, there was an ICRD agent stationed there permanently as a liaison.'

Tanta's feeling of unease increases. She doesn't like where this is going.

'The liaison post has been empty for some time,' Kenway continues, 'but the distribution centre's Logistics Officer has confirmed that the quarters that come with the role have been maintained.'

'What is the ICRD's recommendation, Director Kenway?' the conduit asks. He sounds testy to Tanta, but that's probably her imagination.

'That Tanta become Sodis's new ICRD Liaison Officer,' Kenway replies. 'She and her technical consultant can continue their investigation in the field, using the distribution centre as their headquarters. Reet will manage them remotely, and they will remain there until the region is stable.'

The news drops through Tanta's ears and straight down to the pit of her stomach. She watched Kenway playing Dr Friend just minutes ago, and this move has still come as a horrible surprise. He has upped his game since their interview this morning; he must have been planning this all day – reaching out to contacts, calling in favours.

'But—' she starts, the word slipping out before she can stop it.

She's made a serious faux pas. It's not her place to question the orders of her direct superior – worse, it's not something an obedient, Harlow Programmed Corporate Ward would do. The conduit turns her way, his expression unreadable.

'Is there a problem, Agent Tanta?'

Tanta swallows, forcing meekness into her voice and posture before she replies. 'Are you sure I'm ready for such an important assignment, Director?'

It's the best she can manage. She never saw this coming, and just like Dr Friend, there is nothing she can say. On the face of it, Kenway has just given her a promotion. Tanta will be one of the most senior figures in Sodis – there's no way that a model employee like her could turn down such an opportunity. Tanta knows this as well as Kenway does. She also knows that InTech's regional distribution centres are where careers go to die. They barely qualify as company towns: they're just huge warehouses in the Unaffiliated Zone, surrounded by a smattering of flats for employees. Kenway has assigned her to this one 'until the region is stable', but that's a meaningless term. The region will be stable again exactly when he wants it to be, and she has a feeling that in this case, that's never.

Kenway smiles at her. 'Your qualifications speak for themselves, Agent. There's no need to be modest.'

The conduit takes longer to reply. For a few glorious seconds, Tanta hopes he is going to ignore Kenway's suggestion. But then the man nods, sealing her fate. 'Acknowledged. Continue to update us daily until this matter is resolved.'

Tanta has never lived outside the city before, has barely travelled outside it, save for her field excursions into the Unaffiliated Zone. Everything and everyone she knows is here; it's her home. Now Kenway is forcing her to leave, and who knows when she'll be able to return? She and Cole have been exiled.

Part 2

Chapter 15

Once Kenway has won his point, he's keen to get rid of Tanta as quickly as possible, ordering her and Cole to set off for their new posting first thing the next morning. Tanta doesn't dare demur, especially given her earlier slip-up, but she wishes she could ask for a day's grace. She has had no time to prepare herself for this move, and already it is upon her. She nods along through the rest of the meeting, wanting only for it to be over as quickly as possible. She's on the clock now, each hour bringing her closer to the moment she will have to leave the city, possibly for good. She doesn't want to waste the precious time she has left talking to Kenway.

It ends, at last. As Tanta and Cole walk out of the ICRD into the drizzly twilight, he darts a glance at her.

'So, that was intense. Thank you, by the way.'

'Don't mention it.'

He wants to say more. Cole has had something on his mind since she brought him the drone the previous night – Tanta can see it weighing on him. It'll have to wait, though. They have a single evening in which to make all the arrangements necessary for their transfer to Sodis; their meeting with the board's conduit was just the start of a whirlwind of briefings, requisition requests, and last-minute calls that will consume the rest of it.

The only advantage of her packed schedule is that it doesn't leave Tanta any time spare for worrying about her last meeting of the night – a briefing with her team leader. Reet is still dodging her calls, and as the hours rush by, Tanta finds herself dreading the moment when her lover will be forced to stop avoiding her.

She can no more put it off than she can delay her departure, however. Ten pm finds Tanta walking back into the conference room on the ICRD's fourteenth floor. She knows as soon as she enters the room that something is wrong. Reet stands facing her on the other side of the wide table, but she refuses to meet Tanta's eyes. She's staring steadfastly into the middle distance, focused on something on her 'scape's reader.

'You and Cole will be setting out at five am tomorrow,' she tells Tanta, without preamble. 'You should report to Goods Warehouse Six, by the Outer Gate.'

Reet's tone is so cold, her expression so wooden, that Tanta finds herself almost afraid to reply. 'Will our car be waiting for us there?' she asks, her voice unusually timid.

'Not a car: a heavy goods vehicle. Douglas wants you to accompany it as a security escort.'

That makes sense. InTech doesn't have many trucks – the bulk of their trade infrastructure is made up of UAVs – but given the attacks, Tanta can see why the corporation is switching up its supply chains.

'The zeppelin is docked just outside the city limits at the moment as a security precaution, so latency on the road will be high,' Reet continues. 'You may not be able to communicate with Sodis en route, but your contact should be waiting for you there when you arrive. He's the Logistics Officer in charge of the centre, Edward Smythe.'

The zeppelin houses one of InTech's backup servers, and it usually floats over the Unaffiliated Zone, ensuring consistent network speeds even in areas where InTech doesn't have ground infrastructure. Without it, Tanta and Cole will be lucky if they can even use MindChat. Tanta nods. 'Understood.'

There's an awkward pause. Reet still won't look at her, but she doesn't dismiss her, either. Tanta hesitates; she has no more idea what to say to Reet than she did before, but she has to say *something* – she might not get another chance.

'Reet,' she begins.

'This will be your last briefing from me,' Reet cuts in. 'I've asked Douglas to take me off the case.' Her tone is as expressionless as before, but her fists are clenched by her sides. 'I've been reassigned to another investigation. You won't have to answer to me anymore. I guess that's what you wanted.'

The news knocks the wind out of Tanta. She expected Reet to be angry, but it never occurred to her that she'd recuse herself from the case. She scrabbles for a response. 'It's not what I wanted at all,' she says. 'Reet, I—'

'Just shut up, Tanta. I don't want to hear another word from you.'

Tanta does shut up. She feels like she's been struck; Reet has never spoken to her like this before.

'What the fuck is wrong with you?' Reet asks. 'Don't the ICRD's rules mean *anything* to you? Don't *I*? My first time as a team leader, and you went behind my back. You broke protocol, and it happened on my watch. Douglas is furious; I'm lucky he didn't fire me! Working in the ICRD is my dream, Tanta. You *know* how important this is to me!'

Reet's voice breaks over the words. A desperate sense of guilt claws at Tanta's insides.

'I tried to talk to you first about getting Cole involved,' she says. 'But you—'

'I told you not to? Yeah, Tee, I did. In fact, I *ordered* you not to. And you should have listened!'

'Reet, I'm sorry,' Tanta stammers. Her own voice wavers with suppressed tears. 'I never meant to undermine you. Or to hurt you. That wasn't my intention at all.' The words sound flimsy and inadequate.

Reet obviously thinks so too. For the first time since the meeting started, she looks Tanta in the face. There are tears streaming down her cheeks, but her eyes are blazing. 'Then why'd you do it, Tee? Because I've been thinking about it all day and honestly, I'm stumped.'

Tanta opens her mouth. Closes it again. She cannot answer Reet, however much she wants to. A silence falls over the briefing room, charged with missed opportunities. Then Reet speaks again.

'I – I'm glad you're leaving,' she chokes out. She sounds almost surprised at herself. 'Because I never want to see you again.'

After the briefing, Tanta goes home alone, walking so fast she is almost running. She bites her lip as she goes; the pain focuses her thoughts and keeps her from crying. By the time she reaches her block of flats, she can taste blood. At the top of the stairs, the tears start despite her best efforts, brimming in her eyes and blurring her vision. As she shuts herself inside, a sound escapes her, part scream, part howl, and the dam breaks completely.

She sobs audibly, abandoning herself to the awful luxury of despair. It's not something she's ever done before, and she can't keep it up for long. The volume and fury of her own weeping soon embarrasses her into silence, though it's longer before she can bring herself to move from where she is sitting, huddled on the floor with her back against the door. Moving would mean thinking again, and she's not ready to do that yet. As long as she stays very still, and very quiet, she can pretend that Reet hasn't left her.

At length, she forces herself to rise and begins, mechanically, to gather up her clothes and pack them into a duffel bag. She tries to pack her feelings away at the same time, to put all thoughts of Reet into a box in her mind, to be opened only when she has time and leisure to do so. This is harder. The Reet thoughts don't fit as neatly; they spill out over the edges of the space she has assigned to them, demanding her attention.

This kind of compartmentalisation used to be second nature to Tanta, but she's been finding it more difficult ever since she lost her programming. She wonders, as she has many times before, whether she'll still be able to do her job without it, or whether everything that made her a good agent – her focus, her resilience – was just part of the Harlow package, along with the unquestioning obedience and the euphoria she felt whenever she received praise from a superior. This thought brings a question with it, one that Tanta hasn't asked herself in a long time: *would I be happier if I had it back?*

Being in control of her own mind has only made her life harder. Things that used to bring her peace and satisfaction make her angry, and things that used to be simple are muddy and uncertain. And now she has lost Reet, the most important person in the world to her.

Even as she asks the question, Tanta realises she already knows the answer. Of course she'd be happier – but that doesn't mean it's what she wants. The Harlow Programme was designed to foster contentment, to remove unpleasant ambiguities about ethical responsibility and make the path of duty smooth and clear. Now that Tanta has seen the truth behind those lies, she can't go back.

And as long as that's true, there's no future for her and Reet. On some level, Tanta has known that for a while, though she didn't want to admit it. How can they be lovers, or even friends, when Reet's mind is not her own? Tanta is sad – desperately sad – that things have ended the way they did, but the ending itself was inevitable.

The knowledge holds no comfort; knowing that she and Reet were doomed to failure is not the same as accepting it. Their parting is raw and stinging in Tanta's mind, and she can't turn away from it as she would have been able to two months ago. Then, she would have had her love for InTech to sustain her, giving her courage and determination. Now, she has only – what? *The case*, she thinks. *I have the case to focus on. And getting Cole out of here before Kenway changes his mind about him.*

That thought at last gives her the motivation to continue with her preparations in earnest. She may have negotiated Cole a reprieve for now, but she's acutely aware that his freedom is conditional on her success. If she doesn't deliver the results the board want, how long will it be before Dr Friend requests him back in the city, under lock and key – and they agree?

Once she's finished packing, she pins her new role to her profile, so that any colleagues looking her up will know where she's stationed. That done, she runs through her list of contacts on MindChat to see if there's anyone she needs to inform personally.

It's not a task that's well-calculated to improve her mood. It's the first time she's checked her contacts since the Ward House fire, and it's sobering to see how many of the names on her list belong to the dead. She accesses one or two of their profiles; they look exactly the same as they did when the wards were alive, listing their names and professions, their CB scores. Some of them have a status below their names – inconsequential things about their love for their corporate family or their excitement at a new posting that have now taken on the weight of valedictions. She tries to call one of them, out of a morbid sense of curiosity, but only gets an error message: <<Unknown

error: User not found.>> The profiles are like ghosts that haven't realised they're dead yet.

Seeing them makes Tanta cry again. It's partly grief, and partly loneliness: these wards were her colleagues, her family, but there's none among them that she counted as a friend. The realisation makes her bleak and numb. Leaving the city feels earth-shattering to her, but what is she actually leaving behind? There's only one person she'll really miss, and she'd be lost to Tanta even if she stayed.

A knock on the door breaks in on Tanta's thoughts. She dries her eyes on her sleeve and goes to answer it. It's Cole, a wheeled suitcase in his hand and an apologetic look on his face.

'The flat was making me nervous,' he says, by way of explanation. 'Kept worrying someone was going to lock me in. I even wedged the door open with a shoebox, but it didn't help.'

'Will the sofa be OK?' Tanta asks.

'More than OK. Thank you, Tanta.'

Tanta waves him inside, where he hovers awkwardly in her hallway. She walks through into the living room, gesturing for him to follow her, and begins stacking up her sofa cushions to make a headrest.

'You might regret passing up the chance to spend one last night by yourself, you know,' she says over her shoulder. 'We'll be sharing the same accommodation at the distribution centre for who knows how long.'

Her tone is light, but Cole doesn't reply. When Tanta turns, she sees that he is watching her, his brown eyes intent.

'Tanta, you remember I said I needed to talk to you?' he asks. 'Well, there's been a . . . development, and now I *really* need to talk to you.'

Abruptly, Tanta remembers the unspoken something that's been on Cole's mind ever since last night. She's about to ask him what it is, but instead she says, 'Could it wait until tomorrow?'

She's a little ashamed of herself – it's not like her to delay discussing something that's clearly important – but the thought of another difficult conversation so close on the heels of the last one overwhelms her with tiredness. They have to be gone before first light, and it's already late enough that they won't be able to snatch more than a few hours' sleep. Whatever Cole needs to tell her sounds serious, and she's not equal to it right now.

'Tomorrow sounds good,' Cole replies. He relaxes, and it's only then that Tanta realises he wasn't looking forward to the conversation any more than she was. He crosses to the sofa and lies down.

'I hope it's comfortable,' Tanta says.

'It's great. Though given that the last time we were roomies we were sleeping on junk mattresses in a condemned building, the bar isn't that high.'

That makes Tanta smile, despite the night she's had. Kenway may be exiling her to the arse end of nowhere, but at least she isn't going alone.

Chapter 16

Tanta wakes Cole before dawn. She doesn't want to give Kenway any excuse to make their lives more difficult than he already has; they stagger into Goods Warehouse Six, bleary-eyed and blinking, at five am on the dot to join the heavy goods vehicle they'll be escorting to Sodis.

It's an articulated lorry, its steel-reinforced chassis ancient and rusted. InTech relies on drones to keep its trade and delivery system running, so most of its HGVs are outdated models, close to retirement. Even so, Tanta is dismayed at the state of this one. It's just like Kenway to assign them the most decrepit truck in the fleet, especially when the roads they'll be travelling are long and dangerous. She and Cole exchange dubious glances at the sight of it, but dodgy suspension and rusty bodywork are hardly reasons for delaying their departure.

The lorry is self-driving, like all InTech vehicles, but there are still seats in the cab for guardians working security. The body armour Tanta has insisted Cole wear is making it difficult for him to move; she gives him a hand up into the raised cab, which is cramped and smells of stale sweat.

'I can barely move my arms!' Cole grumbles. 'How am I supposed to fire a gun?'

'I'm not giving you a gun,' Tanta replies. 'You'll have to leave the security work to me.'

'That's smart,' he concedes.

Factory sleepers are still loading the last of the truck's cargo into the trailer, their movements swift and mechanical. While they work, Tanta looks over the equipment she has requisitioned from the ICRD's kit department. In addition to the body armour she and Cole are wearing, she asked for a pair of infrared field lenses, a sniper rifle, and a handgun. She double checks the weapons are loaded before tucking them into her duffel bag, which she stows in the footwell. Kenway has made his animosity towards her abundantly clear, and she wants to make sure he hasn't 'forgotten' to include anything vital. She sweeps the cab for bugs, too, though she's not expecting to find any. This truck is seldom used, and most of its journeys are probably made unstaffed.

They leave too soon. The sun isn't even up before the truck turns out of the warehouse and onto the bare, floodlit stretch of road that leads to the Outer Gate. Just beyond it, Tanta can make out the dark bulk of InTech's data zeppelin, docked at a tall mooring spire against the city wall. Seeing it reminds her of her meeting with Reet; she bites her lip, forcing the thoughts back down.

It's the first time Tanta has been outside city limits since the summer. She takes a deep, slow breath as the cab of the lorry passes beneath the gate, feeling again that sense of liminality, of transition, that always strikes her when she leaves the city.

Once they're through, she turns her attention to the view from the windows, alert for potential threats. The trade road they're on is well-lit, making the dark landscape of the Unaffiliated Zone to either side of it even harder to see, so she slips the field lenses into her eyes. After a second of blurriness, the view becomes a sea of colour. Tanta scans the darkness beyond the road, looking for the orange-red of warm bodies and campfires amidst the green.

'I've checked for bugs,' she says quietly, her eyes still on the front windscreen. 'We're OK to talk. So, what did you want to tell me?'

She feels Cole tense beside her. 'You remember Jeanie's man on the inside?' he murmurs. 'He finally got in touch.'

Tanta doesn't want to drop her guard for even a second, but she can't forbear glancing at Cole in surprise. It has been so long since Yas's visit to Cole's flat that she had concluded that Jeanie's strange message had come to nothing.

'When?' she asks.

'Two days ago. It was Neal Ortega – the guy who came with us to the ICRD yesterday.'

'The CorpWard?' Tanta says sharply. 'How can *he* be working for Jeanie? I thought he was...' She trails off. The knowledge of the Harlow Programme is like a wound in her thoughts; talking about it stings.

'You thought he was Harlow Programmed?' Cole asks.

She nods.

'Well, he is. Sort of. But he wasn't two days ago.'

'That's impossible. The – my—' Tanta stumbles over the words. What Cole's saying makes no sense. Her own Harlow Programming was installed when she was an infant; it shaped the landscape of her thoughts and emotions over the course of almost two decades, a process as insidious as it was time-consuming. Surely not even Cole could design a programme that did all that overnight. 'How could that have happened so fast?' she finishes.

Cole takes a ragged breath. 'Neal and I took a trip to Arthur's lab the night before last,' he says. 'Arthur has been ... studying the Thoughtfront agent's corpse: I think he found something in her MbOS that allowed him to speed up the process.'

Tanta's gorge rises. Suddenly, she's back in the smoke and flames of the Ward House, standing over the operative's slumped body. She thinks of that body on a slab in the Black Box, violated by scalpels, and feels a wave of nausea.

'The software he's devised doesn't produce the same results as the original,' Cole continues. 'Like the Thoughtfront agent's programming, it's a brute force solution – it compels obedience rather than encouraging it through selective reinforcement. The board seem happy with it, though: they want to roll it out in two days' time.' He lowers his voice further. 'Arthur's calling it Harlow 2.0.'

'Who is it for?' Tanta asks. Her mouth is dry.

'That's the thing. From what happened to Neal, it's clear that this new Harlow Programme can stimulate pseudotransmitters in the limbic system without the need for dedicated pathways.'

Tanta gives him a look. 'Meaning?'

'Meaning it doesn't need additional hardware to function – it works on the Inscape system as is. Arthur told me it wouldn't be going out to the Directors or the board, but other than that, it's—' Cole swallows. Tries again. 'It's for pretty much *everyone*.'

Tanta gropes for a suitable reply. What can she say? What does Cole expect her to say? His discovery is like a meteor – too big for her to grapple with, even piecemeal. And like a meteor, there is nothing she can do about it. She can only watch, in pity and horror, as it bears down on her.

'Are you sure?' is what she comes up with in the end. It's a weak response. Cole wouldn't be telling her this if he wasn't.

'You saw Neal for yourself,' Cole replies. 'And I can promise you he wasn't like that when he joined the Black Box.'

Something about what Cole is saying doesn't add up. 'But if Neal was given this new programming *after* you and he' – Tanta makes a gesture to fill the gap in the sentence; saying the words *broke into Dr Friend's office* aloud feels dangerous – 'then has he told Dr Friend what you did?'

'I don't think so. I spoke to him about it in the car on the way to the ICRD; I think the procedure affected his memory.'

'You don't *think so?*' Fear squeezes Tanta's chest. She whirls around to stare at Cole. 'Cole, you could be detained again. And I don't think InTech would put you under house arrest this time!'

Cole opens his mouth to reply. And then there's a bang like a gunshot, and the cab plunges downwards. Tanta's seat bucks beneath her: she's thrown into the air, her head hitting the roof with a painful thud, then yanked back down. Her seatbelt feels like it's going to cut her in half and for an instant, the edges of her vision darken. Then she's back in control, unstrapping herself and pressing her face to the window. Five red figures are standing in the middle of the road. They're wearing old-fashioned gas masks, giving their profiles a creepy, alien uniformity. One of them steps forward, hefting something that looks like a—

'DOWN! NOW!' she yells to Cole, rolling from the seat and throwing herself into the footwell. The grenade hits the window a second later.

The sound of the explosion is a physical thing, a giant hand that slaps Tanta to the floor and boxes her ears, leaving them ringing. In the whining silence that follows it, she rises into a crouch and takes stock. Are these attackers the same bandits who have been targeting InTech's UAVs? It seems likely; if so, this marks a change in strategy for them – they've never hit a lorry before. A small part of Tanta's mind is cataloguing these questions and considerations, storing them away for analysis; a much larger part is focused on ensuring she survives long enough to answer them.

'What was that? What was that?!'

Tanta has to read Cole's lips to understand him. <<It's going to be all right,>> she sends. The message takes a moment longer to go through than it should – probably the latency issues Reet mentioned – but at least on MindChat, they'll be able to understand each other. <<Stay down; I'll handle this.>>

She sounds completely calm because her thoughts are moving too fast for emotion to keep up with them. She strategises rapidly and without panic, assessing the situation before her. The windscreen of the cab has been blown to pieces, leaving her and Cole exposed. The truck has stopped; several warning messages blink on its AR display: {*Emergency stop initiated; obstructions detected; multiple punctures detected*}. Tanta knows a little about the AI that runs InTech's vehicles: it won't move until the obstruction in the road ahead has been cleared – whatever it is. It could be a spike strip, or caltrops. Either way, it's clear this ambush was planned in advance. Was their lorry the intended target, or just the first one that happened along?

Another explosion shakes the cab; this one blows off one of the doors. The truck is sturdy, despite its age, but it won't hold out for much longer. At best, Tanta and Cole have minutes before the bandits shoot the cab to pieces. At worst, a bullet could catch the fuel tank, ignite the hydrogen inside, and set the whole truck on fire in an instant.

Tanta sets the combat analytics on her 'scape to triangulate the bandits' positions from the direction of their shots. Usually, this would be a near instantaneous process, but to her frustration, the programme whirs and hums to itself, taking its time. While the analysis runs, she takes out her field lenses, pulls the sniper rifle out of her duffel bag and sets it on the dashboard above her. She slides its long barrel out through the hole where the window used to be and syncs her 'scape to the camera on the end of its muzzle.

The road ahead comes into focus, framed on either side by

a steep, wooded verge. From her position crouched inside the footwell, Tanta can see that the surface of the asphalt has been strewn with jagged shards of metal. A hundred yards from the truck, the bandits have erected a temporary barrier, a black, domed thing that looks like the canopy of an umbrella. There are a couple of small holes in its surface, through which they're firing. Though they used a rocket launcher for their opening salvo, they seem to have exhausted its ammo, and have switched to pistols to finish the job. The gunfire is so loud that it's more a texture than a sound, heavy and brittle in the air.

A chime in her 'scape tells Tanta that her combat analysis is finally ready. She gestures, bringing up the bandits' locations. Her MbOS highlights them as AR silhouettes in her vision, limned in orange, each one tagged with a set of coordinates. They're crouching behind the umbrella, but that's no matter: Tanta's rifle is carrying armour-piercing rounds, specced to penetrate bulletproof glass to a thickness of ninety millimetres. Steadying her breath, she puts one of the bandits' heads between her crosshairs and remote-activates the rifle's trigger.

The bullet splashes against the barrier as though it's a drop of water. Tanta narrows her eyes, using the rifle's camera to zoom in on the point of impact. There's no mark on the umbrella at all – not even a dent. The bullet, meanwhile, has fallen to the ground, flattened into a pancake.

Tanta feels the first stirrings of alarm. Her mind flicks back to the Thoughtfront agent and her strange, thin body armour, far stronger than it should have been for its weight. There was never much doubt in her mind as to who was arming these attackers – there's none at all, now. The barrier is the closest thing to impenetrable she's ever seen. What can she do against the bandits when their temporary shield is stronger than the truck, with its chassis of reinforced steel? They'll shoot the HGV to pieces without ever emerging from cover, and Tanta and Cole will be trapped inside like livestock in a pen.

Only, it's not a pen. Tanta turns to Cole, struck by a desperate idea.

<<Cole? I need your help,>> she sends. Cole is staring past her with a blank expression. He's not remotely prepared for situations like this, yet she sees him rouse himself as her message arrives in his mind, refocusing on her with visible effort. <<Can you override the truck's emergency stop protocols?>> she asks. <<All of them?>>

<<I – yes. Are we making a run for it?>>

<<Not exactly.>> With the truck's wheels blown out, they wouldn't get far. <<I need you to reprogramme the truck to follow a set of moving coordinates.>> Tanta tenses as she waits for Cole's reply. She's not sure that what she has asked him to do is even possible; the truck's destination was programmed in at the warehouse, and neither of them is authorised to alter it.

Cole frowns, drawn in by the puzzle despite the bullets tearing through the upholstery inches above their heads. <<I think I can do that. I should be able to reset our destination as a formula that refers to a moving point, if that point is supplied by Inscape software.>>

<<It is. I've got it here.>>

<<In that case, I just need a key to whatever programme you're using.>>

Tanta pings him the details he needs; Cole's hands shake as he accesses them. Outside, the tempo of the gunfire slows, then stops. Through the ringing in her ears, Tanta hears voices. She turns her head to one side, enhancing her 'scape's audio to zero in on the sound.

'Is she dead? Did we get her?' The voice is breathless, young, and male. There's something in it of the lilting cadences of the unaffiliated, but Tanta can tell from his accent that this bandit isn't from the city.

'There was two of them.' Another man's voice. 'He didn't tell us there'd be two of them.'

'The guy doesn't matter. We were just supposed to get the girl, right?'

'Whatever. We must've got them both by now.'

'Cole?' Tanta hisses. Cole's hands race through the air.

<<I'm done,>> he sends. <<But Tanta——>>

<<Then get us moving. Now!>>

Cole taps the AR console, and there's a rumble as the engine kicks back in. Sparks leap past the cab's windows as the truck starts to move, dragging itself over the spikes blocking its path on tyres that have been flayed down to their metal bones. The air fills with the noise of metal grinding against asphalt. To Tanta, it sounds sweeter than birdsong.

<<Tanta,>> Cole sends again, <<these coordinates are only a hundred yards away. If we're not running, then what——>>

<<Brace yourself,>> Tanta interrupts. <<And don't look.>>

As the lorry lurches forward, the bandits scatter from behind the barrier, firing as they go. That's good, because the gunfire is what Tanta's 'scape is using to triangulate their locations – and as long as she knows where they are, the truck's AI does too. The truck accelerates, veering to follow the bandits' path. They try to run, but even with its wheels blown out, the lorry is faster. It flings the first man aside like a rag doll, breaking him against the metal barrier that runs along the road's central reservation. The second goes under the wheels with a sickening bump that's like hitting a pothole.

'The verge!' a voice barks. This one Tanta hasn't heard before. It's a girl, her tone commanding. 'Get onto the verge!'

The surviving bandits must heed her advice, because an instant later the truck swerves sharply to the left, barrelling off the road as it tries to follow them. Through the rifle's camera, Tanta sees three figures fleeing up the wooded bank. She would be impressed with the bandit girl's resourcefulness, if she had the time to appreciate it. As it is, it's just put the truck on a collision course. The cab lists dangerously, its metal wheels losing their already tenuous grip on the asphalt.

Tanta severs her connection to the camera with a sweep of one hand; with the other, she grabs hold of Cole. She leaps out of the ragged hole where the cab's left-hand door used to be, dragging him with her. They hit the ground in a heap of jarred limbs, but Tanta is on her feet again in an instant, pulling Cole free and urging him into a run. They're ten paces from the truck when it hits the verge. The cab, already weakened by the gunfire and the grenades, folds in on itself with a final groan of tortured metal. Behind it, the trailer swings round and to the right, describing an almost leisurely arc, before smashing into the central reservation. When she hears the crash of the impact, Tanta hurls herself and Cole forward, throwing them clear of the truck as it tips onto its side. It crashes onto the tarmac with a final, resounding thud.

Silence – true silence, not the deafness of the firefight – falls at last. Tanta picks herself up, inspecting herself and Cole for injuries. Cole looks shaken, but not seriously harmed. Tanta thinks she may have a mild concussion – the ringing in her ears hasn't subsided, and she did hit her head quite hard on the roof of the cab – but otherwise, she's unscathed. Ignoring the ache in her head and the bruises blossoming on her skin, she forces herself to make a sweep of the area.

The truck is lying across half of the dual carriageway, a beached whale. A little distance away from it lie the broken bodies of the two bandits. Tanta collects their bulletproof shield, and their weapons. The pistols are light and sleek, beautifully designed; she recognises them as Thoughtfront guns immediately.

She finds no sign of the other three shooters. They have vanished into the trees that line the bank.

Once she has satisfied herself that the immediate danger has passed, Tanta ventures back into the overturned truck to retrieve the sniper rifle and her and Cole's bags. When she emerges, Cole is bent over by the verge, dry heaving into the grass. She fishes out her canteen and a towel from her duffel bag and offers them to him; he takes both gratefully.

'I'm sorry,' she says.

'For what?'

'For making you do that. I should have explained.'

'There wasn't time.' Cole takes a swig of the water, grimaces and spits. 'And it needed to be done. It was...'

'Them or us.' Tanta finishes the sentence for him when it becomes clear he isn't going to. 'It really was, Cole. We didn't have a choice.'

They sit together without speaking after that, catching their breath and waiting for the adrenaline pounding through their heads and hearts to drain away. Tanta tries at intervals to contact the ICRD and request an extraction, but receives no response to any of her hails. She's not sure whether this is due to the high latency on the road, or whether Kenway is ignoring her on purpose. She tries hailing Edward Smythe at Sodis, too, with the same result – comms are down, then, and with the zeppelin docked outside the city, there's no telling when normal signal coverage will resume.

Gradually, the ringing in her ears subsides, replaced by the mounting sounds of the dawn chorus. Watery light begins to illuminate the wreckage of the lorry, and the wreckage of the bandits. Curious birds land on the road, inching closer to the bodies in a series of hops and flaps. Tanta tries not to look at them.

'The bandits were here for me,' she says to Cole. 'One of them said so.'

'Shit. Do you think Kenway sold us out?'

Tanta considers the question. 'It's unlikely.' Kenway is a monster, but a strictly bureaucratic one – a move like this isn't his style. She files the question away for future reference, though. Somehow, the bandits had known that she'd be travelling in the HGV – just as they always seem to know the routes and schedules of InTech's drones.

'So, what do we do now?' Cole asks. 'Request a tow-truck?'

'I'm trying,' Tanta says, 'but the ICRD isn't taking my calls.'

Now that her head has cleared, she realises just how urgent their need to get out of here is. They've been sitting by the side of the road for too long already. Three of the bandits survived, and they were here to kill Tanta – how long before they come back to finish the job? Hitching a lift is not an option. There's not much road traffic through the Unaffiliated Zone at the best of times – most corporations prefer the speed and certainty of air travel – and now their crashed truck will be broadcasting its location to any other cars that are in the area, instructing their AIs to reroute. It could be hours before another InTech vehicle passes this way – and even longer before they encounter one with passengers willing to stop for them.

Cole darts her a quick, thoughtful glance. 'There might be another option,' he says. He opens his suitcase, pushing aside layers of clothes. Tanta watches over his shoulder. At the bottom, hidden inside a shoe, is Jeanie's communicator, the one Yas gave him two months ago.

'Yas said I should use it if there was ever an emergency,' Cole says. 'I think this qualifies.'

Tanta stares at it, feeling uneasy. With comm links to the city and the distribution centre down, Cole's suggestion is not a bad one – there may be no one else they can call. Even so, she doesn't like the thought of asking someone from outside InTech to help them, especially someone working with a known defector. She's still processing the things Cole told her before the ambush about his contact with Jeanie's agent and their discovery of Harlow 2.0. Getting in touch with her directly feels like a huge step – one Tanta isn't sure she's ready to take.

'We don't know anything about Jeanie,' she says. 'What she wants, how she knows you. I'd rather get the answers to some of those questions *before* we talk to her.'

'Neal told me some things about her. She seems to be a … well, I suppose you'd call her a freedom fighter.'

Tanta can feel her headache growing at the edges of her awareness, like storm clouds gathering on the horizon. 'A "freedom fighter" sounds a lot like what InTech would call a terrorist.'

'I don't think she's violent,' Cole protests. 'She just wants to expose corporate atrocities. Things like the Harlow Programme.'

'Violent or not, we still have to be wary of her.'

Cole looks annoyed. 'Because she wants to hold the corporations to account? That's a reason for InTech to be wary, not us.'

'We *are* InTech, Cole. It's our corp. Do you think Kenway will accept "I don't think she's violent" as an excuse for our associating with an anti-corporate agitator?'

'OK. I take your point,' he replies, 'but I don't see that we have any other option. She's the one who tipped us off to the existence of Harlow 2.0. We'll need her help to stop it.'

This brings Tanta up short; she hadn't planned that far ahead. Harlow 2.0 already feels too big to think about – the idea of *stopping* it is overwhelming. A part of her wishes Cole had never told her about it in the first place. Things were just starting to get back on track for her: she's made it back into the ICRD and managed to secure Cole as her partner again – and now both those things, which she has worked so hard for, are at risk. Cole's meeting with Neal Ortega and their break-in at the Black Box have put Tanta in a very difficult position, though it feels childish to complain about it given everything that's at stake here.

All in all, she has a whole bag of mixed feelings about this. But Cole is right on one count: they have no choice *but* to speak to Jeanie. Tanta wishes that Harlow 2.0 wasn't on her radar, but now it is, she and Cole need to find out more about it. Jeanie might have useful intel. And in the shorter term, it's not like Tanta has a better idea for getting them out of here.

'OK,' she says at last. 'Make the call.'

Cole looks nervous. As though, despite it being his suggestion, he wasn't expecting to have to use the communicator so soon. 'What should I say?'

'Just that we need help.' Tanta pauses. 'Or *you* need help. It's probably safer not to mention me.' If Jeanie really is a freedom fighter, Tanta doubts she'll be thrilled by the prospect of giving a lift to an ICRD agent.

Cole spends another minute deliberating, rubbing the button in the centre of the communicator with the pad of his thumb. Eventually, he presses it. There's a musical chime, then silence.

'Um. Hello,' he says. 'I – my name is Cole. Yasmin Das told me to use this if I was – if there was an emergency. Well. There's an emergency.'

There's no response for so long that Tanta begins to think the pendant has malfunctioned. Perhaps its batteries have run down, or they are out of range of whatever signal it's trying to receive. Then the chime sounds again, and she hears an unfamiliar voice.

'You see the switch on the side of the device? Turn it on and it will send me your location.'

Cole turns the communicator over, flicking the tiny switch.

'Stay put,' the voice instructs. 'I'm sending someone now.'

Chapter 17

Fliss runs through the trees, her breath loud and ragged in her ears. The formless fears that have dogged her ever since she met the strangers have taken terrible shape, and the worst part is that she has only herself to blame. She always knew the strangers and their gifts came with strings attached; she allowed those strings to wind themselves around her neck, and this is the consequence.

The back of her neck prickles as she sprints. She's expecting at any moment to feel the bite of a bullet between her shoulder blades, but the only sounds of pursuit come from Sonia and Josh, crashing through the verge in her wake. The van is parked in an overgrown field on the far side of the embankment. Fliss throws herself towards it and wrenches open the door.

'Fliss! Wait!' Sonia shouts. She draws level with the van, her face taut with terror. 'Ben – and Gabriel,' she pants. 'We can't go – we don't know if—'

'We know,' Fliss says. She wouldn't be leaving if there was even a chance the rest of the crew were still alive – she saw their bodies herself. 'Put that out of your head, Sonia. They're gone.'

Josh catches up with them an instant later and Fliss leaps

inside, flooring the gas. The van lurches forward, jouncing over the rutted ground.

'Where are we going?' Josh asks. In the rear-view mirror, his eyes have the same hectic, excited look they did when he shot up the car back in Albourne.

'Back to camp,' Fliss mutters.

'But we didn't get them! And I heard them crash,' Josh urges. 'They'll be sitting ducks now.'

When no one answers him, he repeats himself, adding: 'We should go back. Gabriel would've wanted us to—'

'You don't get to tell me what Gabriel would've wanted,' Fliss says.

She says it quietly, but there must be something dangerous in her tone, because after that, no one says a word. Sonia cries softly; Josh turns away from her, staring out the window with a thunderous expression. Fliss keeps her tears inside and her eyes on the road. She can't allow herself to feel the loss of Ben and Gabriel as deeply as she wants to – the grief might kill her, and not figuratively. The people who mowed them down could be coming after her, Josh and Sonia even now. Survival comes before sadness; it has to.

What builds in her instead, during the long, silent drive back to camp, is a simmering rage. It's partly at herself: she ignored her own misgivings about this situation, and now Ben and Gabriel have paid the price for her bad bargain. The brunt of her anger, though, is reserved for the strangers, who duped her and the crew into doing their dirty work in the first place. They pitted Fliss and her friends against a threat the crew was too small to withstand, dropping them into a conflict they must have known not all of them would survive. Fliss realises, too late, that her mother was right: you can't win against the corporations, and you definitely can't bargain with them. She never should have tried.

★

Fliss drives the remnants of the crew back into camp to find the man waiting for them. He doesn't look concerned to see only three people get out of the van; nor does he bother to ask what happened to the other two.

'Is it done?' he asks, the syllables clipped and precise.

'No. Your mark had backup,' Fliss replies. 'She got away. The rest of my crew weren't so lucky.'

'That is unfortunate.' The man doesn't sound surprised. Fliss wonders whether he even expected the crew to succeed, or whether he was just throwing them at his enemies to slow them down.

'There will be other opportunities, however,' he continues. 'Stand by; I need to discuss this with my colleague. You'll receive details of your next target shortly.'

'No, we won't,' Fliss says. 'We quit. The crew are out.'

She's planning to pause there and see what the stranger has to say for himself, but all the pain of the last hour comes welling up in her eyes, in her throat, and she can't hold her rage in check any longer. 'Now take your drones, get back in your fancy car, and GET THE FUCK OUT OF OUR LIVES!'

There's a long silence. The stranger looks at Fliss like he is examining an interesting species of biting insect. 'It can't have escaped your notice that my colleague and I control your weapons,' he says. 'She's at our base of operations now, waiting for my call. One word to her and your pistols, your net gun, even your phone, will all be turned off permanently. Without our support, you will be without resources and drone coordinates. Soon enough, you will find yourself without food and supplies as well.'

'We managed before,' Fliss shoots back.

The man flicks a disdainful glance at Fliss's old gas mask, which she's still holding. 'I'm sure you did. But I wasn't finished.

Before our partnership, you shot down any UAVs you could get – including ours. That is an activity I cannot permit you to resume. Your faces are in our system now. If you renege on our agreement, the next time you set foot in one of our company towns, or pass by one of our roadside defence turrets, our systems will mark you as hostiles – and respond accordingly. It's entirely out of my hands.' The stranger holds them up in the air, as if to demonstrate. 'It's just how our security algorithms work. You'll be known – and hunted – anywhere we own. And Thoughtfront's territories are extensive.'

Fliss says nothing. Her throat has closed up. She'd long suspected the man worked for Thoughtfront, of course, but hearing her suspicion confirmed is its own kind of terrifying, like finding out that the monsters of her childhood nightmares really have been lurking beyond the campfire all this time.

'I raise these points because I don't think you've fully considered the implications of your position,' the stranger says, his tone indifferent. 'I imagine your surviving crewmates may feel the same way. Hadn't you better put it to a vote?'

'We can't make it on our own anymore, Fliss,' Sonia says, her voice timid. 'Not without—' She can't bring herself to finish the sentence.

'I'm with Sonia,' Josh says. 'I'm not going back to shooting drones with a handgun.'

Fliss doesn't reply immediately; her mind is reeling. She didn't call this vote, so it shouldn't count, but she realises, in a distant, panicky way, that she isn't in charge anymore – she hasn't been since she accepted the strangers' bargain. This knowledge has been hovering uneasily on the edge of her thoughts for a while; now, it comes into sudden and frightening focus. The power dynamics of the crew have shifted beneath Fliss's feet, like tectonic plates. Like so many other things recently, she hasn't noticed the change until far too late.

As rocked as she is by this silent coup, there's something else on Fliss's mind besides the tenuousness of her own position. One of the stranger's threats has snagged on her attention, leaving a dangerous thought behind. *My colleague and I control your weapons*, he had said. *She's at our base of operations now.* It's the first time he's ever acknowledged the power he has over the crew's firearms – and in the same breath, he has given Fliss a hint about how she might wrest it from him.

Faintly, like the light at the end of a mineshaft, Fliss begins to see a way out of this catastrophe, one that might even leave her, Sonia and Josh better off than they were before. It's only the bare scraps of an idea – it barely merits the dignity of being called a plan – but she has precious little else to cling to right now. She glares at the man, holding his dispassionate gaze.

'*I* call the votes,' she snarls. 'Don't fucking forget that.' She turns to the crew; Josh looks mulish, Sonia, abashed. 'And I say we'd do fine on our own – but that's just me.' She forces herself to shrug, dropping her eyes. 'Can't say I'm happy about this, but it's two against one. Send us our next mark, then. We'll be ready.'

The man gives a cool nod. 'You can load your latest consignment of UAVs into my car while you wait,' he says. 'Expect to hear from me once I've spoken to my colleague this evening.'

Fliss nods, making no reply. By this evening, she'll be long gone. And if she's lucky, the crew will be free from her bad bargain once and for all. If the man's colleague can turn the crew's weapons off, then Fliss can turn them back on again. All she needs to do is find the switch.

Chapter 18

After Jeanie's first, terse instruction, Tanta and Cole hear nothing else from the communicator. While they wait on the verge, tense and expectant, Cole passes the time by examining the handguns Tanta recovered from the dead bandits.

'They're Thoughtfront weapons,' Tanta tells him. 'I've seen similar models before. What do you make of them?'

Cole picks one up, holding it by the barrel. He knows nothing about the mechanics of guns, but most modern firearms have some kind of MbOS interface, and that's something he can look into. He turns the guns over, checking them both for AR marker codes. All of their MbOS features are designed to be accessed by the MindEye rather than the Inscape system, of course, but it doesn't take Cole long to reconfigure them.

'They're certainly hi-tech,' he says, once he's had a look. 'They have MbOS-compatible micro-cameras in their muzzles – and that's just for starters.'

Tanta nods. 'My sniper rifle has something similar.'

The features on these Thoughtfront guns make Tanta's InTech-issued rifle look like a child's toy, but Cole refrains from pointing that out – it's the kind of comparison she's likely to take amiss.

'They've got AR targeting systems, too,' he says instead. 'And also … huh. That's interesting.' Amidst the data readouts and tactical information cluttering Cole's Array, one icon has caught his eye: there's a red key on the AR display for both weapons.

'What's interesting?' Tanta asks.

'It looks like there's a lock on these,' he replies.

'Can you remove it?'

Cole gives one of the keys an experimental tap; it flashes angrily at him. 'I'm sure *I* could, but the bandits wouldn't have been able to,' he says. 'It's baked into the guns' MindEye settings – no one without an MbOS would even be able to see it.'

To demonstrate, he points one of the guns at the ground and pulls the trigger. Tanta claps her hands over her ears, but there's only a soft click.

She frowns. 'If the guns are locked, then how did the bandits fire on us?'

'Give me a minute,' Cole replies. 'I'll check their logs.'

He pulls up the usage data for both guns, placing the readouts side by side on his Array. They're filled with grey space – it seems that the weapons spend more time locked and offline than in active use. Cole swipes a few commands on the air, filtering the data before him to show only the times when the guns' locks are off. The readouts fill with date stamps in neat rows, surprisingly uniform. He viewshares them with Tanta.

'It looks like the bandits' weapons are being controlled by a third party,' she says slowly, staring at the logs. 'Someone who's turning them on only at specific times.' She catches his eye, looking excited. 'This is excellent work, Cole. If we could cross-reference these logs with records of the bandits' other attacks, then—'

She stops, turning from him to look up the road. A moment later, Cole hears what has distracted her: the low hum of an engine.

Cole feels a mounting sense of anticipation as the car

approaches. The prospect of meeting Jeanie fills him with equal parts nervousness and excitement. She's the first tangible link to his past he has found – the only person, besides Arthur, who seems to have known him well before his MindWipe.

In some ways, Cole has already filled in the most pertinent gaps in his memories. He knows about his role in the Harlow Programme and the foray into anti-corporate terrorism that followed it, and perhaps those two shameful incidents tell him everything about his past self that he needs to know. But two incidents from several decades of missing time are not a lot to go on; he's hungry for the rest – however ugly it might be. Cole cannot relate to the man he used to be at all, but if he's ever going to make amends for the choices he made, then he's going to have to try and understand him. Jeanie can help him with that: she may be the only person who can.

The car reaches them more quickly than Cole was expecting, coming to a screeching stop yards from where they are sitting. It's armoured, with a matt-black chassis that's faceted like a diamond. Cole squints through the windshield, trying to get a look at the passenger, but the glass is tinted almost to opacity. Then a window rolls down and Yas leans out. For an instant, he is disappointed.

'Hey, Tanta,' Yas says. She turns an accusatory look on Cole. 'You should have mentioned you were back with the ICRD.'

Tanta takes a step forward. 'Agent Das—'

'Spare me the formality. I'm not an agent anymore.'

'Yas. I know you weren't expecting to see me here,' Tanta continues, her voice level. 'But Cole and I could both use your help.'

Yas pulls a face. 'What *I* was expecting doesn't matter. My orders were to retrieve Cole. I don't think my employer will be thrilled to find he has an agent in tow.'

'You're working for Jeanie, then?' Tanta asks.

'You're working for InTech,' Yas rejoins, 'so you'll forgive me if I don't answer that question.' She opens the door and steps out. Her black hair is longer than when Cole saw her last, and her skin has tanned to a darker shade of bronze. An old-fashioned rifle, one with no MbOS interface, hangs from a holster at her belt. She doesn't draw it, but she doesn't come any closer, either. She looks from Cole to Tanta, her expression cool and quizzical, before her eyes finally come to rest on the remains of the truck.

'What *happened* to you two?' she asks.

'We were ambushed on our way to the Southern Distribution Centre,' Tanta says. 'We've been stranded here for the last two hours.'

'And you haven't called for an extraction from, you know, your own corp because ...?'

Cole opens his mouth, but Tanta jumps in before he can reply. 'We can't tell you that.'

'Turnabout's fair play,' Yas concedes.

Cole is growing frustrated with this conversation. Tanta and Yas are circling each other like a pair of cats, neither trusting the other enough to get to the point.

'Look, Yas,' he says. 'I'm really grateful you've come, but let's get one thing straight. I've already told Tanta everything, and she hasn't turned me in yet. I trust her. So, anything you or Jeanie have to say to me, you can say to her too.'

To Cole's surprise, Yas gives a snort of laughter. 'You couldn't make this shit up,' she murmurs. She raises an eyebrow at Tanta. 'He's an ICRD consultant and he's never heard of "need-to-know"?'

'Don't be hard on him,' Tanta replies. 'He was a neuroengineer for a lot longer.'

Cole's face heats. This wasn't the reaction he was expecting, but at least it's broken Tanta and Yas out of their holding pattern – even taken some of the tension out of the air between them.

'Well, there's no helping it now,' Yas sighs. 'But as to whether Jeanie will talk to you, that's not my call to make.'

She reaches into her pocket, producing a communicator identical to Cole's own, and presses the button in the centre. 'J?'

'Hey, Yasmin,' Jeanie replies. It's the same voice Cole heard from his own communicator before, a musical voice, its accents rich as deep water flowing over rocks. For some reason, the sound of it makes his skin prickle.

'There's been a development,' Yas says. 'I have Cole, but he isn't alone. He's back in the ICRD and partnered with Tanta again. He's already told her about the update,' – here, she gives Cole an old-fashioned look – 'so that horse has bolted. He wants me to bring her with him.'

'Bring us where?' Tanta asks.

No one answers her. There's a long pause; Cole begins to think he's scared Jeanie off, and has time to feel all the extremes of regret and self-recrimination that idea entails, before she speaks again.

'Yasmin, you know this girl. Can you vouch for her?'

'Now, that's a complicated question.' Yas lets out a huff of air, considering. 'Yeah. I'll vouch for her,' she says eventually. 'She helped me get away from InTech clear, back in the summer. She keeps her word.'

Tanta almost killed her once, too, but luckily, Yas seems to have decided to leave that detail out. There's another pause. The communicator lies in Yas's hands like a stone.

'I don't like this,' Jeanie says at length. 'I don't like it at all. Doesn't sound like I have a choice, though. Bring them both in, Yasmin. If you and Cole trust this CorpWard, I suppose I should at least meet her for myself.'

'And there you have it,' Yas says. She gestures to the car. 'Your carriage awaits.'

'We were supposed to be at Sodis hours ago,' Tanta says. The suspicion hasn't left her voice. 'We don't have time for a detour.'

'Don't worry,' Yas replies. 'This is on the way.'

On the outside, Yas's car looks a lot like an ICRD tactical vehicle – albeit one that has seen better days. On the inside, it is like nothing Tanta has ever seen before. InTech cars all have the same basic layout: four to six seats and a smooth dashboard with a programmable AR interface. The inside of Yas's car looks like someone took that setup and eviscerated it. The right-hand side of the dashboard has been ripped open, and someone has stuck a T-shaped metal bar into the mess of wires within. They've torn up part of the floor, too, revealing two pedals beneath the carpet like misshapen front teeth. Tanta is keen to get moving again, but as she loads her and Cole's bags onto a back seat, she can't help feeling alarmed at the sight of this broken mess.

'Are you sure this thing is roadworthy, Yas?' she asks.

'It got me here, didn't it?' Yas replies. 'Now come on. We're burning daylight.'

'But... how are you going to input our destination?' The car has no AR interface, and the metal bar and clunky floor pedals bear no obvious relationship to its inner workings that Tanta can see.

Yas gives her a look that's part pity, part self-deprecation. 'You have no idea how old that question makes me feel. Would it shock you to learn that I actually know how to drive?'

Tanta is familiar with the concept of operating a car manually, of course: most pre-Meltdown cars had manual steering rigs, and some InTech emergency vehicles still do. She's even seen a few before, rusting out in the Unaffiliated Zone – but she's never used one.

'Where did you learn that?' She asks, unable to keep the scepticism out of her voice.

'It *used* to be part of basic training,' Yas says. 'Time was, all ICRD cars had steering rigs below the dash for emergencies – EMP attacks or server outages, stuff like that. Then InTech started including a backup AI in a miniaturised faraday cage instead – now it's only the older models that have manual overrides at all.' She smiles to herself. 'And only the older models of agent who still know how to use them, apparently.'

Tanta is still stuck on how Yas is going to use the manual override to make the car *go*. 'So ... what's the bar for?'

'The bar turns the wheels,' Yas says, speaking as slowly as if Tanta is five years old. She glances at Cole. 'You get what I'm talking about, right?'

'I understand the principle,' Cole says, looking intrigued. 'I'm assuming one of the pedals goes to the braking system and the other one connects to the engine?'

'Pretty much,' Yas replies. 'It's simple! I'm still a bit rusty though, so you'll want to buckle up.'

She plonks into the front seat as she speaks, positioning her feet over the pedals and her right hand on the metal bar. Cole and Tanta barely have time to obey her instruction before she slides her other hand under the dashboard and the car lurches into motion.

Yas's warning wasn't an idle one. The journey is both jerkier than Tanta is used to and much, much faster. InTech's cars tend to travel at an even thirty miles per hour, unless the traffic management mainframe has marked them as high priority. Yas pushes the car up to three times that, making Tanta's pulse race and her hands ball involuntarily into fists. For large parts of the journey she drives off-road, too, avoiding InTech's roadside cameras, so their breakneck speed is combined with constant bumps as the car races over the rutted and uneven ground of the Unaffiliated Zone.

True to her word, Yas drives them towards Sodis, taking a similar route to the one Tanta and Cole were on before the truck was ambushed. About half an hour away from the distribution centre, an ancient slip-road, built before the Meltdown and long since abandoned, branches off to the left from the corporate-maintained motorway. They pull onto it; the path is so old, and so neglected, that there are trees growing through the asphalt, and the car has to push its way forward through a thickening tangle of undergrowth. After a while, Tanta can only tell they're still on a road at all because of the pre-Meltdown signs, which perch here and there amidst the foliage like exotic birds.

At length, they emerge from the green darkness outside a disused service station. It, too, has been overwhelmed by nature: ivy wreathes its red-brick walls, helping to support a pitched roof that has partially collapsed in on itself. Yas brings the car to a halt on the forecourt and turns to face them both.

'She's inside,' she says.

Cole goes in first; Tanta peers warily after him. It's past midday, and the forecourt is bright, but the interior of the building is dark with ivy and shadows. There's a sort of porch at the front, shards of grimy glass in its windows like jagged teeth, and within, she can make out a seated figure. She takes a breath, smelling earth and growing things. The forest where she fought the Thoughtfront operative rises vividly to her mind; this place smells like that – a heavy, secretive smell. She isn't ready for this encounter – isn't ready for any of the revelations Cole has thrown at her today – but she can't walk away from it. She needs to find out what Jeanie knows; she can figure out what that knowledge means for her later. Together, she and Yas follow Cole inside.

Cole doesn't know what he was expecting Jeanie to look like. In all of his speculation about who she is and how she knows him, he'd never spared it much thought. In the event, she's tall and statuesque, with a waterfall of dark hair. She's sitting cross-legged on the floor, but she rises as Cole walks into the building, coming forward to greet him. When she gets closer, Cole can see that she is about his age. Her white skin is weathered, her eyes a deep, liquid blue.

'Hi Cole,' she says. 'It's good to see you again.'

Just as when he heard it through the communicator, there's something in her voice that gives Cole goosebumps. The effect is stronger here, now that he's standing in front of her; it feels as though there are memories lurking just beneath the surface of his skin, inaccessible, but achingly close.

'I wish I could say the same,' Cole replies. His face heats; he's only just met Jeanie and already he's put his foot in his mouth. 'I mean,' he stammers, 'I – uh, what I meant to say was that I don't remember—'

'I know.' Jeanie smiles; it's a sad smile. 'I've been keeping tabs on you, best I could, and I heard about the MindWipe. I'm sorry.'

Cole doesn't know what to say to that. Jeanie's knowledge of his life was something he thought he was prepared for, but it has still caught him off guard. He's rescued from having to respond by the arrival of Yas and Tanta. They hang back in the doorway; Yas is keeping half an eye on the forecourt outside, but Tanta stares at Jeanie, her expression guarded.

'They're expected at Sodis,' Yas says, 'so we'd better keep this brief.'

'You wanted to talk to us about Harlow 2.0?' Tanta adds.

Jeanie gives Tanta an icy stare. 'I wanted to talk to Cole,' she corrects. 'You're here on sufferance. And I'll be as brief as I can,

Yasmin, but there's some things Cole and I have to discuss first.' She turns back to him, lowering her voice a fraction. 'You must have a lot of questions. We're short on time, but you deserve answers. Are you sure you want the CorpWard here for this?'

Cole nods.

'Then ask me anything you want to know.'

Cole feels a guilty kind of gladness at being the sole focus of Jeanie's attention, especially given her coldness to Tanta. He tries to suppress the feeling and focus on the conversation at hand. He's been longing for this opportunity for the last two months so, of course, now that it's here he has no idea where to start.

Jeanie seats herself again, tilting her head to invite Cole to do likewise. The gesture is easy and familiar, as if they have sat down to talk like this many times before. Something tugs at Cole's throat as he joins her; it takes him a moment to recognise it as regret. Jeanie's manner towards him speaks of friendship and closeness. If those things were ripped away from Cole along with the rest of his memories, then maybe his past wasn't all bad. It's this thought that decides the first question he asks:

'How did we know each other?'

'We used to work together,' Jeanie replies. 'For the Brokerage.'

Cole feels the shock register on his face. The Brokerage belongs to the realm of spies and classified intelligence. He knows what it is, but all of his experience of the shadowy, extra-corporate organisation comes from *after* his MindWipe. Even now, he wouldn't know how to contact the Brokerage if his life depended on it. It's out of his element, to put it mildly.

Something about Jeanie's half-smile tells Cole she is think-ing the same thing. 'I recruited you,' she says, in answer to his unspoken question. 'God knows, you wouldn't have been able to find us on your own. You were pretty hopeless.'

Shaken as he is by Jeanie's news, Cole finds that it fits within the half-finished puzzle of his life more neatly than he might have expected. 'Did my work for the Brokerage have something to do with the false flag attacks on InTech and Thoughtfront's sleeper factories last summer?' he asks.

Out of the corner of his eye, he sees Tanta give him a warning look. He is unabashed; this isn't something she wants him discussing with Jeanie, but he has waited for this chance for too long to be content with only part of the story. 'You said yourself that I must have had an accomplice,' he points out to Tanta. 'There's no way I orchestrated both attacks alone.'

'It would be more accurate to say that you *were* the accomplice,' Jeanie says. 'You developed the viruses under the Brokerage's guidance, and it helped you to distribute them.'

'The Brokerage sells classified intelligence; InTech and Thoughtfront are two of its biggest customers. What would it have to gain by setting them at each other's throats?' Tanta asks. She was standing a little apart from Cole and Jeanie before, giving them space, but she has drifted closer.

'It never occurred to you that the Brokerage has an agenda of its own?' Jeanie retorts. 'One besides making credits, I mean.' The change in her tone is striking – all her solicitude is switched off in an instant, leaving her voice hard and suspicious.

'You haven't answered my question.'

Cole is starting to get annoyed at Tanta's interruptions. He understands why she is turning this into an interrogation, but he wishes she would back off. This is his life they're talking about. If anyone should be leading the conversation, it's him. Jeanie evidently thinks so too, because she doesn't respond, turning her attention back to Cole.

'When I recruited you to the Brokerage, you told me you'd been trying to create a programme that would improve the mental wellbeing of Corporate Wards and that, somewhere along the way, InTech had turned it into an experiment in mind control,' she says. 'By the time you realised the Harlow

Programme's true scope, the board had approved the project and rolled it out to an entire cohort. My superiors and I recognised the implications: if InTech was willing to subject its wards to mental manipulation, then how long before it did the same to its residents – or to the residents of other corporations? You wanted to stop the programme before it got that far, and the Brokerage wanted to help you.'

Cole frowns. It sounds like a noble beginning, but he knows how this story ends – with dozens of deaths on his conscience. He's not sure how he got from the mindset Jeanie is describing to plotting acts of anti-corporate terrorism.

'What happened next?' he asks.

'We got played,' Jeanie says. 'I joined the Brokerage because it recognised the threat corporate rule posed to human liberty and wanted to do something about it. It turns out it was only our goals that aligned, not the means we were willing to use to achieve them. I wanted to stop the Harlow Programme, but my superiors in the organisation saw it as an opportunity to weaken the entire system of corporate control – to drive InTech and Thoughtfront to war. It's why I left.'

Cole feels sick. There's a certain cold logic to the plan that he cannot deny. InTech and Thoughtfront are two of the biggest corporations in the world, and an all-out war between them is one that neither could easily win. They'd destroy each other, probably taking many smaller corps with them in the process.

The next question he has to ask is a difficult one; it catches in his throat. 'But – but I *stayed*?'

'They manipulated you, just like they did me.' Jeanie's tone is gentle. 'I tried to persuade you to come with me, but you weren't having it. You were convinced that what they had you doing was for the greater good.'

Cole knows he has only himself to blame for the burning sense of shame he feels at Jeanie's answer. He was eager to get a glimpse of his past self, but he knew he wouldn't like what he saw. He wishes he could believe Jeanie that he was an innocent victim of forces beyond his control, but he has too much faith in his own intellect to let himself off the hook that easily.

Tanta is speaking again. 'You said your goals align with the Brokerage's,' she points out. 'How do we know you're any different from them?'

Jeanie gives her a contemptuous glance. 'I want a world where people have autonomy over their own lives, yes, and I believe that's impossible within the current system – I make no secret of that. But not all revolutions have to be bloody; that's something the Brokerage doesn't understand. The attack on the sleeper factories was only the start; when I left, they were planning an escalating campaign of destabilisation, from minor acts of sabotage right up to bombing corporate landmarks.'

Cole imagines he sees Tanta standing up a fraction straighter at this. Like him, she must be thinking of the attack on the Needle. Everyone is blaming it on Thoughtfront, but could the Brokerage be involved too? In deference to Tanta's 'need-to-know' rule, Cole doesn't voice the thought aloud, but he makes a mental note to discuss it with her later.

'Like I said: after I left, I tried to keep an eye on you,' Jeanie continues, 'but you dropped off my radar after your MindWipe. At first, I was just hoping I could help you get out of the Brokerage, but by the time I met Yasmin and discovered her connection to you, things with the Harlow Programme had escalated, and I needed your help.'

At this, Yas walks over from the doorway and seats herself next to Jeanie. After a moment, Tanta does the same. It's time to get down to the business at hand.

'Ortega told us what you and he found at the Black Box,' Jeanie says. 'I'd suspected a second phase of the Harlow Programme was in development for a while, but this confirms it. InTech wants to roll the programme out city-wide, just as we always feared.'

Cole's throat tightens at Neal's name. The situation is even more frightening than Jeanie thinks; he's seen Harlow 2.0 in action, and it's far worse than the original.

'About Neal,' he says. 'There's something you should know. After our break-in, Arthur used him as a test subject for Harlow 2.0. He's—' He stops. There's a plug of rage and sadness in his throat that makes it impossible for him to put what happened with the trainee into words. 'He's like a completely different person.'

Jeanie looks grave. 'That's a great loss. But it may not be a permanent one.' She glances at Cole, then at Yas. Finally, her eyes slide to Tanta; for an instant, it looks as though she's in two minds about whether to continue at all. 'I have a theory about how we might reverse the effects of the programme,' she says at last.

Cole's heart lurches; he's not sure whether it's excitement or fear. He was expecting Jeanie to have a plan – she wouldn't have taken the risk of recruiting him on spec – but now the time has come to discuss it, it has taken him aback. After two months of radio silence from Yas and Jeanie, events over the last two days have moved at breakneck speed. Cole has only just discovered Harlow 2.0 even *exists*, and now here he is plotting to sabotage it. The implications of what he's doing – and what would happen to him and Tanta if InTech caught them at it – hit him afresh.

'You really think we can do that?' he asks, trying to keep the tremor out of his voice.

'*Think* is the operative word right now. I'll need to review the software itself to be sure. Before he was compromised, Ortega managed to get it out of the Black Box and into one of my storage points in the city,' Jeanie explains. 'Yasmin is going to retrieve it tonight. Assuming my theory holds water, I'll need your help to implement it.'

'What *is* your theory?' Tanta asks.

'Cole and Yasmin may have vouched for you, CorpWard, but that doesn't mean I trust you,' Jeanie replies. 'One way or another, I'll know about my plan by tomorrow afternoon. That will also give me some time to think about how much I'm willing to tell *you* about it.'

'By Cole's account, that will give us less than a day to implement it before Harlow 2.0 goes live,' Tanta pursues. 'It's unreasonable to keep us in the dark that long: you're asking us to take a lot on faith.'

'And you're not?' Jeanie snaps. 'Before today, I had no idea you were back in Cole's life. If you think I'm going to brief an ICRD agent I've only just met on something this important, no questions asked, you've got another think coming.'

'Tanta has more reason than anyone to want to take down Harlow 2.0,' Cole interjects.

Tanta shoots him a warning look, but Jeanie only tosses her head. 'I said I'd been keeping tabs on you, Cole. I know the CorpWard lost her Harlow Programming. If I didn't, I wouldn't have allowed her to sit in on this conversation.' She turns back to Tanta. 'Yet now you're an agent again. Even you must see why I'm having a hard time sussing out where your loyalties lie.'

Tanta makes no answer to that. Jeanie stares her down, then turns away. 'I'll send Yas to meet you outside Sodis tomorrow afternoon, Cole,' she says. 'I can fill you in on the details then. If you insist on bringing the CorpWard along, make sure she's figured out which side she's on.'

Cole feels another twinge of guilt. He glances at Tanta: her face is as unreadable as ever, but her shoulders are tight. Yas must notice, too; there's sympathy in her expression when she looks Tanta's way.

'Easier said than done, I imagine,' she says, her tone light. 'But fair's fair, Tanta. Till then, the plan is need-to-know.'

Chapter 19

True to her word, after the meeting with Jeanie, Yas drives them straight to Sodis. The distribution centre is further from the city than Tanta has ever travelled before, all the way on the south coast. As they race through the Unaffiliated Zone and she tries to ignore the queasy feeling in the pit of her stomach, she allows her mind to drift away from the difficult conversation she's just had, and the ones likely awaiting her at their destination. Unfortunately, there aren't many places her thoughts can go that aren't equally unsettling. Her usual refuge – Reet – is closed to her; just picturing her lover's face tugs on a knot of misery in the centre of Tanta's chest. When will they speak again? *Will* they speak again? She tries to dismiss these questions. She and Cole are starting a new chapter in their lives: a new case, a new home. She can't change the past, and it makes no sense to dwell on it.

'Don't mind J,' Yas says, snapping Tanta back to the here and now. 'She'll warm up to you. She was spiky with me, too, when I started working for her.'

The comment is a welcome interruption to Tanta's ruminations, but she's not sure how to respond. She's pleased to see Yas safe, and grateful to her for vouching for her earlier, but there isn't much they can safely talk about together. Tanta doesn't like

Jeanie, but she was right about one thing: they're not on the same side. Tanta is an ICRD agent, and Yas is a defector; even if Tanta and Cole end up collaborating with her and Jeanie, that won't change.

Still, Tanta realises, she *wants* to talk to Yas. She's happy to see her again. And this might be her only opportunity to find out more about Jeanie from someone who knows her well.

'How *did* you end up working for her?' she asks. 'After everything that happened in Thoughtfront territory, I thought you'd want to get as far away from the city as possible.'

'Believe me, I tried,' Yas says. 'After I left you, I was planning on joining another corporation – preferably one with headquarters across the channel – but when I reached out to my contacts, no one was biting. Turns out being on the hitlists of two of the biggest corps in the world is a major turn-off for prospective employers – who knew?' She shrugs. 'When that didn't pan out, I went looking for the Brokerage. I thought I might be able to sell them some intel, but it was a long shot. Things were pretty bad. Then Jeanie got in touch, and when she found out I knew Cole, she recruited me to her outfit. As bosses go, she's not bad. She's cagey, sure, but she's better than some.'

Tanta nods; loyalty to your manager is something she understands. And having worked for both Jennifer Ash and Douglas Kenway, she supposes she has no right to comment on Yas's choice of employer.

'It's probably for the best,' Yas adds, after a while. 'The city – this line of work – it's what I'm good at. And I'm too old to change.'

She's smiling when she says it, but Tanta guesses that she's only half joking. Being an agent is what she's good at, too. She can see why Yas would choose to work for Jeanie, if it gives her the chance to keep doing the only work she's been trained for. Perhaps, if she were in Yas's shoes, she'd do the same.

They approach the distribution centre at an oblique angle, so Tanta's first glimpse of it is nothing more than a chain-link perimeter fence topped with barbed wire. She narrows her eyes, zooming in on the compound. She's struck by the sameness of the place. The city was a riotous mixture of old and new; the walk from Tanta's old flat to the ICRD took her past hundreds of years of history, from buildings built long before the Meltdown to modern skyscrapers. By contrast, the homes and warehouses of Sodis are so uniform that they must all have been designed at the same time – streets of reinforced concrete cubes rolling ready-made off a city-sized production line. Whatever coastal settlement used to stand here – if there ever was one at all – was probably bombed into oblivion during the Meltdown. Tanta's gaze skims over the drab buildings, catching at last on the gleaming expanse of the sea. She's never seen it before outside of pictures, and it's hard to tear her eyes away. It's everything the distribution centre is not: chaotic, formless, mercurial. Its grey waves rear and shift, in constant flux, a reflection of Sodis's tower blocks in a funhouse mirror.

Not long afterwards, Yas brings the car to a halt by another ancient slip-road.

'This is as close as I can get you,' she says. 'Any nearer and the car might be picked up by the centre's cameras. I don't want to risk it.'

'You've already gone above and beyond by bringing us this far,' Tanta replies. 'Thank you.'

Yas shrugs awkwardly. 'Let's call it even.'

She watches them out of the car, then rolls down her window. 'Hey, thanks for running with us on this,' she says. 'I know it's a lot to take in. If things go well, I'll see you tomorrow.'

It's half a question, and she's looking at Tanta when she says it. Tanta affects not to notice; she's not ready to think that far ahead just yet. As Yas roars away down the slip-road, Tanta touches her index finger to her temple, checking the map on her Array. They're still a kilometre out from Sodis, and so late for their check-in that the delay is swiftly turning from embarrassing to concerning. She'd like to arrive before Smythe sends out the search parties.

'Come on,' she says, swinging her duffel bag onto one shoulder. 'We'd better get going.'

The walk to the distribution centre is not unpleasant. The weather is cold but crisp, and their route goes through an agricultural zone owned by Bayanto, one of InTech's agro-pharmaceutical trading partners. They walk parallel to the main road, following one of the maintenance paths intended for the use of the sleepers who work in the pastures, fields and greenhouses that fill the area. They spot a few of these workers in the distance, spraying pesticides and operating machinery, but nearer at hand, there's nothing moving save for a few crows.

'I'm sorry for springing this Harlow 2.0 thing on you,' Cole says quietly. 'I really wanted to tell you earlier.'

'It's OK,' Tanta replies. If truth be told, she's reluctant to resume the conversation even now. The whole situation fills her with a bone-deep unease. This walk will probably be their best opportunity to discuss matters unobserved, however, so they can't afford to waste it.

'What did you think of what Jeanie had to say?' Cole asks.

Tanta doesn't reply immediately; her thoughts feel too big and shapeless to be put into words. She has to admit that the freedom fighter's story is a plausible one: she'd already suspected that the Brokerage might have played a role in the false flag attack. She thinks back to her strange encounter with the Brokerage last summer. An unaffiliated street urchin had given her a black tile, a touchscreen device through which she'd spoken to someone claiming to be a Brokerage agent. It was that agent who'd given her Hardinger's name, putting her onto Thoughtfront in the first place.

Jeanie's cause, too, is hard to dismiss, and as Cole said, it's all the more compelling to Tanta for being personal. She's not sure she can stand by while half the city is subjected to a programme from which she only escaped so recently herself, and to which she would never willingly return.

But weighed against all of these considerations is the sheer enormity of the task Jeanie has laid at her and Cole's door. The idea of sabotaging Harlow 2.0 looms in Tanta's mind like a gate. It is a point of no return – if she helps Jeanie and Yas, she'll be a traitor to her corporation. Everything she has built for herself within InTech would be at risk: her fledgling career in the ICRD; the chance, slim enough already, to repair her relationship with Reet. Aligning herself with the freedom fighters would mean turning her back on all the things in her life that are certain, safe and secure, and Tanta has very few of those left. She thinks of what Jeanie is asking of her and feels as though she's teetering on the edge of a precipice, nothing beneath her but air.

'I think we can't trust her until we know more about her,' is all she says aloud.

It doesn't come close to summing up everything that's on her mind, but it's a start. One of the first things Tanta learnt in basic training was that you never walk into a situation blind, and that's exactly what Jeanie expects her and Cole to do. Two days is not long enough to do the groundwork she needs to be sure about this partnership.

'We don't have a lot of time to make our minds up,' Cole reminds her.

He's being diplomatic; he means that *she* doesn't have a lot of time. Tanta can tell that Cole is already on board with Jeanie's plan, whatever it turns out to be. 'I just want to make sure we make the right call,' she says. 'Things are moving very quickly, and we don't have all the facts.'

Cole gives her a quizzical look. 'Isn't the right call pretty obvious? Harlow 2.0 needs to be stopped.'

Tanta's headache is coming back. She rubs her temples. 'I'm not disputing that. Look, I know we're under pressure, but can we shelve this discussion – just for now – and focus on the case? I need some more time to think about this.'

'Well, how much longer do you think you'll need?'

'Will you back off?' Tanta snaps. 'You said yourself that you sprang this on me. I'm not ready to talk about it yet.'

She regrets the outburst as soon as it's happened. 'Just give me a day, all right?' she says, in a softer tone. 'You remember what Jeanie said about the Brokerage bombing corporate landmarks? It might be involved in the UAV thefts and the attack on the Needle, somehow. If we keep working the case and that lead pans out, it could tell us more about how far we can trust her intel.'

It's a shameless ploy for more time, but Cole seems satisfied by it for now. 'I was thinking the same thing. All right, so what's our next move?'

'We need to check in with our contact,' Tanta replies, relieved to be moving the conversation back onto safer ground. 'He's the Logistics Officer: he oversees all the deliveries to and from Sodis, so he should have information on how the thefts have been impacting things there.'

She summons her Array as she speaks, checking Edward Smythe's employment record. He's had a long career with InTech: he flunked out of the ICRD's agent programme in his teens, spent two decades as a guardian, and then moved to the Trade Division. He's been in his post at Sodis for twenty-five years. Tanta suppresses a shudder. Gathering dust as the Logistics Officer of a regional distribution centre for twenty-five years seems a cruel fate; she imagines the brass have all but forgotten about Smythe. She hopes the same thing doesn't happen to her.

'And what do you want me to do?' Cole asks. 'I mean, I'm happy to tag along, but isn't questioning people more your department?'

They're completely alone, walking down a narrow path between two fields, but Tanta still glances around before she replies. 'Can you monitor his vitals through his Inscape while we talk?' she asks, voice low. 'Check if he's telling the truth?'

'The lie detector thing?' Cole asks. 'Sure. But why would he lie to us?'

'I don't necessarily think he will. I'm just covering our bases.' Covering them against Kenway in particular. Short of actually betraying the corporation, there's little he wouldn't do to sabotage Tanta. While she hopes he will be content with the damage he has already done to her career, she wouldn't put it past him to brief against her, even in a place as remote from the city as this.

Sodis has no pedestrian entrance, so when Cole and Tanta get near enough to the centre's main gate, they are forced to walk along the side of the road. There's more traffic on the stretch leading up to the entrance, probably because the cars and trucks all have to slow to a crawl on their way through the centre's gate scanners. Passing beneath the motor cortex immobilisers that line the top of the gate at high speed would be a recipe for disaster. They thread their way carefully through the near-stationary cars, making a beeline for the guardian station on the road's central reservation.

Smythe is waiting for them there. He's a huge, barrel-chested man in his late fifties, with dark skin and a white moustache. His expression is thunderous; Tanta has no trouble guessing why. It's past midday, and they were supposed to be here before 09:00.

Tanta walks up to the window of the booth and shows him the Agent badge pinned to her profile.

'Logistics Officer Smythe,' she says. 'Thank you for waiting for us. My name is Tanta, and this is my colleague, Cole. I'm here to take up the ICRD Liaison Officer role.'

Smythe doesn't bother to return the greeting. 'Yes, I know who you are,' he says. 'Where have you been? And where's the HGV you were supposed to be escorting?'

His peremptory tone nettles Tanta. What does the man want, an apology? She forces her temper back into line with an effort. She *should* apologise. They're very late, and it would be courteous to explain why.

'I'm sorry. We were attacked by bandits on the road. The truck was damaged beyond repair. We had to walk the rest of the way here.'

Smythe doesn't offer so much as a murmur of concern. 'Another ambush? And do you mean to tell me you abandoned the vehicle you'd been assigned to guard? What happened to the cargo?'

Another? Tanta thinks. Reet hadn't mentioned any danger of an ambush when she sent Tanta and Cole out in the truck. She hopes, fervently, that Reet didn't know; the alternative is too painful to contemplate. 'We had to leave the cargo,' she says aloud.

Smythe's frown turns into a full-on glare. 'Why is this the first I'm hearing of this? I should have had an incident report the moment it happened! Don't they follow protocol in the city?'

Tanta bites back a snappy response. She's not going to start this new chapter of her life by getting into an argument with her contact. 'Comms in the Unaffiliated Zone are down, Logistics Officer. Otherwise I would, of course, have informed you straight away.'

This seems to mollify Smythe. 'My engineers did say something about the damned zeppelin being moved,' he admits. 'I can't wrap my head around all that signal coverage jargon. Well, I suppose it can't be helped. I'll send a team out to retrieve the cargo – if there's anything left of it by now.' Belatedly, he extends a meaty paw, seizing first Tanta's hand, then Cole's, in a bone-crushing grip. 'Welcome to Sodis, Agents.'

If the distribution centre looked nondescript from a distance, it's positively dreary up close. Smythe ushers Cole and Tanta into a car that takes them up a straight, grey road into a straight, grey town. Sodis is laid out in an enormous grid of office blocks, flats, and warehouses, everything perfectly aligned with every-thing else. Tanta could stand by the gate and shoot someone on the other side of town, simply by lining herself up with the gaps between the buildings.

His annoyance at their late arrival past, Smythe seems pleased they're here. Tanta gets the impression that Sodis doesn't get many visitors of note – her and Cole's visit must be the most exciting thing that has happened in the distribution centre for some time.

'I flirted with becoming an agent once, you know,' Smythe tells them. 'Even signed up for the training programme. Wasn't for me – too much sneaking around. Prefer the guardians, myself – more direct.'

Tanta nods politely and says nothing, thinking with amused pity of Smythe's employment record. The car makes another ninety-degree turn, taking them down another row of identikit buildings.

'That's the Trade Division's data centre,' Smythe comments, gesturing to a particularly large tower. 'It's something of a local landmark.'

He points out a few other 'landmarks' as they drive. To Tanta, they look exactly the same as all the other buildings in Sodis. One big, squat box is the centre's first warehouse; another, smaller cube is its clinic; and on and on until, when she shuts her eyes, all she can see is blocks of grey concrete. At least Smythe's loquaciousness gives Cole plenty of opportunity to access his 'scape unnoticed. The next time the Logistics Officer turns to the window to point out a site of interest, Tanta darts her partner a quick glance.

I'm in, he mouths, giving her a discreet thumbs-up.

Tanta is hoping the car will drop them off at their accommodation – she'd like the chance to drop off their bags and change her clothes before she and Cole get down to work in earnest – so she's disappointed when they pull up at last in front of an austere office block. There are bars over its windows and a security shutter above the door.

'And this is my base of operations,' Smythe announces grandly. 'The Logistics Office.' He climbs out of the car, beckoning for Tanta and Cole to follow him. 'I think you'll find the arrangements inside are quite impressive, even' – he turns to throw a knowing look in Tanta's direction – 'in comparison with what you're used to in the ICRD.'

He leads them into a wide lobby. 'When I took up my post here, the security protocols were in a dreadful state,' he continues. 'I had them completely overhauled – put infrared motion detectors at all the main entry points, pressure plates on the staircases, and a system of weight sensors in the shelves of the archive that I've been told is cutting edge even by the standards of...'

Smythe is gesturing as he speaks, pointing out sensors and cameras with proprietary pride. With a sinking feeling, Tanta realises that he intends to deliver a lecture on all the security measures in the place. 'Logistics Officer,' she interrupts. 'I was hoping to discuss InTech's recent bandit attacks with you. Perhaps you could tell me more about Sodis and its internal security afterwards?'

That checks Smythe's enthusiasm, but only for a moment. 'The case – of course!' he says. 'We'll talk in my office.'

He leads them through a door to the left, into a drab room with a wilting pot plant in one corner. 'So, what's our play?' he asks, dropping into a chair. 'You were attacked on the road, yes? Did you manage to take any of them out?'

Tanta hesitates. She's in a tricky position with Smythe: he's not her manager, but she's in his jurisdiction here, and technically, he outranks her. She doesn't like his 'our', or what it implies. Whatever Smythe says about the ICRD not being for him, he's got a chip on his shoulder about the size of a missing Agent badge, and Tanta suspects he's trying to counteract the boredom of his provincial role by playing spy.

'At the moment, I'm just looking for answers to a few questions,' she says, laying a slight stress on the *I*. 'Have you seen any unusual activity around Sodis over the last two months?'

'No, nothing unusual. I've doubled security patrols around the perimeter, but we haven't seen any bandits at all.'

Tanta glances at Cole, who gives a fractional nod. She barely needs this confirmation of Smythe's honesty – he's clearly eager to be as involved in the investigation as possible. He hasn't fully answered her question, though.

'What about unusual behaviour from colleagues?' she asks. 'Unscheduled leave, bouts of unexplained sickness? Anything like that?'

'If you mean to suggest that one of my staff could be involved with the thefts,' Smythe says sharply, 'then you're on a hiding to nothing. We don't harbour traitors in Sodis.'

'I didn't mean to imply that you did,' Tanta says, 'and treachery isn't the only explanation for leaks. Sometimes, simple carelessness can—'

'I will not discuss this any further with you, agent. Sodis is above reproach. Besides, Director Kenway interviewed many of the workers here personally. He ruled out a leak himself.'

Tanta already knew that, of course, but she's still taken aback at the defensiveness of Smythe's response. 'In that case,' she continues, after a pause, 'it would be helpful if we could review the records of the UAVs that were attacked, if you have them.'

Smythe nods, a touch stiffly. 'I'll escort you down to the archives.'

'Aren't the records digital?' Cole asks.

'Of course they are,' Smythe snaps. 'But for security reasons, they can't be accessed remotely.' He can't forbear adding, 'You'll see no carelessness about classified information in *this* office.'

The archives are in the Logistics Office's basement, a vast, dim room with an exposed ceiling. It takes Tanta several seconds to get used to the darkness. Then Smythe clicks on an old-fashioned physical light switch and rows of strip lights blink on overhead, dazzling her again. The sides of the room are lined with floor to ceiling stacks, so densely packed that there is no room to move between them. The end of each unit of shelving is fitted with a crank; Smythe crosses to the nearest one and starts to turn it.

'The stacks are operated manually,' he explains. 'Outmoded, I know, but we don't have a city budget to work with here.'

There's a creaking sound as the shelves roll sideways, moving on runners set into the floor. When the gap between them has widened to about half a meter, Smythe folds himself into it like a hermit crab. Tanta cranes her neck; she can see him running his hands up and down the shelves, on which are stacked row upon row of boxes. He re-emerges a minute later, a data card pinched between finger and thumb.

'These are the details of all our shipments to the city for the last year,' he says.

He waves Tanta and Cole over to a couple of chairs and a

desk set against the wall by the door. Tanta runs through the contents of the data card in her 'scape's reader, filtering the readout to show information for the last two months. Columns of figures scroll before her eyes: all of Sodis's UAV shipments, along with the times they left the distribution centre and the times they were scheduled to arrive in the city. The stolen drones are highlighted in red. She passes the data card to Cole.

'Can you cross-reference this with the times the bandits' weapons were unlocked?' she murmurs. Smythe is still hovering behind them; he's busying himself with setting the shelves to rights, but she has a feeling he's listening.

While Cole compares the two sources of information, Tanta gets up and walks back into the stacks. The archives are bigger even than they first appeared; the strip lights Smythe turned on illuminate only a small portion of the room. She stops at the edge of the pool of light and peers out into what lies beyond. Shelves stretch away into the darkness. For all she knows, they could go on for miles.

She's about to step out into the gloom when a heavy hand on her shoulder makes her turn. Smythe is behind her. She almost pulls away from his touch – he moves more quietly than she was expecting, and she hadn't realised he was so close – but restrains herself.

'The archives are classified,' Smythe says. 'You can requisition individual files from me directly if you need them, but I can't let you wander around down here without an escort.'

'Are all of these precautions really necessary?' Cole asks.

It's the wrong thing to say. Smythe bristles. 'Sodis is not merely some regional haulage operation,' he says. 'We house the data centre for the entire Trade Division. Our engineers maintain the servers on the zeppelin itself. And you're standing in InTech's principal regional archive. The documents we store down here are highly sensitive.'

Smythe's reply sparks a memory – something Kenway said when he assigned Tanta to the distribution centre. *There has been unrest in the area before.* Sodis looks so dull, so unremarkable, that it's hard to imagine it ever having been a site of anything as interesting as 'unrest'. But Smythe's security measures – and his caginess – suggest otherwise.

Cole shrugs. 'I was just asking. I'm all done,' he adds. He gets up as he speaks, the chair scraping back against the concrete floor with a dull shriek.

Tanta returns to his side. 'What have you got?'

'I think we should talk about this elsewhere,' Cole mutters. 'You're not going to like it, and neither is Smythe.'

Chapter 20

Tanta manages to hold in her questions while Smythe shows them back up to the main office and into the car. Thankfully, it's a short trip to their accommodation. Their new flat is located in what passes for Sodis's town centre, a few blocks away. The building is yet another big grey box, indistinguishable from the ones to either side of it save for the AR marker that tells Tanta it's theirs.

The flat itself is much like the edifice that houses it – square and anonymous. It could be any one of a million furnished corporate lodgings. Tanta recognises the same fridge-freezer and plain wooden dining table that adorn her old flat in the city. They don't make the place feel any more like home, reminding her of the metropolis she has left behind without conjuring up any of its atmosphere.

She and Cole dump their bags in the hallway and then sweep the flat for bugs together, working swiftly through long practice. It's clean; Tanta is torn between relief and discomfort at the discovery. Being able to talk unobserved is a rare blessing, one she's learnt to treasure, but it's also another sign that Kenway really does intend to leave them here in the sticks to rot. Tanta is back within signal range, so he must have received the messages she sent while she and Cole were stuck on the road by now, but she has heard nothing from him – not even a query about the fate of the HGV.

Although the bandits are operating close to the distribution centre, it's clear that Kenway has assumed Sodis itself is a dead end – he wouldn't have sent Tanta and Cole here otherwise. At first glance, he would appear to be right. Kenway has already ruled out a leak in Sodis as the source of the bandits' intelligence; what can Tanta glean from the place that he hasn't discovered already? She has an advantage on Kenway, though: she and Cole have the weapons Tanta recovered from the dead bandits to help direct their investigation. Their encounter on the road nearly cost them their lives, but it was also a significant development in the case.

Kenway may have written her and Cole off, but Tanta is by no means so pessimistic about their chances. She *will* complete this assignment, and then perhaps the board will allow her to leave this concrete graveyard of a place and come home. Of course, before *that* can happen, she and Cole must figure out what to do about Harlow 2.0. The threat of the update still swirls in Tanta's thoughts like a gathering storm, but she averts her mind's eye firmly from the sight. One challenge at a time.

Cole has just finished checking the last pillow on the plush beige sofa for concealed cameras. He straightens up, and Tanta turns to him expectantly. 'What did you get from Smythe?' she asks.

Cole frowns. 'Well, I don't think he was lying to us about anything. He got pretty nervous when we were down in the stacks, though. Especially when you tried to explore.'

That confirms what Tanta already suspected. There's something odd about the Logistics Officer – his defensiveness and obsession with security both speak to a man with something to hide. She isn't sure yet whether that something is connected to the drone attacks, but it's a possibility she can't discount.

'What about the file he gave us? Did you find any links between the thefts and the logs from the bandits' weapons?'

'I did,' Cole replies. 'But not the ones I was expecting.'

He viewshares a graph with Tanta. It's covered in a cluster of dots, a few of which are standing proud of the others. 'I rigged this up while we were in the archives,' he says. 'It shows the relationship between the times the stolen trade shipments were sent out, and the times the bandits' weapons were activated. *These*' – he highlights the rogue data points – 'are instances when the weapons were unlocked, but no theft took place.'

Tanta peers at them. 'Could the bandits have been going after some other target at these points? Maybe a shipment from another corporation?'

'That's what I thought at first, too, but it's a strange pattern if so. Over 90% of the time, the data Smythe gave us matches the bandits' weapon activity very closely. If the bandits spend so much of their time and energy targeting InTech's supply lines, then it's more likely these anomalous results represent occasions when they were trying to do the same thing, but something went wrong.'

Tanta follows the logic. 'OK, so what went wrong?'

'That's the thing you're not going to like,' Cole replies. 'I had another look through Smythe's file, and this time I also checked the details of shipments that *weren't* stolen. A few of these turned out to be from UAVs that were never sent: they were entered into the trade servers, given a time slot and a serial number, but never shipped out from a warehouse. In all likelihood, they were cancelled at the last minute, but never removed from the system.'

Tanta only nods. She has an idea of where Cole is going with this now.

'When I cross-referenced the anomalous data points with the cancelled shipments,' he continues, 'I got a perfect match. At all of these times, a shipment was scheduled, and the bandits' weapons were unlocked *in anticipation*. Then, when no drone was sent out, they were locked again.'

Tanta can see why Cole wanted to wait till they were alone before dropping this bombshell. If whoever is controlling the bandits' weapons knows to unlock them the moment a UAV delivery is scheduled, they must have access to the trade servers themselves – or know someone who does. A thought occurs to her: another thing the bandits had known in advance was that she would be in the HGV they ambushed.

'Do the trade servers store records of delivery vehicle security escorts?' she asks.

The same conclusion she has reached is written across Cole's face. He nods, his expression grim. 'Most shipments don't have an escort, but the ones that do all have a note of the lead guardian's name on their manifest. I think we can guess whose name was on the manifest for the truck we rode in on.'

'But Kenway ruled out a leak,' Tanta says slowly.

She calls up the meagre case files Reet sent her yesterday evening as she speaks. They confirm what Smythe and Reet have both told her already: the first thing Kenway did to investigate the thefts was an elimination test, where he suspended entire departments of the Trade Division one by one to see if the attacks continued in their absence. They did – and everyone in Sodis took their turn, Smythe included.

Cole shrugs. 'Looks like Kenway was wrong. Unless you can think of another way the bandits know where InTech's drones are going to be before they even leave the warehouse.'

Tanta thinks about it. Kenway's elimination test was a smart way to detect a mole among Sodis's staff, but there are scenarios it hasn't ruled out, such as the possibility someone from outside the corporation is hacking into the Trade Division's data centre. It's vanishingly unlikely – InTech's cutting edge security protocols make such incursions almost impossible – but there's a way they can be sure.

'The bandits may have some other way of accessing the data centre,' she says, 'something we haven't considered yet. If we could monitor the servers in real time, during an attack, we could find out for ourselves.'

'I could do that,' Cole replies. 'I see two issues, though: one, Smythe will never go for it, and two, how are we going to know when the next theft will be?'

He has a point on both counts. Smythe has made it clear that any internal investigation into Sodis itself is something he won't tolerate. Tanta could try arguing the toss with him, but she doesn't want to take the risk. If he *is* involved in the attacks, then the last thing she wants to do is tip him off to her suspicions. Her face heats. She has a solution to both of Cole's problems, but it's the kind of thing he's likely to tease her for.

'We need to track the bandits on two fronts,' she says. 'If I can tempt them into making an attack on a fake delivery, and you can monitor that delivery on the trade servers, then one way or another, we'll find out how they're getting their information.' She pauses. 'We only need to tell Smythe about the first part of that plan, though. My agent privileges should grant me access to the data centre – I can let you in myself.'

Cole smirks at her. 'For an ICRD agent, a lot of your plans involve circumventing corporate authority.'

She glares back. 'Pot, kettle.'

'My first point still stands, though,' he pursues. 'Getting access to the data centre is only half the challenge. How do we know the bandits will even attack the fake shipment you send out? We still don't know anything about how they pick their targets.'

'We know one thing,' Tanta corrects. 'And they won't be attacking this shipment because of its cargo. They'll attack it because my name will be on the manifest.'

Chapter 21

Fliss already has a scheme in mind, and a rough idea of how she's going to pull it off. The only thing her half-baked plan needs now is a distraction. Luckily, the stranger gave her the start of one himself when he instructed her, Josh and Sonia to load the drones into the boot of his car. This is something the crew do regularly, and it was a time-consuming process even before they lost two of their members. They hunt a lot of drones in a week, and the business of taking them apart, boxing them up, and stacking them in the boot causes a bustle of talk and activity that Fliss can exploit.

She takes Sonia into her tent to get the drones, sending Josh away to clean and oil the weapons. He may be part of the crew, but Fliss doesn't trust him enough to bring him in on this. He's always been reckless – never a good quality when there's plotting to be done – but there's a new side to him emerging lately that Fliss likes even less. She keeps thinking of the expression on Josh's face when he shot up that corporate car and killed the guard inside. He gets something from the crew's partnership with the strangers that the others never have, something disturbing, and Fliss can't see him being willing to give it up.

The drones, already disassembled, are stacked in two crates

against the side wall of Fliss's tent. Sonia goes to pick up the nearer one, but Fliss lays a hand on her shoulder, stopping her.

'What's up?' Sonia asks.

Fliss zips the tent closed before she replies. She can't do what she has in mind without Sonia's help, but now that the time has come to ask for it, she's afraid. She and Sonia have known each other since they were kids in Gatwick – she's been in the crew since the beginning, but Fliss is still uncertain whether she'll be on board with this plan. If Sonia balks, the whole thing is dead in the water, and if she peaches on Fliss to the stranger, then Fliss is dead, too. There's no one Fliss trusts more than Sonia, but in their line of work, trust has its limits.

She takes a breath, steeling herself. 'Sonia, I have a game in mind,' she murmurs. 'Are you in?'

As Tanta expected, Smythe is pleased with her plan – the half she tells him about, anyway. It 'takes the fight to the bandits', as he puts it, and seems to appeal to his idea of spycraft. She's back in the Logistics Office for the second time that day, struck once more by the stark contrast between it and the sleek chrome-and-glass headquarters of the ICRD.

'Yes, yes, a sting operation; I see the logic.' The Logistics Officer is nodding, his bristly chin resting in his hands. 'And then, with a squad of guardians in tow, you'll take them out?'

Tanta hesitates. But the more involved Smythe feels with her side of the investigation, the less likely he is to ask awkward questions about what Cole will be doing. 'Going alone will give me a better chance of remaining undetected,' she replies. 'The plan isn't to attack the bandits immediately. Once I've located them, I'll place a tracker on their vehicle and trace them back to their base of operations.'

'Why wait?' Smythe asks. 'The board want results, presumably, not excuses.'

Tanta resists the urge to sigh; this shouldn't need explaining, even to a civilian like Smythe. 'The bandits who attacked me and my partner are likely just one cell of a much larger operation. Wiping them out wouldn't stop the thefts, but tracking them might lead us back to other groups, or to their employers. Waiting a day or two to gather intelligence will strengthen our hand, not weaken it.'

Smythe's eyes gleam. 'Or you could just take one of them captive. There are other ways of gathering intelligence. But you're the expert,' he concedes, in a tone that says he isn't convinced on that point himself. 'Going alone is out of the question, though. You'll need backup if things go south. I'll come with you.'

That, Tanta wasn't expecting – though perhaps she should have anticipated it. 'Will that be possible, given your responsibilities at Sodis?' she asks.

'I'm sure the pencil pushers can spare me for an evening,' Smythe barks. 'This is real work – the kind of thing my squad and I used to do all the time.'

Tanta takes the liberty of doubting that, though she doesn't voice her scepticism aloud. The Logistics Officer isn't even a guardian anymore; to say that he's untrained for this sort of mission is an understatement. She could refuse him: she has a feeling it would cause fireworks, but he can't force her to take him on an ICRD assignment. On the other hand, bringing him along could actually work out in her and Cole's favour. Tracking the bandits might give them useful intelligence, but it's not as important a part of Tanta's plan as Cole's investigation into the trade servers. Anything she can do to draw Smythe's attention from her partner and his task, she should.

'*If* you come,' she says, 'you need to respect that I'll be acting as your team leader. Protocol may have changed on some points since the last time you did this kind of work: you'll have to follow my orders exactly.'

Smythe dismisses her warning with a wave of his hand. 'Of course, of course. I'll take my lead from you.'

It's not an encouraging response, but Tanta nods her assent. She doesn't trust Smythe's professionalism – or his motives – but that's all the more reason, perhaps, to keep him close.

'Now,' Smythe continues, 'let's talk terrain.' He brings up an AR map of the region outside the distribution centre, which he arranges across his desk with a flick of the wrist. 'I have some routes in mind...'

Tanta settles into the impromptu tactical briefing with as good grace as possible. It's another unpleasant surprise, but it looks like there's no helping it. Smythe drones on, and she fixes her face in an expression of polite interest, preparing herself for what looks likely to be a lengthy discussion.

A quarter of an hour after she entered Fliss's tent, Sonia emerges alone. She shoves two crates through the opening, then picks one of them up, staggering a little under its weight. Josh wanders over.

'Where's our glorious leader?' he asks.

'In her tent.' Sonia lowers her voice. 'She's crying.'

Josh snorts. 'I'll keep out her way, then. Those the drones?'

'Yeah. Give me a hand, would you? They're fucking heavy.'

Their voices drift to Fliss's ears, muffled by the wooden walls of the crate in Sonia's arms. She's crammed inside like a sack of potatoes, her knees hugged up to her chest and her head tucked into her chin. Sonia has arranged some packing material on top of her and closed the lid over her head. It's cramped and airless inside, but from without, there's nothing to give away her hiding spot. She waits in the sawdust scented darkness, her breathing shallow. The box jolts up and down as Sonia walks, grazing Fliss's elbow painfully with each step. There's a couple of muted thuds as she and the other crate are placed into the bottom of the car, followed by the much louder bang of the boot being closed.

After that, Fliss can't hear much of anything. Sounds are dulled by the double barrier of the boot and the crate, making her feel as though she is hearing the voices outside from underwater. If the man asks where she has got to, he must be satisfied by Sonia's response, because after a few minutes Fliss hears another thud–click as his door closes. There's a low growl and the car begins to thrum. She's off.

The crates in the boot knock against each other as the car rumbles through the wasteland, bumping and jarring Fliss at every rut in the uneven ground. She holds herself as still as she can, taking deep breaths to keep the nausea at bay, and tries to plot her next move. As flung together as her plan has been so far, she's thought even less about what comes next. All she knows is that within the strangers' base is the switch that controls the crew's weapons, and if she can find it, she can put the three of them back in charge of their own fortunes.

Fliss isn't sure what the switch will look like, but she knows enough about the corporations and their technology to realise that it probably won't be anything like the kind you'd find on a solar lamp. It's likelier to be some kind of touchscreen, or even a virtual button, something that's only accessible by corporate headware. She thinks through the different scenarios, planning her response to each in turn. If the switch is something small and physical, then Fliss can steal it. If it's big, or virtual, then perhaps she can jam it or break it. She has brought her handgun with her, tucked into its holster on her belt: whatever form the switch takes, and whatever Fliss ends up doing to it, she'll be able to test instantly whether or not it has worked. And if things really go tits-up and she gets discovered, the gun will also come in handy to clock one of the strangers with before she legs it.

With their weapons back under their own control, she and Sonia – and Josh, if he's minded to stick with them – would be free again. They could run from the crosshairs of the corporation that hired them, and the corporation it pitted them against, and start over somewhere else. Where exactly they'd go is another matter Fliss hasn't considered yet. Certainly, they'd have to leave the wasteland; perhaps they'd even have to flee the country. The man told Fliss that if she reneged on her bargain, the crew would be hunted wherever Thoughtfront had territory, but even with that threat hanging over her head, Fliss is sure that they could find some turf to call their own. Anywhere would be better than where they are now, with two corporations breathing down their necks, and the stranger's gun to their heads.

After an hour or so, the car turns onto a smooth, corporate-maintained road. This affords Fliss some relief from the seasick motion of the crate, but by this point, she's facing a bigger problem. It was cold outside when she left the camp, but now the sun is up, and the boot is starting to boil. Beads of sweat trickle down her sides and prickle uncomfortably on her skin. She hasn't eaten or drunk anything since last night – she's thirsty, and there's a dizzy ache in her head that's making it hard to think.

She cracks open the lid of her hiding place, in search of fresh air, but the ceiling of the boot is too low for her to even sit up fully. She catches herself wondering how much air there is in its stifling confines, before batting the thought away. If she lets herself think like that, she'll panic, and then she's liable to find out the answer to that question the hard way. She forces herself to take small, shallow breaths, like sips of water. It doesn't do anything to help the spinning in her head, but telling herself that she's rationing whatever air she has left at least stops the seeds of hysteria from taking root.

Time stretches and warps in the blackness. Fliss lies as still as possible, feeling the walls of the crate pressing in against her. She's drowsy, but afraid that if she drifts off, she won't wake up again. She fights against the tug of sleep with pain, digging her nails into the palms of her hands.

After what feels like hours (though it's impossible to tell), the car turns off the road. The crunch of twigs and leaves beneath the tyres jerks Fliss back to full consciousness. She has been lying in a daze, one arm flopped halfway out of the crate like a dying fish. Awareness of the danger she's in filters through to her slowly. The car is slowing – she needs to hide. She drags her arm back inside the crate as their speed drops to a crawl. It's all she can do to let the lid fall closed – the confinement is becoming unbearable. If the stranger were to open the boot and discover her right now, she'd be so grateful for the rush of air and space that she doesn't think she'd care.

The car rolls to a stop. There's a thud, then more crunching: footsteps, coming her way. Fliss holds her breath, coiled in the bottom of the crate like a snake, but the footsteps continue right past the boot, halting a little distance away.

'It's Hardinger,' the stranger says, speaking to someone Fliss can't see.

'How did it go?' The second voice is distorted and alien. Fliss can't be sure if it's the woman who accompanied the stranger the first time she met him, but it seems a safe bet.

'They failed,' the man – Hardinger – replies.

'Come down. We'll talk inside.'

There's a screeching, metallic sound, like a gate opening on rusty hinges, then silence. Fliss strains her ears until they ring, but can hear nothing more: Hardinger has gone. The woman, too. It takes a moment for her fuzzy thoughts to grasp just how bad this is. She had assumed that Hardinger would unload the car immediately and carry the crates into his base. Fliss was planning to sneak away and begin her search for the switch after he'd brought her inside. Instead, he's left them in the boot – and her with them.

She pushes the lid off the crate, light-headed with terror. The thought that she only needed to hold out in this airless box until the car had stopped was the one thing holding her panic at bay; now that they're parked, and she's still trapped, claustrophobia closes in. She forces both arms through the narrow gap at the top and reaches for the door of the boot, scrabbling at it like a mouse trapped in a wall. Her hands encounter nothing but the ridged metal of the car's chassis. She abandons her measured sips of air, her breathing becoming loud and rapid. She's stuck in here – she could *die* in here. She's going to pass out and when the man comes back he'll find her body and—

A soft *thud* brings Fliss back to herself. In her struggle, something has slipped free from her jeans pocket and wedged itself between her and the back of the crate. She reaches for it, blind hands patting herself down until they make contact with something smooth and hard. It's the smartphone – the one the strangers gave her. She'd forgotten she had it with her. She pushes the button on the side with trembling fingers. Weak blue light floods the interior of the crate. When she shines it through the crack at the top and into the boot, it reveals what her frantic search in the dark could not: a plastic lever, just above the lock. She strains towards it, yanks it, and the boot pops open.

Fliss scrambles free of the crate, slithers out of the boot and collapses on the ground, dragging in deep, grateful lungfuls of air. For a delicious half-minute she lies still, letting her panic ebb away and enjoying the cold, damp earth pressing against her skin. She won't allow herself to savour her freedom any longer than that: Hardinger and the woman could come back at any moment. She staggers to her feet and closes the boot. It's only then that she looks around her for the first time.

The car is in a clearing in the middle of a forest – an ancient one, with a thick canopy that paints the ground with shadows. Fliss scans the oaks and yews, the undergrowth and climbing ivy, at a loss. Hardinger works for Thoughtfront: she was expecting his base of operations to be in London. In her plan, she had envisioned it as some kind of corporate office block or laboratory – a·building she could search, one room at a time, until she found what she needed. This wood has no human boundaries or purpose that Fliss can see: she has no idea where to start.

She stands still and listens, alert for any sign of human activity. The only thing she can hear, close at hand, is a high, threatening buzz. The noise sets her teeth on edge: there must be a wasp nest nearby. She edges around the side of the car, moving slowly for fear of disturbing it…

And leaps back in horror, a cry of alarm dying in her throat. Her first thought is that the mass in the centre of the clearing is a swarm of bees the size of cats. The ground and the air are black with them, immense bodies weaving in and out in a complicated dance. Then Fliss spots the rotor blades and the black, spindly legs, and her eyes reprocess what she's seeing. The clearing is swarming not with bees but with drones – and not just any drones.

Many of them have been modded with additional hardware – Fliss catches sight of mounted guns, long nozzles, and cameras, appearing for brief flashes before they vanish within the throng – but the basic design is one she has encountered hundreds of times before. She knows, now, what Hardinger and his colleague have been doing with all the UAVs the crew have captured for them.

They've turned them into a flying army.

Smythe suggests sending the decoy truck out at dusk, giving them the rest of the afternoon to prepare. Tanta approves of this, the only downside being that the Logistics Officer's idea of preparation runs directly counter to her own. She needs to let Cole into the data centre so he can get to work on the second half of their plan, but Smythe keeps her in his office for the best part of two hours, poring over maps and drilling her in the details of a strategy that she came up with.

At long last, he works his way around to the only essential order of business on his agenda: creating a manifest for the fake delivery truck and entering it into the system. As soon as he's done, Tanta murmurs a goodbye and tries to slip away. She's halfway out of the door when Smythe seizes her arm.

'Before you go,' he says, 'we ought to discuss gear. Sodis has an equipment room with some firearms and vehicles we might find useful for an assignment of this nature.'

Tanta forces a smile. 'I should brief my partner on these developments first, but—'

'Nonsense. This will only take a second.'

Smythe is already towing her out of his office. Something dangerous stirs in Tanta. She'd expect this sense of entitlement to her time from a manager, but Smythe has no authority over her and she's growing ever more tempted to remind him of that fact. She stifles the urge to jerk out of his grip. Smythe could make her and Cole's stay in Sodis very difficult if he chose to; she needs to keep things civil.

Tanta knows enough about Smythe by now that she's not surprised when he leads her down a corridor at the back of the building and into a room like a military bunker, with no windows and a steel-reinforced door. There's a garage door at the back, too, a rolling steel shutter big enough to drive a truck through. The equipment room has enough assault rifles and riot shields to quell a small army and, in pride of place, three armoured tactical vehicles. They're an old model, similar to the one Yas was driving, though in far better condition. Someone – Smythe, probably – has spent a lot of time polishing their black chassis. They gleam like oversized stag beetles, and they look about as out of place. In fact, the room and all the equipment in it would be more appropriate on the front lines of the Meltdown Wars than in an administrative building in a regional logistics centre.

Smythe opens his mouth. Tanta has nightmare visions of the encomium he's doubtless about to deliver on the racks of weapons, armour and crowd control equipment that surround them.

'None of this gear will be necessary,' she says. 'All we need is a GPS tracker. Do you have those?'

The Logistics Officer deflates, but gestures towards the back of the room. There's a worktable back there with a kind of junk drawer of superannuated ICRD gadgets. By dint of much searching, Tanta finds what she's looking for – a serviceable magnetic tracker that she can attach to the underside of the bandits' car. She takes a sheaf of flex cuffs, too, in case of emergencies.

'What do you think about bringing a couple of assault rifles along?' Smythe asks.

'We'll take handguns. Weapons of this –' Tanta searches for a tactful word '– calibre will be too bulky for a stealth mission. As will the armoured cars,' she adds, before Smythe can suggest they take one of those, too. 'I need to tell my partner about our plan now,' she continues, desperate to forestall the Logistics Officer before he picks up another weapon or, worse, suggests another meeting.

Smythe frowns at her. 'Are you sure you're treating this seriously enough, Agent? If I were in charge of an assignment of this importance, I'd conduct a more careful examination of the tactical gear at my disposal.'

Tanta breathes in through her nose. 'You're not, though, Logistics Officer: I am. So you're going to have to let me be the judge of what an assignment of this importance requires.'

She walks quickly to the door. She's already been blunter than she intended; if she doesn't leave now, she might say something she can't take back.

The drones have made Fliss's legs go weak and watery. A single UAV is a quirky sight – an oversized mechanical insect; a swarm of them is deeply disturbing. She edges behind an oak tree, putting its wide trunk between her and the murmurous cloud. Perhaps if she can circle the clearing, hiding in the treeline, she can get behind the swarm and see what they're guarding. She has only taken a few tentative steps into the woods, though, when she hears the screeching again. She throws herself back against the trunk, pulse pounding. Voices rise over the humming of the drones; the strangers have come back.

Fliss peers through the tree's thick branches. Hardinger and the woman have reappeared as suddenly as they vanished. They are walking towards the car, the cloud of drones hovering in the woman's wake like a train of ravens. Fliss curses them both. When she needed Hardinger to open the boot, he was nowhere to be found, and now he's returned just as she was about to start her search in earnest.

'—disrupted some extremely sensitive operations of ours last summer, destroying plans that had taken years to put in place,' Hardinger is saying. His voice, usually so hard and cold, has a wheedling note of unease in it. He opens the boot as he talks, lifting out one of the crates inside. 'If we have another shot, we should take it.'

The woman watches him, the drones hovering around her

head. She doesn't offer to help. 'There's no need to be coy, Hardinger – we know more about those "sensitive operations" than you think. And we have our own plans for dealing with the CorpWard, but if you want to go after her again, be my guest.'

Hardinger turns back towards her. 'You said she'd be alone this time?'

'Yes.'

'And you're sure of your intelligence?'

'The Brokerage is always sure.'

Fliss listens to their conversation, interested despite herself. She had always assumed the strangers both worked for Thoughtfront, but by the way they talk to one another, that doesn't seem to be the case. She's never heard of the Brokerage before – it could be another corp. Perhaps Hardinger and the woman have made a bargain of their own.

'Her leaving Sodis so soon after she arrived is suspicious, however,' the woman continues. 'It could be she's trying to draw you out.'

'That's irrelevant,' Hardinger snaps. 'The subcontractors are expendable.'

His words snap into sudden, terrible focus. Fliss's interest sublimates into alarm. Hardinger must be talking about the girl he sent Fliss and the crew to kill this morning – and he wants them to try again. All thoughts of finding the switch are forced to the back of her mind. Taking control of the crew's weapons won't matter a damn if the crew are all dead. She can find this place again if she has to; right now, she has to get back.

The woman shrugs. Then she takes a phone from her pocket, the clone of Fliss's own. 'I'll send the alert out now, then.'

Fliss realises what's about to happen a second before it does. She's still holding her own phone tightly in one hand. She fumbles it around, jabbing desperately at the buttons on the side, the cracked screen, but she has never needed to switch it off before – the only thing she's ever used it for is to check the coordinates the strangers send. She's about to hurl it into the trees when it starts to beep.

The sound pierces the swarm of drones like a balloon. They scatter, exploding out and into the trees with terrifying speed. Fliss shoves the phone into her pocket and runs, but she's only made it a few steps when a mechanical body bobs down in front of her. The drone has two misshapen black eyes boring directly into her own. One is a camera; the other is the barrel of a gun.

From behind the tree, Fliss hears the woman's distorted voice. 'It appears we have company.'

Fliss dives, throwing herself under the drone and rolling to her feet on the other side of it. Then she ducks her head and bolts. She hears the cough of the gun an instant later. The blow knocks her face-first into the dirt, but the body armour the strangers gave her shields her from the worst of the damage. Adrenaline picks her back up and forces her into a sprint. She's not dead yet, and as long as she's not dead, she has to keep running. She zigzags through the woods, chunks of bark and dirt exploding to either side of her as bullets pepper the air. Her head is tucked into her chest, her shoulders drawn up around her ears. She runs bent over, making herself as small a target as she can.

The buzzing intensifies as more drones join the hunt. Fliss risks a glance behind her: they're flying low to the ground in an arrow formation, darting through the trees. She thinks there's five of them following her, though it's hard to tell. She tries to make for the parts of the wood where the undergrowth is thickest, so that the drones are forced to slow down as their sensors identify a route through the tangled vegetation. It's hard – she's going so fast that branches keep rushing up to meet her and she has to veer out of their path – but she has lived her whole life among the woods and urban wreckage of the wasteland and is used to such treacherous terrain.

Even with this advantage on her side, though, Fliss knows she's fighting a losing battle. One drone falls to her stratagem, snared by a thicket of brambles that stop its rotors much as the net gun would have done, but the other four glide right over its twitching carapace and keep coming. Fliss's chest is burning with the effort of her sprint, and her back aches from where the first drone shot her. She thinks of what Hardinger said about Thoughtfront and its facial recognition technology. The drones know who she is, and they won't stop until she's dead. They are tireless, unerring, inexorable – and she can't run forever.

Her thoughts have distracted her; a branch smacks Fliss in the chest. She stumbles, arms pinwheeling to keep her balance, and a sharp pain explodes in her left ear. She darts a hand up reflexively to the side of her face: it comes away bloody. Terror whines in her ears as the drones close in. Fliss shakes her head, clearing the fear away. The near miss has rattled her, but it has also given her an idea. Rather than resuming her weaving course through the trees, she grabs the branch that just hit her with both hands and hauls herself up and onto it, climbing into the canopy.

Fliss has climbed enough trees as a lookout that she can let instinct guide her. She scales the tree – a sprawling yew – with practiced ease, leaping from limb to limb as she goes so as to put the branching trunk in between her and her pursuers. Bullets thud into the red-brown bark, but the tree is huge, and its broad boughs conceal her from the drone's cameras.

Twigs and needle-like leaves scratch at Fliss's arms and wreak red agony on what remains of her ear, but the drones fare worse. They have been flying low precisely to avoid the dense canopy of the trees. There's a crash as one of them smashes into the yew's thick foliage, its rotors making a buzz-saw hum as it struggles to free itself. Another follows, and a third gets tangled in a branch that catches in its landing gear. It spins on the spot like an insect with an injured wing, spitting bullets at the ground.

Fliss climbs on past all of this, gritting her teeth through the pain in the side of her head. The limb she's on branches and narrows, so she kicks off her shoes and continues barefoot, using the soles of her feet to grip the peeling bark. She doesn't stop until she's so deep within the tree's ancient crown that it's difficult to see the world outside. Here, she pauses. The yew's trunk is pitted with hollows and she drops into one, letting the cavity between the branches conceal her. She is in the green heart of the tree, a sap-scented cocoon of bark. It's as good a place as any to make her last stand.

The last drone comes on with more care than its fallen fleet mates. Fliss can hear it buzzing beyond the curtain of leaves. It fires a volley of exploratory shots into the foliage, but they whizz by over her head. After that, it stops shooting and whirs to itself, as if in thought.

That's right, you fucker, Fliss thinks. *You're going to have to come in and get me.*

She crouches in the hollow, shadows stippling her face, and waits. There's a ragged gap in the tree's crown to her right, a beam of sunlight slanting through it. After ten minutes, the light is blocked out by the body of the drone as it lowers itself through the narrow gap. It hovers in the green shade, the twin eyes of its camera and its gun swivelling as it searches among the leaves and branches for a human face.

Fliss rears up in its blind spot, her handgun raised above her head. She'd thought this morning that she could clock someone with it in a pinch; she wasn't expecting to use it to smash a drone to bits, but it works for that just as well. She brings the gun down on the flight computer in the centre of the drone's carapace with a sharp crack. The drone manages to get one more shot off, but its gun is facing away from her. Fliss pounds her own weapon up and down on its plastic shell like she's grinding spices in a mortar, working some of the terror out of her system. When she's finished, the drone is a crushed mess of exposed wires and twitching rotors.

Fliss leaves it in the hollow of the tree and climbs back down to the ground. Her breathing is laboured; there's a throbbing ache in her back, and blood running freely down the side of her face. She isn't full of bullets, though, and that has to count for something.

Now that she is safe, for a given value of safe, her thoughts turn back to Sonia and Josh. She has to warn them. She pulls the phone from her pocket, checking the details the woman sent her. The second attack on the girl is scheduled for tonight. Fliss swears; it took her hours to get to this forest by car! Now, she's on foot – bare feet, at that – and the day is over halfway done. By the time she makes it back to their camp on the downs, the crew will have already left.

She knows where they're going, though. Fliss checks the map again: her own blue marker blinks in the middle of a forest to the south of the city. The red arrow of the crew's new target is some distance away, but closer than Ditchling. It will be a long walk, but Fliss can make it there if she leaves now. She gives herself a moment to catch her breath, steeling herself for the journey ahead. Then, at long last, she takes her mother's advice. She turns her back on the forest – on Thoughtfront, the Brokerage, and their cruel machines – and she runs, as far and as fast as she can.

Chapter 22

Tanta is shut away in the Logistics Office for so long that Cole is beginning to think they'll have to delay their sting operation till tomorrow. That's not ideal: Jeanie wants to brief them tomorrow, and they're unlikely to have time to help her *and* track the bandits. He's considering sending Tanta a message to this effect when he hears hurried footsteps in the corridor outside their flat and she walks in.

'I don't have long,' she says. 'Smythe's bound to want me back in a minute for another "tactical briefing".'

'He's on board with the plan, then?' Cole asks.

Tanta pulls a very un-Tanta like face, rolling her eyes. 'Too on board, if anything. He's coming with me into the field tonight.'

'And here was me thinking you and I were partners for life. I'm hurt.'

She shoots him a look. 'Come on. We have to get going.'

They walk to the data centre; it isn't far. There's no way Cole would have been able to find it on his own — all the buildings in Sodis look alike to him — but Tanta was paying more attention during Smythe's guided tour than he was. It's a huge tower, with no windows and only one door — a dingy service entrance for maintenance personnel. The lack of windows suggests that the building operates under a lights-out protocol — common practice for InTech's data centres. Everything inside will be fully automated. This is good for Cole in that there will be no staff around to notice or object to his presence, but bad in that he'll be working in the dark.

There's an AR keypad shimmering in the air in front of the building. Tanta uses her agent override to bypass the lock, and the door clicks open.

'I'll check in with you when I can,' she says, 'but I need to keep an eye on Smythe, so we'll have to keep chatter to a minimum. I'm sending you the ID code for the manifest now.'

'Thanks,' Cole says. He backs inside. Tanta is framed in the light from the doorway, watching him in. 'Hey, good luck,' he says.

'You too.'

She closes the door, then, sealing Cole into a darkness that at first seems total. After a few minutes (which he spends standing very still, afraid of walking into or off the edge of something), his eyes adjust to the gloom and he sees that there are dim lights running along the floor.

The place is a labyrinth of data, rows of servers like corridors stretching away into the blackness. Cole looks up and sees more – the floors and ceilings are made of perforated metal to improve airflow. The whole centre is cool as a walk-in refrigerator; Cole's skin prickles, his flesh coming out in goosebumps. *Now, where to start?*

The servers are highly secure, but most of their safeguards are designed to protect against remote-access hackers. Now that Cole is actually inside the building, getting into the system should be simple. All he needs to do is find an MbOS port. In this dark maze of servers, that's a challenge in itself, but there must be one around somewhere – InTech's engineers need a way to physically access the system in case of problems. It will be somewhere that's relatively easy to get to, so Cole begins his search at the edges of the room. He takes his time, working his way up one row and down the next. When he has searched the whole of the ground floor, he finds a metal access staircase bolted onto the far wall, climbs it, and repeats the process one storey up.

He finds the port at last, attached to a console at the back of the room on the second floor. There's a rickety old office chair plonked in front of it, the data centre's one concession to the comfort of its engineers. Cole sits down, slips the port over his eyes, and checks out the system's innards. The labyrinth inside the servers is far vaster and more complex than the room they're stored in. This data centre handles InTech's trade and logistics operations for the entire region, and it takes Cole a while to adjust to the scale of it. He's used to working with the Inscape system – a complex beast in its own right, but small and contained compared to a data centre that handles millions of queries a second.

Once he's become acclimatised, Cole sets to work, instructing the data centre's VI to send him details of all the Inscape accounts that have access to the trade servers. It's a huge number, comprising most of the people in the distribution centre and thousands of others besides – everyone in InTech's Trade Division, for starters. As a list of suspects, it's too large to be helpful – searching through it would be a lot like diving into the ocean to fish for minnows – but Cole has several ways of cutting it down.

First, he excludes all the sleepers. The Trade Division employs thousands of them, as warehouse operatives and shelf-stackers, mostly. While they're at work, they are linked into the trade servers at all times, processing a constant stream of data. They're also unconscious, their bodies filling orders and organising stock as directed by the sleeper rig in each warehouse that transmits them their instructions. A single delivery manifest entered on the InTech trade servers could pass through hundreds, if not thousands, of sleepers' routers as it is logged, packed up and sent off. These irrelevant transactions will only obscure the kind of suspicious activity Cole is looking for; sleepers are too low-level to have the security clearance to view sensitive trade data in their waking lives, so he can safely eliminate them as suspects.

Next, he turns to the ghost accounts. When an InTech employee transfers to another division or retires, their account is simply removed from whatever databases, buildings and servers they had access to. When someone has died in post, however, the sysadmins can get lazy – or sentimental. A dead person can't pose a security threat, so there's no need to revoke their clearance. In some cases, deactivated accounts can hang around in a system for years. When Cole worked in the Black Box, he'd sometimes see the account of a neurotech who suffered an aneurysm on the job popping up on employee lists, a grisly digital spectre. Some of the other techs in the office had been fond of him and wanted to keep him around. The gesture always struck Cole as more creepy than affectionate. Even dead, the guy couldn't clock out.

With the sleepers and the ghost accounts gone, Cole is pleased – and a little unsettled – to see that the size of the list has more than halved. He wasn't expecting to cut out so many suspects in a single stroke, and while it's progress, it's also a depressing reminder of how many people in The Trade Division have literally worked until they dropped. It's what InTech demands of its employees, of course. Only the very best paid wagers can afford to retire before they're forced to bow out due to ill health or incapacity. Many never do.

<<I'm all set up,>> he sends to Tanta. She responds with a mental nod.

Next, he enters the ID code for the fake manifest Tanta sent him. Instantly, the details of the 'delivery' flash before his eyes. The ID number is followed by Tanta's name, a route code, and a delivery status bar, which currently reads *pending*. He places these details on one side of the MbOS port's viewing area, and his list of Inscape accounts on the other.

<<Alert me if any of the accounts on this list access the details of this delivery,>> he instructs the VI.

If one of his suspects so much as glances at the manifest, he'll know about it.

This done, Cole adjusts his position, settling himself more comfortably in the old office chair. He could be in for a long wait.

Tanta and Smythe leave at nightfall, as planned. Tanta needs to keep a close eye on her surroundings, so she instructs the car to set out at a crawl. It drives through the gates of the distribution centre at sunset, a mile ahead of the empty HGV they're using as bait. The dawdling pace grates on Tanta's nerves. She has nothing to say to Smythe, but this doesn't stop him from pointing out every tall building, hill, or particularly large rock they pass, as if a bandit might be lurking behind each one.

Tanta finds his interruptions annoying and distracting but they're not the worst of it. The long journey is the first stretch of time she's had to herself since her and Cole's meeting with Jeanie that morning, and the thinking space isn't welcome to her. The freedom fighter said she'd have more information for them tomorrow afternoon. Tomorrow is fast approaching, and Tanta has no more idea about how to deal with Jeanie and Harlow 2.0 than she did before.

'Did you see that flash?' Smythe asks, startling Tanta's thoughts away. She looks out the window again, annoyed with herself. If the Logistics Officer has spotted a sign of the bandits she missed, she must be losing her touch. The HGV is still lumbering safely along behind them, though. Their own car is driving off-road now, parallel to and ahead of the truck. The aim is to spot the bandits before they spot the HGV, then get in close while they're attacking it and place the bug on their getaway car. Their route is through overgrown fields, but in the distance, Tanta can see the remains of a pre-Meltdown settlement, its buildings looming shadows in the night.

The truck will drive past it – Tanta was careful to plot a route that stuck as far as possible to open ground, to give the bandits fewer places to hide. Still, if Tanta were going to try and ambush a lorry, this is probably the place she'd pick. She squints, enhancing the view before her and zooming in on the details.

Before the Meltdown, the city was a lot bigger than it is now, sprawling outwards for many miles in a wide skirt of suburbs. Those suburbs were all abandoned long ago, but their bones remain. This settlement is better-preserved than most, and Tanta doesn't like the look of it. It didn't appear on her maps, which tend to have scant information on pre-Meltdown structures in general; now she sees it, she wishes she'd plotted a different route for the truck. The buildings offer too much cover, and they're taller than she'd like.

One in particular stands out, a large, concrete cuboid. Its sides are open to the elements, but crisscrossed with metal girders, giving it the appearance of being covered in scaffolding. Through this metal fencing, Tanta can make out a dark interior, filled with stone support columns. The structure is about half the height of the Ward House – plenty tall enough to allow someone on the top of it to shoot at a vehicle on the road below.

As Tanta zooms in on it further, in fact, she *does* see someone standing on top of it, as if her premonition has summoned them into existence. They are balancing a rocket launcher on the lip that runs around the edge of the building. Tanta has to give credit where it's due. Smythe's 'flash' was more than just a trick of the light.

'Did you see it?' Smythe asks again. 'What is it?'

'It's them.' Tanta captures the image and pings it to Cole. <<We have a visual,>> she sends. <<They took the bait.>>

She inputs a few commands on the car's AR interface, ordering it to speed up. Now they know where the bandits are going to strike, the sooner she catches up with them, the better.

Time hangs heavy in the windowless confines of the data centre, with nothing but whirring servers for company. Cole gets one alert from the VI early on, when Smythe himself accesses the listing, then nothing.

While he waits, he examines the servers for bugs and weaknesses, leaving the VI to notify him of any more activity on the manifest. Tanta trusts Smythe about as far as she can throw him – which in her case is probably pretty far, but the point still stands. He was nervous when Tanta asked him about the archives during their meeting this morning; it's possible that there's some security flaw within the data centre that he's been hushing up. Cole's probing doesn't bear out this hypothesis, however. The centre's security protocols are up to date, and his sweep for system errors and data breaches returns zero results. Either Smythe has covered up the breaches in a way Cole can't detect (and Cole is almost certain this is impossible) or the bandits really do have someone on the inside.

After the first hour, Cole has run out of avenues to explore. After three hours, he's beginning to think the plan is going to be a bust. Perhaps the bandits have missed this shipment. Or perhaps, somehow, they know enough to be suspicious of it. The cool air of the data centre makes it impossible to doze off, but staring at unyielding readouts until his eyes ache has almost put him into a stupor when Tanta's message startles him back into alertness.

<<We have a visual. They took the bait.>>

Alarm spikes through Cole. He hasn't seen anything; could he have missed a notification from the VI? He checks, but there's nothing. OK, so he wasn't completely asleep at the switch. But if the bandits have tracked the HGV, how did they find out about it? Cole's next thought is that the VI must have made an error. Anger at himself turns into annoyance at the machine.

<<Has anyone accessed the delivery listing I asked you to monitor?>> he asks it testily.

<<Yes,>> the VI interface replies. <<Since your last query, the listing has been accessed three hundred—>>

<<I meant anyone on my list?>> Cole amends.

<<No.>> To Cole's ears, the pleasant voice has a hint of acerbity.

'But that makes no sense,' Cole mutters. The bandits have turned up, so *someone* has to have viewed the manifest. Unless he was wrong, and they're getting their information some other way.

Cole likes to think he's no more arrogant than most people, but he knows his strengths. His analysis was accurate, he's sure of it, and Tanta agreed that his conclusions were sound. He chews this over. He could be wrong, or the VI could be in error, but there's also a third option. One Cole didn't even bother considering before, because it seemed impossible.

<<Show me the access requests from the accounts that aren't on my list,>> he instructs the VI.

It whirs for a second, and then all three hundred and fifty-two of them flash up before his eyes. Cole scrolls through them; they all appear to be from sleeper routers, as he expected. He checks their accounts manually, querying each sleeper's status with the data centre. He's too intrigued by the conundrum to resent the dullness of the task. Sleepers are unconscious while they're at work. Unless one of them has figured out a way to hack the servers when they're not on duty, it shouldn't be possible for them to see any trade data with their waking eyes.

It takes Cole a long time to satisfy himself on this score. Tanta pings him while he works, letting him know that she and Smythe are on their way back to Sodis – he's been so absorbed by his own investigation that he's missed her side of the plan entirely. In the end, and after the best part of two hours spent squinting in the dark, he's convinced that it *is* impossible. One by one, his checks on the sleepers' accounts indicate no red flags of any kind. All of them were on duty and functioning normally at the time their access requests came through. He's three hundred and fifty-one accounts in before he finds an answer to this mystery. It must be the solution, by a process of elimination, as it's the only option left, but it's even harder for Cole to wrap his head around than the idea that one of the sleepers was responsible. The final user to have accessed the listing was an anonymous ghost account. And ghost accounts belong only to people who are, well, ghosts.

<<Are you broken?>> he asks the VI. <<How is this user profile still active? And where are the rest of their details?>>

<<Information unavailable,>> the VI simpers. Which Cole was expecting, but he's surprised when it adds, <<Access denied. Profile is classified under case number #1436.>>

The person responsible for the data breach is dead. And buried so deep that Cole can't even find their name.

Chapter 23

By the time Fliss reaches the mark, the sun has set, and she's running on fumes. Without any equipment on hand, she hasn't been able to disinfect and bandage her damaged ear as her mother taught her to. She's had to settle for ripping off the arm of her jacket and wrapping it around the wound, which has stemmed the bleeding but done nothing for the pain. Her bare feet are blistered and sore, and she can feel a bruise blossoming on the small of her back. When the last of the light dies out of the sky, she stops using the map on the phone to navigate and points its screen at the ground instead, where it casts a feeble glow over her path.

She figures out where the crew will be a few miles before she reaches them, when she gets to the outskirts of an abandoned settlement. She recognises the place: they've hunted drones here before, setting up in a multi-storey car park on the edge of town that overlooks a corporate road. Fliss remembers the vantage point, which stuck in her mind at the time as being a good one. The car park was solid concrete and looked like it could withstand an apocalypse – as in fact it has.

She slows her pace as she enters the town, looking warily around her. She slips the pistol from her pocket and thumbs the trigger, but it hasn't been switched on. She doesn't know how fine-grained a control the strangers have over the crew's weapons. Will it activate with the rest of the guns when the mark comes by, or has it been switched off forever? She keeps it drawn all the same; if Hardinger is here, she doesn't want to be caught unprepared. As she steps through the ground floor entrance of the multi-storey car park, she hears voices. She can't tell who's speaking at this distance. The emptiness of the building catches and distorts the sound, bouncing it off the concrete pillars and the rusting hulks of the few remaining cars.

Fliss pads across the ground floor of the car park towards the ramp that slopes up to the next level. The crew will be on the roof if they're here at all. She's pleased to see that Josh and Sonia have at least planned this strike sensibly. They're not going to make the mistake of trying to waylay the truck on the road, like she did last time. They've picked a good, high vantage point, one from which they can shoot without putting themselves in the line of fire. Of course, the woman said this mark was likely a trap, so their precautions won't make a difference. But Fliss can't help feeling a kind of pride in her crew's good planning, all the same.

The voices grow louder the higher Fliss climbs, though not more distinct. The car park is more of a framework than an enclosed structure, metal railings crisscrossing a concrete skeleton, and the wind sighs as it moves through its bones in a way Fliss finds disconcerting. She's never felt, as some do, that the structures of the pre-Meltdown world are haunted by the ghosts of that long-ago past. The demands of the present have always been too pressing to allow her to indulge in that kind of magical thinking. But if she was tasked with imagining a haunted place, this is probably what her mind would conjure up.

It's a relief to pad up the last ramp and out into a drizzly night. Fliss can just make out a figure leaning on the edge of the roof, fifty metres away from her. Josh is staring through the sights of the rocket launcher, which he has propped on the lip of the building. Fliss's heart leaps. It's good to see the little shit again. She doesn't announce herself immediately. Instead, she stops where she is, letting her eyes play over the rest of the space. The car is parked at the far end of the car park, right up against the stairwell, a darker shape in the darkness. After a minute, she sees Sonia too, crouching at the base of the wall with her gun drawn. There's no sign of Hardinger anywhere.

Reassured, Fliss takes a couple of steps forward. Her footfalls, which splash in the puddles on the roof, send Sonia and Josh whirling around, as she knew they would. Sonia points the gun her way. Fliss raises her hands, in case they haven't recognised her from this distance.

'Relax,' she calls. 'It's me.'

'Fliss?' Sonia replies. She sounds incredulous. Neither of them shifts their positions.

'Who else would it be? Listen.' Fliss takes another step. 'We have to get out of here. We've been played.'

'We thought you were dead,' Sonia says. 'I mean, *he* said you were dead.'

'Well, I'm not.' Fliss doesn't know what else to say. Nerves jump and twist in her stomach. Why aren't either of them moving? And why is Sonia still pointing that handgun at her? 'We have to go,' she says again. 'That girl, the one from this morning – she's coming back.'

'We know. He told us.' Sonia looks wretched. 'We got a new plan now, Fliss. We can handle the girl.'

'Like fuck you can,' Fliss shoots back. 'This whole setup is a trap! I heard the strangers talking about it. They're just rolling the dice with us, Sonia. *They* don't even think you can handle her, and they sent you here.'

'You shouldn't have come back, Felicity,' Josh says, speaking for the first time. He sounds strange, like he's trying to make his voice deeper than it really is. Usually, Fliss would laugh at him for acting the big man. Right now, that doesn't seem like such a good idea. She scans the car park roof. Just to her left, close to where she emerged from the ramp, a section of the wall surrounding the structure has crumbled away. She takes a half-step towards it, her hands still in the air.

'And why's that?' she calls, though she already knows the answer. It's in the feeling gnawing at the pit of her stomach. That, and the fact that Sonia still hasn't lowered her gun.

'Because while you were gone, there's been a change in management.'

'Oh really? He put you in charge, did he?'

It's hard to tell in the dark, but she thinks Josh puffs out his chest. 'He did.'

Stupid, stupid Josh. Fliss doesn't do business this way, but if she did, and she were in his position, she would have shot the old boss as soon as she walked onto the roof. If you're looking to step into the leader's shoes, you don't leave them alive long enough to brag about it. But he's always been a show-off. Meanwhile, Fliss has used his little speech about management, which sounds like he lifted it wholesale from a gangster flick, to take a few steps closer to the side of the building. She risks a quick, sideways glance over the edge. It's a long way down.

'That's funny,' she says. 'I never had him pegged as a complete fuckwit.'

She can see Josh stiffen from all the way across the roof. 'Just shoot her,' he snaps. Sonia hesitates, turning to look at Josh for confirmation. Fliss feels a flicker of affection. She doesn't blame Sonia for falling into line; she can see which way this is going, and it takes a special kind of stupid to join the losing side out of nothing but love and loyalty.

But Fliss loves her for her moment of indecision. It's more

than most people get. It also saves her life. As Sonia turns back, her finger already going for the trigger, Fliss steps off the edge of the roof.

The truck is still a good half hour behind them when Tanta's car turns off the road and heads towards the abandoned town. She doesn't want to drive too close, in case the bandits hear them coming, so she directs the car to stop a few minutes' walk from the building where she saw the figure. She's about to step outside when Smythe taps her on the arm yet again.

'Why have we stopped?' he hisses. 'I thought the plan was to plant a tracking device on the bandits' vehicle. Have you seen it?'

'Not yet. I'm going to approach the car park on foot. I'll draw less attention that way.'

'I see.'

Tanta opens the door on her side. Smythe does likewise. She stops. Even in optimal conditions, remaining hidden from people who are actively on their guard against intruders is difficult. With Smythe in tow, Tanta thinks it may be impossible. 'Wait in the car,' she orders him. 'If the bandits spot our tracker, we'll need to be ready to pursue them.'

Smythe nods. 'Good idea.'

She heads off, her footsteps slow and deliberate. She's still in sight of the car when Smythe pings her.

<<What's the hold-up?>>

Tanta grits her teeth. <<The bandits are close. I'm moving slowly to avoid making a noise.>>

<<Ah. Carry on, then.>>

When she reaches the bottom of the car park, Tanta makes a careful circuit of the building. She's anticipating scouts stationed on the ground floor but finds none. They must all be inside – that, or the bandits are an even smaller crew than she thought.

<<What are you doing now?>> Smythe asks.

<<I think their car is parked inside,>> she returns. <<I'm going in.>>

The interior of the multi-storey car park smells of mildew and rust. It still appears structurally sound, but years of exposure to the elements have cracked its walls and ceiling, and carpeted its floor with patches of moss. The moss makes it easier to disguise her footsteps, though it's slick underfoot, forcing her to walk even more slowly as she explores the dark space.

There are several cars down here, but they're all rusted hulks, left over from before the Meltdown. The same is true of the second and third storeys. Tanta has a good idea of where the bandits' vehicle is likely to be, and it's not going to make her job any easier.

<<They must have parked on the roof,>> she sends to Smythe.

Keeping their getaway car so close at hand is a smart move. Tanta calls up her earlier image capture, calculating the best angle of approach. If she takes the ramp up to the top of the building it will bring her out directly opposite the figure she saw and she'll be spotted. A door on the far side of the car park catches her eye and she creeps over to investigate. It creaks when she eases it open, but she's glad she checked it – it leads to a stairwell. Better still, there's a panel in the door. The glass is grimy with age and dirt, but if there's one at the top of the building too, Tanta can use it to scout out the roof before she emerges.

She's not sure how many bandits are up there. If they've left someone by the car, it will be almost impossible to get close enough to attach the tracker. It's dark, though, and the night is overcast and foggy. If luck is on her side, she may still be able to pull this off. She mounts the stairs, which she's pleased to see are made of the same concrete as the rest of the building, and too solid to creak or give way.

She's hoping Smythe will have the good sense to leave her to her work uninterrupted, but it's less than a minute before he pings her again.

<<Have you seen anything? Do you need backup?>>

Tanta sends back a quick negative and then, in sheer frustration, mutes the channel. How can Smythe expect her to discover anything if he won't stop messaging her?

As she approaches the door, Tanta hears voices. That's good. If the bandits are talking, they'll be less likely to notice her. She enhances the audio on her 'scape and edges forward to peer through the panel on the door. The car park's roof is flat and open; with her enhanced vision, she takes the whole scene in at a glance. There are three figures on the roof – two by the wall to her right and one immediately opposite her, a girl. She can't see the car from her vantage point; she's just wondering if there's a way for her to get a better view when the girl steps forward. The two figures to Tanta's right turn to look at her. While they're distracted, Tanta edges the door open a fraction and slips out.

'Relax. It's me.'

Tanta tunes out the bandits as she scans the rooftop. The stairwell is in a concrete box that juts out into the car park. At the very back of the roof, tucked behind and to the left of the stairs, is a black van. Its modern design marks it out immediately as a corporate vehicle, doubtless supplied to the bandits by Thoughtfront, just like their weapons.

It's no more than five metres from where Tanta is standing but getting to it is going to be tricky: the space is in full view of the rest of the roof. Many peoples' natural instinct would be to run, trying to cover the distance as quickly as possible, but years of training have rid Tanta of such misplaced impulses. The human eye is more sensitive to motion than almost anything else, especially at night, when there's less visual information available. If she bolts, she'll be spotted immediately. No, the only way forward is to move as slowly as possible. She checks her 'scape – still fifteen minutes till the HGV is scheduled to pass by. That should give her plenty of time to plant the tracker and get back into cover.

She sticks to the shadows, crouching low to the ground to make her silhouette harder to identify. As she moves, she allows the bandits' conversation to come back to the forefront of her awareness, monitoring it for any warning signs.

'You shouldn't have come back, Felicity,' one of the bandits is saying.

'And why's that?'

'Because while you were gone, there's been a change in management.'

That catches Tanta's attention. Without halting her progress, she glances sideways. Are the bandits talking about Thoughtfront?

It's only when she's looking at the three figures properly that Tanta notices the tension in their stances, and the way their guns are pointing. It seems she has walked in on the middle of some kind of internecine struggle. That's bad. It does mean the bandits will be that much more distracted, but the last thing Tanta wants is to get caught in the crossfire. She'd like to monitor this situation, to see what has caused this change in management, and what its likely consequences will be, but there's no time. She quickens her pace, taking advantage of the distraction to dart behind the car. She fishes the tracker out of the pouch on her belt as she moves. The powerful magnet pulls against her hand as she slips it underneath the chassis.

<<I'm done,>> she sends to Smythe. <<There's a situation developing out here, so—>>

The sound of gunfire interrupts her message. She peeks out from behind the car, just in time to see the girl to her left plunge off the edge of the roof. At first, Tanta thinks she's been hit, but no — she dived a fraction of a second *before* the gun's retort. The muted pops are followed by a howl of rage. And then the door bursts open. Smythe is standing in the entrance, gun in hand.

<<What are you doing?>> Tanta sends frantically. <<Stand down. STAND DOWN!>>

Smythe's hand falters, but the decision isn't his anymore. The bandit with the gun has heard the creak of the door and she spins in the direction of this new threat. The sharp, uneven cracks of Smythe's semi-automatic pistol meet the muted noise of her silenced handgun, and Tanta is forced to duck back behind the car to avoid the hail of bullets.

Smythe fires six shots. Tanta risks a glance from behind the car. One look is enough to tell her that the mission is in shambles. One of the bandits is dead. The second is running for cover. Smythe flings himself back through the door to reload. A millisecond later, another barrage of shots peppers the air where he was standing. They thud into the door, splintering the wood and breaking the window.

<<You weren't responding to my messages,>> Smythe sends reproachfully. <<I thought you might need backup.>>

Tanta feels something welling up inside her, like water boiling in a kettle. She isn't sure whether it's tears or screaming. She hopes Cole has fared better than she has, because her side of the plan is a catastrophe. Even if any of the bandits survive, there's no way they'll return to the car now. With time and careful planning, Tanta could have taken down their entire operation; Smythe's thoughtless aggression may have robbed her of that chance.

<<That showed them!>> Smythe adds. He sounds like a child playing in an arcade. <<Won't attack our shipments again in a hurry now, will they?>>

Tanta bites her lower lip, pressing so hard that she tastes

blood. There is one way she can salvage something from this train-wreck of an assignment. She dashes across the roof, making for the gap in the wall where the girl disappeared. It's too late to track the bandits – Smythe destroyed that idea in a haze of bullets. But she can still take one of them prisoner.

She reaches the edge and peers over. No body at the foot of the structure, which means the girl didn't land there – there's no way she'd have walked away from a fall from that height. But Tanta sees the framework of metal girders that crisscross the sides of the building and realises where the bandit has gone. She climbs over the edge, using the metal railings like a ladder, and swings through them and onto the floor below.

Evidently, she's far slower at climbing than the bandit is. Before she's had a chance to get her bearings, a bullet hits a car beside her, shattering its windscreen into shards of crystal. Tanta ducks and rolls behind the car's front bumper, drawing her own handgun.

'Your mark's getting away!' A voice calls. 'Fuck off and follow it, OK?' The girl must have mistaken Tanta for one of her comrades in the dark. Another shot follows the words, but she's way off this time – it takes a chunk of concrete out of the wall on the other side of the car park.

The bandit isn't trying to kill her: she's running away. Tanta rolls back out from behind the car and pursues. She catches up to her at the ramp, putting on a burst of speed that leaves her chest and shins screaming. She tackles the girl to the ground; the force of the impact knocks the gun from the bandit's hand, sending it skittering away across the floor.

'Stay down!' Tanta shouts, training her gun on the girl's back.

'Oh, shit,' the bandit mumbles.

Tanta ignores her, frisking her for concealed weapons. She can see the outline of a rectangular object in the bandit's jacket pocket; she tugs down the zip and reaches for it. Her fingers touch something smooth, cool, and unaccountably familiar. She pulls it free. It's a black tile, its screen scored with cracks. It could have broken in the fall, but Tanta doesn't think so.

'Why do you have this?' Tanta asks her. 'Who gave it to you?' But she already knows the answer; she recognises the slim device with its cracked black screen.

It's the same one she used to talk to the Brokerage almost a year ago.

Chapter 24

Tanta cuffs the girl and walks her out of the car park at gun-point. Now that she has the chance to look at her properly, she can see that the bandit is in a bad state. There's a makeshift bandage tied around the side of her head and her black hair is matted with blood. There's blood on her face, too, crusting her left cheek. She's east Asian, with a tanned, rounded face, and she's dressed in a strange hodgepodge of different clothes – old, dirty jeans and a torn puffer jacket that looks as if it's been lifted from a pre–Meltdown shopping centre, but underneath that Tanta can make out the contours of body armour. Tanta's tackle has left her dazed; she's unsteady on her feet and does not try to run.

Tanta pushes the girl into the car, locks the doors, and returns to the roof to help Smythe. One of the bandits who shot at him – a teenager with red hair – is lying dead on the ground; the other has fled. Tanta removes the now–useless tracker from the bandits' car, then sets about collecting their weapons and gear. In addition to the rocket launcher and the handgun they abandoned on the roof, the boot of their vehicle is a cornucopia of firearms and protective equipment – a net gun, several gas masks, and another of those folding shields the bandits used when they attacked the truck. Cole can examine it all later, though Tanta doubts these new weapons will tell them anything they don't already know. Smythe keeps up a steady stream of prattle while she works.

'I think this venture was a huge success, all things considered. I told you taking a prisoner would be the most straightforward way of doing things.'

'It wasn't the plan,' Tanta snaps. 'And I told *you* to wait in the car.'

Smythe looks offended. 'You could do with developing a little more flexibility, Agent. It's a useful skill in our line of work.'

Tanta doesn't bother to reply to that. She's too tired to challenge Smythe's nonsense again — and too preoccupied with her own thoughts.

The bandit girl was carrying a Brokerage device. That means the Brokerage *is* involved in the UAV thefts — which is exactly what Jeanie's story suggested. Tanta isn't sure what she thinks about this vindication of the freedom fighter's intel, though she doesn't trust the woman herself any more than she did before.

Nor has this revelation done anything to address her other misgivings. Harlow 2.0 needs to be stopped, but by working to bring it down, Tanta would be setting herself in opposition to the corporation she calls home. It's been a long time since she thought of InTech with the love and loyalty she once did, but it's a far cry from her current scepticism to turning traitor. These thoughts chase each other round and round in Tanta's head like fish in a bowl, getting her nowhere.

She and Smythe put the weapons and other gear they have collected in the boot and begin the journey back to Sodis. Tanta pings Cole as they leave, warning him that they're on their way back; if he isn't finished with his side of the plan already, he'll have to hurry it up. Cole acknowledges her message with a mental nod, but sends no other reply. If she knows him, he's probably still neck-deep in data, with no attention to spare for chatting.

Smythe, by contrast, will not shut up. He's using MindChat now that they're in the car with the bandit. <<Yes, a captive really is much better when you think about it – a bird in the hand, and all that. We'll let her sweat a bit in one of the inter-rogation cells, and then we can—>>

<<I'm sorry, Logistics Officer,>> Tanta interjects. She's not so distracted that she's about to let this stand. <<The prisoner is wounded. We need to take her to a clinic before we do anything else. And I'll be conducting the interrogation with my colleague, Cole, not you.>>

Smythe turns to her with an expression of venomous surprise. <<You are posted in my distribution centre, Agent. I have as much right to conduct this interrogation as you do.>>

'No,' Tanta says aloud. 'You don't. This is my assignment, Logistics Officer, and I'm trained to engage with non-corporate hostiles. Are you?'

Airing their conversation in front of the prisoner like this crosses the line from blunt into downright unprofessional, but there's only so far that Tanta's tact and caution can stretch. She's had more than enough of Smythe inserting himself into her work, and on this issue, she won't budge. She already has an idea of how the Logistics Officer thinks an interrogation should go, and it makes her flesh crawl.

'You think I've never dealt with hostiles before?' Smythe's tone is icy. 'Let me tell you, I've seen things you wouldn't believe. I've—'

He stops. Tanta's mind flicks back, once again, to Smythe's paranoid security arrangements, and his bizarre collection of ICRD paraphernalia. For a moment, her curiosity overcomes her dislike, and she's moved to ask, <<Are you talking about something in particular?>>

<<Never you mind,>> Smythe replies curtly.

That seems to signal the end of the conversation. Smythe never answers Tanta's question, but nor does he refer again to trying to run the interrogation himself. Overall, Tanta thinks it's a good bargain.

He doesn't speak again until they reach Sodis. As the car pulls up outside the clinic, he sends, <<We have three emergency holding cells on the first floor of the Logistics Office. You can keep the prisoner there, but you'll have to question her in the conference room.>>

<<That will be fine,>> Tanta replies. <<Have a guardian escort her to the office after her wound has been treated. I'll talk to her then.>>

There's a charged silence. Smythe glowers at her. <<I don't much like your attitude, Agent,>> he sends. <<I've got half a mind to speak to your manager about it.>>

And Tanta is sure Kenway will be only too happy to discipline her – though what more he could do, having already exiled her from the city, she isn't sure. <<Do,>> she fires back. <<And I'll tell him how your flagrant disregard for protocol almost jeopardised the entire assignment.>>

Before she makes any report to Kenway, though, she needs to talk to Cole. They agreed to reconvene back at the flat; he's there by the time Tanta arrives, and she can tell by the suppressed eagerness in his expression that he has had more success than she has.

'What did you find?' she asks.

'A ghost!'

'Meaning?' Tanta's tone is terse. Any other night, she'd have patience for Cole and his enigmatic style of explaining himself, but right now, she doesn't have the energy.

'A ghost account,' he clarifies. 'It accessed the manifest for your truck a few hours before the bandits showed up. A ghost account is a 'scape profile that belongs to someone who's—'

'I know what it is,' Tanta cuts in. She thinks, with a shiver, of the all the CorpWards who perished in the Ward House fire, their profiles still filling up her contacts list. 'How is that possible?'

'It *shouldn't* be.' Cole must see the doubt in Tanta's expression. 'I'd think I was crazy too, if I hadn't seen it happen.'

'Who did – does – the account belong to?' Tanta asks. They can figure out how on earth this is happening later; right now, all they need is a name.

'That's where it gets really weird. When I tried to get more information, the VI told me the profile was classified – something about case number 1436.'

'A case number is a really good start,' Tanta says eagerly. 'If we've got that, we can look up the case files themselves in the archives. Our culprit will be in there.'

Cole grins. 'Then all we need to do is get in. I imagine asking Smythe for access would be a mistake, though. You remember how nervous he got when you tried to wander off into the archives before?'

Tanta was thinking the same thing. Whatever Smythe is hiding, this could well have something to do with it. Unfortunately, that's going to make their job a lot harder.

'Come to think of it, going over his head probably isn't a great idea, either,' Cole adds.

She nods. Talking to Kenway about this would be even worse than confronting Smythe. At best, he'd send one of his more trusted deputies to investigate in Tanta's stead (she thinks of Reet coming to Sodis, and quails). At worst, he'd sit on her intelligence until the window of opportunity had passed. Tanta doesn't quite think Kenway capable of sabotaging the entire investigation for spite – it'd be his career on the line as well as hers, after all – but she doesn't want to bet on it.

'Another break-in, then?' Cole asks brightly. 'I'm free tonight.'

'We have an interrogation to conduct first,' Tanta replies.

Briefly, she relates her own limited success, and the failure that preceded it. By the time she's finished, Cole looks thoughtful. Tanta knows what's on his mind. When he asked her what they were going to do about Jeanie and Harlow 2.0 this morning, she told him she wanted a day to look into the former Brokerage agent's story. Now that day is almost over: she has run out of thinking time.

'That bears out what Jeanie was telling us,' Cole says. He gives her a meaningful look. 'Did you think any more about what we were talking about earlier?'

'Our investigation isn't finished yet,' Tanta replies. She's abashed by the petulance in her own voice. 'Once we've checked out the archives...'

She trails off. She can't finish the thought, because it doesn't have an end. She'd put this conversation off forever if she could.

'Jeanie needs an answer from us by tomorrow,' Cole prompts. 'We can't keep delaying this discussion.'

Tanta casts around for a response in a kind of panic. 'It might be better for us to try and work out a solution to Harlow 2.0 without Jeanie's help,' she says at last. It's the best thing she can come up with.

Cole gives her a look of pure bewilderment. 'What? Tanta, the update is going live in two days. There's no way we could work out *anything* in that timeframe! Jeanie already has a plan.'

'A plan she's refused to tell us anything about. We've only got her word for it that she knows what she's doing. Working with her is a huge risk.'

'Well, it's better than the alternative!' Cole rejoins, his voice rising. 'We can't do nothing.'

'That's not what I'm suggesting.'

'Then what are you suggesting?'

Tanta opens her mouth. She shuts it again.

Cole waves a hand at her. 'That sounds like nothing to me.'

'Maybe if you'd help me think, rather than putting your faith in a woman we know nothing about, I'd be able to come up with something,' Tanta replies testily. She can feel her own temper rising to meet his. Cole's trust in Jeanie is naïve – and a little insulting. The freedom fighter may have been cordial to him, but she treated Tanta with open contempt, and that doesn't seem to bother him at all. 'We still have no idea what Jeanie's motives are,' she continues.

'You're missing the point!' Cole bursts out. 'We don't have any other option. Besides, she *told* us her motives. We're all trying to achieve the same thing – what's the point in doing it separately?'

'She *says* she's trying to achieve the same thing as us, but we can't just take her at her word!'

Cole stares at her. 'Would you be saying that if she was an InTech employee?' he asks.

Fury races through Tanta. Bringing her own Harlow Programming into this, and the instinctual trust of InTech and its representatives it instilled in her, is a low blow. Her anger is made all the worse by a queasy awareness that Cole has a point. She thinks again of the bomb attack on the Needle, when she wasted precious seconds waiting for a corporate authority figure to approve her actions, as though obtaining InTech's sanction was more important than saving lives.

Her hesitation then was proof enough that unless she guards herself closely, her thoughts and behaviours are all too apt to fall back into the old grooves that the Harlow Programme has left in her mind – especially when the stakes are high. Tanta doesn't like Jeanie at all, and she doesn't trust her, either, but how far are those first impressions her own? She can't be sure. She may never be sure. And whose fault is that?

'I don't know, Cole,' she snaps. 'You're the expert on the Harlow Programme. Maybe you should tell me.'

Cole drops his gaze, his posture sagging. If Tanta was looking to wound him, she's succeeded. It was a vicious thing to say. She doesn't care. He opens his mouth – probably to apologise – but she cuts him off before he can speak.

'InTech wouldn't even have this software if it wasn't for your research,' she spits at him. 'Did it ever occur to you that I wouldn't want to risk my career over your mistake?'

'You're right,' Cole says simply. 'It *is* my mistake. I just... thought you would want to help me fix it, I suppose. After what InTech did – what I did – to your mind, I thought you'd want to prevent the same thing from happening to anyone else. If you don't, I'll stop asking. But I'm going to – with or without you.'

The anger has gone from his voice. In its place is a conviction that's marrow-deep. Tanta searches for a way to answer him, but finds nothing. Her flash fire of rage has died away as quickly as it came, leaving her ashamed. A message from one of the distribution centre's guardians saves her from having to reply: the bandit is ready for questioning.

'I have to go and speak to the prisoner now,' she says, rising to her feet.

She turns on her heel, striding out of the flat before Cole can say anything else. It's a flimsy excuse; what Tanta is really doing is running away, and she knows it. Cole is right: she can't delay this conversation forever. She can postpone it for another hour, though.

The Logistics Office's makeshift interview room is a conference space opposite Smythe's office, its only furniture a large, square table and twenty straight-backed chairs. It's manifestly unsuitable for an interrogation, but Tanta supposes she'll have to make do. In the absence of a cuff bar bolted to the table, she shackles the bandit to the chair she's sitting on.

The girl watches her do this with dark, blank eyes. The clinic has cleaned her up and put a fresh bandage on her wounded ear, but she still looks shellshocked – she may even be mildly concussed from when Tanta tackled her. Interrogation is not Tanta's specialism, but she covered the essentials in basic training. She can see the bandit is frightened, and the altercation she witnessed on the roof of the car park suggests that she also has no one to protect – her co-conspirators have all either died, or turned on her. In other words, she's primed to talk; all she needs is the right incentive.

Tanta decides to start by building a rapport. She sits down opposite the bandit and smiles at her. 'Your name's Felicity, right?' she asks.

'Fliss,' the girl corrects.

'Fliss. I'm Tanta. Would you like a drink? Or something to eat? You must be tired.'

At first, Tanta thinks Fliss is still too dazed to understand the question, but then she asks one of her own.

'What happened to the rest of my crew?'

Tanta is surprised she cares. They didn't appear to be on the best of terms last time Fliss saw them. She can see that the information matters to the bandit, though; her expression is more focused than it was before. Anything a prisoner wants is something you can withhold from them in return for informa-tion, but Tanta knows what it's like to lose colleagues. She can't keep this from Fliss, even if she is an enemy of InTech.

'One of them died,' she says. 'The other ran away.'

Fliss leans forward in her chair – as far as she can, given the cuffs. 'Which one ran? Was it the girl?'

Tanta nods, and an expression of relief crosses Fliss's face. 'I didn't realise they were your crew,' Tanta adds. 'I'm sorry for your loss.'

The bandit glares at this. 'No, you're not. And you mean "I'm sorry I killed them", don't you?'

It's a slap in the face, but Tanta doesn't flinch. She does feel a twinge of frustration, though – not at Fliss, but at Smythe. No one was supposed to die on this assignment. 'I didn't, for what it's worth,' she replies. 'It was my colleague.'

'Same difference.'

'I'm not going to ask you to turn on her, you know,' Tanta says, voice soft. 'InTech isn't interested in you, or your crew; I only want information on your employers.'

'You're not interested in us? Well, thank fuck for that,' Fliss replies. 'I know some dead people who'll be really glad to hear it.'

Tanta pauses, considering her next move. She's trying to encourage Fliss to trust her and talk to her, but it's clear the bandit regards her as an enemy. Tanta isn't fazed by the hostility, but she's going to have to try a different approach.

She takes the touchscreen device from her pocket and slides it across the table. 'Who gave you this?'

Fliss folds her arms. 'What's that information worth to you?'

This response, at least, is something Tanta can work with. 'If you answer all of my questions honestly,' she replies, 'there's no reason why you shouldn't walk out of here free and clear at the end of this interview.'

Fliss draws in a sharp breath. She looks suspicious, but the glimpse of freedom has done its job. 'You'd let me go back to the wasteland?' she asks.

'Better than that,' Tanta tells her. She has a duty to keep InTech safe from bandits, but she also has a responsibility to do right by informants who cooperate. In this case, there's an easy way to achieve both ends. 'If you give me accurate information, then I'll give you something in return: a place in the city, with InTech.'

'No deal. If you want to know what I know, you have to let me go.'

Tanta is confused. Has Fliss not understood her? 'I *am* going to let you go. The community guardians – that's InTech's peace-keeping force – may want to monitor you for a while to make sure you're not a security risk, but you won't be imprisoned. You'll have a job and a home.'

Fliss stares at her. 'And say I wanted to go back to the waste-land instead. Could I refuse your oh-so-generous offer?'

It's such an unexpected question that for a moment, Tanta doesn't know how to answer it. She hadn't considered the pos-sibility that Fliss *would* refuse, especially given the likely alterna-tives. Tanta caught her red-handed about to attack an InTech delivery vehicle. She's hardly in a position to bargain.

'Well, no,' she admits. 'But I don't see why you'd want to. This is for your safety as much as InTech's security. Your crew turned on you. Even if I could let you go back into the Unaffiliated Zone unsupervised, what do you think would happen to you there? I'm offering you the chance to start over. A new life.'

'You're a liar, then,' Fliss retorts. 'You're not "offering" me anything.'

Tanta tries to see things from the bandit's perspective. 'The city isn't a bad place to live,' she says. 'I've lived there my whole life.'

'And you seem so well-adjusted. I said no deal. I want to go back to the wasteland.'

'You must see why that isn't possible,' Tanta persists. 'There's a reason your crew are dead. Their actions – yours, too – have threatened the peace and security of my corporation and all its residents. You've put lives at risk.'

'I've put lives at risk?' Fliss says. 'Oh, that's a good one, cor-porate girl. You killed my crew. But *I'm* the threat?'

'You tried to kill me,' Tanta points out. She taps the device. 'I found my photo on this. I know it was you and your crew who ambushed the HGV I was travelling in.'

'And yet here you stand. My crew weren't so lucky.'

'If you and your crew didn't want to go up against InTech, perhaps you shouldn't have stolen from us.'

To Tanta's surprise, Fliss bursts out laughing. 'What's the view like from that high horse you're on?' she hoots. 'What do you think InTech does when it sees something it wants? You ever wonder why the wasteland's chock-full of nothing? It's because the corporations took everything worth having. Don't go calling me a thief when you started it.'

Tanta is beginning to get exasperated. She has allowed Fliss to steer this conversation off course; she needs to get things back on track. 'How do I even know your intelligence is any good?' she asks. 'You've told me nothing so far to indicate you know anything useful.'

A gleam comes into the bandit's eye. 'I know plenty,' she says. 'I know where the Brokerage is, for starters. And I know Hardinger.'

That catches Tanta's attention. 'Where did you hear that name?' she asks sharply.

Fliss only smirks. 'Let me go, InTech,' she says. 'Then we'll talk.'

Tanta calls a halt to the interview not long after that. It's never a good idea to question a suspect when your own emotions aren't under control; that's in the ICRD procedural regulations. She takes Fliss up to the holding cells on the first floor and locks her in, leaving strict instructions with the on-duty guardian that no one is to talk to her but Tanta herself. The touchscreen device and the weapons, armour and gas masks she and Smythe gathered from the bandits she puts into a holdall, which she leaves in Smythe's equipment room. That done, she goes for a walk. She needs to clear her head.

She had been expecting the interrogation to go very differently. She'd had a plan going in: build up a rapport, drop a few implicit threats, and then win the bandit over with the promise of a job and a home, a place in corporate society, in return for her compliance. She'd assumed that these were things Fliss would want. Wouldn't anyone? The girl's laughter, her open scorn, took Tanta completely by surprise. At first, she couldn't fathom why Fliss would turn down an offer that would see her set up for life in circumstances far more comfortable and secure than any she could have experienced before. She understands now, though the knowledge discomfits her. The bandit can't see a home within InTech as an incentive when the corporation has only ever been a threat to her. In Fliss's view, InTech is full of thieves and liars. Tanta has to admit that she's not wrong.

Tanta was hoping the interview would take her mind off her argument with Cole, and the impossible choice she needs to make, but it's had the opposite effect. The longer the interrogation lasted, the more Tanta found her thoughts drifting back to Harlow 2.0. Talking to Fliss has only reminded her of all the other things InTech is capable of. She can't bury herself in her work to escape this problem because her work is part of the problem, and she can't hide from it elsewhere because she carries it with her, lurking beneath her own skin.

Tanta has struggled with the question of who she is ever since she lost her Harlow Programming, but she's not in doubt about what she wants. She wants to get Reet back; she wants to live in the city with her; she wants a career in the ICRD without Kenway breathing down her neck. She knows that some of these desires are based on lies, on programming that was put into her head without her consent, but that doesn't make her want them any less.

Working with Cole and Jeanie to sabotage the rollout of Harlow 2.0 will put all of that at risk. More than anything, when Cole asked her to make that choice, Tanta wanted to avoid it, to pretend, if only for a little while, that she doesn't know the things she knows, and that life is simple. She was only delaying the inevitable, though. Even when she bargained with Cole for more time, Tanta realises that, on some level, her mind was already made up.

Because she also wants to do the right thing. It used to be that the right thing was whatever InTech wanted her to do, but that isn't true anymore – it hasn't been for a long time. She has been pretending that she can square the circle, that she can continue to serve InTech's interests and follow her own conscience, but she can't do that any more than she can avoid the threat of Harlow 2.0. The update will subject everyone in the city to the programming that stole Tanta's own mind from her. She can let that happen, or she can take a stand against it. When she looks at it like that, the choice is no choice at all.

Her walk has taken her back to the flat. She takes the lift upstairs and finds Cole pacing the room, as he always does when he's anxious. As soon as he sees her, he stops, looking at her with worried eyes.

'Tanta. Look, I'm sorry about what I said.'

'Don't be,' she replies. 'You were right. I'm ready to help.'

Part 3

Chapter 25

Kenway has not forgotten about Tanta so completely as she supposes. In fact, the meeting he's on his way to now is all about her. He arrives punctually, walking in through the steel-reinforced door of the Black Box at one pm on the dot. Arthur meets him in the lobby and escorts him to his office, where they sit in awkward silence for a few minutes while an intern makes them both tea.

Kenway doesn't like any of his fellow Directors. At best, they're irrelevant to him, and at worst, they are potential threats to his own career. Arthur falls into the former category, though. He's a harmless old coot, more interested in the innards of the Inscape system than political manoeuvring. For this reason, Kenway doesn't waste any time on circling the issue. He knows Arthur will be more than willing to talk to him about the topic he has on his mind.

'I had some questions for you,' he says, 'about the Harlow Programme.'

Arthur's eyes brighten. 'Of course,' he says. 'The new version, or the old one?'

'The old one.'

That makes the old man sag a little – the original Harlow Programme was Cole's creation, after all, not his – but his scientific interest in the subject soon wins out. 'What did you want to know?'

'It inspires complete obedience in its subjects, yes?'

'Not exactly.' The doctor shifts in his seat, assuming a musing expression. 'The foundation of the Harlow Programme is affection. The programmed wards feel intense love and loyalty to InTech – and its representatives, of course. The obedience follows as a natural consequence.'

'So, it should be impossible for a Corporate Ward to, say, double-cross her manager?' Kenway asks.

Arthur's brow creases. 'Are you concerned about one of your wards?'

Despite his faith in Arthur's political neutrality, Kenway isn't willing to risk giving him that information up front. 'I am merely speaking hypothetically. I want to understand how far they can be trusted.'

The doctor's frown deepens. 'They can be trusted absolutely. But your question is a difficult one to answer. If a manager is engaged in conduct that's detrimental to the corporation, and a programmed ward learns about it, they'll likely report the manager in question.'

'Likely?' snaps Kenway. That's too equivocal for his tastes.

'It's not an exact science,' Arthur says. 'The wards are programmed to feel loyalty to InTech *and its representatives*. If one of those representatives turned out to be corrupt, a ward's programming might well leave them torn. They're only as good as their handlers, after all. We have an excellent example in Tanta's exposure of Jennifer Ash,' he adds. 'I imagine Tanta was very conflicted about her actions, but, in the end, her loyalty to the board won out. Probably because she'd met the board's conduit in person.'

Since Arthur has brought Tanta up himself, Kenway doesn't see any reason not to keep the conversation focused on her.

'Is that the result you would have expected?' he asks.

'It wasn't *unexpected*.'

'But you wouldn't expect Tanta to do the same thing again to a manager who *wasn't* corrupt?'

'Certainly not! A programmed Corporate Ward is the most loyal of agents.'

Kenway hesitates. But he's going to have to take the plunge sooner or later. 'What about one whose programming is defective?'

'I see what you're doing, you know, Douglas,' Arthur says.

The response confuses and nettles Kenway. 'I'm not doing anything. I have some concerns about Tanta's programming that I'd like to discuss with you, that's all.'

The doctor gives him an unpleasant smile. 'Oh, really? It's no secret that the board are dissatisfied with you. You have every reason to be worried about your position, but if you think casting aspersions on the work of *my* division is going to distract from your own incompetence, you're mistaken.'

Belatedly, Kenway thinks of all the times he has tried to do exactly that. He imagines seizing the old man by the throat and throttling him. Of all the moments for Arthur to decide to grow a spine! 'You mistake my intentions,' he says, through gritted teeth. 'If you'll hear me out—'

'I've heard more than enough already.' Arthur glares at him. 'Do you think I don't notice your attempts to make me your whipping boy? Jennifer Ash used to do the same thing. It didn't work out well for her, and I doubt it will end much better for you.'

'This is different,' Kenway growls. 'My misgivings are genuine. Tanta's behaviour—'

'Tanta's behaviour is the very thing that means I have no doubts about her programming whatsoever. I've sat in on the same meetings you have. She's been a model employee. And her

actions towards Jennifer Ash prove her loyalty beyond question.'
Arthur rises to his feet. 'I'll show you out, Director.'

Kenway seethes all the way out of the compound and back onto the street. It isn't *fair*. He knows he's right about Tanta, and he's got more than his own mistrust to go on. She's not behaving as she should, and if Arthur would only put political grievances aside long enough to *listen* to him, he would see that.

His progress is checked by a sharp tug on the sleeve of his coat. He looks around, bewildered – in his anger, he hasn't been paying attention to his surroundings – then glances down. There's a child standing in front of him; an unaffiliated beggar, no doubt.

'Get out of my way,' Kenway snaps.

She doesn't budge. 'Douglas Kenway?' she asks. 'You've been asking questions about Tanta and the Harlow Programme?'

Kenway is startled into a nod. 'How do you—'

'The Brokerage has answers for you,' the girl says. 'Come with me.'

The one advantage of her exile, Tanta reflects, is that it's far easier to meet with Jeanie than it would have been from within the city. In her old home, Tanta was used to reporting on everything she did and everywhere she went, first to Jen and then to Reet and Kenway. But while security within Sodis is as tight as Smythe can make it, all of his care and attention are lavished on the inside of his little kingdom, not on its borders. Once Tanta and Cole have stepped beyond the distribution centre's chain-link fence, they're completely unobserved.

Even so, Tanta walks them a kilometre and a half from the gate before she will allow Cole to use his communicator to summon Yas. She picks a spot that's shielded from passing traffic by the huge stanchions of a defunct bridge, and they wait in its shadow. Yas arrives half an hour after Cole makes the call, pulling up beside the bridge at a jaunty angle, like a hat on askew. She rolls the window down and sticks her head out. She looks genuinely pleased to see Tanta.

'Hey, you made it!' she calls. 'I'm glad you came around. I was getting lonely as the only ex-agent in Jeanie's outfit.'

'I'm not an ex-agent,' Tanta says through gritted teeth.

Yas whistles. 'A double agent, then? That's impressive. Takes more guts than I have, that's for sure.' Her expression softens as she sees the look on Tanta's face. 'I'm just kidding,' she says. 'Look, Jeanie told me all about the original Harlow Programme, what it did. That's ...' She trails off, letting the silence speak for her. 'If you've got mixed feelings about leaving InTech, that's more than fair. We still appreciate the help.'

Tanta makes no reply; she doesn't want Yas's pity any more than she wants her quips.

'Though life on the outside isn't so terrible, you know,' Yas adds. 'If you're ever thinking about defecting—'

'I'm not,' Tanta snaps. 'I want to help, but once this is done, we part ways. For good, this time.'

Yas gives her a strange look, but she doesn't push the issue further. The car takes a different route from last time, driving up into the rolling hills that surround the distribution centre.

'Aren't we going back to the service station?' Tanta asks.

Yas shakes her head. 'Jeanie's got a lot of safehouses.'

They've been driving for less than twenty minutes when Yas pulls up just within a copse of trees and stops the car. Tanta peers out of the window; they're high on a rise, and the view is excellent. She can see the distribution centre, far below and just to the east, but there's no sign of a base at all.

'Is it underground?' she asks.

Yas grins. 'Something like that.' She strides deeper into the trees. When she has gone about forty paces, she raises her fist and knocks on the empty air. It looks like she's issuing some kind of strange haptic command to her 'scape, but Tanta hears the blows land, as though Yas is knocking on solid wood.

She's trying to figure this out when something even stranger happens. A doorway opens in the middle of the copse, a slice of air and trees swinging away to reveal a rectangular entrance and, within, Jeanie herself.

Tanta is too much the agent to show her feelings at this development, but Cole has no such scruples. He whistles. 'Cool hideout! How are you cloaking it like this?'

'Come over here,' Jeanie says, beckoning.

As she and Cole approach, Tanta notices a shimmering in the air, like a heat haze. When she's inches from the doorway, the illusion breaks down completely: for a fraction of a second, there's a building in front of her, small, square and low-roofed. Then she blinks and it's gone.

'The AR skin is most effective at long range,' Jeanie explains. 'Once you get within spitting distance, you get glitches. No one corporate ever comes up here, though, so it works well enough to cloak me from people in the valley.'

'I've never seen an AR skin this realistic before,' Cole marvels.

'It's my own design,' Jeanie replies, without arrogance. 'Come inside.'

The interior of the building looks like a museum exhibit on retro technology. There are several freestanding legacy comput-ing units on tables, and the floor is carpeted with a jumble of wires. A battered armchair in front of the closest unit attests to where Jeanie must work. Its fabric upholstery is covered with a crocheted blanket, and there's a small fridge beside it. The air hums with the sounds of extractor fans and a boiling kettle. There's a curtain at the back, leading to another room. All in all, there's something incongruously homely about the scene.

'These are genuine, pre-Meltdown "desktop" computers, aren't they?' Cole asks, his eyes shining.

Jeanie nods. 'Neat, right? It took me years to scavenge them all, and even longer to get them working, but it was worth it.'

Tanta can see why. Models this old must be undetectable to most of the digital signature scanners employed by InTech and the other corps, making them ideal for someone flying under the radar. Cole walks over to the nearest one, gazing at its black screen and bulky plastic casing with naked yearning.

'Shall we get started?' Tanta asks. Cole looks disappointed, but he can poke around on the legacy units after they've discussed the issue at hand.

There's a stack of folding chairs leaning up against the side of the wall. Jeanie sets three out and gestures for them all to take a seat, then slumps into the armchair. She looks more like a hostess welcoming them to a party than a co-conspirator. Again, Tanta is moved by how comforting this place feels. She wonders if the room at the back is where Jeanie sleeps; for all its strangeness, it has the air of a home about it – something Tanta hasn't encountered in a long time. Then Jeanie flashes her a look of intense dislike, shattering the feeling.

'I'm surprised you came,' she says to Tanta, with withering disdain.

'I said she would,' Yas replies. 'You owe me ten chit, J.'

Tanta is grateful for this attempt to lighten the mood. Cole is looking at his feet, embarrassed. 'I want the same thing you do,' she says. 'To circumvent—' *sabotage*, a voice in her head corrects – 'Harlow 2.0.'

Jeanie sighs. 'Fine. But for the record, that's not something I need *you* for, CorpWard.'

'You said you had a way to reverse the effects of the update?' Cole prompts.

'Yes and no,' Jeanie replies. 'It really all depends on you.' She stares at Cole. 'How much do you remember about the creation of the original Harlow Programme?'

Cole shifts on his chair, looking as uncomfortable as he always does when his role in the Harlow Programme is mentioned. 'Nothing at all,' he admits. 'It's a blank to me.'

'That's what I suspected.' A look flashes across Jeanie's face, gone before Tanta can identify it. 'You and I were in contact throughout the last few years of the programme's development. I was your Brokerage handler, and we spoke about it a lot.'

Cole spending years as a double agent is something that Tanta finds hard to imagine, but not to believe. She's had time to come to terms with the fact that the Cole she knows now is very different to the man he was; she barely recognises Jeanie's description, but she acknowledges its accuracy. Judging by the expression in Cole's eyes, he feels similarly.

'Before the Brokerage came up with the false flag attack, they had another plan,' Jeanie continues. 'They asked you to build a backdoor into the Harlow Programme, a—'

'A self-deletion protocol?' Cole asks, catching her meaning. He glances at Tanta – *can I talk about this?* – and she inclines her head in a nod. Much as she dislikes rehashing this sequence of events, there's no point in concealing them from Jeanie now.

'When Tanta lost her Harlow Programming, over the summer, I found a self-deletion protocol in her 'scape while I was examining the damage. I thought it was a security measure.' Cole is speaking rapidly, his voice animated.

Tanta doesn't begrudge him his enthusiasm – she knows he can't help it – but she finds she has trouble meeting his eyes. She looks at Jeanie instead – and sees the same interest animating her face.

'Had she been anywhere near an unvetted broadcasting device beforehand?' Jeanie asks.

Both Cole and Jeanie turn to Tanta simultaneously. She thinks again of the black tile, the same one she found in Fliss's pocket.

'I took a call on a pre-Meltdown device from someone claiming to be a Brokerage agent,' she admits.

Jeanie switches the hundred-watt bulb of her attention back to Cole again. 'That would explain it,' she says. 'I know you gave the Brokerage a way to access the backdoor remotely through a wireless signal. They might have used it on Tanta in an attempt to derail her investigation, especially if she was sniffing around after their activities.'

'I always wondered how it was triggered!' Cole's brow furrows, the implications of what Jeanie is saying catching up with him. 'The self-deletion protocol almost killed Tanta,' he says, speaking more slowly. 'Was that the – my – intention?'

'No, no,' Jeanie says. 'It was an unforeseen side effect – you were trying to iron it out, but I wouldn't put it past the Brokerage to use it against someone who was on their tail.'

Tanta is getting tired of this conversation, which is about her but does not include her. Still, Jeanie's interest in her as a convenient source of experimental data is at least preferable to the hostility and distrust that preceded it.

'So, what does the backdoor in the old Harlow Programme have to do with Harlow 2.0?' Cole asks.

'That's what I needed the software itself to check,' Jeanie says, 'It turns out, Harlow 2.0 has the same weakness. Friend designed the update using a combination of the Thoughtfront agent's programming and your Harlow Programme as a template. Now that I've had a chance to examine the code myself, it's clear that he copied a lot of it wholesale from the original – and he left the self-deletion protocol intact. He may not even have realised it was there.'

'That sounds like a significant oversight. Is it possible?' Tanta asks, addressing Cole. He looks almost surprised at the interruption, as if he had forgotten Tanta was in the room.

He considers her question carefully, though, before

committing himself to a reply. 'You remember when we broke into the Black Box last summer,' he says. 'Arthur was jealous of my work on the Harlow Programme and from what I've seen of the update, he hasn't been able to match it. The amount of code involved in the original programme is vast – it takes up more CP power than any other Inscape programme I've seen – and Neal told me that Arthur was on a tight deadline to adapt it for Harlow 2.0. Given that there are no problems with it that he knows of, I wouldn't be surprised if he'd replicated some portions of the code without going through them line by line.'

He turns back to Jeanie. 'This is huge,' he says. 'If Harlow 2.0 has a backdoor of its own, then reversing it could be as simple as updating the trigger signal to recognise the change in native interface.'

'Could we have this in English, please?' Yas cuts in.

'If the original Harlow Programme can be disabled by a signal, and the new one can be too, then we just need to update the signal to match the new programme, then broadcast it to as many people as possible,' Jeanie says.

Yas frowns at that. 'If Dr Friend's software fails without warning, I imagine he'll have some questions about it. What if he finds the backdoor and removes it? There's nothing to stop him from sending out the update again.'

'Even if Arthur figures out what happened, we'll at least have bought ourselves some time to develop a more permanent fix,' Cole replies. 'And the board may not give him the chance. A last-minute software error of this magnitude would make him look completely incompetent. In a best-case scenario, InTech might decide to mothball the whole project.' He glances at Jeanie. 'I'm more worried about the side effects. We can't trigger the self-deletion protocol if it's going to fry people's brains.'

'My intel indicates that Harlow 2.0 has already been uploaded to InTech's servers,' Jeanie says. 'If we can infiltrate whichever location is being used for the software rollout, you can fix the problems with the backdoor before the update has even been sent out to residents' 'scapes. We can embed the signal key in the same update packet.'

'The programme will uninstall itself as soon as it goes live,' Cole summarises. He beams at Jeanie. 'That's clever.'

'I can find out the location, and get you inside,' Tanta says. She's a little shocked to hear the words coming out of her mouth. But she wanted to help, didn't she? Cole and Jeanie's technobabble is incomprehensible to her, but this is something she can do.

Jeanie shoots her a look of pure scorn. 'Excuse me if I don't leap at the chance to leave an ICRD agent in charge of the most crucial part of this plan.'

'Who better than an ICRD agent to gain access to an InTech server centre?' Tanta counters. 'I can use my privileges to get you in and out before anyone realises anything is amiss.'

'Tanta's right,' Cole says. 'No one will question us being there if she's with us, and she's better trained for this than any of us.'

'Hey!' Yas protests.

Tanta knows Cole is trying – however belatedly – to defend her, but she, too, is stung by this praise. She's trained for the exact opposite of this – she's supposed to be protecting InTech's interests, not subverting them! *You want to do this, remember?* Knowing that this is something she has chosen – perhaps one of the first things she has even had the power to choose – doesn't make the guilt needling Tanta's insides go away completely, but it does help.

'I'll consider it,' Jeanie says at last. 'But let's cross that bridge when we come it, shall we? We still have to adapt the signal key so that it'll work. When that's done, *then* we'll talk about what comes next.'

Tanta has to accept that answer, equivocal as it is. She's on

Jeanie's turf, and has no choice but to play by her rules. It's not a situation she finds comfortable, so she's not sorry about what she has to say next.

'Cole and I should get back to the distribution centre before someone notices we're gone,' she says. 'We can use the communicator to keep you updated on Cole's progress with the signal key, then meet again when he's finished adjusting it.'

There's an awkward pause. 'Actually, I think it'd be better if I stayed here,' Cole says. His eyes flick to hers, then away again. 'I could use Jeanie's help with this.'

<<Are you sure that's a good idea?>> Tanta sends. She's not about to voice her concern aloud – she doesn't want another dressing down from Jeanie – but the thought of leaving Cole alone with the freedom fighter makes her uneasy.

A flash of annoyance crosses Cole's face. <<We've been over this, Tanta. I trust her. You don't need to babysit me.>>

Tanta hurts, though she conceals any trace of it. 'OK,' she says. 'I'll see you later, then. Ping me when you're done.'

'Will do.'

Cole turns back to Jeanie as he speaks, his attention already elsewhere. Tanta is about to suggest a code they can use over MindChat in case of any important developments, but Jeanie and Cole are discussing the signal together in low, excited voices, her presence all but forgotten. Yas rises from her chair, giving an elaborate stretch.

'And that's our cue to leave,' she says. 'Come on, Tanta. I'll drive you back.'

When they get outside, Yas pulls a face at her, rolling her eyes. 'Scientists,' she says.

Tanta smiles dutifully, but she barely registers what Yas is saying. She shouldn't be upset by Jeanie's suspicion – it is mutual, after all – but she can't help but feel isolated by it. She *has* chosen this – has chosen to turn her back on her training, on

Reet, and on her home – and her reward for that leap of faith is hostility and scorn. Yas and Cole have jumped ship and been accepted – welcomed, even – into this new life. Why hasn't she?

Maybe because you've still got a foot in both camps?

And that's the crux of the problem, isn't it? Tanta's loyalties are divided, and Jeanie can see that.

The problem with divided loyalties is they spread you thin. It's been a long time since Tanta really felt she belonged with InTech. She'd been hoping that feeling would subside, but it's only grown. And now she knows that there's no more a place for her outside the corp than there is within it. She is profoundly alone. A touch on her arm calls her back to herself. Yas is looking at her with that strange expression again, the one Tanta can't quite place.

'I'm sorry,' Tanta says. 'Did you say something?'

'I was just saying that it's nice to have another agent around.' Tanta must look sceptical, because Yas holds out her hands and adds, 'I mean it. Jeanie's more of an engineer, and she doesn't have much in the way of ground troops. It's mostly me, and I think she only hired me because I knew Cole.' Yas's lips quirk upwards in a half smile. Her crooked nose gives the expression an air of puzzlement. 'You know what it's like to be in the thick of it. And you had my back when we worked together. When you weren't trying to kill me, I mean. I'm glad you're here.'

Tanta returns her smile, but says nothing. It seems like Yas is the only person who is.

Chapter 26

Cole is gladder than he'd care to admit when Tanta and Yas finally leave. It's not just that he is eager to explore this Aladdin's cave of technology uninterrupted – it's also Jeanie herself. Cole was drawn to her before he even met her because of what she seemed to represent, and the answers she held about his past. Since then, his interest has only intensified. And now, for the first time he can remember, they are alone together.

Jeanie swings the door of the safehouse shut and turns to him, her expression expectant. Cole knows he ought to say something pertinent to the task at hand, like suggesting a starting point or advancing a theory, but as soon as her eyes meet his, his mind becomes a perfect blank. It is as if he has never thought or said an intelligent thing in his life.

He snaps himself out of this stupor with an effort of will, reminding himself sternly what is at stake here. Figuring out a way to reverse the rollout of Harlow 2.0 could be the most important thing he ever does, saving an entire population from a lifetime of mental control. He can't let his interest in Jeanie get in the way of their shared goal. He tries to look like he has his shit together; hopefully, if he can feign presence of mind well enough, it will come back to him in time.

'So, where should we start?' he asks her. It's a good question, he thinks: work-focused, business-like. The fact that he's only asking for an excuse to talk to her is knowledge that he tries to suppress.

Jeanie leads Cole to a worktable at the back of the room. The gadgets that litter its surface are more modern than the pre-Meltdown tech that fills the rest of the hut – there's an AR smart screen, a few MbOS ports and, in pride of place, a strange little contraption like a silver bird's nest. Cole has seen such things before: it's a dummy 'scape, an external version of the Inscape system that allows neurotechs in training to hone their skills on a real MbOS without running the risk of giving anyone brain damage.

'There's a copy of Harlow 2.0 in a walled garden on here,' Jeanie says, gesturing to it. 'I know enough about the software that I can recognise the backdoor, but I don't have the skills to analyse it properly. Could you take a look? I'm hoping it's similar enough to the protocol in the original programme that we can apply the same workaround.'

The way Jeanie talks about the update and her plans for circumventing it makes it clear she is familiar with how mind-based operating systems work. Cole is impressed; encountering someone so conversant with MbOS terminology outside of his office in the Black Box feels a little like finding someone who speaks the same language as him in a foreign country.

'That sounds like a plan,' he says. 'It's nice to be working with someone who understands this stuff.' Then he blushes, feeling as though he has betrayed Tanta with the comment. Tanta is a great partner and an even better friend, but there's a reason she needs him. He's her technical consultant; it's his job to interact with the Inscape system in ways she isn't trained to. Cole is so used to oversimplifying his explanations for her and her managers that he can't help but find Jeanie's surefooted grasp of his field refreshing.

'Sounds like you know a lot about the Inscape system,' he says, to cover his embarrassment. 'Do you have a background in neuroengineering?'

'Just regular engineering,' Jeanie says. 'But you and I used to talk about these things all the time when we worked together. You taught me a lot.'

That makes Cole's face heat even more. He's been betrayed into self-aggrandisement, though it wasn't his intention.

'You sent me copies of some of your research papers,' Jeanie continues. 'I've still got them all in an external hard drive back at my place.'

'This isn't your place?' Cole asks, surprised.

'You thought I lived here?' Jeanie laughs. 'It's a little cramped. I do crash here sometimes, when I need to be close to Sodis, but my main base is elsewhere. That's where most of my tech is. This' – she gestures at the banks of computers – 'isn't even half of it.'

The computers in the safehouse are more pre-Meltdown tech than Cole has ever seen in his life. The thought that Jeanie has even more is thrilling.

'I'd love to check it out,' he says. 'The tech, I mean.'

'I'll take you there sometime. I think you'd like it.' She flashes him a shy smile. 'Well, you've been before, and you liked it then.'

Behind his nerves and confusion, Cole feels a profound sadness. He and Jeanie seem to have shared so much, and all of it is lost to him.

'I'm sorry I don't remember,' he says. 'I wish I did.'

'I do, too,' Jeanie replies.

'Still, it sounds like I was a shitty person back then, so maybe it's for the best.'

'I wouldn't say that. But then, you don't know the old you like I did.'

Cole's heart suddenly feels like it's trying to climb out of his throat. He turns away and connects to the dummy 'scape, burying his turbulent feelings in his work. He locates the walled garden at once and accesses the software inside it.

The first thing that strikes him about the code for Harlow 2.0 is that it is strangely incoherent – probably because it has been cobbled together from so many different sources. Cole recognises a lot of his own work in the software, but there are changes. Another hand has made holes in the edifice he built and filled them in with a hodgepodge of materials, in several different architectural styles. Like an essay written by a student in a rush, there's very little about the update that's original. Cole's programming and the repurposed Thoughtfront code are doing most of the work, with Arthur's contributions merely bridging the gaps between them. Cole is not surprised. He knew Arthur didn't have an innovation like the Harlow Programme in him; he had to rely on Cole to create the first version, and this is a far shoddier follow-up.

After he's inspected it for a while, Cole can trace in the software before him the behavioural changes that he saw in Neal first-hand: his constricted affect, his conditioned obedience. There's no immediate explanation in the code for the memory loss Cole noticed, though it's possible it was caused by the trauma the intern must have experienced during the update itself. Cole feels a fresh surge of grief and anger at the thought, which he pushes firmly aside. He needs to focus – for Neal's sake as much as anyone's. He turns his attention elsewhere, searching for the self-deletion protocol.

He goes looking for it in the same place he found it in Tanta's 'scape. It doesn't take him as long to locate it as it did the first time – he knows what he's looking for now. It's where he expected it to be, curled within the centre of the programme like a worm at the heart of an apple, ready to demolish the whole thing from the inside out. It's no wonder Arthur never noticed it was there. It's so small as to be virtually undetectable; if Cole hadn't known what he was looking for, he doubts he would have found it himself.

In Tanta's 'scape, which he was only able to get a good look at after the self-deletion protocol had done its work, there was not much Cole could figure out about its mode of operation. Now, he has the chance to examine the backdoor while it's still intact – and he can see at once that it is very straightforward. At the moment, it's inactive, waiting for the signal that will set it in motion. On receipt of that trigger, it will hatch like a wasp from a cocoon, and devour the rest of the programme with the same rapacity.

Cole can see, too, why this process almost killed Tanta over the summer. The flaw in the self-deletion protocol's design is that it's too simple: it has no brakes or safeguards at all. Once it begins, there's no stopping it, and it swiftly snowballs, causing a huge drain on the core processor of the Inscape system. This was what caused Tanta's 'scape to overheat, and there's every reason to assume the same risk is present in Harlow 2.0. Cole is confident he'll be able to fix it, if Tanta can get him access to wherever the update is going live from – but as Jeanie said, he'll have to cross that bridge when he comes to it.

'What do you reckon?' Jeanie's voice comes from closer at hand than Cole was expecting. He looks up with a start to find her at his elbow. For a moment, he can't answer her. Her hair is brushing his arm, and he's transfixed by the sensation.

'Arthur seems to have copied the self-deletion protocol over wholesale,' he tells Jeanie. 'It's almost identical to the original.'

'Do you think you'll be able to design a signal that will trigger it?' Jeanie asks. She's close enough that Cole can feel her breath on the back of his neck.

'Yes,' he manages. 'It could take me a while, though.'

'Sounds like fun,' she grins. 'Let's get to it.'

There's that smile again: shy, sidelong, and ... inviting? Cole's mouth goes dry. For an instant, he allows himself to entertain a dizzying possibility, one that makes him simultaneously want to dance for joy and find a cave to hide in forever. If his feelings for Jeanie were the only issue in question here, Cole is sure he'd be able to ignore them far more effectively than he is doing. No, the prospect that makes his head spin and his breath catch in his chest is far more alien to him: if he didn't know better, he'd almost think that Jeanie liked him back.

Back at the flat in Sodis, Tanta tries to pick up where she left off. It's hard at first; returning to her official ICRD investigation is like acclimatising to a change in air pressure or gravity. She's been focused all morning on Jeanie and Harlow 2.0, so her return to the world of bandits and ghost accounts is a jarring one.

It isn't helped by her uncomfortable sense of duality. Her double life doesn't sit well with her, however temporary she hopes it's going to be. As Yas said, being a double agent is stressful. It's not that Tanta fears detection – not imminently, at least. Manipulation and duplicity are essential tools in her arsenal, and she's good at them. She's confident she can see both her missions through and leave Smythe, Kenway and the board none the wiser as to her involvement with Jeanie. But doing so costs her: she feels stateless, split down the middle.

She shakes off these feelings as best she can, trying to focus on where she and Cole left the case. Her next step is to find out the identity of the ghost account Cole discovered on the trade servers – and figure out how on earth the source of the leak within Sodis can be a dead person. If she can find the account, and get Cole to deactivate it, the bandits' operations will be significantly hampered. Without their man – or ghost – on the inside, they won't be able to target InTech's trade shipments with the uncanny accuracy they've displayed so far. It will be a huge success for Tanta, if she can pull it off – maybe even big enough that she could use it to convince the board to let her return to the city.

Of course, rooting out the source of the bandits' intel won't tell Tanta any more about the motivations of the people arming them. She is still puzzled on this score: Thoughtfront's role in the bandits' activities has never been in question – the fact that Fliss seems to know Hardinger only confirms it. What she can't figure out is why the Brokerage is helping the rival corp. The false flag attack was the Brokerage's doing, too, and that was designed to hurt Thoughtfront just as much as InTech. Thoughtfront may not know that it *was* a false flag attack, of course; if the corporation across the riverbed still believes InTech was responsible, the Brokerage could easily have capitalised on its anger and fear to build an alliance. The shadowy organisation has already set the two corporations at each other's throats; perhaps the only aim of this new partnership is to inflame tensions even further. If, as Jeanie claims, the Brokerage wants to sow chaos and destruction, then Tanta can't say it isn't working.

Tanta's thoughts are interrupted by a notification popping up on her Array – she's getting a call from Douglas Kenway. She sighs; Kenway is the last person she wants to talk to right now, but she returns his hail with a decent pretence at civility.

<<Director. What can I do for you?>>

<<Tanta. I'm calling to check in. Have you made any progress on the assignment?>>

Kenway's tone is unexpectedly cordial. Tanta pauses before she answers; she's wary of revealing to him just how far she's come. She'd rather present the closed case as a *fait accompli* when it's done. Let Kenway know how close she is to success, and she's sure he'll find a way to snatch it from her grasp.

<<Things are progressing well,>> she sends. <<I'm working on a number of leads. Nothing definitive yet, but I hope to have an update for you soon.>>

<<Good work.>> The Director sounds like he's barely listening. <<I have a question for you.>>

<<Go ahead.>>

<<It's about your work for Jennifer Ash last summer.>>

Tanta's unease increases. Kenway has already quizzed her extensively on the events of last summer. What more can there be to discuss?

<<I've been reviewing your service record, and I see that you were hit by an EMP device in the line of duty,>> he continues. <<Did you notice any side effects afterwards?>>

Tanta swallows. <<What kind of side effects do you mean?>>

<<Changes to your 'scape, perhaps?>> There's a pause. Tanta tugs at the collar of her shirt, which feels as though it's tightening around her neck. <<Mood swings?>>

<<No,>> Tanta replies. Her collar is noose-like, now, cutting off her air supply. <<I never noticed anything like that.>>

<<Even so, I think it would be best to check,>> Kenway returns. <<I'd like you and Cole to come back to the city tomorrow, please: I've scheduled you a check-up with Dr Friend.>>

A roaring starts up in Tanta's ears. Kenway knows. She doesn't know how he has found out, but he knows.

<<I'm sending Reet to pick up the investigation where you left off,>> he is sending. <<She'll arrive tomorrow morning. I'd like you to turn over all records relating to your investigation to her. She'll escort you back to the ICRD.>>

<<Director, I don't understand. Why do I need to see Dr Friend?>>

<<It's just a check-up,>> Kenway replies. <<To make sure

your Inscape system is functioning as it should. Nothing to worry about.>>

Tanta doesn't know how she responds to that; before she knows what is happening, Kenway has disconnected the call and she is alone again with the chaos of her thoughts. Two days ago, she would have leapt at the chance to return to the city; she couldn't feel more differently now. Bringing Cole back, before he and Jeanie have worked out a way to circumvent Harlow 2.0, would destroy him. And while he is exposed to the new Harlow Programme, Tanta will be subjected to the old one. Kenway must know that she has lost her programming – and if he doesn't, Dr Friend will soon figure it out. Tanta curses herself. She was too careless in the way she handled Kenway. She tipped her hand to him, and now he has discovered her secret.

She stands stock-still in the middle of the flat's living room, overwhelmed with terror. She is going to lose herself, and this time, there is nothing she can do to escape it. She and Cole are being dragged back to the city as unwillingly as they left. They could run, of course, become defectors, like Yas. But Tanta doesn't want to run. The corp may have lied to her, betrayed her and used her, but it's the only home she has ever known. She cannot turn away from it so easily even now, when the choice before her may well be between staying within InTech and staying herself.

Last summer, Tanta was able to rise above everyone's suspicion because of her outstanding conduct. Her exposure of Jen, her valiant actions in the Ward House fire, proved her loyalty to InTech beyond question. Could she pull off the same trick twice? It would take another achievement of similar magnitude. She would have to solve the case, then use that success to somehow convince the board to overrule Kenway's order. It's a desperate hope, but it may be the only one she has. And with

Reet arriving tomorrow, she has less than twenty-four hours to pull it off.

She is going to have to break into the archives tonight.

Cole stretches, feeling an unpleasant collection of clicks and pops. It's a few hours shy of dawn, and he's pretty sure he's cracked it. He and Jeanie have been up all night trying to design a key to the backdoor in Harlow 2.0 that has a decent chance of working. It's been a long, tiring process, but not an unwelcome one – not least because Jeanie has stayed by Cole's side the entire time.

While Cole has collaborated on research projects with colleagues before, it's always been a dry, transactional kind of relationship, with little in the way of conversation. He would read his fellow neurotechs' comments on the code they'd send him, and leave his own in return. He's never had an actual partnership before, someone with whom he could discuss his work in detail, asking their opinions and offering his own. It's a completely new experience to him – one that he finds as heady and intoxicating as Jeanie herself.

It's mostly thanks to Jeanie that the work has gone as quickly as it has. Cole is sure that without her there to listen to his theories and pronounce them sound or shaky, he'd still be scratching his head over the backdoor even now. As it is, he finally has some code for the key that's halfway useable. Now, there's just the small matter of testing it out. He reconnects to the dummy 'scape and runs a diagnostic: all systems are greenlit, including Harlow 2.0. When he transmits the new code he has devised, it should cause the software to unravel, just as Tanta's programming did last summer.

'Ready for the moment of truth?' he asks Jeanie.

She grins at him, eyes sparkling. 'Ready as I'll ever be.'

Cole takes a deep breath. Then he picks up the data card

on which the key is stored and uploads it to the nest of wires before him. The effect is instantaneous and dramatic. Cole's diagnostic detects critical system errors immediately; they flash yellow, then red, and then disappear as the dummy 'scape's core processor shorts out completely.

The physical effects are even more extraordinary. Cole wasn't expecting to *see* anything outside of the system logs on his Array, but the hardware of the dummy 'scape itself is actually changing shape, its hundreds of hair-like wires melting and bending as the core processor overheats. Cole has never seen anything like it. He watches transfixed, torn between horror and fascination as, over the course of half an hour, the Inscape collapses in on itself. Wires fuse to the processing chip and to each other, until the whole thing is a tangled ball of molten metal.

'I'm guessing it worked, then,' Jeanie says drily.

Cole can't help laughing, though it's a reaction born as much from shock as amusement. Was this what was happening to Tanta's 'scape last summer? It looks even worse playing out on the model. He checks the diagnostic tool again. Harlow 2.0 has indeed been deleted, though that's hardly a surprise. Nothing could have survived the catastrophic MbOS collapse that he and Jeanie have just witnessed. If this 'scape had been in a human head, it's owner would likely have suffered seizures, stroke and aneurysm, followed by swift brain death.

'Oh, it worked,' he replies. 'Now we just need to sort out the deadly side effects.'

To do that, Cole will need to work on Harlow 2.0 directly, which won't be possible until he and Jeanie can access InTech's servers. He is by no means disheartened by the task. Getting the software to interface with the signal key in a way that isn't potentially lethal will be difficult, but he's confident he can do it. He'll take the measures he used to save Tanta last summer as his starting point, automating and integrating them with the new software. It will be a challenge, but a satisfying one, both in itself and in its effects. It will also give him a convenient excuse to spend more time with Jeanie.

'I'm looking forward to it,' Jeanie says. 'That's a problem for tomorrow, though. We should get some rest. As much as we can, anyway.'

She touches his arm, her hand brushing against his bare skin. A shiver runs the whole length of Cole's body. It's as though Jeanie is a Van de Graaff generator; her touch was the lightest and briefest of caresses – there and gone again in an instant – but it was enough to make his hair stand on end. He wants her to touch him again. He wants...

Before Cole knows what he's doing, he finds himself leaning towards Jeanie, like a plant drawn to the sun. The gentle pressure on his arm returns, and this time it does not subside. Every instinct Cole has screams at him to stay still and say nothing, to enjoy Jeanie's touch for what it is, and not ask for anything more. He's terrified of breaking whatever strange spell this is, of saying something awkward or doing something clumsy that will make Jeanie move away again. But if he does nothing, the moment will pass and Jeanie will go to bed, and he'll lose the chance to find out what could have been, possibly forever.

'Jeanie,' he says. His mouth is so dry it's an effort to get the words out. 'When we worked for the Brokerage together, were we...?'

Jeanie is looking at him intently. She does not finish his sentence for him, much to his embarrassment. He tries again. 'I mean, did we ever...?'

A smile tugs at her lips. 'Yes. We did. Many times. Never in here, though. Why do you ask?'

Cole's thoughts turn dizzy cartwheels in his mind. He's not sure whether he's overjoyed or terrified. 'Well, I, um. I mean. Would you like to...?'

Jeanie sighs. It's a soft sound, like waves breaking on a deserted beach. 'I thought you'd never ask,' she says. She leans in and kisses him.

After that, Cole forgets to think for a while.

Chapter 27

Tanta watches from the flat's narrow windows as dusk falls over the distribution centre. When it's late enough that she judges most of the personnel in the Logistics Office will have gone home for the night, she pins her hair back out of her eyes, puts on the darkest clothes she owns, and takes the lift down to the ground floor. She steps out into a downpour that drenches her within minutes. Far from resenting the freezing deluge, she welcomes it. There's no moon tonight, and the rain is so heavy it is like a curtain drawn across the air, shielding her from view. She scuds across the streets like a cloud in a high wind, keeping to the shadows.

She spends the trip to the Logistics Office racking her brains, trying to dredge up everything she can remember about the place. She wishes now that she'd been less dismissive of Smythe's boastful lecture about the building's security arrangements when she and Cole arrived at Sodis; if she'd known she was going to have to break into it the following evening, she would have paid more attention. All she can remember with any certainty is that the place is a fortress, stuffed with more alarms and monitoring systems than InTech's holding cells in the city.

The security shutter is down when Tanta reaches the office a few minutes later, but since it's secured with only a physical lock, she can circumvent it easily enough. She takes her time making sure she isn't observed, loitering opposite the office and watching the empty street. The rain soaks through her clothes and into her skin, making her shiver. When forty-five minutes have passed without her seeing another soul, she creeps up to the door and uses her hairpins to pick the lock. It takes two pins, one to apply pressure on the barrel and the other to slide into the lock and raise the lock pins one by one. It's a satisfying activity – listening for the click of the pins and feeling for the subtle motion as the lock gives way gradually to the application of pressure and patience. Once she's in, she slides the shutter up, cracks the door open and slips inside.

The interior of the Logistics Office looks different at night, darkness rendering its wide lobby and potted plants unfamiliar. Tanta stands still, conjuring a mental image of what the place looks like during the day. Her memory is good, but she wasn't expecting to be returning under cover of darkness the last time she visited.

She's sure Smythe mentioned motion sensors, and she *thinks* she remembers their locations – one over the doorway of his office, another opposite it. She gets her 'scape to calculate the sensors' likely range; two red cones appear in her vision a foot in front of her, meeting in the middle of the floor. That means she's safe here, plastered against the door, but as soon as she steps into the room, she'll trigger an alarm. Luckily, she can take precautions to conceal herself from where she is.

Most motion sensors don't really detect movement at all. What actually triggers them is rapid changes in infrared radiation, which for Tanta's purposes means heat. A tree in a strong breeze casting a moving shadow on the wall won't cause the alarm to trip, but a warm body walking through the room itself will. It's the reason Tanta took so much time to get over here. Chilled to the bone from her wet clothes and walk through the rain, she's already in a reasonable position to fool the sensors. She sets her 'scape to monitor her body heat and compare it with the ambient temperature. They're close — whether close enough that her own heat signature will blend into the background, she's not certain.

She doesn't have any time to waste, though. Now that she's indoors, she's only going to get warmer. She drops to all fours and crawls forward, her chest tight and her hands curled into fists. She can feel the blind eyes of the motion detectors above her, boring into the back of her neck. She strains her ears so hard listening for an alarm that the silence itself becomes noisy, filled with the ringing sound of absence. In a way, the quiet is worse. Tanta catches herself worrying about silent intruder alerts: what if Smythe has already received word of her presence here via his 'scape? She brushes her anxieties aside with an effort. There's no point to them; Smythe will discover her treachery, or he won't, and that's all there is to it.

After what feels like an age, Tanta makes out a rectangle of darkness ahead of her — the stairs down to the archive. Here, she pauses, trying to remember what Smythe said about this part of his unasked-for tour. Pressure plates! That was it. She inches forward another few feet and the tile floor gives way to carpet, supporting the hunch. Pressure sensors don't work under hard floors, so if Smythe has put them anywhere, it's here.

She looks around, trying to find a way past this new obstacle. But Smythe has placed the pressure plates well. She has no way of detecting them other than by triggering them, so she has to assume there's one on every step. The staircase stretches downwards, into a darkness so complete that even Tanta's 'scape-enhanced vision cannot penetrate it. It's long and steep: there's no way she could clear it in a single jump, and even if she could, the fall would injure her too severely to make continuing the assignment possible.

A spindly handrail on the right-hand wall presents the only way around the problem Tanta can see. It doesn't look like it will take her weight for long, but perhaps she can use it to get close enough to make the leap to the bottom of the staircase. She removes her shoes and climbs onto the rail gingerly, like a cat. It creaks, but does not give way. Moving slowly, wary of losing her balance, she rises to her feet and tightropes down the bannister. She has seen vids of people doing this at insane heights, walking a wire stretched out between two high-rises. The bannister may be closer to the ground, but the stakes here are scarcely any lower. One false move will send her plunging onto the pressure sensors, setting off an alarm that will bring all the guardians in the distribution centre to her location. They'll be armed and, if Smythe is any indication, trigger happy. They might wait to check Tanta's profile before they shoot but Tanta doesn't want to bet her life on it.

She walks like a monkey, placing each foot deliberately and using her toes to improve her grip. But no amount of balance on her part can make the thin rail better able to take her weight. The metal groans, beginning to buckle. She increases her pace and, just before the supports securing it give way completely, she springs, throwing herself to the bottom.

She twists as she falls, tucking her head in and drawing her arms and legs close in a protective ball. It's vital she doesn't touch the stairs with any part of her body, but a bad fall could kill her just as easily. She hits the ground on her side, with an impact that jars through her. It hurts, but that's good: the floor she has landed on is hard tile, not the soft carpet that conceals the pressure pads.

Tanta lies on the ground for a moment, checking herself over for injuries. When she is satisfied that she can walk, she puts her shoes back on and rises to her feet. Behind her, the handrail is hanging loose from the wall, sagging dangerously close to the stairs. Before her is the door to the archives.

The archives are pitch-black, with an exposed ceiling that sucks all the heat out of the room. Tanta lowers into a crouch and moves forward slowly, in case there are more motion sensors in the walls. Rows of shelves stretch away into a distance she cannot penetrate.

She creeps over to the stacks nearest the door, scanning them for an AR label that might give some clue as to their contents. There's no AR tag that she can see, but about halfway up the closest shelf she can just make out a paper index card with something scrawled on it in black ink. She dials up the contrast on her 'scape, trying to make it out. The note is in Smythe's handwriting and says, simply, 'Income'.

Tanta boggles. The index card isn't even dated! This laconic classification system is going to make her job even harder. Doubtless that's the intention – she suspects that only Smythe truly knows where everything in the archives is. Still, she has a starting point: the classified files are sure to be labelled with their case numbers, if nothing else. Case number #1436 will hold the answers she's looking for. All she needs to do is find it.

She creeps on, feeling the deep chill of the place seep through her soaked clothing and settle in her bones. She has to grit her teeth to stop from shivering – it's better that she stays cold to mask her heat signature, and she also wants to avoid any unnecessary movement. She checks the labels on the stacks as she goes but sees nothing worth looking into for a long time. Rows and rows of shelves all bear the same label – 'Income' – sometimes with the addition of a year. There's also 'Orders', 'Returns', and the unhelpfully labelled 'Correspondence'. She finds several stacks devoted to 'Staff', but after laboriously moving the wheeled shelves back far enough to access their contents, she finds that the data cards inside contain only commonplace records of performance reviews and disciplinary proceedings.

The archives are vast – more like a wide tunnel than a single room – and the deeper in Tanta goes, the less used they seem. Around the forty-five-minute mark, she starts to feel dust tickling her bare feet, which she scuffs as she goes to obscure her footprints. It gets thicker the deeper she progresses; no one else has been this far into the archives for a long time.

After an hour and a half of fruitless searching, she's getting anxious. She can't be found here when the Logistics Office opens – she has no way to explain her presence – but if she can't find what she's looking for and solve the case, the consequences will be even worse. Reet is coming to take her back to the city. She may already be on her way. And once she arrives, Tanta will lose her one, slim chance at continued freedom.

Tanta is struggling against the first stirrings of panic when her eye is caught by something she hasn't seen before. Two stacks are yoked together by a thick metal chain. One index label serves for both. It is marked with a single word in all-caps: 'CLASSIFIED'.

Tanta's pulse quickens. This is it. The chain is secured with a padlock, one so old and rusted that she is spared the trouble of picking it. She gives it a sharp twist and it snaps, the chain slithering off the hand winches of the stacks like a dead snake. Tanta stows it out of sight under the nearest cabinet, then cranks the shelves apart and steps into the narrow aisle between them. The data cards within are stacked in boxes in orderly rows. Each box is labelled with a handwritten case number.

Tanta runs her eyes along the rows of boxes, looking for the one she needs. *1436. 1436.* She finds it at last at the very end of the middle shelf, a battered cardboard box that looks as old as the lock on the stacks. It has a sheet tacked to the front, bearing the names and affiliations of the people who have accessed it. Sure enough, no one seems to have so much as looked at it for twenty years. Tanta is surprised to see several people from Intracorp on the list of accessors. Intracorporate Affairs is InTech's internal investigatory force; their agents conduct surprise inspections of InTech facilities and deal with cases of embezzlement and misappropriation of corporate assets. If they've been involved with whatever Smythe is hiding, then it's no wonder he's so cagey about it. She's even more curious to see, at the very bottom, the name *Dr Arthur Friend*. What was the head of Inspire Labs doing here?

Well, there's one way to find out. Tanta seizes the box, sliding it free from the dusty shelf. The lights slam on, and a piercing alarm shatters the stillness. A wave of fear sweeps through Tanta, bringing a memory with it. The one security protocol of Smythe's she had forgotten: the weight sensors in the shelves.

For an instant, Tanta's mind is filled only with light and noise. The blaring alarm is sounding not only in her 'scape but also through speakers on the walls, and the lights are dazzling, flooding the room with white. Then her training kicks in. There's no way to shut the alarm off; the guardians will be converging on the archive even now.

She wrenches the lid off the box and flicks frantically through the data cards inside, looking for the one or two she will need. They've all been labelled by hand, though, in spidery handwriting that's impossible to decipher at speed. She checks the clock on her Array – thirty seconds have elapsed already. There's no time; she'll have to ride this out and come back to the box after the guardians have gone, if she can.

She's about to jam it back onto the shelf when another idea occurs to her. The alarm has already been set off – the guardians are going to know that *something* has happened here, but not necessarily what. The shelves this far back in the archives are old, their metal rivets weak. Perhaps she can make this look like an accident, one in which no intruder was even involved. Tanta drops the box, then brings her fists down hard on the others, pounding them again and again. The shelf beneath them groans, creaks, and gives way with a crash. Boxes thud to the floor, spilling data cards everywhere.

In the midst of the chaos, Tanta rakes her eyes to and fro, searching for some means of escape. The archives look a lot smaller in the glare of the overhead lights and, though they are filled with shelves, she can't count on them to hide her: the guardians' search will be too thorough for that. Nor can she make it to the door before the guardians arrive. She is hopelessly exposed, pinned in place by the unforgiving brightness like an insect on a board. She squints upwards, and the strip lights stare back at her. But there's something else up there as well.

Quick as a squirrel, Tanta scales the cabinet closest to her, climbing the undamaged shelves like the rungs of a ladder. At the top, she raises her arms and jumps upwards, feeling for a handhold. Her fingers catch on a length of piping and she hauls herself up into the innards of the exposed ceiling. The strip lights hang from the ceiling on metal cables and are shaded from above. The door bursts open a second after she has pulled herself into cover and six guardians stream into the room, fanning out as they make their way between the shelves.

Spread-eagled in the shadows of the ceiling, bracing herself against a metal pipe on one side and a ventilation duct on the other, Tanta waits with breath held in and limbs tensed.

'Clear!' One of the guardians calls, reaching the end of a row of stacks. His cry is repeated by several others.

The guardians sweep the room with maddening slowness. Almost imperceptibly, the pipe supporting Tanta's left arm begins to sag.

'There's something here!' a woman shouts. She has reached

the cabinets Tanta was searching. From above, Tanta watches the woman scratch her head, trying to make sense of the mess. *Don't look up don't look up don't look up.* Other guardians converge on the woman's location. Tanta's limbs are aching; she can't hold herself in this position much longer.

'What do you reckon?' the woman asks her colleagues.

There's an agonising pause.

'Probably one of the shelves gave way,' a man replies, at last. 'These things are ancient.'

'Smythe's a fucking cheapskate,' the woman replies. 'Figures we'd all be pulled out of bed for equipment failure. False alarm!' she yells. 'Shut it off. And someone order a cleaning crew down here for tomorrow.'

Tanta would heave a sigh of relief, were it not for the fact that the tension holding her body rigid is the only thing keeping her from dropping from the ceiling like a stone. As it is, she just closes her eyes in a fervent but silent prayer of gratitude. There's a little more milling about, and an abortive attempt to repair the broken shelf, but the guardians are all keen to get back to their beds and they quickly disperse. As soon as the lights go out, filling the archive with blessed darkness once more, she drops from her hiding place. Now that all the boxes are on the floor, she can examine the files from case 1436 at her leisure – relatively speaking – and then leave the box where it fell. The cleaning crew may puzzle over the broken handrail and the snapped padlock when they discover them tomorrow, but it's unlikely they'll piece together what happened here tonight – and even less likely that anyone would think to point the finger at Tanta.

She seats herself cross-legged on the ground and reopens the box. Rows of data cards in plastic holders stare back at her. Tanta flicks through them, looking for anything that might identify the owner of the ghost account. She pauses on one marked

317

Incident Report and loads it on her 'scape's viewer. It's a video file, showing two men talking in a room that looks a little like the conference room in the Logistics Office, a floor above where Tanta is crouching now. As she examines the scene, Tanta realises that she recognises both men. The first is Smythe. The other is the board's conduit. The conduit looks much younger. His eyes are brighter and the paunch that Tanta is used to seeing around his waist has gone, but the likeness is unmistakable.

'Report, Logistics Officer,' the conduit says.

'The software update did not go as foreseen, Representative,' Smythe replies. 'We uploaded it to the participants' Inscapes this morning, but there were side effects. Director Friend's team didn't warn me about the bloody—'

'We have already been apprised of the side effects,' the conduit interrupts. 'What has been done to contain the situation?'

'We've put a comms blackout in place, but there wasn't much we could do about the rest of the centre finding out,' Smythe says bitterly. 'There's about a hundred of them out there now, waving their damn placards. You must have seen them on your way in.'

The conduit stares at Smythe impassively. 'The dissidents are an inconvenience. What is your damage limitation plan?'

'Damage limitation plan? With respect, Representative, what do you think I've been doing all morning? It's only thanks to me and my team that the riots have been contained to Sodis,' Smythe replies.

There's a long pause while the conduit takes this in. Tanta knows from her own experience with him that the board must be locked in debate on what orders to issue next. She's about to fast forward the recording when the conduit speaks again.

'It is the board's decision that all knowledge of this incident be suppressed, Logistics Officer. Director Friend will make sufficient MindWipe headsets available for this purpose. Is that understood?'

'Perfectly, Representative. But I'm short-handed here already, and thanks to Director Friend's blunder, I've lost the trust of the staff. Convincing them all to submit to the procedure voluntarily may be beyond my resources.'

'Failure to comply is to be met with force. Additional resources will be provided if required.'

Smythe considers this; Tanta can almost see his greedy eyes twinkling. 'I'll need some armoured tactical vehicles to round them all up. And assault weapons for the troops. Maybe a—'

Tanta shuts off the recording there. She knows already what the outcome of Smythe's request for more 'resources' was. The over-supplied equipment room, filled with enough firepower and armoured vehicles to take over a small country, bears witness to the fact that the board granted his request in full. It gives Tanta a queasy feeling in the pit of her stomach to think that all these weapons of war were supplied for InTech to use against its own employees. Something bloody happened here, and it wasn't a terrorist attack or an incursion from an enemy corp. No, InTech did this to its own.

But why? Smythe mentioned something about an update. If the distribution centre was used to pilot a new piece of Inscape software – one that appears to have gone terribly wrong – then that would explain what Dr Friend has to do with all of this. It still doesn't tell her who the ghost account belongs to, or how it is still active after all this time, but if Inspire Labs is involved, there's bound to be documentation in here somewhere about the update's purpose – and the names of the people on whom it was tested. She flicks through some more of the holders until she finds one labelled *Research Papers*. She takes the holder out and summons her Array so she can scan the contents of the cards inside. As she works, she lets her focus soften and expand, taking in as much information as possible.

Experimental modifications

Thirty-seven participants

New update to increase processor speed

In light of the deaths

Tanta stops, her attention narrowing to a point again to focus on the words that have caught her eye:

In light of the deaths and their possible impact on employee morale, it is the recommendation of the researchers that these records be sealed.

She tracks back, looking for more details. The sentence that arrested her attention is from the conclusion of a paper entitled 'Processing Speed Updates to the Inscape System: A Software Change Impact Analysis'. She scrolls back to the top of the article to find the abstract.

The trial was of an update to the Inscape system, she reads, *designed to increase system speed by 3%. It was estimated that this would lead to a significant uptick in worker efficiency. Thirty-seven participants were selected from the Trade Division's Southern Distribution Centre.*

Tanta wonders whether the participants were given the choice to take part in this trial, or whether they were as ignorant of their involvement as she was of the Harlow Programme.

She reads on. *The update works in theory, but in practice several serious failings were discovered. Thirty-two participants experienced haemorrhagic stroke due to cascading system errors. A further five were rendered catatonic.*

A chill spreads through Tanta, one that has nothing to do with the temperature of the room. If these are the skeletons in Smythe's closet, they are grisly indeed. A covert experiment on human subjects – one that led to dozens of deaths – it's no wonder he wants these secrets buried forever. Evidently, InTech does too. The corp has suppressed all memory of this dark chapter in its history very effectively. These records probably only exist for the benefit of researchers like Dr Friend and his team at the Black Box.

Suddenly, Tanta understands why InTech would pick someone with ICRD training to head up Sodis. Smythe may not be good enough to be a field agent, but he's sufficiently well-versed in security protocols to guard the archives – and the sensitive documents they contain. She's ashamed of her oversight: there was more to the Logistics Officer's security arrangements than paranoia and ego-stroking all along, and she was too disarmed by the man's apparent idiocy to see it.

She is sickened by the things she has seen and read, but not shocked – a realisation that is almost a shock in itself. Has she become so habituated to her corporation's cruelty? It has been a gradual process, one so slow and so insidious that she has barely noticed it. Less than a year ago, Tanta had believed InTech could do no wrong, and now here she is – learning that the corp used her colleagues as guinea pigs and concealed all knowledge of their deaths – and she isn't even surprised. This is what InTech does. She has seen enough over the last two months to have learnt that lesson thoroughly. It takes care of its own only until it is more convenient not to do so.

She hasn't got time to dwell on her growing cynicism, however. Whatever this report says, clearly at least one of the thirty-seven participants in InTech's software experiment survived, and went on to access the trade servers again. The owner of the ghost account must be among the supposed dead; Tanta is sure of it. She now also has some idea of what may be motivating them to aid the bandits and the Brokerage – though she's not sure why they've waited until now to strike. The deaths happened twenty years ago. Where has the owner of the ghost account been during that time, and what have they been doing? Tanta continues flicking through the document, looking for a list of the study's participants.

It's at the end of the paper, in the appendices. Thirty-seven names, and thirty-seven photographs. There is no other clue as to the lives these victims lived, or the people they left behind. They have been forgotten – worse, erased – by the corporation they served. This afterthought of a list, appended to a paper that spends more time talking about the future of the research programme they were sacrificed to than it does acknowledging their deaths, is the only memorial they have. Only, of course, one of them is still very much alive.

Tanta reads the names slowly, letting the weight of what was done to them settle on her shoulders. Time is short, and she knows she should hurry. But she will not rush this.

Her sombre pace does nothing to lessen the shock when she reaches the end of the list to find a name and a face she recognises.

The back room of Jeanie's safehouse is warm and softly lit, and the curtain separating it from the workspace next door draws a comforting veil across the world outside. That world has never felt more remote to Cole. He could happily stay here forever, and let Harlow 2.0 and the bandit attacks, even Tanta, blur into an uneasy dream. Lying on Jeanie's rickety fold-out bed, wrapped in Jeanie's arms, he drowses, utterly content.

This feeling lasts for about twenty minutes – possibly a record. Cole has never been the kind of person who can enjoy lying still and doing nothing for long. His mind is too active. Even now, in the midst of the greatest sense of peace he has known in a long time, his restless thoughts are soon on the move again, questioning, exploring, and worrying.

He wriggles around, turning to face Jeanie. She is awake too – and watching him through half-shut eyes. Cole smiles to see her. His shyness has dissipated. Although none of his memories have returned, he has a romantic notion, one that isn't wholly without scientific merit, that he never truly forgot Jeanie. Even when he didn't know her, his body remembered her. That they are together again, however unexpectedly it has happened, feels natural.

'We should get in touch with Tanta and Yas,' he tells her, half-regretfully. 'Let them know we've cracked the key.' As sorry as he is to leave the bed, he's also keen to let Tanta know what they've achieved – and to move forward with the next step in their plan.

'Mm. I suppose so,' Jeanie grumbles. She stretches, releasing Cole, and rolls to her feet. 'But first...' She vanishes into the other room. When Cole follows her out, she is holding two tumblers filled with something golden and bubbly. 'We should celebrate! Don't worry,' she adds. 'It's non-alcoholic.'

She offers one of the glasses to Cole and he takes it gratefully. His mouth is very dry, and he can't remember the last time he ate or drank anything. They sit down together, Cole on one of the folding chairs, Jeanie in the armchair.

'A lot of people have made a lot of sacrifices to get us to this point,' Jeanie says. 'We're on the home stretch now.'

Cole clinks glasses with her. 'To defeating the Harlow Programme.' He downs his drink in one long swallow. It tastes nice: mildly sweet, with an undertone of something he doesn't recognise.

· Jeanie takes a sip of her own drink and looks at him. 'I wish you could know how hard you worked for today,' she says. 'You've wanted this for a long time.'

Cole nods, conceding the point. Even when he planned the false flag attack, he was still trying, in a roundabout way, to bring the Harlow Programme down. He can't tell if it gives him any comfort to know that his past self was once motivated by the same thing that drives him now. Probably not, given how things turned out the first time around. The thought makes him gloomy.

'Sure,' he says. 'And the terrorism was just because I got a little side-tracked.'

'Let me get you another drink,' Jeanie replies.

She gets up and walks back into the bedroom. Cole is expecting her to reappear immediately, but she's gone for some time. While he waits for her, he looks around the room again. Jeanie's hideaway really is like a cave, he decides. The bulky shapes of the old computers cast strange, angular shadows on the walls that look a bit like rock striations, if he tilts his head to one side and squints one eye. He's still doing this when he feels a cool glass being eased into his hand. He gives Jeanie a grateful smile.

'To Neal,' he says. His voice sounds rougher than he intended it to. 'We couldn't have done any of this without him.'

'To Ortega,' Jeanie replies gravely. 'He was a good soldier.'

A question bobs into Cole's head, then. It's one that has been nagging at him all night. 'About Neal,' he starts. The words come out slurred, which makes him forget what he was going to say. 'Are you sure this isn't alcoholic?' he asks.

Jeanie laughs. 'You're just tired, Cole. And no wonder. You've worked hard. Harder than you remember.'

That pushes the question back into Cole's mind. 'Neal didn't remember our break-in at the Black Box, or you, or anything,' he says slowly. 'I thought the memory damage was a side effect of the update, but I've looked at the software, and it wasn't.'

Jeanie meets his gaze. 'You're right,' she says. 'It wasn't.'

This strikes Cole as an odd response, though he can't put his finger on why. He sits in silence for a little while, waiting for the reason to come to him. It seems to be travelling from some distance away. Eventually, it reaches him.

'How do you know that?' The words feel too thick for his mouth, somehow, angular and misshapen as the shadows on the walls. And his head feels heavy. *Really* heavy, like someone has stuffed his brain full of lead.

'I always tell my soldiers to do a full MindWipe when the job is done,' Jeanie replies. There's a sad little smile on her face. 'The Brokerage never uses the same agent twice. It's the only way to protect my identity.'

Cole's head is too heavy for him to hold it up. It sags sideways, and the rest of him follows it. Jeanie is not in the armchair anymore, but at his side, guiding him down off the chair and onto the floor. Cole heard what she said, but he didn't quite understand it. The lead in his brain is making it hard to think. Even through the weight in his mind and in his limbs, though, he's dimly aware that she has told him something important.

'M – MindWipe,' he says. 'My ...?'

Jeanie leans over him. Her face is blurry. She lifts a hand – feathery motion trails follow it as it moves – and lays it over one of Cole's own. 'Yes,' she says. 'Even you, Cole. I'm sorry.'

Chapter 28

Tanta stares at the photograph for a long, terrible moment. The universe is spinning like a child's pinwheel, and she is its axis. She stands at the centre of the vortex, and everything she thought she wanted shifts around her, until the landscape of her life and hopes is no longer one she recognises.

In the space between one heartbeat and the next, the things that drove her to break into the archives are rendered irrelevant, beside the point. She came here hoping to salvage her place within InTech, her chance at a home and a career. None of that matters now; it all comes a distant second to the little file photo of Jeanie, and the terrible truth it represents. Jeanie never left the Brokerage. She *runs* the Brokerage. The ghost account belongs to her: she has been coordinating the bandits the entire time – the same bandits that tried to kill Cole and Tanta on their way to Sodis. And now, she and Cole are alone together.

Tanta has to get to him. This thought breaks the spell that's freezing her limbs in place; she climbs to her feet and sprints for the door, hailing Cole as she goes. He doesn't reply; there's nothing on their channel but dead silence. At first, reaching Cole and making sure he's OK is the only thought in Tanta's mind, but other considerations crowd in hot on its heels. If Jeanie lied about her connection to the bandits and to the

Brokerage, then what else is she concealing? A memory comes back to her from yesterday morning, when Smythe was showing her around the Logistics Office for the first time: *we don't harbour traitors in Sodis*, he had said.

Jeanie has been lurking on the distribution centre's servers for years, right under Smythe's nose. And she's been biding her time. Once Tanta has rescued Cole, she realises, she'll need to stop Jeanie – because whatever she's really doing with Harlow 2.0, Tanta doubts it has anything to do with saving the residents of InTech from it. The Brokerage wants to destroy the entire corporate system – Jeanie said so herself. Everyone in InTech's part of the city could be in danger and, right now, Tanta is the only one who knows about it.

She has reached the stairs. Rather than waste time with the tightrope walk up the handrail again, Tanta keeps right on sprinting. She feels the click as her foot touches the first pressure plate, but she's prepared for the alarm that follows. She runs through the noise, letting it wash through her consciousness without focusing on it. She'll have two minutes before the building is swarming with guardians again – maybe more, if the ones who responded last time are still on duty and inclined to write this off as another false alarm. That's not a lot of time for what she has in mind, but it's enough. When she gets to the lobby, rather than making for the door, she continues up to the first floor and the holding cells.

She meets Fliss's guard on the landing. It's Smythe himself, which is lucky: he recognises her, and for a split second, she sees him assume that she is here to respond to the alarm, rather than being the one who triggered it. Smythe is a big man, and he's had some of the same training Tanta has; she doesn't want this to come to a fight. She keeps her eyes locked on his face, her hands relaxed at her sides as she runs up the stairs towards him – *I'm not a threat.*

'I'm glad you're here, Agent,' Smythe says. 'Someone—'

Tanta punches him in the solar plexus. He goes down with a soft grunt – the sound of all the air leaving his body at once. Tanta hops over his prone form, feeling a mixture of guilt and satisfaction: she's wanted to hit Smythe almost since she met him.

There are many blows she could have landed that would have killed the Logistics Officer outright, but she's not about to use lethal force on a colleague, even a monster like him. He'll be in a lot of pain – enough to make him black out, by the looks of things – and she may have broken his sternum, but he'll survive. Of course, he'll also recover far quicker than he would have done from a blow to the head. Tanta estimates she has five minutes at most before he's back on his feet and pursuing her. She dashes past him and into the holding cells.

Fliss has not been idle during her day in the holding cells. From the moment her guard shut her inside, she was already planning how she'd walk out again. Getting out of her cuffs was easy. The guard took her belt and her jacket before he left, but he couldn't take her teeth. As soon as she was alone, Fliss had simply gripped the end of the zip-tie in her mouth and pulled it as tight as she could, straining her wrists in the opposite direction. It hurt like hell and has left gashes in her skin like red bracelets, but it snapped the zip-tie in two.

After that, she had turned her attention to the cell itself. Escaping this is a trickier proposition, one she's still ruminating on now. The cell is empty apart from a toilet, a sink, and a bed, which is really no more than a slab of poured concrete jutting out of the wall. There's a foam mat on it, but no blanket or pillow Fliss could shred and use as a rope. Even if there was, there's no window in the bare room, and the door is solid metal, with nothing more than a barred peephole at the top.

Her best bet, Fliss decides, is to wait until someone visits her. Perhaps the guard will bring her dinner – then she can pretend to choke on whatever crap she's given. There's no way she can break out of here alone, but if she can trick a guard into coming inside, she might be able to garrotte them with the snapped off zip-tie, or at least smash them over the head with her food tray. As a plan, it's an oldie but a goodie. Fliss has seen it in movies before; how hard can it be?

She's thought out her exit strategy so far when the alarm goes off for the second time that night. It makes Fliss wince, but it's good news. Another alarm means chaos, and chaos is something she might be able to use. After a minute or more of ringing, she hears footsteps on the stairs. She plasters her back against the wall next to the door, pulling the zip-tie taut in her hands. This could be her ticket out of here; if someone's coming to check on her, she's determined it'll be the last thing they ever do. There are sounds of a scuffle from outside, and then the door swings open. Fliss leaps into the doorway, her improvised garrotte raised in both hands, and runs at her warder.

Only it's not her warder. She collides with Tanta, the InTech agent. Fliss is holding the zip-tie too high – she was expecting to be fighting one of the bulky guards, not the girl, who is much shorter. She goes to lower it, but the girl is faster. Before Fliss knows what is happening, she has been spun around, forced to the floor, and one of her arms has been twisted painfully behind her back. The zip-tie flaps uselessly from her pinned hand.

'Stop that,' she hears from behind her. 'I'm not here to fight you.'

'Fucking funny way of showing it,' Fliss growls. She twists around, trying to bite Tanta's arm, but Tanta brings her other hand up, fending her off as easily as if she's a fly.

'If I let you up, will you hear me out?' Tanta asks.

'That depends on what you've got to say.'

'I'm here to agree to your terms: I'm releasing you from InTech's custody. In return, I want you to take me to the Brokerage.'

Fliss stops struggling against Tanta's hold. It's more surprise than acquiescence on her part. Her 'terms', as Tanta puts it, were the result of sheer bravura. She's confident she *can* get back to the place where she overheard Hardinger and the woman talking – she spent long enough staring at the map on the smartphone that it's more or less burnt into her brain – but she wasn't seriously expecting to have to make good on the offer. She's not sure why InTech has released her – she wouldn't, in its shoes. As soon as she goes limp, Tanta lets go of her arm. Fliss springs to her feet and turns, eyeing the agent warily.

'Why the change of heart?' she asks.

'I'll explain on the way,' Tanta replies. 'If you want to go, we have to leave *now*.'

Fliss *does* want to go – more than anything – but the agent's reply almost makes her resolve to stay put. She doesn't like being rushed, and she has no idea what this girl's agenda is. She plants her feet and folds her arms. 'Answer my question first. Or how am I supposed to know I can trust you?'

For the first time since she met her, Fliss sees an expression on the girl's face that's halfway to human. She looks exasperated – fair enough, Fliss often inspires that reaction – but she also looks afraid.

'I punched out your guard,' she says, her voice low and urgent. 'More guards are on the way. We've got about a minute to get out unseen, and I *really* don't want to have to kill anyone. So can we talk later?'

That's when Fliss notices the bulky body on the stairs. Now, that is interesting. Tanta's answer has only given her more questions than she had before, but Fliss can see that now isn't the time.

'All right, InTech girl,' she says. 'Last one down the stair's a rotten egg.'

At first, Tanta is concerned that Fliss is going to make a run for it, but it turns out she needn't have worried. The bandit springs down the stairs quicker than a cat, but when Tanta catches up, it's only to find her waiting by the door.

'We're not leaving that way,' Tanta tells her. Guardians will be streaming through that entrance any minute. She points down the hallway, past Smythe's office and towards the back of the building. 'There's another exit down here.'

She leads Fliss towards the equipment room, her heart pounding in her chest. As they round a bend in the corridor, she hears the heavy footsteps of the guardians arriving. Luckily, they're headed in the opposite direction: up the stairs and into the holding cells – for now, at least. They'll find Smythe immediately, and he'll tell them about Fliss's escape and Tanta's involvement. After that, they'll lock down not just the building, but the entire distribution centre. Worse still, Smythe will doubtless red-flag Tanta's 'scape. Before long, she won't be able to so much as buy a coffee with her MbOS wallet without the ICRD knowing about it. She and Fliss need to make it out of Sodis before that happens. Tanta has a plan for how to do that, but it's a desperate one.

She taps in the internal code on the door to the equipment room – the same one she saw Smythe enter yesterday – and wrenches it open. As soon as she and Fliss are inside, Tanta runs to the drawer where Smythe stores the magnetic GPS trackers, grabs one, and slams it in place over the door and the doorframe. The powerful magnet will act like a deadbolt, holding it shut. It won't buy them much time, but it will at least slow their pursuers down. Next, she grabs the holdall full of the bandits' weapons and gear that she stored here earlier; they might come in useful.

The equipment room is as cluttered with oversized weapons and combat gear as Tanta remembers it. In the middle of it sit the three armoured vehicles. Tanta turns to Fliss; she's not happy about it, but a significant portion of her plan hinges on the bandit. Loath as she is to admit it, she needs her help.

'You can drive, right?' she asks. In different circumstances, Tanta could simply programme a destination into the car using her 'scape, but not without alerting Smythe to where she was going.

Fliss shoots her a dirty look. 'Not one of these I can't. Your cars don't have steering wheels.'

'These ones do.'

Tanta pulls open the door of the nearest car and jumps inside, swinging the bag of weapons onto the back seat. The interior looks identical to Yas's car, except that the dashboard and floor are unbroken. She runs her hand over the dash, trying to picture where the metal rod and the pedals were.

'Are you stupid?' Fliss says. 'There's nothing there.'

'Old models like this have a manual steering rig hidden inside the dash. For emergencies.'

Tanta says this as though it's obvious, though in fact, she's only parroting what Yas told her. As she speaks, she feels a thin line beneath her fingers. There's a panel in the dashboard, virtually invisible in the matt black surface.

'Hand me something I can use to lever this open,' she mutters. 'We don't have long.'

To her credit, Fliss hops out of the car quickly, returning moments later with a huge combat knife. Tanta takes it off her and jams it under the dash. She feels the panel pop free and Fliss lifts it away. The cavity beneath is filled with wires, cables, and other parts that Tanta can't put a name to. Jutting up from the centre of this mess is a thick metal bar with a hole in the top. There's another secured to the side of the dash; Tanta pulls it free and slots it into the hole to make the T shape she remembers seeing in Yas's vehicle. Then she gets down on the floor of the car and feels around. There's a handle in the footwell; she takes hold of it and lifts a section of the floor away, revealing two pedals.

'There,' she says to Fliss. Despite the urgency of the situation, she can't avoid a note of triumph creeping into her tone. 'There's your "steering wheel".'

Fliss looks at her like she is utterly deranged. 'Where's the ignition?' she asks.

Tanta's stomach clenches. 'What's an ignition?'

'It's what makes the bloody car start!' the bandit shouts. 'Shunt over,' she orders, pushing Tanta to one side and assuming her place in front of the steering rig. 'Where'd you see someone driving one of these?'

Tanta is taken aback at the sudden authority in Fliss's tone. 'It was one of my colleagues,' she says.

'OK. Before she drove off, did she do anything? Like push a button, turn a key – something like that?'

Tanta rakes her mind back, trying to remember everything about that harrowing car journey to the distribution centre. An image comes to her – Yas reaching her hand under the dashboard. 'I think there's a button!' she says. 'Under there.'

Fliss reaches her hand where Tanta points and Tanta hears a click, followed by the low growl of the car's engine turning over. Fliss rolls her eyes. 'You corporate types. Honestly—'

A loud thud cuts her off mid-sentence. Someone is pounding on the other side of the door. The bandit is about to punch the pedal to the floor when a thought occurs to Tanta.

'Wait!' she says. She hops out of the car, still holding the long knife.

'What the fuck are you doing?' Fliss hisses. 'Don't you want to get out of here?'

'Just wait,' Tanta replies. The tyres on an armoured car are usually bullet resistant, but they're just as vulnerable to other kinds of damage as the normal variety. A quick slash with the knife across the tyres of the other two cars, and Tanta is confident she will have delayed their pursuers by at least a couple of minutes. She dives back into the front seat. The car leaps forward before she's even shut the door.

The roller door leading out of the equipment room is steel panelled, blast resistant, and braced with solid beams; it probably weighs about two hundred pounds. Any car hitting it from the outside would be flattened like a tin can, but all its reinforcements and security precautions are designed to stop people from breaking into the building, not out of it. The armoured car hits it head-on, and sweeps through it as though it's a cat flap. There's a squadron of guardians just rounding the corner of the building, coming to secure the back entrance; they scatter in confusion as Tanta and Fliss shoot out of the Logistics Office and off into the rainy, pre-dawn darkness.

'Which way?' Fliss asks.

Tanta summons her Array, calling up a map of the distribution centre. 'Right,' she says. The car swerves, clipping one of the floodlights on the street corner. 'Careful!' Tanta adds.

Fliss gives her a withering look. 'You think you could do better?'

'If we crash, we're dead for sure.'

'And if we don't get out of here sharpish, we're just as dead!'

Tanta doesn't have a reply to that. An explosion of gunfire behind them fills in the silence. Glancing back, Tanta sees the guardians standing in front of the open doorway, high-calibre rifles in their hands. The bullets ping off the car's reinforced chassis.

'WHICH WAY NOW?' Fliss yells.

Tanta checks her clock. Seven minutes have elapsed since she triggered the pressure alarm in the Logistics Office. If Smythe is half as security conscious as she thinks he is, the main gate of the distribution centre will already be locked, and a team of guardians dispatched to guard it. It's the exit route Smythe will be expecting Tanta and Fliss to take; the gate is the weakest point in the perimeter fence, after all. They can use that expectation to their advantage. She cross references the road ahead with the map on her Array. There's a stretch of road that runs parallel to the western side of the fence for about a mile, leading up to the main gate at the end.

'Go right at the fork and then straight ahead,' she says, 'but get ready to swerve off-road when I tell you.'

She's expecting Fliss to say something sarcastic in reply, but the bandit only nods. Tanta hears sirens, faint at first, but growing steadily louder. The sound is soon accompanied by flashing red lights, and then the outlines of cars behind them, distant, but gaining. Fliss keeps her eyes on the road ahead, her jaw set in concentration, while Tanta watches the force massing at their backs.

'Are you going to tell me why you changed your mind now?' the bandit mutters, after a minute has elapsed in tense silence. 'You didn't seem so keen on my offer before.'

'There was a new development,' Tanta replies.

'As in you suddenly "developed" a strong desire to hightail it out of town in the middle of the night, and you needed a driver?'

Something like that, Tanta thinks. Aloud, she says. 'I'm not at liberty to discuss that with you.'

Fliss snorts. 'Says who? Your boss? I think discussing it with me is the least of your worries.' She flicks a glance at Tanta. 'If

335

you won't tell me what's going on, how can I trust you're going to keep up your end of the bargain?'

'You said it yourself,' Tanta snaps. 'Does it look like I'm in a position to take you back into InTech's custody? We'd both be detained if I tried it.'

It's something Tanta already knew, but saying it out loud sends a weight plummeting into the pit of her stomach, like a stone dropped into a well. She's just broken a prisoner out of holding, and now they're on the run, pursued by what looks like all the guardians in Sodis. There's no way back from this for her. Her dreams of a career in the ICRD, a home in the city, were over the moment she punched out Smythe.

The entrance to the distribution centre comes into sight, hazy through the driving rain. Tanta can make out more cars up ahead, and a crowd of guardians on foot with riot shields. Smythe may even be among them, spoiling for round two. If she and Fliss wait much longer, they'll be cut off and surrounded. Tanta accesses the car's AR interface, still visible on the left-hand side of the dash, and turns the headlights off.

'Sharp left,' she says. 'NOW!'

Fliss jerks the bar and the car veers off the road, throwing Tanta to the right. She bumps into Fliss, who curses. They can see nothing at first, and then a looming shadow reveals the fence, coming up to meet them. There's a terrible, grinding screech of metal against metal. And then they're through, trailing a pole and a strip of chain link fencing behind them like industrial bunting. They're free.

'They'll follow us,' Tanta says. 'Do you think you can lose them?'

Fliss gives a snort in response that Tanta has to assume means yes. 'And then you want me to drive you to the Brokerage, right?' the bandit adds.

'Not yet,' Tanta replies. 'We have a stop to make first.'

Chapter 29

Sensations come back to Cole before consciousness does. He isn't sure where, when, or even who he is, but he knows that his heart is beating a mile a minute and his mouth tastes like bile. He tries to move, but his body feels nerveless and slack, like a puppet he doesn't know how to control. He lies on the ground, feeling the panic of paralysis coupled with a gnawing, sick sense that he has forgotten something very important. He focuses on his breathing, trying to ride the *in-out, in-out* rhythm to something approaching calmness, but his heart is beating so hard he's afraid it may burst out of his chest.

The thick numbness seeps out of his limbs gradually. In its place, he gets pins and needles, which are painful, and the butt-ends of memories, which are worse. Something bad happened; he isn't sure what it was, but he knows it was bad. He and Jeanie were talking. She had just brought him a drink. And then...

With an effort, Cole cranks open his eyes. It's dawn, and Jeanie is gone. The flood of memories intensifies. She drugged him! He sits bolt upright but immediately keels over again. He hits something solid – he thinks it's the leg of a chair – and uses it to support himself, slumping against it like an ailing plant while he tries to recall the events of the previous night. He had just finished work on the key to the backdoor in Harlow 2.0, and they had stopped to celebrate. His drink tasted funny...The memory is fuzzy around the edges. It feels like it happened to someone else.

Cole digs in his pocket until he feels the small shape of the communicator and drags it free.

'Jeanie?' His voice sounds slurred and strange.

There's a long silence. Cole has concluded Jeanie is going to ignore him – or perhaps she doesn't have her communicator on her – when the device crackles and she says, 'I really am sorry, Cole. I would have preferred to do this as partners, like last time.'

'You MindWiped me,' Cole says. The memory of their conversation comes back to him as he speaks. 'You're the reason I forgot about the Harlow Programme.'

'You MindWiped yourself.' Jeanie's voice is sad. 'But I asked you to, yes. It wasn't the original plan, but you were about to be captured.'

Cole thinks back to Tanta's confrontation with Arthur Friend in the Black Box last summer. Cole *was* captured, of course – probably mere hours after he set the false flag attack in motion – and when it became clear to InTech's Directors that he had no memory of what he'd done, they had partnered him with Tanta to see if he could help to solve the crime he had committed. He did it all at Jeanie's instigation, and yet InTech never even learnt of her existence: she made sure of that.

And that's not all she's done. Cole thinks of the ambush on the way to Sodis. If Jeanie runs the Brokerage, then that was her doing as well. 'You tried to kill me and Tanta!'

'Cole, you have to understand, I didn't know you and the CorpWard were partnered again,' Jeanie replies. 'I thought I saw a way to take out a persistent problem of mine. If I'd had any idea you would be in that truck, I never would have sent the bandits after it.'

She sounds genuinely remorseful. Cole isn't sure how she can think her explanation changes anything. 'I was only trying to kill your friend, not you', is so far from being a reasonable defence that it's on a different planet. He doesn't even know how to respond to it. He leans his head against the cool metal of the chair leg, fighting back tears. The drugs in his system combine with his own heartbreak to fill him with an over-whelming sense of loss. He has been so deceived by Jeanie, and he still doesn't know why she has done any of this – or where she has gone, for that matter.

The thing he's leaning against is not a chair but a table, Cole realises – the desk he was working at last night. He hauls himself up it, rising unsteadily to his feet. The surface of the worktable looks the same as he remembers it – there's the melted wreck of the dummy 'scape, the scattered piles of tech projects in various stages of completion – with one exception. The data card containing the Harlow 2.0 key is gone. Panic stabs through Cole; it isn't helped by whatever drug Jeanie gave him, which is still making his heart go crazy.

He allows himself to drop back to his knees (it isn't difficult) and scans the space underneath the desk. Maybe the card fell down somehow when he lost consciousness? It isn't there, either; Jeanie must have taken it. That's bad. The key is only half of what's needed to sabotage Harlow 2.0: without Cole to readjust the backdoor in the software itself, the signal will melt the 'scape of anyone who receives it. He stabs the button on the communicator again.

'Jeanie, you need to come back,' he mumbles. 'You won't be able to reconfigure the self-deletion protocol without me.'

'I know,' Jeanie replies. 'I don't intend to.'

A terrible possibility worms its way into Cole's mind. 'Then what are you trying to do?'

'Destroy the Harlow Programme, of course. Like you always wanted.'

'I didn't want to do it like this!' Cole shouts. 'That key is deadly on its own – it'll kill anyone who downloads it!'

Jeanie sighs. 'That's the point. I admired the sentiment, Cole, but it's like Yasmin said – undoing the rollout harmlessly would have been a temporary solution at best. Eventually, InTech would have found the backdoor, fixed it, and run the update again. There was only ever one way to shut the programme down for good.'

'I don't understand,' Cole says. His pulse pounds in his ears, louder than the static on the line. The Jeanie he knew – or thought he knew – cared about freedom. She can't emancipate the dead. 'You'll kill half the city!'

'I'd estimate closer to thirty-five per cent,' Jeanie replies. Her tone is as calm as though she and Cole are comparing notes on a tricky piece of code. 'With treatment, I'm sure many people will survive, just like Tanta did. Whatever you may think of me, mass murder isn't my aim; I don't like the short-term suffering any more than you do, but in the long run, it will make things better. We should never have let the corporations assume as much power as they have. It's the proliferation of MbOS technology that has made this kind of mass population control possible; what I'm doing will ensure the public never trust organisations like InTech to grub around in their heads again.' She pauses. When she resumes speaking, her voice is pleading. 'There was a time when you understood how important that was.'

Cole tries to think of something – anything – he can say to get Jeanie to turn this hellish plan around. She must still care about him: she clearly has no regard for human life in general, so he'd be dead if she didn't. Is there some way he can use that to convince her to change her mind?

'I do understand,' he says, trying to keep his voice level. 'I understand everything you're saying, but if we could just sit down together and *talk*, I'm sure we could find another way to achieve what you – what we both – want. *Without* bloodshed. Where are you right now?'

Jeanie chuckles ruefully. 'Nice try, Cole. You couldn't come after me even if you knew: I've locked you in. Don't worry – all my safehouses are shielded from MbOS traffic. You'll be safe from the update when it goes live. I'll come back when I'm done. Then we can talk as much as you want.' There's a pause. Dead static crackling on the line like a building burning down. 'The old you would have been on my side here. I hope, one day, you will be too.'

Then the line goes dead.

The first thing Cole does is try the door, but it's a wasted effort. Jeanie has lied to him about a lot of things, but she wasn't lying about it being locked. It's only now that he finds himself trapped in the little cabin that Cole realises what an effective prison it makes. The windows are boarded over, and it's too remote from civilisation for anyone to hear him if he shouts. He tries hailing Tanta on MindChat, but only gets a network error. He works his way around the walls, looking for some chink in the armour of the place, but finds nothing. If Tanta were here, she'd be able to pick the lock. But then, if Tanta were here, she would never have fallen for Jeanie's cheap trick with the spiked drink in the first place. With a rush of shame, Cole thinks of the last time he saw Tanta. He was so wrapped up in talking to Jeanie, he barely even noticed her leave. He should have gone with her.

Cole makes a sound, then, an inarticulate yell of fury and despair. He cared for Jeanie, fell for her in every sense of the term, and she played him – and has been playing him from the start. His self-recriminations are all the more bitter because he's pretty sure this is the second time it has happened. The mastermind behind the false flag attack was right in front of Cole all along, and he was too besotted to see it. He may have been manipulated into working with Jeanie this time around, and conspired with her of his own volition the last, but it makes little difference to the outcome. He was her willing attack dog once, and she had him wipe his own memory to destroy the evidence. And then, when she needed him again, he could not remember enough to stay away.

His attempt to make amends for his bloody past has only betrayed him into a worse and more wanton act of destruction; once again, people are going to die and, once again, it's his finger on the trigger. The irony of his situation is not lost on Cole, though he's in no state to appreciate it. Tears prickle his eyes, blurring his vision. Through them, he begins searching the safehouse for another way out. He can't give in to self-blame and heartbreak. Wherever she's going, Jeanie hasn't uploaded the key yet, which means there's still time to stop her, if Cole can only figure out how to do it. He surveys the hut, looking for something he can use to force the door. Perhaps if he can unscrew one of the legs of the desk, he can use it as a makeshift crowbar.

Cole is just contemplating how best to do this when the door bursts open of its own accord, flying back against the wall with a crash. Tanta is framed in the doorway, dark against the grey sky outside. How did she get here so fast? And how did she know he was in trouble? The relief and confusion of seeing her is so intense that for a moment, it leaves Cole speechless. She closes the gap between them, running inside and wrapping him in an uncharacteristic hug. Cole returns her embrace.

'I'm really glad you're OK, Cole,' Tanta says, her head buried in his chest.

'I'm fine,' Cole reassures her, 'but, Tanta, we need to go. Jeanie lied to us. The false flag attack was her idea, and now she's taken the key and she's going to—'

'Wait.' Tanta holds up a hand. 'I want you to tell me everything, and there's a lot I need to tell you, too. But while we talk, you need to disable the location tracker in my 'scape. Yours too.'

'He can do that?'

Cole looks up at the unfamiliar voice and starts. There's a girl standing in the doorway; someone he has never seen before.

'Yes, he can,' Tanta replies, without looking round. 'He's a neuroengineer.'

'Um, Tanta, who is that?' Cole asks.

'Who're *you*?' the girl retorts, with a contemptuous toss of her head.

Tanta beckons the girl into the room. 'Cole, this is Fliss,' she says. 'She's the bandit I was telling you about. Fliss, Cole is my colleague. Like I said, we have a lot to talk about.'

Cole has a thousand questions, but he shelves them for the time being and does as Tanta asks. Her request is unexpected, but not impossible. Most neurotechs would find it prohibitively difficult – the Inscape system is considered by many to be tamper-proof – but he's not most neurotechs. Also, this isn't his first rodeo. He has tampered with his and Tanta's location trackers before, when they broke into Inspire Labs last summer, spoofing their locations to make it look as though they were at home. While Cole works, he tells Tanta about what Jeanie has done – and what she is planning to do.

'That tallies with what I've found out as well,' Tanta replies, when he has finished. 'I looked into the ghost account – it's Jeanie's. She was injured in an experimental update to the Inscape system and left to die. Only she didn't. She's had access to Sodis ever since. I don't think she ever left the Brokerage. In fact, I think she might *be* the Brokerage. She was probably the agent I spoke to last summer, too.'

She jerks her head towards the bandit, Fliss. 'When I realised what was going on, I got Fliss out of holding and came straight here.'

The implications of this statement are not lost on Cole. If this is what he thinks it is, then Tanta has given up everything she values just to make sure he is safe. 'Fuck, Tanta. Is this why you needed me to turn off your location tracker? Are you …?'

'I'm a fugitive from InTech, yes,' Tanta says.

'I'm sorry.'

'Don't be. If we can't stop Jeanie, it's not like either of us could return to the city anyway. If we go to the Brokerage, we might be able to catch her before she leaves to upload the key – or work out where she's headed.'

'Jeanie did mention she had a main base elsewhere,' Cole says. 'I don't know where it is, though.'

'Fliss does. She's going to take us there.'

'Yeah, about that.' It's the first time the bandit has spoken since she came in. Cole and Tanta both turn her way. 'I'm going to need you to do something for me in return.'

'That wasn't the deal,' Tanta replies, glaring at her. 'I already did something for you when I let you go. You promised you'd take me to the Brokerage in exchange.'

Fliss matches her stare for stare, completely unruffled. 'I'm renegotiating the deal,' she says.

'You can't do that.'

Fliss folds her arms. 'I can if you can! I asked for you to let me go, not bust me out.'

Cole feels a swell of anger on Tanta's behalf. 'You're splitting hairs,' he says. 'It's the same thing.'

'It's not the same thing at all,' the bandit fires back. 'InTech is going to be after me the rest of my life for this. I get too close to the city, or any of their outposts, and they'll pick me back up again – or worse – before I can blink. I'm on the run for good. Right?'

Cole opens his mouth, then shuts it again. Fliss has a point.

'Yeah. Thought so,' she says. She turns her attention back to Tanta. 'When I struck that deal with you, I was talking to InTech. But you don't speak for them anymore.'

Tanta shrugs, a gesture of defeat. 'Fine. What do you want?'

To Cole's surprise, Fliss turns her piercing stare on him. 'You're a corporate scientist, right?'

Cole nods uncertainly. 'Right,' he replies. 'Well, I was.' He supposes that technically, the term 'corporate' doesn't apply to him anymore. If Tanta's on the run, then so is he. Even if the ICRD aren't looking to arrest him, he's not leaving her to face a life of exile alone. Besides, as Tanta said, with Harlow 2.0 about to go live, he couldn't go back to the city if he wanted to. Even if he managed to avoid the initial rollout, his Inscape would just download the software as soon as he got back in range of InTech's servers.

Fliss waves a hand, dismissing the distinction. 'Do you know your way around a gun?' she asks.

At first, Cole is confused by the question. Does Fliss expect him to fight her? 'That depends,' he answers. 'I'm a neuro-engineer by training, so mechanical systems aren't my speciality. But MbOS synced weapons... yes, I know about them.'

'I didn't understand any of that,' Fliss says. 'But I think you can do what I need. When the Brokerage woman – your Jeanie – recruited me and my crew, she gave us some fancy new weapons. Only there was a catch: they only work some of the time.'

Realisation dawns. 'The lock!' Cole exclaims. 'I found it when I was examining the guns we got from—'

He was going to say *from the bandits we killed*, but he stops himself. Fliss shoots him a paint-stripping glare. 'Yeah,' she says.

'The lock. I want you to get rid of it. *Then* I'll take you to the Brokerage.'

'If you've got the weapons with you, I can do it on the way,' Cole replies.

Tanta frowns at Fliss. 'One of those weapons is a rocket launcher. That's a lot of firepower to simply hand over to you.'

'How about this, then,' Fliss counters. 'You give me the weapons, and I'll help you take down Jeanie and Hardinger. Sounds like we all want them gone. You might need a rocket launcher on your side for that.'

There's a pause while Tanta considers this. 'The weapons would be useful,' she admits.

''Course they will be,' Fliss says easily. 'It's why you brought them with, right? And I'll be useful, too. Jeanie has a bunch of drones following her around – nasty fuckers. And there's no one better at taking out drones than me.'

Tanta raises an eyebrow at this. 'An army of drones. Where did she get those, I wonder?'

That shuts the bandit up, but she's already won her point.

At first, the route to the Brokerage closely mirrors the one Tanta and Cole took to Sodis two days ago in reverse. Fliss drives them north, back towards the city, keeping off the corporate roads to avoid any patrols that might be out looking for them. Tanta and Cole sit in the back seat, both overwhelmingly relieved to see each other again, neither saying much about it. Cole works on picking the digital lock on the bandits' weapons, and Tanta watches him.

Cole is quiet, lost in reflections that Tanta can tell from his downcast eyes are unpleasant ones. He trusted Jeanie more than Tanta ever did; her betrayal must hurt him deeply. Tanta wants to say something encouraging – to show Cole that she is here for him, just as he was there for her when she discovered the

346

way she had been used and manipulated by InTech – but she can't find the right words. Fliss's presence in the car prevents her from speaking as openly as she would like to. The bandit may be helping them, but Tanta doesn't trust her enough to discuss something so personal in front of her.

Ordinarily, she would simply hail Cole on MindChat, and she does catch herself reaching for her temple to summon her Array a few times, before she remembers with a crushing feeling that she can't take the risk. Cole may have disabled his and Tanta's location trackers, but InTech can still read their MindChat communications. Now that she's a fugitive, they'll be on high alert for any clue as to her whereabouts: her private chat with Cole would likely end up pored over and dissected by the whole of the ICRD. In the end, she takes Cole's hand instead, letting the gentle pressure convey what she cannot put into words.

After about an hour, Fliss turns the car to the west. Tanta has no idea what to expect of the Brokerage. She has known of its existence since the earliest days of basic training, but when she tries to picture it, all she can conjure up are vague images of hidden bases and shadowy double agents. She has no sense of its location or appearance; it could be a fortress in the mountains or a bunker beneath the sea, could be hiding in plain sight, like Jeanie's cabin, or protected from the world by mile-high walls and machine gun turrets. She has no expectations to be met or not, so she is not surprised when she realises that the route Fliss is following is familiar to her. She has been this way once before: her first time out in the field.

That mission, the red assignment that began her brief career in the ICRD, had been in a forest to the south of the city. Tanta soon begins to see landmarks she recognises, and before long, the forest itself is before them, as dark and ragged as the night she first saw it.

It seems fitting to her that the Brokerage should be near here, where she first fought the Thoughtfront agent. It's as though Fliss is driving Tanta back into her own past, to the place where all of this started. In fact, Fliss takes them to a point just west of the section of forest that Tanta and her team searched all those weeks ago, bringing the car to a wobbly stop at the base of a thickly wooded hill.

'It's up there,' the bandit says, pointing at the summit. 'We'll have to keep a sharp eye out. The drones already know my face, and I reckon they probably know yours, too.'

That sounds ominous. Tanta takes one of the newly unlocked handguns from the holdall before she leaves the car, and gives Fliss one, too. She treads carefully as she follows Fliss into the trees, but the forest is still and eerily silent. There's none of the humming, whirring and buzzing that Tanta was expecting, the noises of a wild space populated by mechanical life. The only sound is the pattering of rain on leaves, and even that is muffled by the forest's thick canopy. The quiet is jarring, setting all their nerves on edge. Tanta strains her senses and feels her pulse quicken with every snap of a twig or rustle of a branch.

Fliss guides them through the darkness, surefooted and insouciantly confident, until they reach a clearing near the top of the hill. Here, she pauses, turning on the spot.

'It's around here,' she says.

'Around here?' Tanta whispers. 'I thought you said you were going to lead us right to it!'

'I have!' Fliss insists, instantly defensive. 'When I followed Hardinger, he parked here. Then I heard this shrieking. He was gone by the time I got out the car.'

'It could be cloaked, like the safehouse,' Cole suggests.

Tanta's inclined to agree, but hypothesising won't get them very far if they don't know where the entrance is.

'Let's search the area,' she says. She inches forward, scanning the clearing for the telltale flicker of an AR skin.

Her eyes are on the trees ahead, so she doesn't see what hits her. All she knows is that one minute she's upright, and the next there's a warning yelp from Cole, and something smashes into her back, driving her face-first into the dirt.

Chapter 30

Tanta's instincts kick in with a surge of adrenaline. She bucks beneath the weight on her back, trying to push herself to her feet so she can confront whatever or whoever has knocked her over. A hand grabs her right arm and twists it behind her, the motion practiced and swift. The person grappling her (*Jeanie?*) straddles her, their free hand pressing down on the top of Tanta's head.

If it is Jeanie, this could be Tanta's best – perhaps her only – chance to stop her and her plan in its tracks. Her assailant has her at a disadvantage, but Tanta has had practice in how to break a hold. She drives her left hand into the ground (the motion sends a twinge of remembered pain through her recently healed fingers) and pushes upward, twisting her body sharply to one side. It works, and for a second, she feels the pressure on her back ease as her attacker is thrown off balance.

A second is all Tanta needs. She rolls onto her side and aims a kick behind her, wrenching herself free from the woman's grasp. She spins as she lunges to her feet, her right hand going instinctively for the gun in her belt, and rounds on her attacker. They recognise one another at the same instant.

'Tanta?' Yas says. Her tone is incredulous. She doesn't change her stance, but she does take a step backwards, giving Tanta space. 'When the proximity alarm went off, I assumed it was another squirrel,' she adds. 'How the hell did you get here?'

For a moment, Tanta considers taking advantage of the fractional lowering of Yas's guard to rush her. Agent Das may have been her idol once, but now she's working for Tanta's enemy, and Tanta needs to get into the base she is guarding. Then a memory darts through her thoughts: her arm across Yas's throat, Yas's eyes rolling back into her head. It's all Tanta needs to knock some sense back into her. With a conscious effort, she wrenches her mind out of its old track, the track that separates the whole world into InTech and everyone else. There are other ways to see the world – she knows that – and the knowledge has been too hard-won for her to abandon it now.

Yas may be working for Jeanie, but it's clear she doesn't know everything about the freedom fighter's plan – the fact that she's talking to Tanta right now, rather than trying to kill her, proves it. Tanta takes a deep breath and, against every instinct in her body, raises her hands slowly into the air. She has no desire to fight Yas; that's something she hopes never to have to do again.

'Fliss showed me the way,' she replies. 'Cole, Fliss: it's OK. You can come out.' She glances behind her and her companions emerge from the treeline, looking nervous.

Her answer to Yas's question is half a test, a way of gauging how much Yas has actually been told. The older agent starts at the sight of the two of them, and gives Cole an uncertain nod, but there's no recognition in her eyes when she looks at the bandit. She probably wasn't involved in the drone thefts, then – or the attack on the Needle.

Yas frowns. Then, slowly, she relaxes her stance, dropping her arms. This is not the time to be getting sentimental, but Tanta finds herself unexpectedly touched by this gesture of faith. She thinks back to the night Yas defected from InTech – back then, she'd been so wary of Tanta that she'd continued to view her with naked suspicion, even after Tanta had saved her life. Somehow, amidst the loss of her corporation, her lover and her home, Tanta has gained her hero's respect. It's not something she takes lightly.

'OK, I'm lost,' Yas says. 'Who's Fliss?' She turns to Cole, 'And aren't you supposed to be with Jeanie right now?'

Tanta had been hoping Jeanie was still in the Brokerage getting ready, but Yas's question puts paid to that idea. It means Jeanie has even more of a head-start than she did before – and they still don't know where she's going.

'Cole and I found out some things about Jeanie tonight,' Tanta replies. 'Things we think you should know.'

She explains the situation to Yas as circumstantially as she can, omitting no detail that there is time to include. They're short on time, but also on allies. If she can convince Yas to help them, it could make a big difference.

'Everyone with an Inscape is at risk,' she finishes. 'Including the three of us. We have to stop Jeanie from uploading that key.'

'Shit,' Yas says. 'That's ... a lot to take in.'

'If it's too much, I wouldn't blame you,' Tanta says. 'Maybe you know where Jeanie's going, or you want to help us locate her. Maybe all you want to do is get as far away from the city as possible before the update goes live – it would be a smart move. There's no judgement either way, but whatever you decide, the rest of us are staying here. We have to try and stop Jeanie. We've done too much to help her already.'

Cole drops his eyes as she says the words. Fliss rolls hers. 'Speak for yourself,' she says. 'I've got my own reasons.'

For a long moment, Yas hesitates. Her expression doesn't change – she used to be an ICRD agent, after all – but Tanta can guess at the invisible struggle playing out in her mind by her fixed gaze and the tense sent of her shoulders. At length, she sighs.

'Well, looks like I'm out of a job either way,' she says. 'OK. If we're doing this, we should do it properly. You'd better come inside.'

As it turns out, the Brokerage is not in the forest but under it. Yas walks to the edge of the clearing and lays her hand against the gnarled trunk of one of the trees. There's a creaking sound and a section of grass rises from the ground, the turf lifting away. A rectangular metal platform emerges from the earth, its surface mottled with rust. Yas steps onto it, motioning Cole, Fliss and Tanta to follow her. As soon as the four of them are standing on the platform, it sinks again, with the same screeching of ancient gears.

'Jeanie didn't build this, did she?' Tanta asks.

'I don't think so,' Yas replies. 'She's always been cagey about how she found this place, but I think it's a pre-Meltdown military installation.'

The lift carries them down into a garage. From there, Yas leads them along a corridor lined with dozens of doors. The Brokerage is a huge space with a surprisingly high ceiling – a bunker carved out of the innards of the hill itself – but the whole place has a claustrophobic air, probably because it has no windows. The walls are grey, with strip lights providing a harsh, artificial light. Tanta has no trouble believing it was once a military bunker. What it is now, though, is something else. Through doorways, she glimpses bedrooms, a kitchen, and some kind of underground garden – racks of plants growing under glaring LEDs. At the end of the corridor there's a control room. Like Jeanie's safehouse near Sodis, it's filled with pre-Meltdown computing units, old-fashioned screens and cluttered worktables.

'This place is amazing,' Cole marvels. A spasm of emotion constricts his face. 'Jeanie – she said I'd like it. She wasn't kidding.'

353

Tanta, too, is impressed. The Brokerage is enormous, sophisticated, and right under the city's nose. Some of her surprise must show, because Yas turns to her, answering a question she hasn't yet asked.

'It's entirely shielded from MbOS traffic, too,' she says. 'From the corps' perspective, it's invisible – no digital signature, no heat output, nothing. In case you were wondering why you don't have any MindChat signal,' she adds.

When they're all gathered in the control room, everyone sits down at once, as if at an unspoken signal. Cole sinks into a battered swivel chair. Yas perches on the desk beside him. Fliss lowers herself to the floor. The same signal makes them all look at Tanta, even the bandit. Tanta stares back at the three expectant faces; she's never felt less ready to lead. She opens her mouth, unsure of what words are going to come out of it until they do, sounding a lot more confident than she feels.

'If we're going to stand a chance of stopping Jeanie, we need to know three things,' she says. 'Where she's going, what she's armed with, and how much time we have.'

'I know the answer to number three, at least,' Yas pipes up, 'and it's not long. Our last intelligence from InTech was that the update is scheduled to go live at noon.'

Tanta nods, acknowledging the intel. She's alarmed, though she doesn't show it. That's not long at all; by the clock on her Array, it's already eight am. Jeanie was planning to send out the key in the same update packet as Harlow 2.0 itself – they have to catch up to her before the rollout.

'Cole, if we can find her in time, is there anything you can do to stop her?' she asks him.

Cole wrinkles his brow. 'In theory, I could just carry out our original plan,' he replies. 'If I can get access to the Harlow 2.0 update packet, I can tweak the self-deletion protocol in the software to allow the key to interface with it safely.'

'So when Jeanie uploaded the key, it would work as you intended it to: uninstalling Harlow 2.0 without causing casualties?'

'Exactly. It won't be easy, though. Hacking a secure InTech server is a challenge at the best of times, and it'll be even harder if' – he swallows, scrubbing a nervous hand across his mouth – 'if Jeanie's there already. Especially if she has backup.'

Tanta sees the tremor in Cole's hands, the suppressed emotion in his eyes that talking about Jeanie brings on. She gives him what privacy she can in these close quarters by turning her attention – and the conversation – elsewhere. 'Which brings us to question two,' she says. Firepower. Given that the forest was empty of UAVs on their way in, it seems Jeanie has taken the bulk of the Brokerage's defences with her. 'Fliss, what can you tell us about these drones you mentioned?'

'The fleet?' Yas asks. 'Ooh, I know this one too! Jeanie's been collecting them for ages – from scrap heaps, she told me. They're how she gathers a lot of her intel.'

'Me and my crew have been collecting them for her for ages,' Fliss corrects. 'And they're not just for snooping. Like I said, they're nasty: she's modded them with guns and cameras.'

'Does Jeanie control them?' Tanta asks. If she does, they might be able to circumvent the drones by taking out Jeanie herself.

Unfortunately, Yas is shaking her head. 'They're autonomous,' she says, 'piloted by AIs.'

'We should be able to get around them, though,' Fliss adds. 'They're jumpy: make a noise, or show your face, and they'll go straight for you.'

Tanta considers this. 'Then we might be able to separate them from her, if we can engineer a big enough distraction. Do you think you can handle that?'

The bandit grins. 'I have a few ideas. I'll need a hand, though.'

'I'll help you,' Yas says grimly. 'Blowing up the fleet's as good a way as any of handing in my notice.'

That only leaves the question of where Jeanie is going, and on that score, Tanta is still clueless. When she and Cole discussed the plan with Jeanie in the safehouse, she had claimed not to know which server centre Harlow 2.0 would be launched from. Finding out had been Tanta's job, and without her agent privileges – and full access to her 'scape – to help her, that's no longer as easy as it once was. Clearly, the freedom fighter lied about her ignorance, but Tanta's no closer to knowing the location of the software release than she was before.

'Did Jeanie mention where she was going to either of you?' she asks Cole and Yas. Both shake their heads.

'She just told me she'd handle it,' Yas says. 'But if she kept any records, this is where they'll be.'

They make a search of the control room, hunting through the cluttered desks and old machines. Cole, fascinated despite his misery, boots up one of the legacy units and pokes around in the entrails of its code. They turn up much of interest – hundreds of files of classified intelligence that, in other circumstances, Tanta would dearly have liked to peruse – but no mention of server centres, or of Harlow 2.0 at all, for that matter.

Even as Tanta looks, she knows it's hopeless. The location of the rollout may well be hidden somewhere in this treasure trove of data, but they'll never find it in time. Rather than continuing with the search, she racks her brains, casting her mind back over her and Cole's conversations with Jeanie and scouring them for clues. Reviewing their interactions with the freedom fighter reminds her of how little they ever really knew about her, and how artfully she manipulated them. She feels a pang of frustration. There was never a moment in their relationship when Jeanie wasn't in control. She presented Tanta and Cole with a timebomb that only she could disarm, and then she fed them exactly what she wanted – reeling Cole in, freezing Tanta out, widening the distance between them by incremental degrees.

Beside Tanta, Yas shuts an ancient filing cabinet with a sigh. 'It couldn't be the Needle, could it?' she asks. 'That's where InTech's main server room is, right?'

'Unfortunately not. The servers there were damaged,' Tanta replies, without thinking. And then she stops, struck by a sudden idea.

Jeanie is the one responsible for the drone thefts, which means that the attack on the Needle was her doing as well. Tanta had always assumed that the target of that attack was the Foundation Day party, and all the execs and Directors gathered there, but what if that was never what Jeanie was aiming for?

Something Smythe said to her bobs back into her mind. When Cole had questioned the Logistics Officer's overzealous security arrangements, he had been vocal in justifying them. *Sodis is not merely some regional haulage operation*, he'd said. *Our engineers maintain the servers on the zeppelin itself.* And Jeanie was one of those engineers, once. What if the data centre within Sodis is not the only InTech installation she can still access?

'I've got it,' Tanta says aloud. The others look up at her, surprised. 'I know where Jeanie is. Get ready, everyone: we're going back to the city.'

Chapter 31

If Jeanie's fleet reminded Fliss of a swarm of giant wasps, then the zeppelin is their hive – an immense, swollen structure that hangs over the city, pendulous and menacing. On the approach to the wall, she turns off the corporate road and slows the car to a crawl, creeping through the ruined suburbs that surround London like a skirt. The sneaking pace eats into what little time they have, but the wreckage of the wasteland conceals them from searching eyes.

Fliss doesn't need to explain the need for stealth to anyone. They can all see the horde of drones from where she parks the car in the crumbling shadow of an office block. The fleet is gathered around the bottom of the zeppelin's mooring spire, just outside the wall. Once they've climbed out of the car, they can all hear it, too. The buzzing of rotors, distant but threatening, makes the hairs on the back of Fliss's neck stand on end.

As the only one of the group to have successfully fended off the fleet before, Fliss is in charge of this part of the plan by mutual consent. She brings them all closer cautiously, edging from one piece of cover to the next, checking she hasn't been spotted, and then motioning for the others to follow her. Her brush with the drones in the forest is still fresh in her mind. She's sure they're on high alert for any movement in their vicinity, and they already know her face. If they spot her before she's ready, they won't need to waste any time on deciding whether or not she's a threat – they'll shoot her on sight.

There's a sort of no-man's-land just outside the wall, a narrow strip of scorched earth where the city ends and the wasteland begins. Within it, the pre-Meltdown buildings have all been demolished, leaving the ground bare of anything but weeds. When they've reached the edge of this barren zone, Fliss gets everyone into position behind the wall of a tumbledown house and scouts out their target. The docking tower is a spire of reinforced steel. The zeppelin hangs like a swollen tick from the top of it; at its base, the drones swarm.

Fliss turns, then, to face the others, surveying them dubiously. They're not the crew she would have chosen for a job like this. Tanta and the other agent, Yasmin, are both capable enough fighters, but Fliss has never seen them shoot before. The scientist is old and looks like he's never held a gun in his life. All three of them are sleek and well-fed in a way that Fliss distrusts. In short, none of them could hold a candle to the crewmates she has lost, but they'll have to do.

Fliss opens the bag full of the crew's weapons, now unlocked and useable, and doles them out. She gives the net gun to Yasmin and a pistol each to Tanta and Cole, just in case.

'All right, everyone, pay attention,' she barks. 'None of the rest of you have ever done this before, so you need to stay sharp. Tell me your roles.'

Yasmin hefts the net gun. 'I'm running interference with the UAVs.'

'You're a shooter,' Fliss corrects. 'And I am, too. Normally, that'd mean we picked a nice, safe position to line up a shot, and we stayed there. There are too many drones for that, though, and these ones have teeth on them, so the plan this time is to shoot first, then run like hell and try not to get got. Clear?'

Yasmin nods. 'Crystal. I wish all my briefings were that succinct.'

Fliss turns to Tanta and Cole. 'And you two are the runners,' she says. Though on this job, they'll be running past the drones, not to them. She takes a pair of the crew's old gas masks out of the holdall and hands them over. The masks are not to protect them from gas cannisters, this time, but from the drones' facial recognition technology.

'These smell like something died in them,' Cole complains, his voice muffled.

Fliss thinks of Josh, with a prickle of grief-tinged nostalgia. 'Can it,' she says. 'If a drone clocks you, the smell will be the least of your worries. Now, is everyone ready?'

There's a series of nods. With their weapons in hand and their masks on, the new crew looks a bit more like the old one. The sight boosts Fliss's confidence. They're short-handed – they're missing a lookout, and Fliss would have preferred to have left someone waiting in the car so they could make a quicker exit – but with luck, they might just be able to pull this off. She and Yasmin might even survive it. She's not so sure about the other two. All she and Yasmin have to do is leg it, but Tanta and Cole must get past the drones, into the bowels of the zeppelin, *and* take out whatever Jeanie has waiting for them inside.

'You two should get into position over there,' she says, pointing Tanta and Cole towards a house on the far side of the ancient street. 'Yasmin and I will draw the drones away from you while you run, but that won't buy you much time – you'll have to be ready to bolt soon as I give the signal.'

'Understood,' Tanta replies. 'What's the signal?'

In response, Fliss reaches into the bottom of the holdall and draws out her own weapon, propping it on the sill of one of the house's empty windows. When she was attacked by the drones in the woods, only five of them came after her; the rest stayed behind to guard the entrance to Jeanie's base. This time, she'll need to summon all of them at once – Tanta and Cole will never make it to the mooring spire if she can't – and for that, as Tanta said back in the Brokerage, she'll need a much bigger distraction.

Fliss slots a rocket-propelled grenade into the wide bore of the launcher and sights through its scope.

'Take a guess,' she says.

Tanta leads the way to the house Fliss indicated, crouching low to avoid catching the attention of the drones. They're still buzzing around the entrance to the mooring spire in a black cloud, watching Jeanie's back. In any other circumstances a collection of UAVs this size – and this heavily armed – at InTech's gates would be sure to draw the attention of the corporation's automated defence turrets. Unfortunately, these drones were stolen from InTech itself, and their idents still mark them as friends, not foes.

The heavy gas mask is hot against Tanta's face, the rubber sticking to her skin. Through the tinted glass of the eye holes, the world appears distorted and strange. The bare strip of Unaffiliated Zone that separates them from the zeppelin stretches out, looking wider than it really is. The dirigible is docked just outside the city wall, a hundred feet above them and twice as far away.

Tanta could sprint the distance in less than five seconds, but with Cole in tow, it will take them longer, and all of that time, they'll be exposed. If even one drone spots them, their desperate plan could be over before it's even begun. Once again, she's reliant on Fliss – and Yas, of course – to ensure that doesn't happen. Tanta doesn't like having to depend on the bandit, but she has to admit that she knows how to handle herself. She's also had more than enough opportunities to betray Tanta – or at the very least, to run from her – and so far, she hasn't taken any of them. Gradually, and against her better judgement, Tanta is learning to regard Fliss, if not with trust, then at least with the beginnings of it.

When they're in position, Tanta glances at Cole, trying to catch his eye. It's the first time they've been alone together since she bid goodbye to him at Jeanie's safehouse yesterday. He has barely looked at her in all that time; Tanta can almost see the guilt radiating off him in dark waves.

'Hey,' she says, softly. 'It's going to be OK.'

Cole gives a nervous start. He turns to face her, then, his anxious brown eyes meeting hers. 'Tanta?'

'Yes?'

'If we don't make it—'

'We will.'

'But if we don't . . .' Cole trails off, but he doesn't need to finish the sentence for Tanta to intuit what's in his thoughts.

She wants to tell him not to blame himself. She was right that Jeanie couldn't be trusted, but he wasn't wrong when he argued that working with her was their only option. And as for Cole's less rational motives for wanting to get close to the freedom fighter (which Tanta can take a good guess at), she had just as many driving her away. If Cole had listened to Tanta from the beginning, Jeanie's plan would have failed – and she never would have had the chance to hurt him as she has. But then again, if Cole had listened to Tanta, they would have done nothing, and their best chance to prevent the rollout of Harlow 2.0 would have slipped through their fingers.

Tanta looks over to where Fliss and Yas are standing, ten metres away. Yas gives her a thumbs-up. Fliss is sighting along the grey barrel of the rocket launcher, her tongue protruding between her teeth. There isn't time to put all that she's thinking into words. She smiles at Cole instead, putting as much reassurance and understanding into the expression as she can.

'We're going to put it right,' is all she can say.

Then there's a pop from the rocket launcher, and Yas and Fliss vanish in a cloud of grey smoke. Two hundred feet away, the drones stop with one mind, their cameras turning to follow the trajectory of the rocket as it sails towards them. A fraction of a second before it hits the ground beneath the swarming mass, they burst outwards, as if prefiguring the explosion to come. At the same instant, Tanta pulls Cole out from behind the house and takes off running.

They sprint in a wide arc, skirting the rocket's blast radius. Even so, the explosion almost knocks Tanta over, slamming into her with a force she's become depressingly familiar with over the last week. Cole stumbles, but rights himself quickly, and they run onwards. Out of the corner of her eye, Tanta sees the black bodies of the drones sheeting past them, following the path of the missile back to its source. As Fliss predicted, they ignore Cole and Tanta completely, their facial recognition software fooled by the alien contours of the gas masks. As Tanta watches, a net hits one in mid-flight, plucking it out of the air.

She can't spare any more of her attention to see how Fliss and Yas are faring. She forces her eyes front again, measuring the distance between them and the entrance to the mooring spire. The path ahead is clear; the rugged ground vanishes beneath her feet. She runs next to Cole, matching her pace with his. They're forty metres away. Thirty metres...

They're within the zeppelin's broad shadow, in sight of the door, when Tanta hears a high buzzing behind them. She flings herself sideways, shoving Cole clear. The shot, when it comes an instant later, grazes her arm. The drone that fired on her is the vanguard of an army: behind its spindly body, she can see the rest of the fleet coming their way. There's no time to speculate on what has attracted the UAVs' attention, or to search the landscape for a sign of Fliss and Yas: Tanta hopes that they're OK, but she has nothing more than hope to spare.

She helps Cole back to his feet, urging him onwards. 'GO!' she yells.

As soon as Fliss has the drones' attention, she bolts. Yasmin follows her, turning a few times to fire the net gun over her shoulder as they run. They have to: within seconds, they're fleeing before a storm of bullets, staying ahead of the onslaught by the thinnest of margins.

They sprint away from the bare ground outside the city and into the ruined buildings of the wasteland, letting the crumbling facades cover their retreat. This is the kind of landscape Fliss has known all her life, and she runs through it like water, weaving through houses, leaping walls and diving through windows with barely a thought. Occasionally, she glances to her left to see Yasmin keeping pace with her. Fliss has to give credit where it's due: the woman can run. She doesn't have the same familiarity with the terrain that Fliss does, but she makes up for it with sheer athleticism. At one point, Fliss sees her trip on an over-grown paving stone and go down: she rolls into the fall, regains her feet, and keeps going without even breaking her stride.

Their plan is to retreat to the car, taking out as many drones as they can on the way, and then to pick up Tanta and Cole at the base of the mooring spire – assuming they all make it that far. What with the bandage over her left ear and the ringing from the explosion in her right, the only sounds Fliss can hear are warped and muffled, which is probably why it takes her so long to realise that the plan has gone wrong. In the end, Yasmin has to dart over to her and tug on her arm before Fliss twigs that the barrage of muted pops coming from behind them has slackened and ceased. That's not good: they don't want to lose the drones completely – they'd be a poor distraction if they did. Fliss slows, glancing behind her. The fleet is flying back the way it came.

'Shit!' she curses. She swings back out through the window of the house she just entered and runs into the middle of the rutted, pre-Meltdown road, squinting down it at the airship. She can just make out the dwindling figures of Tanta and Cole in the distance; they've almost made it to the docking tower, but the drones are gaining on them. Fliss takes off sprinting again, reversing her course. She sticks to the centre of the road this time, no longer bothering to dodge and weave between the buildings now that the fleet isn't on her tail.

'What … now?' Yasmin shouts, drawing level with her. 'Can we distract them with the rocket launcher again?'

'We can try,' Fliss pants. 'I don't know—'

She doesn't see the car so much as feel it. It's a low vibration in the soles of her feet, something her body registers before her conscious mind notices anything amiss. It's a good thing it does. Fliss stops short; her right arm shoots out, pushing Yasmin back, and even then, she's not quite quick enough. The car screeches out from between two houses, into the space where she and the agent were standing a millisecond before, and Fliss feels a sickening crunch as its front tyre runs over her bare right foot. Blinding pain shoots up her leg. She fights through it, stumbling backwards. They have to get out of here. The car's windows are tinted black, but Fliss has seen it often enough that she knows who's inside immediately.

As always, Hardinger has turned up at the worst possible time.

Cole isn't sure how he covers the distance between him and the mooring spire. All he knows is that his arms are pumping like pistons, his chest is filled with white-hot agony, and he's never moved so fast in his life. He can only assume that the stress of the situation has given him temporary super speed. 'Temporary' being the operative word: as soon as he has made it inside the tower, he collapses, his legs liquidised by the pressure of the dash.

Tanta throws herself through the doorway an instant later. As usual, she displays more presence of mind in the face of disaster than Cole can muster: while he kneels helplessly in the lobby, trying to get his breathing under control, she slams the door closed. As it thuds into place, Cole hears the ping of bullets ricocheting off its metal frame. The sound is reassuringly muffled: the walls of the mooring spire are thick and the fleet, for all its deadly weaponry, doesn't have a way of getting inside that Cole has seen.

'That ... was ... horrible,' he gasps. They've made it, though. They're in.

The spire is a narrow, circular tower, barely wide enough to accommodate the lift shaft that takes up most of its space. Cole summons the lift as soon as he can find the strength to move again; as confident as he is that the drones aren't going to develop opposable thumbs any time soon, he still wants to put as much distance between himself and them as he can.

The lift is an old-fashioned, bare-bones model, designed for no more illustrious passengers than the engineers and maintenance workers who keep the zeppelin fuelled and the servers running. It has a physical interface rather than an AR display, which makes sense given that it has just two buttons. There's only one floor it can travel to: the bridge leading to the zeppelin's gondola, a hundred feet above. When both he and Tanta are inside, Cole jabs the 'up' button and they begin their ascent.

'Do you think she knows we're here?' he asks.

Tanta gives him a look: it's a stupid question. Yas and Fliss just launched a rocket at Jeanie's fleet. She may not have seen Cole and Tanta themselves, but Cole's sure she can put two and two together.

Cole's mouth is dry, his palms sweaty. Physically, these sensations are similar to the ones he felt last night, when he and Jeanie were getting close, but his thoughts could not be more different. He doesn't know whether to be afraid of Jeanie, or afraid for her. He wants to confront her, to throw her lies back in her teeth and watch her choke on them. At the same time, he wants to protect her from what's about to happen. Their romance – and the betrayal that followed it – happened too quickly for Cole to even begin to process his feelings about either. And now, he may never get the chance. He glances, sidelong, at the pistol in Tanta's belt. Jeanie's an engineer, like him – there's no way she'll survive an encounter with the best agent in the ICRD. He hates the thought of what is coming.

The lift comes to a juddering stop. Cole forces his thoughts to a halt along with it. He can't allow himself to think about this anymore; defeating Jeanie is Tanta's task – he has one of his own. The lift lets out almost directly onto the bridge, a narrow, windswept structure that's altogether too exposed for Cole's liking.

'Don't look down,' Tanta cautions him as they step outside.

Cole hadn't intended to, but the warning draws his eyes inexorably over the edge. The city is spread out to his right, the Unaffiliated Zone to his left. Both are impossibly far away. He ends up crossing the narrow platform in a kind of shuffling run, his hands attached to the safety rails as if by glue.

The gondola's gangplank has been lowered. Its entrance yawns ahead of Cole, a black hole leading to the interior of the airship. It's the clearest sign yet of Jeanie's presence on board. He shivers as he steps inside: the space is as cold as the data centre in Sodis. From the ground, the gondola looks tiny, dwarfed by the body of the zeppelin itself. It seems far larger now that he is standing within its air-conditioned depths.

It's dark and quiet, save for the low hum of the servers.

Somewhere in here, Cole knows, Jeanie is uploading the key that will kill half the city. He has to fix the backdoor within Harlow 2.0 before she succeeds. Tanta brushes past him; he tries not to look at the gun, which is now in her hand. Forcing himself to attention, he follows her inside and gets to work.

He encounters his first problem almost immediately. As soon as he has found an MbOS port and slipped it over his eyes, he's confronted by a red error message: Jeanie has locked the system. His hands fly across the air as he tries to circumvent her. Picking her digital lock, he soon sees, is an achievable task, but one that will waste time they simply don't have. Usually, Cole would search for a clever workaround to an obstacle like this, something he could do to slip soundlessly into the servers without tipping Jeanie off. Right now, though, there's no time to be smart. He pries his way in by brute force, feeling more like a housebreaker than a cat burglar.

It isn't pretty, and Jeanie definitely knows he's here now, but he manages it, at least. With the main server room in the Needle down for maintenance, the backup servers are abuzz with activity. Requests and responses fly past Cole's eyes like a vid of an ant colony playing at triple speed, packets of data whizzing in and out at breakneck pace. He ignores all the motion, picking his way through it till he reaches the heart of the nest, the place where the pending updates are stored. There's just one update packet waiting inside, and it's a big one. Cole recognises the jagged contours of Harlow 2.0 immediately. A timer attached to the packet is ticking down the minutes and seconds until it goes live: three hours and counting.

Jeanie is here, too, in the virtual space of the servers. Cole notices her immediately – her presence is as compelling in the digital world as it is in the real one. She's trying to worm the key into the update packet; Cole can intuit her presence from her access requests, which keep getting denied – the packet is locked to all employees below the level of Director. For now, Cole has the same task Jeanie does – to get around this security arrangement and into Harlow 2.0 – and it's equally impossible for him to do it without being seen.

He takes a deep breath and dives in anyway, inputting haptic commands with frantic speed. He and Jeanie edge around the update packet in lockstep, each trying to find a way in, each aware of the other's presence. Once again, they are working towards a shared goal – but this time, they are in competition. Their struggle for access, silent and intense, feels to Cole like a kind of ghastly parody of their evening together back at Jeanie's safehouse.

There's one thing Cole is dreading more than anything else about the task before him, and he hasn't been working long before it happens. A message comes in through the MbOS port over his eyes. It's marked as a code note from the system administrator, but he knows who it's really from before he even opens it.

<<Don't do this, Cole.>>

Cole ignores Jeanie's appeal, though it blurs his eyes with tears that he struggles to suppress. Jeanie is a monster – a murderer. He shouldn't feel for her as he does. He bites his lip, repressing the urge to shout – whether in anger or in warning, he can't tell. He has to keep quiet. Tanta will find Jeanie and end this; all he needs to do is keep working and keep his counsel.

Another message comes through, flashing before his eyes. <<Your plan won't work. Uninstall the Harlow Programme without casualties, and the corporation will just roll it out again. This has to end in tears. It's the only way people learn.>>

Keep going, Cole tells himself. *She's trying to distract you.* He returns his attention to his search, tuning out Jeanie's messages. After another minute and a half, he finds a crack in the packet's security protocols and slips through it, into the software itself. He's in: Harlow 2.0 is before him. He locates the backdoor and flexes his fingers, preparing to get to work in earnest.

A sigh sounds in his mind, one that makes every hair on his body stand on end. <<I warned you, Cole. Now you've forced my hand.>>

Jeanie's message is followed by a hollow chime – the sound of an access request being granted. It sends a spike of unease through Cole before he even knows what she has done. Then he catches sight of the timer at the top of the update packet, and his heart almost stops. It's no longer three hours till Harlow 2.0 goes live – it's thirty minutes.

Cole had decided going into the zeppelin that he wasn't going to speak to Jeanie – it would be too painful. He's forced to break his own rule, however.

<<Are you insane?!>> he sends, speaking through the server system, as she did. <<If the update goes live while we're still up here, we'll *both* be caught in it.>> If that happens, they'll either die from Jeanie's deadly key, or end up cheerful corporate slaves, like Neal. Cole isn't sure which is worse.

<<You should leave, then,>> is Jeanie's response. <<There's still time. I've got no wish to kill you, my love. Get back to safety. This will all be over soon.>>

But Cole can't do that. Frantically, he returns to his work. Reconfiguring Harlow 2.0 in three hours was a tall order; doing it in less than a sixth of that time may be impossible. He has to try, though – the alternative doesn't bear thinking about. He accesses the backdoor, his hands trembling as he begins the process of adjusting it. That's when two gunshots ring out in the quiet gondola, shattering all his thoughts into pieces.

Cole's first thought is that it's over, and Jeanie is dead. The tears come back, as unwanted and unavoidable as before, but another message from her comes through an instant later.

<<Back off, or the next time I shoot the CorpWard, it'll be fatal.>>

Fear clamps a hand over Cole's heart. Jeanie is bluffing. She has to be.

'Tanta?' he shouts.

Fliss has no sooner stumbled clear of the car's path than it comes at her again, its wheels skidding on the road as it swerves round to ram her. This time, rather than leaping backwards, she goes sideways, taking cover in one of the abandoned houses on the side of the street. Out of the corner of her eye, she sees Yas do likewise, the agent diving right while Fliss goes left.

Hardinger follows her, the body of the car smashing through the doorway of the house with a dull *crump*. The car looks like a civilian vehicle, but it must be armoured like a tank – it seems to take no damage from the impact at all. Fliss scrabbles up a staircase in the corner of the building, pain stabbing through her injured foot with every step. She briefly considers trying to fight back, but at this range, it'd be hopeless. She doesn't dare use the rocket launcher in such close quarters – she'd blow herself to bits if she tried it. She scans the structure, looking for an exit instead: if she doesn't get out of here sharpish, Hardinger will bring the place down around her ears. There's a narrow window halfway up the stairs, like a cat's slitted pupil. Fliss starts to squeeze herself through it, feeling the juddering groan of the house collapsing around her. Behind her, she hears the whir of the car's window sliding down.

'I'd been wondering when you'd turn up again,' Hardinger calls. His tone is casual, disinterested. 'I'm surprised you're still meddling in our affairs. Did you know that the rest of your crew are dead?'

Fliss redoubles her efforts to get free. Hardinger wouldn't have opened his window just to taunt her. The first barrage of shots comes as she makes it out of the house. She leaps to the next roof over, grabbing hold of a drooping gutter and using it to haul herself up. Then she zigzags across the moss-covered tiles, trying to put as much distance between herself and the car as possible.

She's at the end of the next roof along when another blast of gunfire takes a chunk out of its chimney. She veers sideways and scrambles across to the adjoining house, risking a single glance over her shoulder. Hardinger's car is back out in the middle of the street, the wide barrel of a machine gun protruding from its open window. She sees Yasmin, too. The agent is on the other side of the road, keeping pace with her. She's not in Hardinger's sights, but with only the net gun in her possession, there's not much she can do to draw his fire.

'There's nowhere you can go that Thoughtfront won't find you,' Hardinger calls. 'There's no point running.'

Over the last two days, Fliss has been chased by drones, shot at, tied up and run over. She's bruised and battered and tired, and she is getting sick of Hardinger hiding in his car and telling her what she can and can't do. Her mum was right about not being able to bargain with the corps, and she was right about something else, too. Men like Hardinger aren't human – at least, not in the way Fliss understands the word. The man sees everyone as a tool to be used; in Fliss's book, that makes him a bit of a tool himself. She has reached the next house over. She spins around, plants her feet, and plonks the rocket launcher down on the stump of the chimney.

Hardinger shoots again, but Fliss takes cover behind the brickwork. Chunks of mortar go flying, but the chimney holds. 'It won't work,' he shouts. 'I've locked your weapons again. All of them.'

Fliss balks. But if Hardinger were sure of that, why bother saying it? She pokes her head around the side of the chimney, glancing at the road below. There was nothing but stone-cold certainty in Hardinger's voice. But he's rolling up his window.

'Wanna bet?' she asks. Then she fires.

The shot is a difficult one, but while Fliss is no Josh when it comes to aiming, she's no slouch, either. The rocket sails in through the narrowing gap in the car's open window, the kind of hundred-to-one direct hit that makes Fliss clench a fist in silent satisfaction. Then the rocket explodes, and the car is blown apart like a piece of overripe fruit.

Tanta stalks through the rows of servers, gun in hand. The inside of the gondola is dark, cold and alien. She moves as quickly as she can through the chill hush, padding along each row in turn looking for signs of Jeanie, then moving on to the next. The terrorist must still be inside – her drones on the entrance prove it – but the gondola is silent save for the humming of the servers. Tanta's senses sharpen, straining through the darkness and the quiet for any hint of her quarry.

This is a fight Tanta knows she can win, but if her ICRD training has taught her anything, it's that she can't afford to get overconfident. Jeanie may not have her combat skills, but she's crafty and almost certainly armed, and the poor visibility in the server room is more likely to work in her favour than in Tanta's since she's had longer to adjust to it. Tanta is the better fighter, but she can't attack an enemy she can't see. And every minute Jeanie stays hidden gives her a bit longer to upload the deadly key to InTech's servers.

Tanta is halfway down the gondola when a shimmer like a heat haze catches her eye at the edge of her field of vision. She darts back behind the nearest stack, just in time – the bullet hits the wall inches from where she was standing.

A memory slams back to the front of her mind: Jeanie's camouflaged safehouse, designed to fool the eye of anyone with an MbOS. She must be using something similar to conceal herself. Tanta disables her 'scape's AR tag reader, cursing herself for not thinking of it before. She whips back around the server and returns fire, but hurried footsteps tell her that Jeanie has already vanished into the stacks. She pursues, trying to guess the direction the terrorist is running in, but the bare, carbon fibre walls of the gondola capture the sound of their footfalls and throw it back at them, making it impossible to pinpoint where Jeanie is, or where she's going.

'Tanta?' Cole's voice is shrill with fear. Tanta pivots towards him, one hand flying to her Array. Using MindChat is a risk right now, but she needs to warn him.

<<Be quiet!>> she sends. <<Don't let her know where you are!>>

It's already much too late for that, though.

Cole realises his mistake as soon as the words are out of his mouth. He has the self-preservation to duck, at least, flinging himself clumsily to the floor. The next shot shatters the server he was working at, blowing its metal casing apart. Spreadeagled on the ground, his ears ringing, Cole tries to collect his scattered thoughts. He needs to find another MbOS port. It's the only imperative his mind has room to grasp. He crawls forward, making his way to the next server along. Jeanie has anticipated him, though, and it explodes before he reaches it, showering him with shrapnel.

Cole dives again, covering his eyes with one arm. And then Tanta is beside him, returning fire.

'Go!' she says, speaking into his ear.

Cole scrambles past her, his mind full of nothing but gunfire. This is his second time being shot at in almost as many days, but the growing familiarity of the experience has done nothing to dull his fear. He inches forward in blind terror, forced to trust to Tanta and the servers to shield him from Jeanie's bullets.

A part of him can't quite believe that Jeanie is trying to kill him, after everything they've shared. *She wants to kill half the city*, he tells himself viciously. *Did you really think she'd make an exception for you?*

He drags himself to the next row along and gropes blindly for another port he can use. His fingers connect with a headset and he rams it over his eyes, diving back into the update packet with a rapidity born of utter panic. While he has been away, the timer has ticked down to twenty-six minutes and eight seconds. Cole runs back into the ramshackle edifice of Harlow 2.0, where the self-deletion protocol lurks like an unexploded bomb. To his horror, he sees that Jeanie is back in the virtual – and she's followed him in through the crack in the update packet's defences. He sees the moment she slips the key into place: it hangs over the self-deletion protocol, digital finger poised on the trigger.

Cole gets to work immediately. Unless he adjusts it, the self-deletion protocol will be fast and catastrophic, a forest fire like the one that ripped through Tanta's 'scape last summer. His task now is to slow that fire down and dig trenches around it, so that Harlow 2.0 won't take the whole Inscape system with it when it goes up in flames. He starts in the same place he did with Tanta's 'scape, setting a path for the course of the destruction that will slow its spread, giving the programme time to uninstall safely without overburdening the core processor. It's a painstaking task, though, and Cole's efforts to complete it are hampered by Jeanie.

She's trying to lock him out of the system again. Cole can feel her probing his 'scape, trying to find a way to revoke the system admin privileges he's managed to steal for himself. It's like her fingers are in his brain – an unsettling sensation. He tries to fight past it and continue with the task at hand, but Jeanie has an advantage on him. She may not have his knack for coding, but she has a right to be here, according to the system, at least – her engineering access codes were never revoked. Everything Cole is doing within these servers, he must do by stealth, fearful at all times of being booted out or red-flagged by InTech's sophisticated security protocols. Jeanie is still a sysadmin and can do as she pleases.

Cole is fighting on two fronts at once – fixing Harlow 2.0 and fending off Jeanie – and it's taking every ounce of his concentration. The timer has ticked down to twenty-two minutes exactly before he realises, with a numb, disconnected feeling, that it's a fight he can't win. Even if he stays here until the update goes live, risking his mind and his life in the process, he won't be able to make the changes he needs to Harlow 2.0 in time. It's impossible.

There is an alternative, though. Cole can't fix the self-deletion protocol – the task is too complex, and Jeanie's interference too effective, but there's something he can achieve that's simpler. And there's no way Jeanie will be expecting it, because as bad as it'll be for her plan, it's just as terrible for theirs.

'Tanta,' he mutters, trying to keep his voice low. 'I need your help.'

She's still firing into the servers, covering Cole as he works. The pistol is silenced, but her focus at first keeps her from hearing him, and he has to reach out with one hand and touch her arm to get her attention. He can't risk disconnecting from the MbOS port long enough to look at her, but he feels her by his side.

'Jeanie has sped up the rollout,' he says. 'We've only got twenty minutes. I – I can't do it – there isn't time.'

He feels Tanta go rigid with shock. 'What can we do?' she asks.

Saying this aloud isn't easy for Cole. His idea may be worse than failing to stop Jeanie outright. He doesn't know – hence why he's asking Tanta for a second opinion. 'I can remove the backdoor entirely,' he whispers. 'Delete the self-deletion sequence.'

There's a horrified silence. 'But that will—'

Cole nods, his hand still on Tanta's arm. Jeanie can't uninstall Harlow 2.0 if the backdoor she was planning to use has been boarded over. Of course, in that case, neither can Cole.

Back in the Needle, five days and what feels like a hundred years ago, Tanta had known what the right decision was without question, but hesitated anyway, waiting for corporate authorisation that was never going to come. Now, there is no right decision – neither of her options is good – and yet she does not pause for an instant.

'Do it,' she says.

Perhaps one day, she and Cole will be able to return and do something for the brainwashed residents of InTech. But they can't save the dead. Beside her, Cole nods, once, and gestures a command.

For a moment, there is nothing but sick, suspenseful silence.

And then Jeanie's howl of rage and dismay echoes around the gondola, bouncing off the walls.

After he has done it, Cole sags to the floor, suddenly limp. He hears Jeanie's shout, but does not respond to it. Tanta shakes his shoulder.

'Cole, we have to go,' she says. 'We have to get out of here before the software goes live.'

She's right: the timer on the update packet has ticked down to nineteen minutes – they barely have time to make it back to the Brokerage before the rollout. Still, Cole doesn't move.

He feels frozen to the spot. He has been so focused, for so long, on trying to thwart Harlow 2.0 and in the end, he has only succeeded in making its hold over InTech's residents more complete than ever. A part of him doesn't *want* to move – wants to tell Tanta to leave him here. Neal didn't deserve to lose his mind to InTech and its insatiable quest for power, but perhaps he, Cole, does. It's his fault this is happening, after all. He has condemned the city's residents to a lifetime of mental control; isn't it only right that he shares in that fate?

'What have you done?' Jeanie's shout ricochets off the walls like a rock slung through a window, hard and jagged. 'You dedicated the best years of your life to undoing the Harlow Programme. Now you've ensured that will *never* happen!'

Cole tries to summon up a retort. He can find only misery. There's no triumph in having defeated Jeanie's scheme. Neither of them has succeeded. He's not even fully convinced that this state of affairs is better than the hecatomb she intended.

Tanta's attempts to move him are growing more and more insistent. Cole realises, distantly, that she will not leave without him. He must rouse himself – if he does not, he'll be condemning her to suffer the rollout along with him. But he can't go without saying something to Jeanie. They've been through too much together – remembered and forgotten – for him to leave her without another word. He sends her a message through the server interface, afraid to let her know where he is by speaking aloud.

<<Jeanie, you have to get out of here. The update's going live, and in a minute, this place will be swarming with guardians.>>

Jeanie's bark of laughter is the bitterest sound Cole has ever heard. Her reply comes through an instant later:

<<It's too late for that, Cole. And I'll be damned if I'm going to end up like Ortega.>>

Then Tanta wrenches Cole to his feet and rips the MbOS

port from his head. She drags him to the door, and at last he follows, breaking into an unwilling run.

He and Tanta are halfway across the bridge when he hears the sharp retort of Jeanie's pistol. By that point, the tears Cole had been keeping at bay are already running freely down his face. He's not crying for her, though, but for everybody else.

Chapter 32

Tanta and Cole stagger through the door of the mooring spire just as Fliss and Yas pull up outside. They dive into the car in an untidy bundle, Fliss punching the gas before they have time to right themselves. There are squads of InTech guardians pouring through the Outer Gate and racing towards the zeppelin, and the remnants of the fleet are still pursuing them, but far worse than either of these threats is Harlow 2.0, which will be going live in a matter of minutes.

Tanta, Cole and Yas need to be out of range of the zeppelin before that happens. And since the zeppelin's range is wide, and their stolen truck won't get far in the time they have, there's only one place they can go.

For the first mile, the last drones of the fleet keep pace with them, but they're a sorry collection by this stage, weakened by the net gun and the rocket launcher, and it isn't long before the truck leaves them behind. After that, the journey would be peaceful, were it not for the terrifying deadline hanging over their heads. Despite her fear, Tanta spends most of the drive with her mind on something else entirely. The Brokerage is shielded from MbOS communications, and once she, Cole and Yas are inside, who knows when they'll be able to leave? She sits hunched in the back of the truck, drafting frantic messages to Reet:

~~Reet, I'm so~~
~~I love you~~
~~I'll miss you~~
~~I hope that one day~~

She stares blankly at her Array, deleting one missive after another. She knows she can't afford to send any of them: she'd be putting more than her own life at risk. She keeps on writing them anyway, keeps on erasing them. She thinks back to her argument with Reet on the day they started working together, of all the things she said to try to manipulate her lover into doing what she wanted, and of all the things she could have said instead. She thinks about how their conversation in the ICRD might have been the last time they ever see one another.

Her regret is an ache deep within her, a wrongness in her bones that feels as though it will never be right again.

They make it back to the Brokerage – barely. Yas leans out of the car to slam her hand against the scanner concealed within the tree trunk, and they drive straight onto the platform as it rises from the ground. Tanta has a timer on her Array counting down to the moment Harlow 2.0 goes live, and it reaches zero forty-five seconds after the car descends into the bunker. There is no sound, no shaking of the earth – no perceptible change at all – to indicate that the update has been rolled out, but the moment it happens, Tanta feels a sick, dull sense of defeat, like a weight on her chest.

It's the first time she has ever failed an assignment. The fact that this particular assignment is one the ICRD would never have endorsed – one which they would have arrested her for even considering – doesn't make the failure feel any better. If anything, it makes it worse.

Tanta has spent most of her life trying to serve InTech's interests. It's only now that she has turned her back on the corporation forever that she finds herself starting to wonder what – or who – InTech really is. When she first joined the ICRD, she worked for Director Ash. When she investigated the false flag attack last summer, she reported to the board. She discharged her duties to both line managers faithfully, to the best of her abilities, and believed that in so doing, she was working for InTech's good.

But InTech isn't its Directors, or even its board of executives. The corporation is legion – made up of tens of thousands of wagers, CorpWards, sleepers and residents – and being an agent is supposed to be about protecting them all. Tanta never imagined, when she joined the ICRD, that the threats InTech's residents would need protecting from might come from their own corp. It's not a possibility she was prepared for, and not one she *could* have prepared for under InTech's aegis.

She tries to draw comfort from that fact, to let it fortify her against the thought of the gruelling months that lie ahead. InTech is a menace to its own populace; she knows, at last, whose side she is on in that struggle, and much as it pains her, it is not a battle she could ever have fought from inside the city. Leaving was inevitable; more than that, it was necessary. Tanta reminds herself of that, and tries to see what is happening now as a blessing in disguise.

It doesn't feel that way.

Fliss's mood, as she drives everyone back to the Brokerage, is out of keeping with the general atmosphere in the car. The others may have failed to stop their software rollout – though just what that was exactly, Fliss still isn't sure – but as far as she's concerned, their hunt went well. They're not dead, and Jeanie and Hardinger are. That's a success worth celebrating, and she's still high on it as she brings the car to a juddering halt in the Brokerage's underground garage.

It is only once the rush of adrenaline and excitement have abated that she starts to wonder what she's going to do next. Sonia is gone – she has no idea where. Josh, Ben and Gabriel are dead, and Fliss herself is on the most wanted list of not one but two major corporations. She has a duffel bag full of fancy weapons, but they're not much good without a crew to wield them. She could go solo, she supposes. It's not like she can't take care of herself. But living in the wasteland on her own would be a sorry sort of life.

That thought brings Fliss down to earth like a felled drone. By the time they've all piled out of the car, she's as grim and gloomy as the rest of them.

'That's it,' Tanta says, as they walk down the corridor to the control room. 'It's gone live.'

'Shit,' Yasmin replies. 'Well, we already knew we were fucked. Guess now it's official.'

'What do you mean? You all got clear, didn't you?' Fliss asks.

'That's not how Inscape updates work,' Cole tells her. 'We're safe for now – the Brokerage is shielded from MbOS traffic, but as soon as we set foot outside, our 'scapes will receive the update and download it – nothing we can do about it. It's like an airborne pathogen. We—' he pauses, as though this thought is only just hitting him with its full force. 'We can't leave.'

'There's a hydroponic garden down here, hooked up to a solar generator,' Yas says. 'We'll be able to hold out for a while, but even so ...'

She trails off, staring into the distance with a haunted expression.

Fliss makes up her mind there and then. She tells herself it's pity. These sorry corporate types are about as much use in the wasteland as a glass handgun: without her to help them out, they'd be done for. Even as she feeds herself the reasoning, though, she knows it's a cover. Since when has she ever cared about corporate types? Or anyone, really, besides her crew? The truth is that Fliss has as few options as the agents do.

'It's a good thing you have me around then, isn't it?' she says brightly.

The rest of them turn to her, their expressions a mixture of surprise and scepticism.

'Why would you stay?' Tanta asks. 'You don't have an Inscape. There's nothing to keep you here.'

'Why would I stay? Good luck getting me to leave!'

Cole raises an exhausted eyebrow at her. The other two seem too tired to even ask the question.

'Look at it this way,' Fliss continues. 'We killed Jeanie, which means this whole operation' – she gestures at the bunker, with its old machines and data banks – 'belongs to us now.' It's not the only reason she's sticking around, but it's true enough. Fliss has seen enough movies – and enough hostile takeovers out in the wasteland – to know how this works. 'We're the new Brokerage,' she says, 'and it's as much mine as it is yours: I'm not walking away from that. Besides,' she adds, with a grin, 'you sad sacks need me.'

And I need a new crew, she thinks, but only to herself.

Barely an hour later and ten miles away, Douglas Kenway is preparing to explain this clusterfuck to the board. The meeting has been hastily convened: he'd no sooner heard the news of the attack on the zeppelin when he received their summons. He now faces the daunting task of explaining a security breach he's only just learnt about himself. He straightens his tie, trying to swallow past the lump of dread in his throat. He can ill afford an embarrassment like this. Once again, he has dropped the ball, failed to anticipate a threat, and the board's patience with him has worn thin enough already.

Reet pings him when he's ten minutes out from the ICRD. She had just departed for the Southern Distribution Centre when the attack happened, and consequently she was one of the closest agents available. She was supposed to be taking charge of Tanta's investigation this morning – and escorting her back to the city so that Arthur Friend could inspect her Harlow Programming – but, urgent as that is, the current crisis takes priority. She's on site now, investigating the carnage.

<<What have you found?>> he asks.

<<The body appears to have been an ex-engineer from Sodis,>> she sends. <<That explains how she got access to the zeppelin. What I can't understand is that it looks like her employment was terminated twenty years ago, but she still has all her system permissions. Douglas—>>

<<Did she damage the servers?>> Kenway interrupts. Right now, there's only one thing on his mind. <<There was a software update scheduled to be rolled out today. If it was affected in any way, it would be very serious indeed.>>

<<It wasn't. The update went live earlier than scheduled, but Dr Friend told me there weren't any issues with it. But Douglas, I just received a message from Logistics Officer Smythe and—>>

<<The Logistics Officer will have to wait,>> Kenway sends. <<You can resume your journey to Sodis once you've finished examining the zeppelin.>>

<<Douglas.>> Reet's tone is desperate. <<There's something else you need to know!>>

Her voice shaking, Reet tells him. It's bad news – the worst yet – but on top of everything else that has happened today, Kenway supposes he shouldn't be surprised.

★

After Reet's report, Kenway orders her to return to the city and meet him in the ICRD; the board may want to question her in person. His own journey takes far longer than it should. His taxi is held up – not by traffic, but by all the pedestrians in the road. The city has stopped in its tracks, much as it did when Jennifer Ash sabotaged the traffic management mainframe last summer – only this time it's the not the vehicles that have ground to a halt, but the people. All along Kenway's route, he sees residents standing on the balconies of their flats, outside shops, in the roads, and looking around with the bewildered air of people who have just walked into a room and forgotten what they were meant to be doing there.

This mass disorientation was expected. Dr Friend warned the board that there would be an adjustment period of several hours for most residents while the security update bedded in. Kenway has been planning the logistics for weeks, and InTech is well prepared to weather the cost and inconvenience of a few hours of city-wide downtime. It doesn't make the blank-eyed automatons in the street any less unsettling. His foreknowledge of Harlow 2.0's effects has done nothing to arm him against the shock of seeing those effects first-hand.

The clerk on duty on the ICRD's front desk is hunched down in her chair, looking confused and distressed, but her face lights up when Kenway walks in.

'Director!' she says. 'Welcome!' Her smile is unnatural, stretching her mouth too wide.

Kenway stalks past her, repressing a shiver as he hurries towards the lifts.

This time, the conduit doesn't even wait till he has walked through the door of the temporary boardroom in the basement before barking, 'Report, Director.'

Kenway does so, though with none of his usual slickness. He's unnerved by the update, wrongfooted by the speed of events and for once, his knack of projecting a confidence he doesn't really possess has deserted him. He tries to put what spin on his account he can, but he can't disguise the naked fact that this should never have happened at all.

The last thing he told the board was that the threats facing InTech were the work of bandits and agitators, armed by Thoughtfront, yes, but driven by nothing more complex than greed and a desire to wreak havoc. He had promised the conduit that he was handling things, but despite his assurances, there has been another attack — worse, one that has blown his working theory to pieces. It's obvious now that the target of the Needle bombing was not InTech's board, but its servers. Thoughtfront has known about Harlow 2.0 all this time and somehow, despite the ICRD's cutting-edge surveillance networks and intelligence-gathering capabilities, Kenway missed the warning signs.

In other circumstances, the report he has to give might not be so poorly received. Thoughtfront failed, after all: the security update went off without a hitch, and the servers sustained no serious damage. None of this was any thanks to Kenway, though, and in light of his other blunders, he's sure the board will be all too aware of that fact. There is no way to disguise how badly he has mishandled this, no way to draw a veneer of professionalism over the failure of intelligence that has happened on his watch.

'Initial reports do suggest that the rollout of Harlow 2.0 has been a success, Representative,' he says. 'The protesters outside the Needle have dispersed already. Given the escalating situation with Thoughtfront, acting swiftly to pacify our own residents was a wise decision.'

If he's hoping the board will be pleased by this tribute to their good judgement, he's disappointed. The conduit dismisses his flattery with a hard stare.

'What progress has Tanta made with her investigation into the drone thefts?' he asks. 'Can she shed any light on these events?'

Kenway swallows. But he was going to have to get to this sooner or later. 'Tanta is gone, Representative. Yesterday, we received intelligence from a Brokerage agent indicating that her Harlow Programming may have been compromised during her assignment last summer. When she was ordered back to the city for a full inspection of her MbOS, she abandoned her post. Logistics Officer Smythe informs us that she broke a prisoner out of holding last night and disappeared.' He pauses, gathering his strength. When he resumes speaking, his voice is barely above a whisper. 'She has taken Neuroengineer Cole with her. They remain at large.'

The silence that follows the end of this report is the longest Kenway has ever experienced. It goes on for well over forty-five minutes. The conduit's jaw goes slack, his eyes widening as a torrent of internal debate floods through his router. Kenway doesn't wonder at the board's consternation. Cole is one of InTech's most valuable assets: the consequences of him falling into the wrong hands would be beyond catastrophic.

While the board are locked in wordless conclave, the door opens and Reet slips in. Her face is pale.

'Douglas,' she murmurs, taking a seat beside him. 'There's something weird going on. On my way here, there were dozens of people just standing in the road, and they looked...'

She trails off. Kenway understands her uneasiness, though he has neither the time nor the inclination to reassure her. 'It's not your concern,' he says.

Then the conduit stiffens, his eyes locking onto Kenway's, and Kenway dismisses Reet from his thoughts.

'Director Kenway, in light of your report, it is the judgement of the board that the divisions under your care require restructuring,' the conduit says.

'What does that mean?' Kenway asks. The words come out louder than he meant them to, his tone sharpened by fear.

'It means that from now on, the ICRD and Residents' Affairs will be run in partnership by you and a Co-Director. She will oversee your work and approve your decisions, supervising you in the discharge of your duties.'

'Representative, I don't think that's necessary!' Kenway blurts. He's appalled at his own audacity – addressing the board's Representative so directly is the height of rudeness – but he can't restrain himself. 'There's no one in the corporation with more experience of these roles than I have. You can't expect me to answer to someone less qualified than myself!'

'Our decision is non-negotiable,' the conduit raps out. 'You will accept it, or you will resign your posts.'

That shuts Kenway up immediately. Resigning is not an attractive option at the best of times and right now, it's impossible. He realises, with a sense of vertigo, that if he stepped down as the head of the ICRD and Residents' Affairs, he'd be giving up more than his directorship. Returning to the ranks of InTech's ordinary residents would also mean he was no longer exempt from Harlow 2.0.

'You are allowing personal considerations to influence your judgement, Director Kenway,' the conduit continues. 'This is precisely why you require assistance. It is not your experience that is in question, but your ability to put InTech's interests before your own. That is a deficiency your Co-Director will amply make up for.'

'And who is this "Co-Director"?' Kenway asks, unable to keep the venom out of his voice.

By way of answer, the conduit turns in his chair, the movement stilted and mechanical. Kenway follows his gaze with a mounting sense of horror. It is as if his worst fears have been given human form. Everything he dreaded has come to pass: it was all just as he predicted. His only mistake was that he was afraid of the wrong Corporate Ward.

'Reet,' the conduit says. There is something in his tone that Kenway has never heard before – something almost gentle. 'We have a job for you.'

END OF BOOK II

Acknowledgements

I wrote the bulk of *Outcast* during the 2020 lockdowns, and finished editing it during the first lockdown in 2021. It was lonely work, which is why I am so very grateful to all the people who supported me through it and helped keep my spirits up. Chief among these was my partner, Camden Ford, without whom I would never have finished the book (and some days probably wouldn't even have made it out of bed). Meg Davis, agent-extraordinaire, was an unfailing source of sound advice and reassurance. My editor, Brendan Durkin, was instrumental in shaping the novel into something I'm really proud of. Our dialogue on the book's progress was both useful and a much-needed source of human interaction. Huge thanks also to Will O'Mullane, Lucy Cameron, and the whole (award-winning!) Gollancz team. Abigail Nathan did a fantastic job on the copy edits, pruning all my unnecessary commas and spotting a good few continuity errors to boot. I'm lucky to have the benefit of her expertise. And, as always, I owe an immense debt of love and gratitude to the Carey clan. David's morning writing sessions over Discord kept me going when the going got tough; Ben's comments on an early draft of the novel helped me to clarify my thoughts on character and plot. Finally, thanks are due to my mother, Linda and my father, Mike, to whom this book is dedicated. They're the best parents, friends and beta-readers a girl could ask for and dad, you gave me the best advice on writing I've ever had. I still follow it to this day.

Credits

Louise Carey and Gollancz would like to thank everyone at Orion who worked on the publication of *Outcast*.

Agent
Meg Davis

Editor
Brendan Durkin
Áine Feeney

Copy editor
Abigail Nathan

Proof reader
Bruno Vincent

Editorial Management
Jane Hughes
Charlie Panayiotou
Tamara Morriss
Claire Boyle

Audio
Paul Stark
Jake Alderson
Georgina Cutler

Contracts
Anne Goddard
Ellie Bowker
Humayra Ahmed

Design
Nick Shah
Tomás Almeida
Joanna Ridley
Helen Ewing

Finance
Nick Gibson
Jasdip Nandra
Elizabeth Beaumont
Ibukun Ademefun
Afeera Ahmed
Sue Baker
Tom Costello

Inventory
Jo Jacobs
Dan Stevens

Marketing
Lucy Cameron

Production
Paul Hussey
Fiona McIntosh

Publicity
Will O'Mullane

Sales
Jen Wilson
Victoria Laws
Esther Waters
Frances Doyle
Ben Goddard
Jack Hallam
Anna Egelstaff
Inês Figueira
Barbara Ronan
Andrew Hally
Dominic Smith
Deborah Deyong
Lauren Buck

Maggy Park
Linda McGregor
Sinead White
Jemimah James
Rachael Jones
Jack Dennison
Nigel Andrews
Ian Williamson
Julia Benson
Declan Kyle
Robert Mackenzie
Megan Smith
Charlotte Clay
Rebecca Cobbold

Operations
Sharon Willis

Rights
Susan Howe
Krystyna Kujawinska
Jessica Purdue
Ayesha Kinley
Louise Henderson